MICHAEL ARNOLD

Michael Arnold lives in Petersfield, Hampshire, with his wife and children. After childhood holidays spent visiting castles and battlefields, he developed a lifelong fascination with the Civil Wars. Hunter's Rage is the third in a planned series of over ten books that will follow the fortunes of Captain Stryker through one of the most treacherous periods of English history. Other books in the Civil War Chronicles are *Traitor's Blood*, *Devil's Charge* and *Assassin's Reign*, available in Hodder paperback.

PRAISE FOR THE CIVIL WAR CHRONICLES

'A dark-hued romp, livid with the scents, sounds and colours of a country on the brink of implosion . . . impressive' *Daily Express*

'Pushed as the "Sharpe of the Civil War", Captain Stryker is a character well able to attract readers on his own merits . . . promises much entertainment' *Sunday Times*

'The most vivid and thrilling book yet . . . Crackling with the sound of musket fire and punctuated with the roar of cannon, this book brings the Cromwellian conflict to life in an intense battle of wits and weaponry' *Press Association*

'Arnold is at his best describing
Cornwell you will like Arnold'

HUNTER'S RAGE

MICHAEL ARNOLD

HODDER

First published in Great Britain in 2012 by John Murray (Publishers)
An Hachette UK Company

Hodder paperback edition 2014

5

Maps drawn by Rosie Collins

A CIP catalogue record for this title is available from the British Library

ISBN 978-1-84854-412-3
Ebook ISBN 978-1-84854-413-0

Typeset in Bembo by Hewer Text UK Ltd, Edinburgh

Printed and bound by Clays Ltd, St Ives plc

John Murray policy is to use papers that are natural, renewable and
recyclable products and made from wood grown in sustainable forests.
The logging and manufacturing processes are expected to conform to
the environmental regulations of the country of origin.

Hodder & Stoughton Ltd
338 Euston Road
London NW1 3BH

www.hodder.co.uk

For my grandparents, Mick and Doreen

Spring 1643

Royalist territory

Parliamentarian territory

Neutral territory

Inverness
Aberdeen
Perth
Edinburgh
Newcastle
Carlisle
Bridlington
York
Lincoln
Newark
Chester
Nottingham
Lichfield
Worcester
Colchester
Pembroke
Gloucester
Oxford
Cirencester
London
Bristol
Okehampton
Taunton
Stratton
Launceston
Portsmouth
Plymouth

N
W · E
S

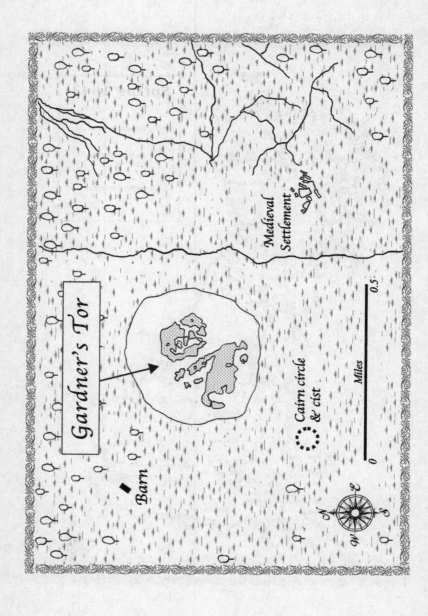

Gardner's Tor

Barn

Medieval
Settlement

Cairn circle
& cist

Miles

0   0.5

N
W   E
S

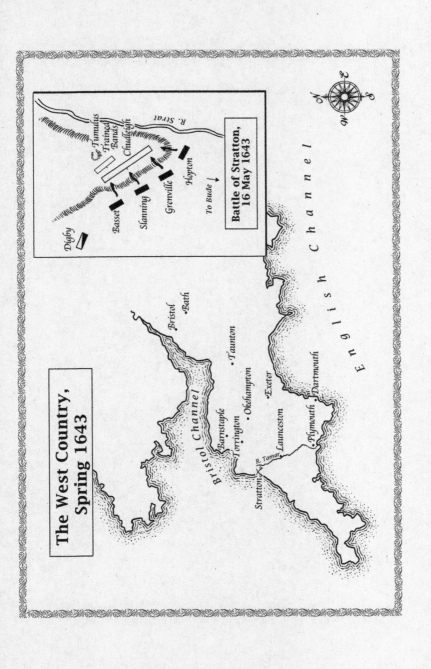

The West Country, Spring 1643

Battle of Stratton, 16 May 1643

PROLOGUE

The soldier had hidden himself well, the thick under-growth at the road's edge providing ample camouflage for a patchy coat of russet and dark green. It was a dry day, the first since the battle, and he was thankful that his back-side would not get wet as he sat on his haunches, waiting impatiently for the cart to arrive.

He checked his twin pistols one last time, ensuring flint, powder and ball were all in place. He was not fond of the weapon, preferring the robust reliability of a musket rather than that of the small-arm, but this brace, stolen from a Swedish cavalryman's saddle holsters, would suffice for today's task. He hefted the pistols in gloved hands, hoping the weapons would lend a fearsome edge to his appearance. The soldier had wanted to burst from the tangled bushes with the ferocity of a demon, all howls and savagery, but he suspected, at just twenty years of age and with a slim frame and long, straight, sable hair, he would appear more feral vagabond than terrifying monstrosity. He had been told that his pale eyes, lupine in their grey depths, gave him a certain roguish quality, but he was beginning to wonder whether that would be enough to cow the men on the cart.

Feeling a tickling sensation cross his knee, he looked down to see a fat bumble-bee crawling across one of the stains that speckled the wool of his breeches. His clothes had collected as many dark, crusty splatter marks as they had lice since he'd enlisted with the company, but this one was different. It still carried that telltale rusty tinge that spoke of its macabre origin. It was a fresh stain and was all that was left of that flashing, screaming, panic-fuelled moment when a man's life had ended. The soldier shuddered involuntarily. His latest kills had been only days before, on a blood-soaked field at the crossroads between three villages whose names he could not even pronounce. The Swedish army, of which the soldier's company of English mercenaries had been a part, had finally triumphed over their enemies in the Catholic League, but at a cost that made him shiver.

Feeling sick at reliving that day of death, he flicked the bumble-bee on to the overgrown grass and forced his mind back to the one thing that made life in this war-torn, hate-filled, plague-rotten part of Europe more bearable.

Beth Lipscombe. He smiled at the thought of her. That fiery hair, the lily skin, the heart-searing gaze, the honey voice.

He tilted his head suddenly. There was a sound of something different and not entirely natural above the gentle thrum of the countryside. He waited, breath held, eyes clamped shut.

There it was again: the creaking of wheels.

The soldier took up the pistols in each hand and thrust himself upwards into a squatting position, careful to remain concealed behind the wild chaos of mouldering bracken and tall grass. The sound of wheels was growing ever louder now, joined in discord by the low murmur of voices and the groaning of wood. Using the muzzle of one of the pistols, the soldier eased the undergrowth apart so that he could catch sight of the road. At first he saw only mud, hoof-churned and undulating like a freshly ploughed field. He let his gaze snake to the right, tracing the road until it reached a gentle bend. And there, drawn by a couple of bored-looking ponies, was the cart. His quarry.

The undergrowth grasped and clawed at the soldier's tall boots as he burst forth from his place of concealment. His knees protested sharply, for he had been concealed there the entire half-hour since sunrise, but the exhilaration of the moment quickly chased the pains away. He turned right as his first boot touched the road, pacing purposefully towards the cart. The driver, he saw, had already spotted him and was desperately hauling back the thin ropes that served as reins. He raised both arms, levelling the twin pistols at the frightened-looking man, and was rewarded to see the lumbering vehicle judder to a slanted stop in one of the road's deep ruts, one of the rear wheels left to spin in mid-air.

The soldier did not stop. He picked up his pace, eager to be up at the cart before its startled occupants had time to respond. He saw four fellows leap awkwardly from the rear, making the cart rock like a skiff in a gale, and immediately trained one of his firearms on them, keeping the other firmly fixed on the driver. The men were all of similar age, though very different in appearance. Two of them, burly of shoulder, rough of face and dressed in everyday shirt and breeches, were clearly locals. Farmers or millers, the soldier presumed. Labourers of some kind.

The other two faces the soldier recognized instantly. Clothed in more expensive attire than their companions – pristine shirts, black cloaks and high-crowned hats – they had softer features and slimmer frames. Both clutched Bibles. The soldier had never met either of them, but had studied them from afar, and knew them to be clergymen of some kind. He hawked up a dense gobbet of phlegm and spat on the road.

'*Was soll das bedeuten?*' one of the priests called out.

The soldier was within ten paces of his captives now, and he brandished what he hoped would be a suitably wolfish grin. 'Don't *sprechen* the tongue, Herr Canker-Blossom.'

The priest, a man perhaps ten years the soldier's senior, pulled a sour expression, wrinkling his hooked, beaklike nose. 'I asked, what is the meaning of this?'

The soldier frowned, as annoyed at the man's evident lack of fear as he was surprised to hear the accent. 'English?'

'Aye, sir,' the priest called back, 'and a saddened one to learn that he may be robbed by his own countryman.'

The soldier shook his head vigorously, sending the dark locks cascading about his shoulders. 'No robbery here, sir. Merely rescue.'

'Rescue?' the black-cloaked man repeated incredulously, but then his small eyes, brown and intelligent, narrowed, and he looked up at the cart. 'And the Lord sheds light.'

The soldier stepped a pace closer, stabbing the air at his front with the pistols. 'Release her, sir, or so help me I'll stick lead in your face.'

The locals, judging by their plate-eyed expressions, probably did not comprehend a word of the exchange, and began stumbling backwards at the renewed threat. The driver stayed in his seat, careful not to move an inch lest he draw the young brigand's attention.

To the soldier's surprise, the English priest stared directly down the mouth of the pistol barrel and shook his head slowly. 'We take this witch to the hanging tree, where she will know God's judgement.'

The soldier gritted his teeth. 'Have a care for your words, fellow.'

'The witch must hang!' the priest bellowed suddenly, his expression darkening with explosive anger. 'Hang, I say!'

A new face appeared then, popping up from within the cart. Narrow and white, with high, delicate cheekbones and glittering hazel eyes, all framed by a shock of flame-red hair that flowed like a sun-dappled waterfall. 'Hang me, you dry old bastard, but then you'll never get your privy member polished.' She grinned; an expression of wickedness and defiance, of pearly teeth and crimson lips.

To the soldier at least, it was a smile of flesh-scorching beauty. He winked at her.

'This wench is a harridan of Satan,' the second priest spluttered. He was fresher-faced than his compatriot, tall and willowy.

The soldier tore his gaze from the girl to meet that of the new speaker, who, to his surprise, was also English. 'She truly looks a frightening creature, sir.'

'She is a witch!' the first priest interjected with outraged indignation. 'I have proof she worships Lucifer.'

A chorus of low mutterings came from the driver and the locals. They may not have been able to comprehend the discussion, but they all knew the name of the Devil well enough. The second priest sketched the sign of the cross over his chest.

'*Proof*!' the girl screeched from up on the cart. 'And I got proof of no wrongdoing!' Her hands were bound in front, but somehow she managed to angle them so that her long, thin fingers could fish for something from within the neckline of her bodice. When she withdrew them, they grasped a glinting disc of metal. 'The king's shilling! Payment for a night's work,' she jerked her chin at the taller priest, 'with this young gentleman!'

'She bewitched me!' the second priest wailed, his tone shrill and desperate. 'Befuddled my senses!'

The soldier's lip upturned in an amused sneer. 'Turn your head did she? She's a rare beauty, I grant you.'

'I—I—' the willowy priest stammered, unable to find a suitable retort.

'What are you, son?' the soldier went on. 'Sixteen years? Seventeen? I bet she befuddled you well.'

'She is the Devil's whore!' the older priest bellowed.

The soldier shook his head. 'She's a whore, certainly, sir. But more angel than demon.'

'*Blasphemy*!' The priest almost spat the word. 'You should have your neck stretched beside her!'

'Perhaps,' the soldier replied casually, 'but at least I can sleep at night. You goddamned priests want her just as any other man, and hate yourselves when you've shot your bolt. You would see her hang to salve your vile consciences.' The younger priest's pale face immediately reddened, and he knew he had spoken true. He glanced up at the cart. 'Beth! Get down here!'

Beth did as she was told. Wrists still bound, she swung her legs over the side of the vehicle and dropped down to the road with a squelch, pushing her way past the indignant men to stand beside her rescuer. She held up wrists that had been rubbed raw by the coarse bindings. He handed her one of the pistols, and she trained it on the group as, with his free hand, the soldier drew a small blade from his belt and cut her bonds.

He grinned as she pecked him on the cheek.

The locals began to mutter their dissent at her release, but they remained frozen to the mud, frightened by the pistols into bovine acquiescence.

The soldier pursed his lips and gave a short, high-pitched whistle. The undergrowth at the road's edge immediately began to rustle and crack as branches, vines, bracken and grass were thrust aside and a bay mare trudged on to the rutted road.

'Get on, Beth,' the soldier ordered, taking back the pistol and backing slowly away from the group.

The younger of the priests simply stared mutely at the ground as the object of his lust clambered up into the waiting saddle, his thin lips working frantically in what looked like silent prayer.

The senior priest took a step forwards, dropping his voice to a low growl. 'She seduced this God-fearing, Christian man, sir. Poisoned his mind with wicked desire. And she *will* swing for it.'

The soldier's angular jaw quivered as he gritted his teeth. 'Not today.'

The shot echoed about the trees as a fat halo of acrid smoke obscured the air around the soldier. He heard the priest scream and knew the ball had found its mark, but did not wait to see the result until he was safely in the saddle, Beth Lipscombe's lithe arms snaked tightly about his waist.

Only when he had holstered the spent weapon and handed the remaining pistol to Beth did he look down at the men gathered around the cart. The priest was rolling in the sticky mud, a hand clutched at the tattered flesh of his backside.

'Let that be a lesson to you, sir!' he called down at the wounded, writhing man. 'And be thankful I showed you the mercy you would not have shown this woman.'

The priest looked up at him, blood seeping through fingers held tight to his breeches, face creased with fury and pain. 'I will find you, witch's helper! I will hunt you down, so help me God! I may not have your name, but—'

'No, sir, you will not!' the soldier called. 'For we will be long away from this cursed country by the time your arse heals! So you may have my name.' He grasped the reins, slashing them against the bay's broad neck, propelling them on in a surge of power and a spray of mud. He crowed his victory to the thick canopy above, glancing back only to shout his name. And they were gone.

CHAPTER 1

Captain Innocent Stryker was in a foul mood. It might have been late afternoon, but it was still warm, too warm for a man in a woollen coat and breeches, and the Devon sky was smothered in a pelt of pregnant clouds that made the skin prickle with humidity. The steepness of the hill seemed to make his pumping chest burn and tightening calves ache. All these things made a march difficult, and, in turn, his mood darken. But worse still, Captain Innocent Stryker was running away. And that, more than any other trial, turned his temper as black and as explosive as gunpowder.

'Maybe we could go back?' a voice came from behind him.

Stryker rounded on the speaker, causing the long line of scarlet-coated soldiers to halt their march. 'God's blood, Ensign Chase! I'll send you back down there alone if you say something so dull-witted again.'

Chase, the man charged with bearing the company standard – a large square of blood-red taffeta, with the cross of St George at the top corner and two white diamonds in the field – stared into his captain's face. That face was narrow, weather-hardened and spoiled by a mass of swirling scar tissue in the place where his left eye should have been. He swallowed hard. 'Sir.'

The tremble of shoulders caught Stryker's lone grey eye. He turned to glare at a man who stood taller than any other in the company, a man whose mottled-toothed smirk immediately vanished. 'And you'll join him, Sergeant Skellen, do not think I jest.'

Skellen's face, layered with dark stubble and criss-crossed with its own creases and scars, became a well-practised mask, blank and unreadable. 'Wouldn't dream of it, sir.'

Stryker turned away to stare back down the road. 'Got out just in time,' he muttered to no one in particular.

They had marched out of Bovey Tracey some three hours earlier, with word of an advancing Parliamentarian unit hastening every step. Stryker eyed the town's thatches, tiny smudges of gold and russet from this distance, huddled at the foot of the tree-choked hill his men now climbed. With the uneasy truce in the south-west close to ending, Hopton, the Royalist general, had become increasingly nervous, and Stryker had been stationed here, at Dartmoor's south-eastern fringe, to guard one of the few routes into the bleak wilderness. But now he had been driven to the hills like a deer in the face of hounds. He swore viciously.

'Least they didn't catch us sleeping,' a new voice reached Stryker from further down the road.

Stryker peered along the line of soaring pike staves and shouldered muskets until he saw the speaker, a man whose hard face and battle-ravaged body belied the fact that he was only in his late teens. Stryker nodded acknowledgement to his second-in-command. 'That is something I suppose, Lieutenant Burton. Still, I hate to turn tail.'

Burton smiled. 'Strategic retreat is not cowardice, sir.'

Stryker glanced at him, single brow raised. 'When did our roles reverse, Andrew?'

'Sir?'

'It was not so long ago that you were as green as cabbage,' Stryker said, though without malice. 'Now you offer me advice.'

Burton absently adjusted the leather sling that cradled his right arm. That arm had been shattered at the shoulder by a pistol ball the previous year and was now withered and next to useless. 'Seen a deal of soldiering now, sir.'

That was true, Stryker reflected. Youthful innocence had been marched, slashed and shot from young Burton, so that the lieutenant was now an extremely proficient officer, and one of the few men Stryker trusted with his life. He was proud of Burton, strange though it was for him to admit.

'We'll rest here,' he ordered suddenly. He looked at Skellen. 'See to it, Sergeant.'

Burton moved to stand at his captain's side as Skellen sent word down the line. The lieutenant kept his voice low. 'What if they send men after us?'

Stryker pulled the buff-gloves from his fingers and scratched at the puckered skin that served as a macabre lid to his mutilated eye socket. 'A force that size? They were to garrison Bovey Tracey. We're of no concern.' He took off his wide-brimmed hat, rapping it with his knuckles to send a cloud of dust into the breezeless air before tossing it on to the grass at the road's verge. 'Besides, if they send cavalry we will be caught. Would you march another hour and be tired when finally they're at our backs?'

Burton shook his head. 'I would rest now and fight them afresh.'

'So we rest.' Stryker unbuckled his sword, dropping it next to the hat, and sank to his haunches. 'And hope the bastards don't come.'

Burton removed his own hat and sat beside Stryker, running a hand across his forehead to shift thick tendrils of sweat-matted hair. 'A good match, wouldn't you say?'

Stryker followed Burton's gaze to where Ensign Chase was attempting to prop the company colour against a broad tree trunk. 'Match?'

'The new coats, sir. Captain Fullwood has some experience in the dying trade, apparently. According to him, getting the right shade of red – or any colour for that matter – is the devil of a job.'

Stryker stared at Chase as the company's most junior officer continued to struggle with the large standard. The regiment had been supplied with new coats after Cirencester had fallen to Prince Rupert earlier in the year. The Stroud Valley was a prolific centre of wool production, and many of the king's regiments had taken the opportunity to replace their threadbare coats and breeches with the sudden availability of material.

'They might have ended up in blue,' Stryker replied eventually. 'There was more blue than anything else.'

Burton sniffed his derision. 'Well I for one am pleased Sir Edmund insisted upon red. Goes with the regimental colours, after all. Slightly darker hue than our flag, I grant you, but it's not too far off.' He glanced down at his own coat, a nondescript shade of brown, and fingered the sleeve of his limp right arm. 'Perhaps I should have taken the opportunity to replace this old thing when I had the chance.'

Stryker shook his head. 'The prince would not have

been pleased.' He might have been an infantry officer, but Stryker and a select group of comrades were often enlisted by the king's nephew, Prince Rupert of the Rhine, for special – often covert – tasks.

Burton chuckled. 'Aye, I suppose he would not wish us parading around in nice, bright red. Still, the fact remains,' he went on, his attention back on the rank and file, 'they look a far more imposing body now.'

Stryker did not much care for coats or colours, and he allowed his thoughts to drift elsewhere. To old battles and fallen friends, to the most recent horrors he had witnessed on the killing field of Hopton Heath, and to the bitter siege he had barely survived before it. And then, inevitably, to the person whose presence had drawn him to the ill-fated little city of Lichfield. A woman with long, golden hair and sapphire eyes. Who could be dainty as a flower one moment and hard as steel the next. A woman who beguiled and infuriated Stryker in equal measure.

'Is she still in Rome?' Burton's voice stabbed through his reverie.

Stryker looked up sharply, and the lieutenant's face paled, his eyes immediately studying the ground. 'Christ, Andrew, but you're becoming as impertinent as Skellen.'

'Beg pardon, sir, I overstepped,' Burton muttered sheepishly.

'Yes, you bloody did,' Stryker replied, though he could feel the anger already begin to seep away. He sighed heavily. 'Aye, she is still in Rome.' The image of Lisette Gaillard leapt back into his mind's eye, and for a second he allowed himself to luxuriate in the memory of her voice, her touch, her scent. But even as those fine thoughts swirled, they were intertwined with sadness. She had left England back in March, shortly after the bloody fight outside Stafford, a fight that saw the last great act of a master fire-worker, the death of an earl, and the restoration of Stryker's reputation. For Lisette was Queen Henrietta Maria's agent. Messenger, spy, assassin. Ever at the monarch's beck and call. And that meant she could never be truly Stryker's. He didn't know if he loved her or loathed her. 'So far as I goddamn know,' he added bitterly.

Burton opened his mouth to speak, but another glance from Stryker's forbidding grey eye made him think twice. Instead he watched Stryker unlace his sleeveless buff-coat and fish out a folded piece of paper. The captain opened the greasy square carefully, staring down at the hand-drawn features adorning its surface.

'Where now, sir?' Burton said after a few moments.

Stryker squinted to discern the black lines of bridle-ways from the paper's myriad creases. He indicated a particular point with a grubby finger. 'We're here. Outside Bovey Tracey.'

'Never to return.'

Stryker thought of the large Parliamentarian force they had seen approach the town and felt a wave of relief that his company had been organized enough to take their leave in good time. 'Aye. And here,' he continued, tracing one of the meandering ink strokes westwards with his nail, 'is the road we'll follow.'

'The Tavistock road.' Burton glanced up. 'Back to Launceston?'

'Naturally. General Hopton will wish to know why we abandoned our post.'

'Will it go bad for us, sir?'

Stryker could sense Burton's concern and he looked up.

'He sends a single company to guard a road, and the enemy appear with a whole bloody regiment.'

'Not a great deal we could do, was there?'

'I fear not.' He leaned back on his elbows. 'Justice will out, Andrew. Hopton's no fool.'

Burton nodded. 'So we must trudge back across the moor.'

Stryker read the bleakness in Burton's expression. 'You do not relish the task?'

'Dartmoor is such a desolate place.'

'You listen to Sergeant Heel too readily, Lieutenant.' Stryker sat up and slapped Burton on the shoulder. 'Tall tales of men vanishing in the mists and swallowed by bogs. The fact remains that we are here,' he said, tapping the map, 'in the south-east, and, as of this morning, so are the enemy. Further east we have Exeter—'

'Rebel town.'

'Indeed.' The captain's finger moved upwards across the page. 'And to the north they hold Okehampton. In short, Launceston is the only safe town for us hereabouts. So we must head due west, back into Cornwall.'

'Across Dartmoor,' Burton said glumly.

'Damn these boots!' Sergeant Skellen's coarse tone – honed in the taverns of Gosport – rang out nearby.

Stryker and Burton looked to where he sat a short distance along the road, long arms wrestling to pluck a ragged-looking bucket-top boot from his huge foot.

'Thought you said they was the best ever crafted,' one of the soldiers said.

'Stitched by the fair hands of a dozen maids, you said, Sergeant,' Lieutenant Burton chimed in.

Skellen let out a heavy breath through his nostrils.

'Indeed an' I did, sir.' He struggled a while longer, amused smirks breaking out all around, and looked up when finally he had relieved his feet of the offending items. 'Took 'em off a dead harq'busier after Kineton Fight. Comfy as a night in the Two Bears down in Southwick.' He closed his small, dark eyes at the memory. 'A buttock banquet before bed, and tits for pillows.'

The men laughed raucously, and Skellen offered an amber-toothed grin.

'What's the matter with 'em now then, Sergeant?' a man asked.

'The wenches at the Two Bears? Absolutely nothin' I hope, lad. For I shall visit them again soon, God willin'!'

'The boots, Sergeant,' the man clarified.

'Kineton were months ago, Harry lad, and I've marched many a night and fought many a day since. Now the buggers are torn up like a pair o' shot-through snapacks, and my feet are sufferin'.'

'And ripe as old milk!' Stryker added, sniffing the air, and was rewarded with more laughter.

'Sir!' The call reached Stryker from perhaps fifteen paces further up the road. 'Horses, sir!'

Stryker scrambled quickly to his feet, spinning on his heel and fixing the nearest men with a look they had come to know well. Wordlessly he gestured that they should stand. Rapidly, and in deathly silence, the red-coated ranks took to their feet, buckled belts, emptied pipes, crammed on helmets, took up weapons and formed into their squads.

The man who had raised the alarm was now at his captain's side, and Stryker looked down at him. He was an incongruous sight, equipped in full military regalia and dressed in the grey coat and breeches of the feared Scots Brigade, for the man's head did not reach a great deal above Stryker's waist. He was tiny, a dwarf whose clothing and weaponry made him appear for all the world like a child playing at soldiers. But it was a sight to which Stryker had grown accustomed in the weeks since Simeon Barkworth had joined his company. He had also grown used to trusting the little man's judgement. 'Certain?' Stryker asked.

''Course I'm certain,' the Scot responded tartly.

Stryker glowered. 'You may not carry rank here, Simeon, but I'll bloody break your nose if you address me like that again.'

Barkworth's eyes were a luminous yellow colour, putting Stryker in mind of a cat, and they narrowed at the taller man's threat. But he evidently thought better than to argue, and instead reined in his temper. 'I apologize, Captain. Aye, I'm certain of what I heard, sir.'

'Good enough.'

And then Stryker heard it too. The soft whicker of a horse, hidden somewhere within the phalanxes of ancient oak. Stryker saw Burton and Skellen staring at him intently, their faces questioning. 'Hear that?' he said, voice quiet now, senses alert.

Skellen frowned after a while, but even as he began to shake his head, a horse whinnied. 'Christ!' he hissed, hooded eyes widening in alarm. 'It can't be!'

Stryker thought for a moment, but shook his head. 'They're not from the town. They'd never have reached us this soon.'

The horse's call carried to them again. Burton pointed to the right of the road, where nothing could be seen for forty or fifty paces through the dense woodland. 'Over there.'

Stryker turned to Simeon Barkworth. 'Take a look.'

Barkworth nodded once and immediately plunged into undergrowth. The company watched as the little man leapt branches and dodged trees, his movements agile but soundless, until his silhouette was swallowed by the gloom.

They waited in near silence for two or three minutes with only the birdsong for company. Stryker studied the sky. It was still warm, the prickling at his sweating armpits all the more irritating now that they were not on the move, but he noted how grey the thick clouds had become, and quietly ordered the men to protect their powder in case it rained.

When Barkworth eventually returned, his expression was one of excitement. 'Land—falls—away—' His voice, throttled to near destruction by a hangman's noose more than a decade earlier, was never more than a rasp, but the sprint had rendered him breathless, and virtually impossible to understand.

Stryker held up his palms. 'Hold, Simeon. Catch your breath.'

Barkworth nodded, took several deeper lungfuls of the muggy air, and looked into his commander's keen eye. 'The land falls away to a shallow bowl. A clearing in the forest. They're there.'

'They?'

'A dozen, cavalry all.'

Stryker's eye narrowed. 'Ours or theirs?'

Barkworth's face creased in an apologetic frown. 'Can't be certain, sir.'

'Field sign?' Lieutenant Burton asked.

Barkworth glanced at him. 'Black feather, sir.'

'A black feather?' Skellen interjected. 'Never heard o' that one.'

Barkworth stared up at him. 'And you're the authority on the subject, you lanky bastard?'

'I'd wager I'm an authority greater than you, you bloody puck-eyed dwarf.'

'Enough!' Stryker ordered. The mostly good-natured sniping between Barkworth and Skellen had become part of the company's fabric since they had first encountered the Scot – working as the Earl of Chesterfield's bodyguard at the time – at Lichfield the previous March, but now he required their undivided attention. 'Simeon, you're sure that was the only field sign? Skellen's right, I've never seen one like that.'

Barkworth nodded. 'That's the sign, right enough, sir. Big thing, too. Pinned between the helmet tail-plates.' He moved a hand across his skull from neck to forehead. 'The plume curves right over, like this.'

Stryker looked at Burton. 'Lieutenant?'

'We assume they're Cropheads until we're certain.'

Stryker nodded. 'Indeed we do.'

Barkworth stepped forward, his yellow eyes suddenly bright. 'Set about them, sir?'

Stryker rubbed a hand across his stubble. 'I'm inclined to let them be, Simeon. I do not wish to draw any undue attention to our small force.'

'Aye, sir,' Barkworth replied casually, 'as you order.'

Stryker stared down at the little man, suspicious at the ease with which Barkworth's notoriously flammable battle-lust had dissipated. 'Simeon?'

Barkworth's gnarled features cracked in a sharp-toothed grin. 'You might like to take a peek at what they have with them, sir.'

Stryker, Burton, Skellen and Barkworth crouched low behind a close-cropped group of trunks and studied the strangers at the foot of the slope. The clearing was indeed the shape of a bowl, a circular patch of sunken, bare land in the forest's depths with wide oaks lining its rim. At its far side was an opening in the trees where a narrow track ran away to the north, quickly swallowed by the darkness.

There were, as Barkworth had said, twelve cavalry-men. All but one was mounted, though there seemed no urgency about their movements. One leaned back to take a long draught from a leather-bound flask, another picked at his teeth with a thin dagger, and at least three were sucking lazily on clay pipes. None of the riders wore their helmets, but those Stryker could see, slung at the sides of saddles or propped under their owners' arms, were adorned with the large black feather Barkworth had described.

Stryker's attention turned to the object that had so excited Barkworth. It was a wagon. An inauspicious affair of half-rotten planks and rickety wheels, drawn by a pair of gaunt nags, and with a nervous-looking man in a brown farmer's shirt who kept his gaze fixed on his reins.

'See there?' Barkworth rasped, indicating the vehicle. 'Worth a scrap, wouldn't you say?'

Stryker eyed the wagon's contents, and his heartbeat immediately began to accelerate. The bed of the vehicle was crammed full of objects. Stout little barrels, bulging cloth sacks, coils of thin rope, and bushels full to the brim with fist-sized orbs. Ammunition. Powder, shot, grenadoes, match.

As he studied the vehicle with growing excitement, Stryker noticed a man emerge from a pit at the wagon's rear. It was narrow, its mouth perhaps a yard across, but evidently deep, for the man had required a ladder to climb out. 'It's an arms cache,' he whispered.

Barkworth evidently read the expression on Stryker's face, for his dirk was suddenly in his little fist and his grin full of murderous relish. 'Fucking rebels.'

'*If* they're rebels,' Burton said soberly. 'And there may be more of the buggers about.'

'Aye, that there may,' Barkworth replied, 'but aren't we to engage the enemy where possible, sir?'

Stryker glanced at them both, weighing up his options. To fight here would be fraught with risk, for the gunfire would likely carry all the way down to the Parliamentarians in the town, but he could not help but think of the rich prize that awaited them. A huge enemy ammunition dump was difficult to ignore. If they were the enemy.

'How do we get close enough, sir?' Skellen asked dubiously. 'Bastards'll ride off soon as they see us comin'.'

Barkworth's grin soured, and he grunted reluctant agreement. 'Ninety-five men ain't on the quiet side, sir.'

Stryker looked at the Scot. 'Aye. If we could get this done with fewer. Twenty perhaps.'

Barkworth's grin returned, his eyes narrowing to gleaming slits. 'Enough to batter this lot.'

'Split the force?' Burton asked.

The question seemed to pour icy water on the fire that was steadily growing in Stryker's belly, and he sighed deeply, impressed with the younger man's cool head. He rubbed a hand across the bristles of his chin. 'You're right, Andrew, of course. I have been in a black mood of late, and my judgement is not what it ought to be.' He turned to Barkworth. 'We should not risk this. There may be a larger troop nearby, and that dozen would send a rider out to fetch them as soon as they heard our approach.'

Barkworth grimaced. 'But sir—'

'And hear us they most certainly would,' Stryker added, cutting Barkworth's protest dead.

The trees began to whisper then. A crackling in the canopy above their heads, as though the branches were passing ancient secrets to one another. Stryker instinctively looked up, wondering at the noise that was already growing louder, more insistent, a chatter rather than a whisper. In seconds it was louder still, a rushing sound that seemed to engulf the forest.

When the first cold drops finally hit his face, Stryker allowed himself a small smile.

'Will, Simeon,' he said as the rain thrashed through the leaves and branches to soak the earth at their feet, 'bring up the men.'

'If they're rebels,' Burton said again as they watched the company's tallest and shortest men vanish with equal stealth into the trees.

Stryker patted the lieutenant's good shoulder. 'Let's find out.'

The two officers met the red-coated ranks some forty paces further back from the clearing. As expected, Stryker saw that his musketeers had wrapped lengths of oiled cloth around their weapons so that the rain would not dampen their firing mechanisms or permeate the black powder within. The pikemen had no such worry, though their lethal staves had to be carried horizontally at waist height to prevent the ash poles, each more than sixteen feet long, from snagging on the boughs above.

'Sergeant Heel,' Stryker said, his voice low, urgent.

Moses Heel, the bullock-shaped native of Tiverton, paced quickly up to his commander. 'Sir.'

'See we're covered.'

'Sir,' Heel said, and abruptly turned to the company. 'Jack and Harry Trowbridge.' He paused as two musketeers, both long-nosed and blue-eyed, with tendrils of blond hair poking out from beneath their pot helmets, stepped briskly out of the line. 'You've got the sharpest eyes, so get your bliddy arses on that road. One north, t'other south.' He looked back at the company. 'Lipscombe and Boyleson, where are you?'

'Here,' was the response as a pair of men came to stand by the Trowbridge brothers. They wore the red coats of the ranks, but instead of pike or musket they carried large drums, slung at their midriffs by thick cross-belts.

'Go with the twins,' Sergeant Heel ordered. 'If they see somethin' worthy o' tellin', hammer it out. Understand?'

'Sergeant,' one of the drummers responded, and the four paced back in the direction of the road.

Stryker nodded acknowledgement to Heel, and turned to Burton. 'Lieutenant, you command the men. Hold them here but spread them wide, and be ready with point, steel and shot on my mark.' His eye winked mischievously. 'I am to go fishing.'

Burton's mouth twitched in half-smile. 'We'll ready your net.'

Stryker led Barkworth and Skellen, chosen for their lack of conspicuous company coats, at a rapid pace towards the clearing. They snaked through the trees, edging ever closer to the black-plumed horsemen, the rustle of their footsteps masked by the rain as it crashed through the canopy. Fat droplets pounded the branches above and the leaves at their feet, exploded against hat rims and raced across the surface of impervious buff-coats.

Stryker halted half a dozen paces before the trees started to thin, knowing the land would soon begin to slope away. He glanced over his shoulder and scanned the trees further back towards the road. He was pleased to see no sign of Burton or the rest of the company.

Skellen appeared at his side. 'What now, sir?'

Without reply, Stryker crept forwards, dropping to the lowest crouch possible as he reached the edge of the clearing. His knees burned keenly as he held the position, but he wanted a moment to study the strangers, to check the group had not been joined by more horsemen in the minutes Stryker had been organizing his approach. There they were: twelve only.

He stood, drawing his sword, easing it slowly from the scabbard's throat so that the rasp was inaudible above the dashing rain. Still the horsemen did not notice his presence. Stryker swallowed hard, took a steadying breath, and stepped out into the open.

A shout went up almost immediately, a high-pitched cry of warning from the base of the shallow bowl, and Stryker wondered whether the cavalrymen would charge him down without pausing to discover his allegiance. But, just as the lobster-tailed helmets were shoved unceremoniously on to their heads and the huge horses were coaxed out of their lethargy, one of the strangers walked his mount out from the group.

Stryker took a couple of tentative paces down the slope, not taking his gaze from the man he presumed to be the small troop's leader. It was difficult to discern age from a face obscured by the three vertical face bars of the helmet's visor, but from the lines at the corners of his eyes, the confident bearing and the thick, pointed beard at his chin, Stryker guessed he was in his early thirties. He, like his comrades, was equipped in the manner of a typical harquebusier, with buff-coat swathing his torso beneath gleaming back- and breast-plates, a long sword at his waist and a carbine slung at his side. Stryker suspected there would be a smaller blade and a brace of pistols about the man's person as well, and he approached with caution.

'Greetings, sir,' he said, keeping his voice loud and steady, for the rain still roared around them.

The leader of the horsemen kicked his mount on a touch, and glared down at the man on foot, pale blue eyes appearing like orbs of glass beneath the coke-black plume of his helmet. 'Who the devil are you, sir?'

'Captain Stryker, Mowbray's Foot.'

The horseman's nose wrinkled. 'I am Colonel Gabriel Wild. Have you no Christian name?'

'None worth mentioning, Colonel,' Stryker said, and stole a furtive glance at the ammunition wagon that was now firmly screened by the dozen harquebusiers. 'King or Parliament, sir?'

25

Wild's expression remained stony. 'The latter, sir,' he said with deliberate slowness. 'And you?'

Stryker could now hear his own heart above the rainfall. 'The former.'

In a flash Colonel Wild's sword was free, its tip levelled at the Royalist's throat. Stryker saw that it was not the delicate, probing rapier he had expected to see, but a brutal, wide-bladed, broadsword. The weapon of a trained killer.

'Hold, sir, I urge you!' Stryker called, forcing the tension from his voice. 'For you are at a disadvantage.'

Those final words gave the cavalryman pause, for he seemed to take a moment to consider the situation, glancing into the trees at Stryker's back. 'How so, Captain?'

'I have men in these trees, Colonel.' With that, William Skellen and Simeon Barkworth emerged from the tree line, muskets trained on the enemy officer. 'You are sore outnumbered.'

'Lies!' Wild spat the word. 'Why are they not here if you have them? You are three only. Nothing more than brigands, wagering at my timidity! You insult my intelligence, sir.'

Stryker ignored him. 'I merely want your wagon, Colonel Wild. Surrender it now, and take your leave.'

Wild tilted his head back so that raindrops soaked his face, and brayed with laughter. 'Such nerve, sir! Such goddamned nerve!' The gesture he made was barely discernible, a mere flick of the wrist that made his heavy sword waver slightly in the air, but Stryker read it and recoiled instinctively, even as one of Wild's men burst forth from the group. The horseman's arm came up, straightened, levelled in line with Stryker's chest, and he saw the glint of metal in the gloved hand. He scrambled back up the slope to the protection of the oaks beyond. The pistol flashed, but the sound was more muffled cough than sharp crack, and he knew the horseman's powder had become damp. The rider looked down in horror at his impotent weapon, and Stryker threw himself on to the higher ground of the forest, screaming at his comrades to follow.

Immediately hooves pounded at their backs, more thunderous than the rain lashing about them, and the three Royalists sprinted for their lives, weaving in and out of the thick trunks of oak, hurdling fallen branches and rotten stumps and powering through grasping thickets of bracken. Stryker's feet and legs and chest blazed with the effort, but still he could sense the cavalrymen gaining, could hear their murder-tinted snarls and imagine the gleaming blades lofted high above their heads, poised for the killing blow.

'Charge your horse and give 'em some fucking steel, boys!' a voice bellowed from somewhere to Stryker's left. He could not see the speaker, for a significant portion of his left side had been left black to him by the bag of gunpowder that had taken his eye, but he knew the voice well enough. He ran towards that voice, immediately rewarded by the black-bearded grimace of the Cornishman, Jimmy Tresick, musket nestled at his shoulder, a seemingly endless length of match-cord wound loosely about his wrist. But the corporal did not pull his trigger for suddenly other men were at his shoulders. Strong men in steel morion helmets hefting long shafts of ash upwards at an angle, the razor-sharp blades embedded in their tips hovering menacingly at eye-level. Or, more importantly, chest-level with a horse.

Stryker threw himself on to the wet earth, rolling under the first of the pike points, and knew that his experienced redcoats would be stepping up to close the trap. He turned just in time to see the first of his Parliamentarian pursuers hit home amid a crow of triumph. But instead of glory, the cavalryman would find only death in this hunt. He was galloping too fast to slow his mount, and though he managed to tear the beast's head back with a savage pull on the reins, the hooves continued unabated and slid in the deepening mud, scrabbling violently for purchase until its heaving chest thudded on to the tip of a waiting pike. The pikeman was driven backwards by the sheer force of the beast, but he did not let the tapered stave go, and the blade drove deeper and deeper. The animal toppled sideways, crashed into the rain-soaked blanket of leaves, and two musketeers, in position behind the pikemen, stepped forward with naked swords. They drove them into the horse's chest, stabbing manically for the heart in order to stop the beast's dangerous thrashing. Its rider was trapped beneath the huge bulk, and he received a blade too, so that both man and horse fell silent together.

Stryker stared left and right, and felt a rushing pride for the men of his company. Burton had hidden them well, and had released them at precisely the right moment, so that the redcoats emerged from behind the trees in two concentric circles, pikes in the front rank, muskets behind. He looked up at the milling cavalrymen, black-plumed heads darting all around, searching for a way through. But he knew there was none. They would see a line of wicked-tipped pikes, offering death to their horses, and, should they break through, they would be cut down in short order by the primed muskets.

Stryker studied each anger-etched face within the circle until he found the one he wanted. 'Do you yield, Colonel Wild?'

Wild turned his mount to face him, and Stryker thought for a moment that the proud officer, incandescent with rage, would launch a suicidal charge, but instead he merely spat a yellow gobbet of phlegm on to the soggy mulch.

'I said, do you yield?' Stryker shouted again.

'Your powder will fail!' Wild shrieked. He lifted his blade, whipping it in a tight circle above the now limp plume of his helmet. 'God and Parliament! God and Parliament!'

But none of Wild's horsemen moved, for their mounts would not charge the hedge of pikes, let alone the muskets beyond.

Stryker shook his head. 'Their charges are dry, sir, unlike your own. For one shot at least. And I think one shot for each of my men will comfortably win this fight, don't you?'

Wild's desperate gaze flicked from one musket to the next and gradually the belligerence began to drain from his face as he noted the oiled cloth wound around each weapon. 'My regiment are nearby, Captain. Four hundred elite horsemen. Four hundred swords that will enfilade your meagre force in a heartbeat. They will be here in minutes.'

Stryker shook his head slowly. 'I think not. You were wrong to give chase, Colonel. Do not make another such mistake, for I would not wish further bloodshed.' He glanced down at the dead rider and his still-twitching horse. 'But be certain I will have the rest of you slaughtered here and now if needs be. I merely want your wagon.

29

Or rather its contents.' He turned to Tresick. 'Fetch it, Corporal.'

With a snarl of pure rage, Colonel Wild flung his sword to the earth, the tip driving into the mud so that the ornate hilt was left to tremble in the rain.

'God and *King*, sir,' Stryker said as he pulled the weapon free.

The languorous frame of Sergeant Skellen came up beside him, a grin splitting the tall man's face from ear to ear. 'And a pox on Parliament.'

A short while later Captain Stryker's Company of Foot were arranged in the formal line of march and ready to take their leave. Stryker was thankful that the rain had finally stopped, for the storm would have made their march into Dartmoor much less bearable.

'You did well,' Stryker said when he found Lieutenant Burton inspecting the heavily laden ammunition wagon. The company had ensured the subterranean cache was truly empty, and now they would take their loot back to the army in Cornwall.

Burton gave a short snort in a futile attempt to hide his pride. 'Men did well, sir.'

'Either way, it was the perfect trap. Exactly as I had imagined.'

Burton went to ensure the bolts at the wagon's rear were locked tight. 'And without a shot fired,' he said when he stepped back.

'That was crucial, Andrew. The wagon is a rare prize, but not one worth losing the company for. Our musketry would have alerted the Roundheads down in the town.'

Burton nodded, perhaps considering the thought of

what horrors might have come from Bovey Tracey had their guns burst into life. 'I still cannot fathom how you knew Wild's powder would be damp.'

Stryker looked at him, acutely aware of the guilt that must etch his face. 'A guess, Andrew.'

Burton's mouth lolled open, but Stryker turned away, unwilling to discuss his folly further. And folly it was, he knew, for he had taken a great risk in gambling on the pistol's misfire. But he had wanted that wagon. He chuckled silently, mirthlessly, chiding himself for a fool. She had made him angry, and he had wanted a fight.

'You are nothing but common thieves, sir!' a bellowed voice carried to him, and in a strange way Stryker was almost relieved to have his dark thoughts brought back to the here and now.

He paced across the clearing and to the edge of the tree line. 'You are alive, sir.'

Colonel Gabriel Wild, stripped of weapons and armour, wrists bound tight at his back and kneeling at the base of a tree, was older than Stryker had thought. Perhaps, he guessed, near forty. His hair was light brown, left long so that it just reached his shoulders, and bisected by a bright streak of silver that ran through the very middle of his head, putting Stryker in mind of a badger. His brown beard had lost its waxed precision amid the chase and the rainfall, but Stryker remembered how well kempt it had been when first he had seen the cavalryman. His grooming, his expensive weaponry, and the well-equipped nature of his troop told Stryker that Wild was a man of status, and of wealth.

'Christ's robes, you damnable peasant,' Wild continued as though Stryker had not spoken. 'I will have every man here hanged by his own entrails!'

Stryker stared down at the line of kneeling, pitiful cavalrymen. 'We are at war, Colonel.'

'War? What do you know of war, eh?'

Stryker heard Skellen grunt in amusement nearby. 'I know enough, sir.'

Wild glared up at his captor, pale eyes glittering with white-hot rage. 'Then you will know that this is not war. It is simple brigandry. You know what I do with footpads on my estates, Stryker? I exterminate them.'

'So I will look forward to when next we meet,' Stryker said, turning to his sergeants. 'Skellen, Heel. The wagon is ready. See Colonel Wild's horses are tethered behind, and his plate and weapons loaded in the rear. We leave now.'

'By Christ, Stryker,' Wild almost spat his words now, 'you will never make it back to your lines! I will hunt you down and use your stones as paperweights, 'pon my honour I will.'

Stryker rounded on the colonel, patience finally at an end, and kicked him square in the chest, so that Wild was flung on to his back, filth spattering in all directions. 'Enough of your threats, you pribbling bastard! Be thankful you lived today, for I am in a cave-dark mood, so help me God!'

Wild kept his mouth shut this time, though his eyes were a veritable blaze of hatred.

'Another mortal enemy, sir,' Simeon Barkworth croaked as Stryker turned away. 'You seem to attract them like flies on . . . well, I'm sure you grasp m' meaning.'

Stryker sighed deeply. 'Aye.'

'Think I'd cut 'em all down here and now, sir.'

'I dare say you would, Simeon,' Stryker replied. 'Which is why I thank God you are on my side.' He glanced back at Wild and his trussed cavalrymen. 'He is no threat now. We have his wagon, his horses, his weapons and his clothes. They have a long walk ahead of them.'

'At least you left them their boots.'

'I might not have, but we do not need them.' A thought struck him then, and he scanned the area for the man whose head he knew would rise above the rest. 'Skellen!'

'Captain, sir,' Skellen said when he had jogged across the clearing to where Stryker waited.

'They lost a man today.'

The sergeant sketched the sign of the cross. 'May God see him rest in peace. A good lad, I reckon, sir. Brave to charge our pikes. And tall.'

'Quite.'

The corners of Skellen's mouth twitched. 'Similar sized feet to mine, I'd imagine, sir.'

'They're yours.'

Skellen affected a deep bow. 'You're a grand man, sir.'

'Spare me, Will,' Stryker said, turning away.

'As you wish, sir.'

Stryker looked to the company. 'Prepare to march!'

CHAPTER 2

Captain Lancelot Forrester found his colonel in a house on St Thomas Road. The dwelling, like so many others in the town, had been commandeered for army use, and its owners could do nothing but suffer in silence and pray the soldiers would march away soon.

Sir Edmund Mowbray – founder, bankroller and commander of Mowbray's Regiment of Foot – was bareheaded and stooped over a paper-strewn desk. He looked up only when Forrester cleared his throat theatrically. 'Well?'

Forrester ignored the colonel's uncharacteristic irritability, for the horrors that had befallen the Royalist army less than forty-eight hours earlier were enough to strain even the most sanguine character. 'You summoned me, sir.'

Mowbray straightened, lifting a hand to worry at the waxed tip of his small, neat beard. 'You know what I want, Captain. The butcher's bill. Spit it out, man.'

Forrester removed his wide-brimmed hat, running a chubby hand through thinning, sandy hair. 'Fifteen, sir, across the regiment.'

Mowbray fixed his fourth captain with a hard stare and chewed the inside of his mouth. 'Fifteen.'

Forrester winced. 'Aye, Sir Edmund, regrettably.'

Just when Forrester thought Mowbray might explode, the colonel took a step back from the table and sighed heavily. 'By God, Lancelot, but that's a heavy toll.'

Forrester thought back to the battle. Just two nights ago, it already seemed like some distant nightmare. The King's Army, triumphant in Cornwall and confident of pressing the advantage all the way to the heart of Devon, had approached the town of Okehampton, only to be cruelly ambushed at a place called Sourton Down. Despite outnumbering the enemy by three to one, General Hopton's Royalists had been hammered by a determined assault and confused by the chaos of nego-tiating unfamiliar terrain in an unusually black night. And then it had rained. To Forrester's mind it had been a storm conjured in the bowels of hell itself, such was its swirling ferocity, and Hopton's hitherto unbeatable army had cut and run. He shuddered involuntarily. 'Might have been a deal worse, sir.'

Mowbray nodded reluctantly. 'Hopton might have lost his entire army in one fell swoop.' The colonel, a fas-tidious little man of compact frame and inexhaustible alacrity, paced across to a sturdy wooden chest in the room's corner. 'Drink?'

'Kind of you, sir.' Forrester watched his commanding officer pluck a bottle and two glasses from the box.

Mowbray filled the glasses and handed one to the taller man. 'Mead. Not my drink, if I'm honest, but needs must.' His brown eyes narrowed. 'You've lost weight, Lancelot.'

Forrester frowned, patting his plump midriff with his free hand. 'Food is scarce, sir. If I am not careful, I shall have no muscle left, and then where will I be?'

Mowbray's mouth twitched slightly. 'Quite.' He turned back to the table, setting his glass down on the cluttered surface, and stared at the largest sheet of paper. 'Sourton was a crushing setback, Captain, I do not mind telling you.'

Forrester chose not to comment on the indisputable truth of the statement. Instead he took the liberty of shuffling closer to the desk, peering down at the object of Mowbray's attention. It was a map. A huge, detailed, exquisitely produced map of the south-western counties; the large block of land that was Devon, the long expanse of Cornwall, tapering westwards into the Atlantic Ocean, and the squirming black line that represented the border between the two. 'Is Devon lost to us?'

Mowbray did not look up. 'Perhaps.' He indicated a spot on the north-west fringe of Dartmoor. It was unmarked, but Forrester knew the location well enough. Sourton Down would be forever etched on his memory. 'They surprised us on those bleak heights. Humiliated us, even. And now we are back here,' he moved his finger several inches to the left, 'in Launceston.'

'Safe here though, sir.'

Now the colonel met Forrester's gaze. 'Safe indeed. And the bloody rebels are safe across the border. We are no better off than we were at Christmas.'

Mowbray straightened. 'Devon is Parliament heartland, Lancelot. Bideford, Exeter, Okehampton, Dartford, Barnstaple, Plymouth. All declared for Pym's vipers, and all sit pretty in their treason. We have not touched a single one, and now we have lost ground, by God.' He shook his head sorrowfully. 'Do you recall how things were when first we came here?'

36

'How could I forget, sir?' Forrester replied, memories of negotiating the Irish Sea still fresh. That torrid, vomit-washed crossing would remain as keen in his mind's eye for as long as the defeat at Sourton. He shuddered slightly. 'We were attached to this army because the truce was ending. Hopton wanted a great push eastwards to secure the south-west once and for all.'

'Such expectation,' Forrester said.

'Such naivety,' Mowbray added sombrely. 'Now, Captain, we are on the back foot. Hopton left scores of good men on that bleak hill, fifteen of them mine, by Christ. And Lord knows what has become of Stryker.'

That thought had not occurred to Forrester until now. His friend had been sent across Dartmoor to watch the eastern roads while the Royalists swept into Devon. He would not yet know of the shock defeat, nor of the Parliamentarian counterattack that was almost certain to follow. He swallowed back some mead, enjoying the sweet flavour of honey and the slight burn at his throat. His nerves were more frayed than he had realized.

Mowbray lifted his own glass to thin lips, drained the contents in one gulp, and fixed Forrester with a level stare. 'Now we must force ourselves out of this mire. Seize the initiative.' The colonel's eyes lit with a sudden spark. 'And for that, we require something—extraordinary.'

'I don't follow, sir.'

Sir Edmund Mowbray's face cracked in a half-smile. 'Come with me.'

The ship thudded into the pitch-dark sea, sending up clouds of salty water to soak the decks. It was a vicious squall – a nasty, vengeful bitch of a thing, the skipper had muttered as he commanded all fare-paying passengers below – so that the *Curlew*'s decks were almost bare. But one person remained at the prow. One stubborn man who was neither sailor nor officer. Like the carved figurehead at the foremost point of a warship, he stood still and silent, wrapped tight in a hooded cloak drenched black by the sea.

Braced against the *Curlew*'s wooden rail, Osmyn Hogg ignored the gale-hewn seamen as they scuttled about behind him like so many crabs. He narrowed his eyes against the stinging spray and ignored the timbers as they groaned beneath his boots. He cared little for the inclement weather, thinking only upon his duty and trusting in God to see the ship safely to port. She was a nimble vessel, or so the captain had proclaimed. A cutter, not ten years out of Buckler's Hard, all sleek lines and snapping sail, yet this morning's squall had given her quite the fight. The fickle wind, pulsing east or west without warning or mercy, tortured the vessel in the choppy swell it conjured, lashing at the rigging and causing even the oldest sailor to stagger across the slick boards.

'Tempest's up, sir!' a voice cried suddenly above the roaring wind. 'She dares us to make our run for Plymouth Sound!'

Hogg glanced to his right to see the craggy features of the *Curlew*'s skipper. 'The Devil does not wish me to reach land, Captain Tubb.'

Tubb, a powerfully built old sea dog with leathery

skin and one milky eye, drew his own hood over thinning brown hair, whipped ragged by the storm, and furnished his passenger with a near toothless grimace. 'He may succeed if you remain here, sir!'

'Do not speak such things into the world, Captain,' Hogg replied acidly, causing the skipper to break eye contact.

'I merely meant it is unsafe, sir,' Tubb muttered, studying the ever-filling horizon.

Hogg followed the stocky sailor's gaze. Land had appeared just after dawn, a black smudge on the grey distance, and he had watched it grow in size and detail ever since. And, though the wind whipped stronger with each passing moment, Hogg had rejected his fear. Even as powerful gusts buffeted the barnacled hull and raced like an army of screaming banshees through the shrouds, he had remained steadfast, keeping his eyes on land and his thoughts in prayer. For the Lord had brought him here, and He would see the *Curlew* came to no harm. But it was not, Hogg reflected, merely the weather that Satan might employ. 'What of the king's ships, Captain Tubb?'

Tubb looked up at the taller man. 'The bastards show 'emselves ever more, sir, 'tis true.'

Hogg nodded thoughtfully, for he had heard as much. Parliament held most of the navy, the squadrons having declared for the rebellion at the war's outset, but a few captains had favoured the king's cause and, bolstered by vessels from Ireland and the Continent, the small Royalist fleet was beginning to grow in strength and self-belief.

'But we're safe enough here,' Tubb continued. 'So close now to Plymouth. The Parliament holds these waters in the main.'

The conversation ended abruptly as the *Curlew* lurched on a big swell, toppling over its white crest and slamming into the next rising wave. They bowed their heads against the blinding spray, only daring to look up when the swell seemed to subside.

'The malignants do not sail here?' Hogg eventually asked.

'Oh, the Cavaliers sail here, right enough, but nothin' of concern. Men o' war, or the like. Small vessels only, prized for speed and seekin' no brabble.'

'Smugglers?'

'Aye. Runnin' powder, shot and men to their Cornish army, or those Pope's turd Welshies.'

Hogg stared back at the dark smear of land and felt his heart surge, for a mass of white sail had emerged from the gloom like a low-lying cloud.

Captain Tubb grinned when he saw his passenger's expression. 'Plymouth Bay, Master Hogg. We shall survive this after all.'

'The Lord provides,' Hogg said, feeling the capricious squall change direction again. He flinched as one of the huge sails cracked like thunder above their heads, and mouthed a short prayer.

'What trade you in, sir, if you don't mind my askin'?' said Captain Tubb.

'I do mind,' Hogg replied bluntly.

'Doctor?' Tubb went on undeterred. 'Some kind o' cleric, perhaps?'

Osmyn Hogg looked down at the captain, fixing him with a look that made Tubb turn away. 'I am a hunter, sir, by God's grace.'

Tubb swallowed hard, and stared out to sea. 'And what is your quarry, sir?' he asked, his voice unnaturally thick.

'Demons,' Hogg replied. 'And the folk who would harbour them.'

And soon, Hogg thought as he watched Plymouth draw ever closer, he would be home. After all these years. And the Devil's minions would suffer.

LAUNCESTON, CORNWALL, 27 APRIL 1643

Sir Edmund Mowbray led his fourth captain into a building some hundred paces along St Thomas Road. Like Mowbray's billet, it was a timber-framed house, though this one was far larger, a great cavernous mansion of big windows, high-ceiling rooms and labyrinthine corridors.

After a minute or two pacing quickly along one of those passageways, the pair reached a thick wooden door guarded by two burly halberdiers. To Forrester's surprise, they received no challenge, the fearsome weapons snapping apart with an impatient wave of Mowbray's hand.

Mowbray grasped the iron hoop that served as the handle and jerked it upwards so that the door creaked ajar. He glanced over his shoulder. 'Hat off, Lancelot.'

Forrester did as he was ordered and followed Mowbray inside.

'Sir Edmund! It heartens the soul to see you well!' The speaker was perched on the edge of a large chair at the far end of the rectangular chamber. He had evidently been leafing through a vast pile of papers, an aide assisting at his shoulder, but leaned back at the sight of the newcomers.

Forrester stared at the man in surprise, for his chirpy voice was rather at odds with his appearance. The man's

41

cropped hair and sombre clothes, plain in cut and colour, made him seem more Parliamentarian than Royalist.

'And you, General,' Mowbray was saying, before indicating Forrester with a snappy nod. 'Please allow me to introduce to you Captain Lancelot Forrester.'

The man at the desk shifted his brown eyes to meet Forrester, and the captain suddenly found himself studying his boots. 'Your—your servant, General Hopton.'

Sir Ralph Hopton, commander of the king's forces in this south-western corner of England, grinned broadly. 'The pleasure is mine, Captain, I assure you,' he said in the rounded tones of Somerset. At the edge of the table sat a wooden trencher holding the remains of a meal of fine bread, cheese and meat pie, the smell making Forrester's stomach growl. 'It is good to finally put a countenance to the name.'

Forrester looked up, unable to hide his surprise. 'Sir?'

'The reputation of Sir Edmund's regiment grows fast and formidable,' Hopton elaborated, leaning back in the big chair and making a steeple of his fingers. 'Many of his officers have received much praise. You among them.'

Forrester felt his cheeks colour. 'Kind of you to say, sir. Too kind.'

'Indeed, I was most impressed to hear of your service with the late Earl of Northampton's force. God rest him.'

'A bloody and terrible day, sir,' Forrester said, thinking upon the battle that had raged on a ridge outside Stafford. 'The Earl fought bravely,' he added, trying in vain not to sound awkward, 'and died a hero.'

Somewhere in the town, the church clock struck nine of the hour. Hopton drew breath to speak, but held it, allowing the toll to run its melancholy course, and Forrester found himself staring at the great man. Though seated, it was clear that Sir Ralph was probably of average height, with mousy hair and moustache and a beard that tipped his chin in a sharp point. He was plump, a fact which surprised Forrester, for the tale of Sir Ralph's death-defying expedition to rescue Elizabeth of Bohemia – Prince Rupert's mother – from Prague had become soldiering legend. But, he reminded himself, that had been more than twenty years ago, and the general would now be in his late forties.

'May I introduce to you gentlemen,' Hopton finally said when the pealing had ceased, 'my commander in Cornwall, Sir Bevil Grenville.'

Hopton glanced over his shoulder at the man Forrester had taken to be the general's aide. He was of a similar age to Sir Ralph, but more athletically built, with light-brown hair that seemed almost bronze. Those locks were curled and left long so that they cascaded beyond his shoulders and across the expensive white collar and silver-laced coat. If Hopton wanted to discuss reputations, then to Forrester's mind, Sir Bevil Grenville was worth speaking of. For all his Cavalier airs, Grenville was a hard-bitten and respected campaigner. A veteran of the Bishops' Wars, he had become known throughout England as a true leader of men, and fearless fighter.

'Well met, sirs,' Grenville said in a broad Cornish accent. 'Your regiment played an active role at Sourton, if I recall correctly. You helped us protect the artillery train.'

Protect, thought Forrester. *Active role*. Words could never describe that hell. The black night, the storm crashing around them, the showers of lead cutting men down, the swords and the hooves and the screams. It had been confusion. Blood-spattered anarchy.

43

'It was, Sir Bevil,' Mowbray replied.

Grenville dipped his head in acknowledgement. 'Then we are friends already.'

'Sir Bevil is my most trusted and able man,' Hopton said. 'Was responsible for driving Parliament's supporters across the Tamar at the war's very birth.'

Grenville's lips twitched. 'Too kind, Sir Ralph, but a small matter in truth. I summoned the posse comitatus and had the devils expelled before they could make trouble.'

'A small matter loyal men failed to achieve in almost every other county,' Forrester said, genuinely impressed.

Grenville offered a small shrug, evidently embarrassed by the attention. 'Cornwall is ferociously loyal, Captain. The number of rebels to be expelled was not great, truth be told.'

'Since then, of course,' Hopton continued, 'Sir Bevil's Cornish army has quickly garnered repute for reckless valour.'

Grenville's jaw twitched as he gritted his teeth. 'A recklessness that has cost us dear of late, I am ashamed to say.'

'There will be time and opportunity to rectify events at Sourton Down, sir,' Hopton replied.

'I pray both come swiftly,' said Grenville.

Hopton looked back at Mowbray and Forrester. 'Where are my manners, eh? Sit gentlemen, please.'

The men drew up a pair of chairs that had been tucked under the general's campaign table, and awaited his next words.

'The Cornish lads are raw, Captain Forrester,' Hopton said after a short time. 'They fight hard enough, by God they do, but they're striplings in the ways of war. Men

44

experienced in soldiering are difficult to find.' He paused then, letting the words linger.

Forrester caught the intimation well enough. 'Men like me, sir?'

'Precisely. I am sending one of my best men, courtesy of Sir Bevil—'

Grenville bowed. 'Your servant, General—'

'On a task of a—' Hopton made a steeple of his fingers again, 'delicate nature.'

'And I?' Forrester prompted.

The general leaned back. 'Escort him, Forrester. See that he is protected should there be trouble.'

Forrester glanced at Grenville.

'We have spoken of my men's tendency to reckless bravery, Captain,' the Cornish commander said. 'They are utterly formidable upon the field of battle, but,' he smiled ruefully, 'perhaps not best suited to tasks requiring a more—subtle touch.'

'Sir Edmund tells me your company is solid as any he has,' Hopton took up the explanation, 'and I understand you have personally undertaken many similar missions for Prince Rupert in the past.'

'Right enough, sir.'

'And he tells me you are rather easily bored.'

Forrester felt his cheeks become instantly hot. 'I—that is to say—'

'It is no bad thing to be a man of energy, Captain. And I expect to remain here for some weeks yet. We have need of respite after our recent—setback.'

'I—I certainly relish a challenge, sir, 'tis true.'

'Then you are indeed the right man. Your company will escort a smaller task force south to the rendezvous point.

Put simply, your role will be to keep him alive so that he might carry out his duty.'

'His?'

Hopton nodded. 'Sir Bevil's man. Perhaps you have heard of him?' Hopton rattled an empty pewter goblet on the table top, and the door at the room's far end edged open, the face of one of the sentries appearing from the other side. 'Show Payne in, Corporal Andrews.'

'Yes, sir,' Andrews murmured, and promptly shrank back.

In less than a minute the door swung open again, this time to its full extent, allowing a man to step through. And Lancelot Forrester wondered if he was trapped in some strange dream.

The newcomer was the single tallest man Forrester had ever laid eyes upon. He had known many men of great stature in his time, had fought with and against several huge Scandinavian mercenaries on the Continent. Even some of the pikemen at Edgehill had appeared like rabid bears on that blood-soaked fair-meadow, and Malachi Bain, one of the villains responsible for Stryker's terrible injuries, had been a rare monstrosity. Yet this man, this colossus, would have simply dwarfed the lot of them. He felt his jaw drop open, and could do nothing to close it.

'Payne,' General Hopton was saying. 'Come in, come in. Forgive me, sir, I regret I do not have a chair that would be—suitable—for you. But come closer.'

Payne had stooped to pass under the lintel, but even now, well inside the room, he was compelled to bend his vast frame simply to remain clear of the ceiling's stout beams. 'My lords,' he said respectfully enough, though in a voice that reminded Forrester of a distant roll of thunder.

46

'Captain,' Hopton said, and Forrester had to force himself to tear his attention away from the giant to meet his commander-in-chief's expectant gaze.

'A—aye, sir.'

'This, Captain, is Anthony Payne. Sir Bevil's—' he glanced at Grenville.

'My manservant,' Grenville replied. 'My bodyguard, my drill-master and my best fighter.'

Forrester nodded mutely and looked back up into Payne's face. It was a face, he realized with surprise, that was not grizzled and fierce, like most of the huge fighting men he had encountered, but open, affable even. Payne's eyes, chestnut in colour and almond-shaped, appeared pleasant enough and twinkled with intelligence. He nodded his huge head of straight brown hair in Forrester's direction.

Forrester removed his hat. 'W—well met, sir, well met indeed.' He swallowed thickly as he noted Payne's arms and legs, thick as culverin barrels. 'My God, man, but you defy all nature.' It was only after the words had passed his lips that Forrester realized what he had said. 'Er—that is to say, I er—' he spluttered, feeling the blood rush to his cheeks, and half expecting the giant to crush him with a single fist.

But Anthony Payne grinned. 'No harm, sir, I assure you. It is the natural response, to which I am well accustomed.'

'My humblest apologies,' Forrester finally managed to blurt, Payne's kindly words doing little to assuage his embarrassment. 'I meant no offence by it, sir, really. My awe compelled the choice of ill-judged words, that is all.'

'Understood, sir,' Payne replied happily, proffering Forrester another white-toothed smile.

'I am merely impressed,' Forrester went on. 'I had heard tell of your—stature—many times, but one dismisses such tales as mere gossip.'

'It is no gossip, Captain.'

'No! Indeed, no. Might I ask—'

'My height?' Payne interjected.

Forrester nodded sheepishly. 'You are asked this a great deal, I shouldn't wonder.'

'Indeed,' Payne nodded. 'I am four inches above seven feet, sir.'

Forrester looked Payne up and down again, marvelling at the man before him. The vast boots, the red coat that might have provided enough material for a man's tent, and the sword that appeared like a twig at his tree-trunk waist. 'My word, sir, but you are surely a modern-day Goliath.'

'Fortunately we fight Roundheads, not Israelites,' Payne observed wryly.

'Ha! Quite so, Mister Payne, quite so. And I thank the good Lord for it!'

'As I have said,' Hopton spoke now, 'Payne, here, is Sir Bevil's man. Like you, Captain, he fought valiantly at Sourton, and I am like to keep him alive.'

Forrester wondered what on earth could kill this man-mountain, but kept the thought to himself. He met his general's gaze, sucking his bottom lip thoughtfully. 'May I know the nature of Mister Payne's mission, sir?'

'You may not, Captain,' General Hopton responded firmly. 'He has his purpose in this, just as you have yours. See that he reaches the rendezvous without hindrance, and see that he returns in good order. You are the ranking officer, Captain,' the general went on, 'and your men will look to your command, but Mister Payne must be allowed full freedom to execute his task.'

Forrester nodded acquiescence, his thoughts in a whirl. 'How many men will we take, sir?'

'Two-score should do it.'

'And I would bring a half-dozen of my most trusted lads,' Anthony Payne rumbled.

'As you see fit, Mister Payne,' General Sir Ralph Hopton agreed, before rising suddenly, offering his hand for Forrester and Payne to shake in turn. 'God be with you, gentlemen.'

They left Launceston at noon. Forrester's forty men – half musket, half pike – and seven Cornishmen, including the gigantic Anthony Payne.

Technically Forrester commanded the company, for the bulk of the troops were his and Payne held no commission or rank to speak of, but knowledge of the local terrain, not to mention the mission's detail, effectively made the giant de facto leader. Forrester did not mind the fact, for he was simply happy to be busy. Mowbray was right when he had told Hopton of the captain's restless nature, and he was only too pleased to be on the road, rather than stagnating in camp. Perhaps, he wondered as he stared at the forest-patched horizon, that was the reason he and Stryker had remained friends for so many years. The pair shared little in common, and Forrester's great love of the arts was something of a mystery to the plain-living Stryker, but they both relished risk. Both preferred challenging danger to languishing in some disease-ridden billet awaiting the next order.

'A happy thought is a precious thing in these dark days,

sir,' Payne's deep voice growled like a warship's broadside across Forrester's reverie.

Realizing he must have been smiling, Forrester craned his neck to look up at Sir Bevil Grenville's famed manservant, whose enormous stride made his own appear like that of a child. 'Your master described the Cornish as reckless, Mister Payne. I was simply reflecting that employing me for this task might not have been a deal safer.'

'Oh?'

Forrester could not help but let out a rueful chuckle. 'Since the turning of the year, I have been embroiled in more quarrels than I care to count, many of which might have been avoided had I been a man of cooler temper.'

Payne's expression was one of incredulity. 'Sir?'

Forrester laughed at that, understanding that the big man would be gazing down at a fellow of average height, round, fleshy face and ample midriff. He patted his belly with a gloved hand. 'I may appreciate the finer aspects of life, Mister Payne, but you can be certain that I am not the tardy-gaited coxcomb you presume me to be.'

'I did not presume so, sir.'

'*Pah*! I have seen your current expression on many a face, sir.'

'Then I am sorry,' Payne said.

Forrester shook his head vigorously. 'It is of no concern, Payne. None at all. I would be lying if I claimed not to have thought you a beef-witted oaf when first I laid eyes upon you.'

It was Payne's turn to laugh, and the sound seemed to reverberate up and down Forrester's spine. 'So you are a reckless Cornishman at heart, Captain?'

'Aye, I think perhaps I am. Why, a mere month ago I was fighting for my life on a cursed field outside Stafford.'

Payne's oval eyes widened. 'You were at Hopton Fight?'

Forrester nodded. 'I was. While you were enjoying your genteel peace accord, I was traipsing around the Midlands dodging rebel musket-balls.'

Payne pursed his lips in thought. 'I did not know Mowbray's were with Northampton's army, sir.'

'They weren't!' Forrester exclaimed. 'That is precisely my point, Mister Payne. I travelled there as a favour to a friend, and events rather overtook us.' He remembered that day. The terrified braying of the horses, the ear-splitting cannon fire, the thundering cavalry charges. A picture of the killing field resolved before him, and the ridge at its summit that was filled with grey-coated Parliamentarians. Aye, he thought, he had gone there for Stryker. And Stryker had gone there for Lisette Gaillard. And she had left him again.

'The difference, of course,' Payne now spoke, and Forrester wondered if the big man could sense the shadow that had fallen across his mood, 'is that my lads aren't over fond o' leavin' Kernow.'

'Oh?' Forrester replied absently.

'Between you and the Cornish, sir. The difference is that your recklessness takes you to wherever the fight happens to be. The Cornish are grand brawlers, make no mistake, but they fight for their county.'

Forrester looked up, a thought dawning. 'That's why I've been chosen for this, isn't it?'

'Sir?'

'It was easier to order me into Devon than any of Grenville's troops.'

Payne's huge head bobbed. 'The Cornish regiments will go where they're told, sir. They will for Grenville, leastwise, for he has their trust. But it is true to say that they would take some persuasion to cross the Tamar.'

'And you?'

'I am not your average soldier, sir,' Payne said bluntly. 'I have served Sir Bevil since we were children.'

'You grew up in his household?' Forrester asked.

'You have it, Captain. He may be my master, but he is also my family. I go where he tells me to go.'

'And where is that, exactly?' Forrester ventured.

Payne's wide mouth stretched in a wry smile. 'Merrivale, sir. We must meet someone there in three days' time.'

'Finally!' Forrester sighed sarcastically.

Payne shook his head. 'But no more detail than that, sir.'

'But—'

'I am sorry, sir,' said Payne, cutting off Forrester's protest, 'but the matter is sensitive. I cannot speak of it further. I trust you understand my position, Captain?'

Forrester sighed again, this time in resignation. 'Do I have a choice?'

CHAPTER 3

Almost any other day, the view from the White Hart was an unremarkable affair. Fore Street, running through the centre of Okehampton, was ever busy; populated by horses and carts, children scuttling this way and that, farmers driving livestock to market, peddlers hawking their wares. The everyday rhythm of life. But not today.

The two men at the inn's large, upper-floor window, its shutters thrown open to the grey dawn, gazed down upon a scene of chaos. Of swirling, bawling, shoving, bustling humanity.

A crowd, large and excitable, had gathered on the road, a roiling dust cloud smudging the air around their ankles, all faced in the direction of a newly erected wooden platform. Men, women and children were there, representatives from all walks of life, from Okehampton's highest ranks to its scrawniest guttersnipes. An army of carrion birds circled above; cawing crows, darting sparrows and majestic red kites.

'Not a real man,' muttered one of the men at the window. He was tall, athletically built, and dressed in a black coat fringed with blue lace. He scratched at his head, ruffling the streak of silver that ran like a badger's stripe through the

53

middle of his otherwise light-brown hair. 'We are at war. We do not need ghoulish killers who hide behind the Scriptures to slake their blood lust.' He stalked back to the empty hearth at the room's opposite side, tall cavalry boots clomping loudly on the floorboards.

The second man remained at the sill, staring down at the jostling throng below. 'Pray, Wild,' he said, without turning round. 'What *do* we need?'

Colonel Gabriel Wild leant against the cold mantelpiece. 'Soldiers, sir. Weapons.'

This time the man looked back from his vantage point. 'You preach to me, Colonel?'

Wild was not easily cowed, but he found he could not meet the challenging gaze of the man before him. Those eyes – small, coal-black, and set deep into a head that carried not a single hair – seemed utterly mesmerizing. He focussed instead on the shining silver lace that snaked its way down the front of his companion's fine green doublet. 'I—'

'When it was you, Colonel Wild,' the green-uniformed man, who might have been anywhere between twenty-five and forty-five years of age, went on. 'You who lost one good trooper, all your kit, all your weapons, a dozen horses,' his tone grew as dark as his eyes, 'and my goddamned arms cache.'

Wild coloured. 'General, I have already explained myself.'

'Then explain again, by Christ!' the general exploded, his hitherto pale face turning the colour of ripe strawberries. 'Or you'll be next on to that scaffold!'

Gabriel Wild gritted his teeth, for it was all he could do not to launch himself at the man in green. To smash his fist into that fragile-looking chin and teach the gutter-born upstart how to address his betters. But he could not, for, despite being of lower birth, Major-General Erasmus Collings was a formidable man. Not only did he enjoy far higher rank – militarily, at least – but it was said that he held the ear of Pym himself. Wild stood rigidly beside the big stone hearth, fists balled, straining to keep his rage-filled body in check.

The corners of Collings's thin-lipped mouth rose to a nasty smirk. 'Do not push me, sir,' he said, and Wild detected no hint of mirth in that icy voice. 'You may hide behind your family's wealth all you like, Colonel, but it is folly indeed to think you might puff up your chest like some pride-swollen peacock and intimidate me.'

Wild did not know if it was the major-general's confident tone, the cutting words, or those lifeless eyes, but he felt the bluster cascade from him like water through a cracked dam. He took a deep, steadying breath. 'We were ambushed, General. By a much larger force.'

'Where did they come from?' Collings said, his tone more moderate now, thoughtful.

'I know not, sir,' Wild said, utterly embarrassed, for he knew his words must appear pathetic in the extreme. 'That is to say, I did not see or hear their approach.'

'But you believe they had marched out of Bovey Tracey?'

'Aye, sir, of that I'm certain.' Wild thought back to his humiliating entrance into the town. It had taken them several hours to trudge down from the hills and into civilization, only to be greeted by a barrage of laughter and abuse. Dressed only in their undergarments, he and his ten horseless troopers must have appeared a hilarious sight for townsman and soldier alike. 'Our people were there,' he said simply, still smarting from the experience.

Collings nodded. 'We have been moving units ever westward since Sourton Fight. Deeper and deeper into the moor. Now that Hopton is forced back into Cornwall, everything east of the Tamar can be ours.'

'Their colonel told me of a Cavalier company that had been in the area for the best part of a week.'

'He saw them?' Collings asked.

Wild shook his head. 'They had fled long before his men reached the town. But the locals described them well enough. Redcoats, near one hundred strong.'

'You're certain they were your assailants?'

'Quite certain, sir,' Wild said, finding the words suddenly difficult to say, for an image of one man in particular had come into his mind. 'The townsfolk described their leader as a hideous creature. A one-eyed monster,' he ran his fingers across the left side of his face, 'with a mass of ugly scars across here.'

'Not a man easily forgotten.'

'Never forgotten,' replied Wild. 'It was he who led the ambush against me, General. Captain Stryker was his name.'

Collings sucked at his hairless bottom lip. 'I have heard of him.'

'You have?' Wild was unable to keep the surprise from his voice.

Collings offered a cold smile. 'How is a mere enemy captain known to a man such as I?' He paused as a great cacophony of excited chatter rose up from below the window.

Wild frowned and paced across the room to retake his position. Three figures moved through the still growing crowd. Two – the foremost and rearmost – were shoving and pushing their way past the bodies, clearing a path to the platform. The man at the front was short, morbidly corpulent, and swarthy-skinned. His hair was long, black as jet, and carried an oily sheen. The man at the rear was taller, of slimmer build, and had marginally lighter skin. His face was cleanly shaven, tapering to a sharp chin and framed with shoulder-length auburn hair that was flecked with shards of grey. He walked with a pronounced limp, leaning heavily on a long, knotted stick. The figure in between, smaller and hooded, seemed a reluctant companion; head bowed, feet shuffling.

'I am a man of intrigue, Colonel,' Collings said when the shouts and jeers began to subside. 'My weapon is not the sword, but the quill.'

Wild looked up from the scene on the street to meet the major-general's beady, almost reptilian gaze. He believed that well enough. Collings was a slight figure. Sallow-skinned, thin-limbed, with bones that looked as delicate as glass. 'Aye, sir.'

'In such a capacity,' the major-general went on, 'I have made it my business to know our enemy. Anyone of significance, at the very least. Stryker is a hard man. Not unlike yourself, I suppose. Experienced, brutal, vengeful. A real devil. And favourite of Prince Robber.'

Wild's eyes widened involuntarily. 'I had not realized.'

Collings stared down at the road. 'A dangerous knave to have encountered, Colonel, make no mistake. The question is: where did he go with my damned wagon?'

Wild made to reply, but found his throat clogged. He cleared it awkwardly. 'Again, sir, I am not certain. Across Dartmoor, I presume, for he must surely wish to convey it to his superiors.'

'Then you had better get it back,' Collings said matter-of-factly, though Wild sensed the threat beneath the plain tone.

Down on Fore Street, the crowd was beginning to stir again. A murmur of voices gradually rose to a great cry as the three figures mounted the wooden platform. At the centre of the structure stood a thick-beamed frame, the shape of an inverted 'L'. From the frame dangled a noose, swaying gently in the breeze.

Wild watched as the fat man drew back the smaller figure's cowl, revealing the face of an elderly woman. He wrinkled his nose in distaste. 'What was her crime?'

'She has made a compact with the Devil!' a bellow came up from the scaffold as if in answer.

The speaker was the taller of the two men. The one with auburn hair, who, Wild now saw, had a long, hooked nose and big teeth that jutted forth from his mouth, giving him an almost equine appearance. His accent was borne of the southern counties, though his skin had clearly seen many more hot summers than England could provide, for it was deeply tanned. The colour, Wild reflected, of the cliffs around his native Exmouth. This was the man whose arrival he had complained about to Major-General Collings.

'You question Hogg's presence here?' the major-general said, evidently reading Wild's thoughts.

Wild looked across at his superior. 'I am a man of action, sir. I do not hold with witch-catchers and their ilk.'

Erasmus Collings chuckled at that. 'Osmyn Hogg frightens the people,' he said, waving a hand at the multitude below. 'The peasants. Soon we will move into

Cornwall, into the very bosom of the King's support. Men like you will crush their armies and burn their homes, but who will turn their hearts, Colonel? Who will bring their minds to our cause?'

'A pact of blood and sorcery!' the man on the scaffold called out. He paused as the crowd took a collective intake of breath. It reminded Wild of an actor on stage. 'But where is my proof, I hear you cry!' Hogg spun on his heel suddenly and pointed at his darker-skinned companion.

'I saw them! Imps in her employ!' the fat man called out in a thickly accented voice.

Wild looked pointedly at Collings. 'Spanish?'

Collings nodded. 'Hogg's assistant, Señor Ventura. A convert to our faith. Quite the crowd-pleaser.'

'I watched the witch in her cell,' Ventura went on. He lowered his voice suddenly as though whispering a secret to the enthralled onlookers. 'They crept in after midnight, a polecat and a toad. Puckrels of the most wicked kind.'

'No!' the old woman spoke for the first time. She lurched forward, beseeching the crowd. 'It is lies! All lies!'

'It is true!' Ventura roared, startling the red kites and crows overhead, so that they veered away in panic. One of his pudgy hands shot out and grasped the woman by her wrist, wrenching her back roughly. He pulled the cloak from her shoulders and thrust her across the platform into Hogg's waiting arms. 'She suckled them as though they were her children!'

With that, Osmyn Hogg took hold of the prisoner and tore a strip of her shirt away, exposing the left side of her body. As the crowd gasped, he lifted her arm, indicating an angry-looking boil just below her armpit. 'See here, friends. Her witch's teat!'

'You sure?' someone from the crowd shouted out. 'Wouldn't catch me sucklin' on them saggy old bubbies!'

The throng erupted in raucous laughter.

'No!' the old woman cried again, desperately drawing up the torn pieces of material to cover her dignity.

'Exodus, chapter 22, verse 18,' Osmyn Hogg called out suddenly, his voice rising above both the woman's shrill cries and the crowd's braying. 'Thou shalt not suffer a witch to live!'

Above, on the upper floor of the White Hart, Colonel Gabriel Wild shuddered. 'I am sorry, General, but I despise his sort. A man who lynches women for keeping cats and making poultices.'

Collings shot him a hard glance. 'In Spain they have the Inquisition. What role do you think it plays?'

Wild shrugged. 'To uphold Papist orthodoxy, sir.'

'Indeed,' the major-general agreed. 'But why is it so vital to the Papacy? People are terrified of the inquisitors, Colonel. The mere thought of those Romish bastards puts ice in their veins.'

Collings furnished the colonel with a white-toothed grin. 'It is a tool. A tool for obedience. And that is why I have invited Hogg to Devon.'

Wild frowned. '*You* invited him?'

'He has spent a decade or more in the New World,' Collings continued, ignoring his subordinate's surprise. 'Weeding out witches and their familiars. Eradicating them. He is strong-minded, clever, and utterly ruthless. A feared man. And now he is here to lend that power to our cause.'

Wild stared down at the scaffold. The mob's joviality seemed to have suddenly vanished as grim reality dawned.

A few dissenting voices rose above the din. One cry of mercy, next half a dozen and then a score. Quickly it became a chorus, a barrage of support for the condemned woman, and the crowd began to surge inwards.

In immediate response, a half-company of green-coated soldiers appeared from a side street to form a forbidding cordon around the platform. They un-sheathed their tucks, daring the crowd to challenge the naked steel. The condemned woman was manhandled to the noose. The fat Spaniard, Ventura, compelled her to stand on a rickety stool, and took her scrawny neck in one hand and the rope in the other. He threaded the loop over her head, fastening the knot so that it fitted snugly, and gave the rope a last tug to make certain it would hold her weight.

The woman screamed. Witch-finder Osmyn Hogg stepped forward and slapped her hard. She began to sob.

'Do you believe it, sir?' Wild asked. 'That he can sense a witch?'

Collings raised his bare upper lip in a sneer. 'It matters not whether I believe, Colonel. Only that the people fear. If a handful of useless old crones must swing for the greater good, then so be it.'

'Is it legal?' Wild asked tentatively. 'Hogg brands a woman a witch and she's lynched?'

Erasmus Collings laughed. 'I am the law here, Colonel. If I say it is legal, it is legal.'

'And what of the local clubmen, sir? It is the kind of matter that would stir them up, I'd wager.'

The major-general casually picked at a speck of dirt under one of his carefully manicured fingernails. 'The clubmen band together against marauding soldiers who would steal their food and ravish their daughters. This old harridan lived alone. Her loss will arouse no feelings of revolt, I assure you.'

Wild and Collings did not hear Hogg issue the final order, but knew it had been given right enough, for Ventura suddenly kicked the stool away. The woman dropped down with a violent jerk. The crowd gasped. Hogg began to intone passages of Scripture.

'Look at them, Colonel,' Collings said, the relish in his voice causing Wild to grit his teeth. 'Marvel at the fear in their eyes. This whole town will do my bidding for as long as I am here.'

Wild swallowed thickly. The black eyes bore into him again, gleaming like nuggets of onyx in that pasty skull devoid of hair, brows, lashes, or even stubble.

'Witch-finder Hogg is more useful to me than your whole regiment,' Collings said with a smug smile. 'Do not forget it.'

Down below, the condemned woman danced. The drop from the stool had been no more than two feet, and had not come close to killing her, so she dangled there, twitching and thrashing and jerking. Her face was rapidly swelling and her tongue lolled, the whites of her eyes dyed blood-red as she kicked her way to a throttled death. Another gasp from the crowd heralded the stream of urine that began to pool on the platform beneath her.

Wild had seen enough, and stalked back into the room's cool interior.

Collings watched him. 'Are your men ready to ride?'

Wild nodded. 'We are ready and eager, sir.' He made a tight ball of his fist at the thought of the one-eyed bastard he had come to hate. 'By Christ, I shall delight in the moment when my dagger meets that knave's stones. He will scream and I will laugh.'

'He will be long gone by now, Colonel,' Collings warned.

Wild shook his head. 'He is on foot, dragging a fully laden cart, which will make him dire slow. And we have squadrons patrolling every road through the moor, which means he must tramp across open country. No, sir, he won't have gone far.'

'Good,' Collings said. 'You may have a hundred men.'

'A hundred, sir?' Wild spluttered, striding purposefully back to the window. 'But they are my——'

'They are *my* men, damn your arrogance,' Major-General Collings hissed, thrusting a long, dainty finger at Wild's face.

'Sir,' was all Wild could say, taken aback by the major-general's sudden ferocity, and he turned away to stare down at the scaffold. The crone's dance had ended, the life suffocated from her. She hung limp now, head canted, rope creaking gently as the townsfolk began to disperse in near silence.

'Certain information was captured at Sourton, Colonel,' Collings said, his flash of ire evidently cooled.

'Information?'

'Intelligence. We have learned that Hopton has been ordered to march into Somerset to merge his army with that of the Marquis of Hertford. Stamford, as I'm sure you can imagine, is eager to confound this plan by striking the enemy first.' Collings's eyes, tiny and black like a pair of apple seeds, seemed to stab through Wild. 'He is mustering our forces at Torrington, and I will not allow you to traipse across Dartmoor with an entire troop. You will retrieve that wagon, sir, and you will do it with one hundred men. If that is not enough, then you are not fit to command them.'

Colonel Gabriel Wild blanched. He despised Collings, loathed his weak body, his penchant for intriguing and his low birth. But, for all that, he feared him. 'I will bring back Captain Stryker's head, sir,' he said simply.

Collings snorted his disdain. 'His sword will suffice, Colonel. And my ammunition.'

NEAR DARTMEET, DARTMOOR, 28 APRIL 1643

'I have it!' exclaimed Simeon Barkworth as he turned the long, black feather in his hand. '*Sgarbh*.'

Beside him, marching at the front of the predominantly red-coated company, a tall, wiry, leather-faced man shook his head in mock exasperation. 'Fucking Scotch gabble. I shall never untangle it, long as I live.'

Barkworth glared up at Sergeant Skellen, eyes bright with indignation. 'Not Scots, you spindly great bufflehead. And you'll no' live long if you call my accent gabble again.'

'Gaelic,' the voice of a younger man broke into the conversation.

Lieutenant Andrew Burton was four or five paces ahead, looking over his shoulder to speak, and William Skellen met his gaze with a confused frown. 'Beg pardon, sir, but I'm not sure them savages have the taste.'

'Not *garlic*, Sergeant,' Burton replied with a withering expression. '*Gaelic*.'

Barkworth proffered the company's second-in-command his shark's grin. 'Aye, sir. *Sgarbh* is the word for

Great Black Cormorant.' The little Scotsman waggled the feather in front of him. 'That's what this is. It's a big old seabird.'

At that, the man at the very head of the company looked back for the first time in more than an hour. 'You remember when we first met, Simeon?' Stryker asked. 'Discussing birds of prey.'

Barkworth chuckled, his damaged throat grinding like metal files on iron. 'I taught you the difference between a buzzard and a red kite, as I remember it.'

Stryker nodded. 'That's right.'

'While he kept us in a cell, as I remember it,' Skellen muttered.

Barkworth glared up at the loping sergeant. 'Be lucky I did'nae skin your hide soon as my lord Chesterfield took you in.'

'Enough,' Stryker ordered, his tone more exasperated than angry. He glanced at the feather clasped between Barkworth's thumb and forefinger. 'Rare?'

Barkworth shook his head. 'But it'll have cost him an angel or three to get enough o' these for a whole regiment.'

'Wild is clearly a man of means,' Burton put in.

'Not only for such a flamboyant field sign, but for their kit as well,' Stryker said, thinking of the equipment they had taken from Colonel Wild's cavalrymen. Equipment that now jangled in piles on the heavily laden wagon that trundled at the centre of his marching column. 'Their weapons are fine indeed.'

An image of Gabriel Wild came to Stryker then. Those glassy eyes, glittering with impotent rage as the colonel was trussed up below a tree with the rest of his near naked troopers. That had been almost two days ago, and he wondered if Wild had made it back to civilization. Since that time, Stryker had led his company – three officers, including himself, two sergeants, two corporals, two drummers, forty-nine musketeers, thirty-six pikemen, and the as yet unranked Simeon Barkworth – ever westwards on the road that would ultimately take them across Dartmoor and into Cornwall. That road, of course, had not been a great deal more significant than a rural bridle-way, and the wagon, its wheels slipping and sliding on the slick terrain, had proven a significant encumbrance.

Happily for Stryker, though, the men had not seemed to care. They had stopped at the hamlet of Ilsington on the first night, having climbed high up on to the moor, and, after making some unfortunate but necessary threats to the villagers, they had taken plentiful supplies for the onward journey. The wagon would now haul sacks of dried meat and fish, and scores of biscuits that Skellen grumbled were as hard as the Devon granite.

They had spent the next day with full bellies and refreshed legs, drinking from streams, gazing out over the magnificent views, and comfortable that they would see an enemy approach from a long way off. And now, having vacated their makeshift billet in a barn at Ponsworthy, they were trudging onwards with a renewed sense of optimism.

'And those nags are some of the best I've seen,' Skellen's droning voice cut across Stryker's train of thought.

Stryker caught the hint in his sergeant's tone. 'No one rides, Will.'

'Just thinking what a nice journey this'd be on horse-back, that's all,' Skellen muttered, glancing back at the eleven magnificent mounts they had taken from Wild and his men. The beasts – eight bays, two blacks and a roan – were tethered in a line behind the cart.

Stryker shook his head. He had a horse, Vos, a big sorrel-coloured stallion, but he had taken the decision to leave him back in Launceston. 'No man rides. I do not want us drawing attention to ourselves. Men on horse-back are too conspicuous on these bleak horizons.'

By noon the column had reached a high point on the undulating terrain, affording an excellent vantage, and topped by one of Dartmoor's many granite tors. Those rocky outcrops, grey-stone blemishes on the bleak plains, provided excellent shelter from the whipping wind, and Stryker ordered they rest in its shadows.

After setting a perimeter of pickets, Stryker went to where his most senior men had gathered. Many of them were lying on the damp ground, propped on elbows, but Ensign Chase was seated on a pale lump of granite. He vacated the perch on his captain's approach.

'Thank you, Matthew,' Stryker acknowledged, and sat on the cold stone, his scabbard clanging against the granite.

Skellen, having lit his pipe, began to sing songs of home. Ditties speaking wistfully of Gosport and Portsmouth, of buxom tavern maids and of the crashing sea.

'How did you know Wild's regiment weren't nearby, sir?' Lieutenant Burton asked after a short time.

'I didn't,' Stryker replied bluntly. 'But it was a reason-able guess. They did not come from the Bovey Tracey garrison, for they'd have passed us on the road.'

'They probably didn't know there was a new garrison at Bovey at all,' Skellen put in, before resuming his lilting tune.

A flock of small black birds raced overhead, changing direction in the blink of an eye, like a mass of speeding thunder clouds. Stryker watched them dart back and forth, amazed at the unison with which they moved. 'So they're a detached unit,' he said when the birds had disappeared from view. 'Mobile and sturdy.'

'When it is'nae raining,' Simeon Barkworth replied with a sharp-toothed smirk.

'They roam where they may, watching the Cornish border, harrying our troops, carrying messages.'

'Recovering arms caches,' Burton added.

'Indeed,' agreed Stryker. 'But if you were Wild, would you use your entire regiment for that task?'

Burton shook his head. 'Not enough food and shelter on the moor to support that many men and horses.' He paused in thought, taking the moment to scratch at his withered forearm with his good left hand. When he looked up, there was a new glint of understanding in his eyes. 'Wild must be based in one of the towns on the moor's fringe.'

'That is my guess,' said Stryker. 'Newton Abbot. Exeter, perhaps.'

Skellen ended his song. 'I'd have still used more than a dozen men though, sir,' he said, with a rearward jerk of his head to indicate the wagon. 'Given the size o' this meaty old stash.'

'They did not expect to encounter you.'

The voice was new to the conversation and the group turned to stare at the speaker. The man, the only one in the company dressed in the drab clothes of a common farmer, was sat, cross-legged, some ten or twelve paces away. It was the man who had driven the rickety cart for

Colonel Wild, and who had been taken with his vehicle as part of the ambush. A man who had not met a gaze nor uttered a single word in the two days since his capture.

'Speak, sir, if you have something for us,' Stryker said when the carter suddenly turned away with a look of sheer terror.

The group watched and waited as the fearful man slowly forced himself to look back at the soldiers. He was of middle age and slight frame. A man whose hard existence of toil and hunger had stripped any vestige of fat from his bones. His hair was fair, though thinning badly, but his teeth and skin were in good condition. His bottom lip trembled violently as he spoke. 'The Roundheads, sir. They had not imagined th—they would run into you.' He swallowed thickly. 'Y—you or anyone else, that is.' He dug his hands into the folds of his threadbare smock and stared at the grass between crossed legs. 'Beg pardon, sirs, I did not mean to pry. Forgive me.'

'Speak plain, sir carter,' Stryker replied calmly. 'You are in no danger.'

The frightened man remained tight-lipped. Barkworth leant forward on the grass suddenly. 'But you'll be in rare bloody danger if you keep your mouth shut.'

The threat seemed to unlock the wagon driver's jaw, for he forced his gaze up to meet Stryker's. 'The rebels, sir. They did not think to meet any king's men hereabouts.'

'Why ever not?' Ensign Chase said in surprise. 'The moor may be Devon land, but it nestles beside the most loyal county in England.'

'And since Launceston,' Skellen added, 'old Hopton's grip tightens daily.'

Stryker nodded agreement. 'You may not have heard,

master carter, but Chudleigh attacked us at Launceston on the 23rd.'

'And he scurried back over the blessed Tamar with two black eyes and his tail twix't his legs!' Skellen growled, eliciting a chorus of boisterous cheers. 'The messenger spared nothing in his bloody account!'

The carter shook his head sadly. 'I fear your messenger was sent out a day too soon.'

Stryker felt his guts begin to churn. 'How so?'

'You have not heard?' the carter said, wincing as he spoke as though the revelation would somehow bring about his own demise. 'There was—a battle. A big battle. Up at Sourton Down. Not two days since your victory at Launceston.'

Stryker and Burton shared a glance.

'Well?' Barkworth snapped.

The carter cleared his throat. 'General Hopton – God protect him – was routed by Parliament's forces. Driven back into Cornwall with mighty losses, I heard.'

And in that moment Stryker understood. He understood why a large rebel unit had strolled so confidently into Bovey Tracey; why Colonel Wild had not expected to encounter Royalist troops; why the furious cavalryman had been so confident that Stryker would never reach the Royalist lines. Those lines, he now realized, were all the way back on the River Tamar.

He cursed angrily.

The carter winced, holding up his palms as though Stryker was pointing a musket at his chest. 'I am sorry, sir. I pass on only what I hear.'

'Fret not, master carter,' Stryker said. 'You are not accountable for this.'

Sergeant Skellen scraped calloused fingers across his dark stubble. 'Now we know why them horsemen were so bloody cocksure. Weren't even checkin' the road for us. Sounds like our boys took a thrashin'.'

'Christ on His cross,' Barkworth hissed.

Ensign Chase sat up straight. 'Does that mean we're alone on Dartmoor, sir?'

'Not alone,' Burton replied morosely. 'We'll be overrun by Parliament men before we reach home.'

'And therein lies our problem.' Stryker glanced at the wagon and its valuable bounty. 'If we're to make haste, we must abandon our prize.'

'And yet,' Burton replied, 'the army will be in dire need of it now.'

Stryker inhaled slowly as he thought. His tawdry mission to watch a quiet rural road had transformed into something far more important. Eventually he exhaled slowly, meeting the gaze of each of his men. 'We keep the wagon. Lieutenant Burton is in the right of it; General Hopton will want us – no, expect us – to deliver it to him, regardless of the danger.'

He paused to allow comment, but none came. 'Of course, we cannot simply march back to Launceston now. If our new friend here speaks true—'

'I do, I do, sir,' the nervous carter blurted. ''Pon my very life.'

'So the moor will soon be swarming with Roundheads. We cannot trust the roads.'

'Roads?' Skellen grunted scornfully. 'There aren't no tracks worth the bloody name hereabouts, sir.'

The group fell silent, and Stryker knew each must be pondering the days to come. It would have been hard enough

71

to drag the heavily laden wagon across Dartmoor's dubious thoroughfares without having to negotiate the bogs and hills of open country.

'Forgive another intrusion, sir,' the carter ventured, 'but I know the moor as I know my wife's face. I could—'

'Hold your tongue,' Simeon Barkworth rasped with sudden venom, the revelation of Sourton Down having evidently eroded what little sanguinity he possessed. He threw a slit-eyed glance at Stryker. 'How can we trust this knave, sir? We found him with the enemy, did we not?'

'Forced, sir!' the carter bleated, once again fearing for his life. 'Forced to drive their wagon, that is all, I swear it! I am a loyal subject of—'

Stryker held up a hand for calm. 'I care nothing for professed allegiances, master carter. Simply know this—'

He made certain the carter's gaze was on his. Transfixed by the single grey eye that, he knew, would appear silver as his expression hardened. The raised palm dropped to his waist and patted the swirling steel of his sword's ornate basket hilt. 'I have need of a new scabbard. If you betray me, it will be your skin I use for the job. Is that clear?'

The carter's jaw dropped, eyes widening and Adam's apple bobbing in a pronounced gulp.

'He says yes, sir,' Skellen spoke for the dumbstruck man.

Stryker's stare did not falter. 'Then we have an understanding that, in my experience, ought to suffice. You know the moor?'

The carter nodded.

'Which route would you have us take, Master —?'

'Bailey, sir,' the carter replied. 'Marcus Bailey.'

'It is a bad idea, sir,' Barkworth warned.

Stryker finally broke eye contact with the terrified carter and glanced at the fiery-tempered Scot. 'Then you would have us stay on the road?' He waited while Barkworth's mouth worked for a moment, but no words were forthcoming. 'I thought not.'

'Over there,' Bailey said, 'less'n a mile thither, is the place where East Dart meets West.'

'The rivers?' Burton asked.

'Aye, sir, you have it,' Bailey nodded eagerly, desperate to please.

'The confluence of two waterways can be a tempestuous place to cross,' Stryker said, his expression sceptical.

'But further up stream,' Bailey went on, 'there's an old clapper bridge over the East Dart. I will show you. When we are over the river, I can guide you to the start of a small track. It runs due north beside the west bank.'

'Taking us away from the West Dart,' Stryker spoke his thoughts aloud, 'and the road.'

Bailey nodded rapidly again, putting Stryker in mind of a small bird pecking the ground. 'It is narrow, near impassable in winter, but not so bad now. Eventually it will sweep westward, taking us through the marshes at Bellever.'

Stryker gnawed his upper lip. 'A difficult route indeed.'

For the first time, Marcus Bailey risked the merest hint of a smile. 'But a safe one.'

CHAPTER 4

The morning was bright, a welcome change from the recent oppressive gloom, and the sun's first rays were quick to burn away the vestiges of dawn mist that lingered like a pale broth on the boggy terrain.

Stryker's company had crossed the ancient stone clapper bridge over the East Dart without hindrance the previous day, and spirits were high as, sure enough, Marcus Bailey's promise of a concealed route through the ancient marshes had come to pass. But the going had been slow after that. It had taken the scarlet-coated column till dusk to negotiate the narrow causeway, marching four abreast and fighting to keep their boots from sinking into the black morass. The presence of the ammunition wagon, placed near the very front of the column, had made things all the more difficult; its big wheels ploughed deep furrows in the viscous mud, which sucked at the vehicle, as if engaged in a tug of war with the horses that laboured to pull it along.

Now, having passed a thankfully mild night huddled around small fires, singing mournful tunes and eating some of the food they had taken from Ilsington, the infantrymen and their precious bounty were on the march again.

After an hour's trudge the track began to zigzag, wending its way around impenetrable bulrush thickets that had been there long before people, and making it impossible to see more than twenty paces ahead. Stryker, setting the pace at the head of the column, stared left and right, ears pricked for any sound that might signal a threat. He had men scouting out in front, and others some distance at the rear, but still he felt uneasy. 'How much further?' he called over his shoulder.

Marcus Bailey, sitting atop the wagon, reins looped in gnarled hands, furrowed his craggy brow. 'A few minutes only, I'd say, sir.' He had promised the track would soon become wider and less suffocated by the maze of reeds and bog as the marsh gave way to one of the larger roads across Dartmoor. And, though the soldiers were nervous of crossing that thoroughfare, they were eager to pick up the pace, even for a short time.

Stryker nodded his satisfaction and turned to face the track again. Suddenly gunfire crackled somewhere up ahead. Stryker glanced sideways at Burton. 'Only a brace, Andrew. Just as easily poachers out for a meal.'

'The lads out front'll bring news, I'm sure,' the lieutenant agreed, though the tension on his face was clear.

Lisette Gaillard. Stryker thought of her again. Of the small details. Her laugh, the way her sapphire eyes wrinkled at the corners when she teased him, the shape of her mouth, the scent of her body, the little white scar that blemished her narrow chin. He quickened his step in an effort to shake her away, hoping the men would assume it was a result of the muffled musketry.

He was pleased when one of the scouts appeared from the dense marshland, for the distraction was enough to regain focus, but immediately the man's expression gave cause for concern.

'Well?'

'Trouble, sir,' the musketeer blurted, stooping slightly as he heaved air into his strained lungs.

Stryker opened his mouth to speak, but the words never came. Because somewhere, someone was screaming.

NEAR PETER TAVY, DARTMOOR, 29 APRIL 1643

Pikeman Tristan Rix had not been a pleasant man. His pinched face, sharp nose, and squinty eyes had given him a stoatlike appearance, and his whining voice, acid tongue, and propensity to thieve had only enhanced the image. The men had disliked him, as had his captain, yet today it was that officer that still held his rapidly stiffening hand.

'He's gone,' Lancelot Forrester said quietly as he moved his free hand to close Pikeman Rix's eyelids.

'Aye,' the man standing behind Forrester replied.

'He didn't cry.'

'No.'

'Said he wouldn't, and he didn't.'

'A brave lad,' Anthony Payne spoke again.

Forrester stared at the gaping hole that a slashing sword had left in Rix's throat, the exposed flesh glistening like a bag of rubies, and noticed that the wound had finally stopped pumping blood on to the soil. He prised his hand free, carefully uncurling the pikeman's fingers, and stood, turning to look up at Payne. 'He was a sour little creature, Mister Payne, God forgive me for saying so. But he stood up to that big sergeant like a damned Spartan.'

Payne nodded, glancing at the corpse. 'Man's a hero, sir. Way he was first 'cross the ford.'

'Right enough,' Forrester said, stooping to retrieve his snapsack and fishing out the pipe from within. He clamped it between his teeth and, after another quick rummage in the snapsack, produced a small plug of dark tobacco that he crumbled between thumb and forefinger, sprinkling it into the clay bowl. 'Light here!' he called through teeth that still held the pipe in place, and one of his redcoats immediately scampered across from where he perched on a nearby chunk of mossy rock. He was a musketeer, and his slow-burning match still carried strong embers, so it took only moments for the tobacco to ignite.

Through the billowing, fragrant pall soon engulfing him, Forrester watched his men. There were thirty-seven of them now, for he had lost three in the fight to cross the River Tavy, and they lounged at ease, drinking from the blood-tainted waterway, eating the stale bread and hard, chalky cheese they had taken from Launceston, or puffing on tooth-worn pipes. Some laughed, some diced, others napped, and he begrudged not one of them. The company, along with Payne and his six Cornishmen, had marched eastwards the day before. Forrester had been kept firmly – and infuriatingly – in the dark as to the exact nature of the mission, but he had gleaned that they were heading for some kind of rendezvous at the village of Merrivale. To avoid the rebel-held Tavistock, they had ventured as far east as Milton Abbot, before veering away from the road and tracing a bridleway to the hamlet of Peter Tavy, whereupon Payne had said they should ford the fast-flowing river and continue south-east across open country. It was only a matter of three more miles to

Merrivale, and, though the terrain would be rough and wild, Payne was keen that they reach the meeting point by midnight.

But the ford had been guarded by a small unit of grey-coated musketeers. Like a gang of folk-tale trolls protecting a bridge, the Parliamentarians had emerged on the Tavy's east bank with a chorus of oaths and challenges. As soon as allegiances were established, the shooting had begun. The defenders had been outnumbered and outclassed, but they knew their duty and stuck to it for as long as reserves of ammunition and bravery had allowed. Forrester's force was larger, however, and his musketeers had lined the western bank and flayed the rebel positions until the return fire almost petered out. They had swarmed across the ford's shallows then, screaming curses and spitting threats, and the fighting – swords, daggers and musket butts – had been swift and dirty. A melee. A gutter brawl. In amongst that Royalist force had been a giant. A man of almost impossible size and strength, hefting a halberd as though it were a twig, and the Roundheads had quailed before him, turning tail at the mere sight of his storm-cloud shadow.

Now the king's men were resting on that coveted east bank, its grass trampled, its defenders routed and scattered, three redcoats and seven rebels dead. Forrester found himself wondering whether the ford had been worth the cost. After all, he did not even know why they were here.

Near the tree line, some thirty paces away, a group of men stabbed and scraped at the cloying soil with swords, heels and jagged bits of rock. A mass grave that would lie unmarked and untended. Nine of the bodies, stripped and pasty, already mottled purple at their extremities, waited by the fresh tomb, and Forrester instinctively turned back to the Tavy's blood-blackened edge where Pikeman Tristan Rix, the last man to die, still lay. To his surprise, he saw Anthony Payne looming over the body like one of the vast standing stones that stood guard over the moor. He watched, transfixed, as the biggest, most fearsome man he had ever seen, crouched suddenly, gently slid his culverin forearms beneath Rix's skinny torso, and hoisted it into the air as though it were no heavier than a willow wand.

Payne caught Forrester's eye. 'Like I said, sir. The man fought bravely.'

Forrester nodded mutely, sucked at his pipe, and watched Payne pace carefully across the slick grass to where the grave was being hastily carved out. The giant knelt slowly, easing Rix's inert body into its place in the line of dead. When he straightened, he noticed the captain's interested gaze, and raised his own dark brow in response.

Forrester felt himself blush. 'My apologies, Mister Payne, I did not mean to stare.'

Payne strode across to stand in Forrester's tobacco smoke. 'Then?'

Forrester offered an embarrassed shrug. 'It is simply not often a man of such—' he waved the pipe in a tight circle as he searched for the word, '—*robust* frame is seen to care for God's creations. Forgive me, sir, but I was impressed by your compassion.'

Payne met Forrester's blue gaze with his large brown eyes. 'O, it is excellent to have a giant's strength,' he said slowly, the depth of his tone vibrating inside Forrester's chest, 'but it is tyrannous to use it like a giant.'

Captain Lancelot Forrester almost dropped his pipe, such was the surprise he felt. '*Measure for Measure*!' he exclaimed, beaming widely. 'Act 2, Scene 2!' He shook his head in astonishment. 'Well I am impressed to the very core of my being, sir, and that is God's own truth. You are a student of the great Bard, Mister Payne!'

Payne offered a wry smile. 'Is it so great a thing for you to fathom, Captain? I am a large fellow, sir, but not a dullard.'

Forrester coloured again, feeling the heat fill his cheeks. He cleared his throat awkwardly. 'It seems I cannot keep my boot from my mouth, Mister Payne.'

Payne's smile grew to a grin. 'No matter, sir. In truth, I am pleased to make the acquaintance of a fellow Shakespeare devotee.' He stooped forward conspiratorially. 'But do not be fooled to thinking my scholarly nature precludes the occasional warlike moment, sir.'

From what he had witnessed during the fight for the ford, Forrester thought, that was fairly unlikely.

NEAR BELLEVER TOR, DARTMOOR, 29 APRIL 1643

The road between Postbridge and Two Bridges was, in reality, no more than a wide bridleway cutting diagonally across the north-west fringe of the ancient marsh. The clawing terrain eventually regained its sticky grasp of the land to the north of the road, but, for twenty paces either side, the territory was flat and drained clear.

Stryker, running at the head of his half-dozen scouts, bounded over a knee-high clump of bowing reeds, slipping as his boot squelched when it hit the soft scrub but managing to right himself just in time to round the body of black water. He emerged into the clearing with mind sharp and senses keen. It was times like these when he felt more wild beast than man. The possibility of danger seemed to hone his sight, amplify his hearing, and make his body prickle with nervous excitement. He drew his sword, comforted to catch the gleam of the red garnet set into its pommel, an ornament that spoke of the blade's reliable craftsmanship.

The pounding of more feet carried to him, and he glanced over a shoulder to see Skellen at his back with a score of redcoats. The tall sergeant hefted his vicious halberd as though it weighed nothing. His arms, Stryker knew, might have been long and thin, but they were knotted with sinew, like the tree roots of the primordial forest they traversed, and were covered by a network of raised veins, telling of the brute power contained within. William Skellen was the best fighter Stryker had ever known, and he never failed to be glad to have him at his side.

He saw the coach first. A big-wheeled vehicle of dark timbers and covered roof, it squatted like a gigantic black toad in the centre of the bridleway. It pointed to his left, westward, and he found himself wondering what business it had travelling in the direction of Royalist territory.

Quickly he scanned the scene. The driver, sprawled over the traces, was clearly dead, the side of his skull an oozing mess of gore. Another man was hanging out of the open door, legs inside the coach, torso out, face turned up at the sky. No one else was clearly visible, but he could see at least three sets of hooves through the gap between the coach and the road, and, as he closed the distance, began to glimpse the heads of riders as they bobbed above the roof.

'Three!' Stryker called to Skellen.

Without reply, the sergeant drifted right, taking half the musketeers with him, and circled round the rear of the coach. Stryker took the rest of the men to the left, passing the moon-eyed stares of the two greys harnessed to the vehicle, and emerged on the far side.

Sure enough, there were three assailants. A trio of horsemen; two bearing swords, one with drawn pistol. At first Stryker wondered whether this was the vanguard of a larger force, perhaps the advancing Parliamentarian army Bailey had warned them about, but their true nature was soon apparent. The men wore scruffy cassocks and battered hats, which alone meant little, but it was unusual for cavalrymen – even dragoons – to wear calf-length boots on their feet. Start-ups, as they were commonly known, were the footwear of agriculture, rarely issued to soldiers, and never, as far as Stryker was aware, given to horsemen. Furthermore, the mounts they rode were small, ill-nourished ponies, not the swift, regal beasts one would expect of a scouting party or vanguard. These were no more than common bandits.

'Ground arms, or you're dead men!' Stryker called.

To his surprise, the man with the pistol, a gaunt-faced fellow of middle age, swung his arm round and fired. Stryker instinctively ducked, shrank backwards, all the while aware that the gesture was futile if the ball flew true. But no pain came, no fire in his flesh, no darkness descending over his mind.

It all happened quickly after that. Before Stryker even had time to straighten up, the world exploded in a maelstrom of noise and smoke. Almost every redcoat had loosed their musket-balls at the man who would dare shoot their captain, and the singing lead minced him. The man's torso shook violently in a series of juddering punches, the balls flattening on impact to form wide discs that left great canals of shredded flesh in their wake. The brigand toppled back from his saddle, his already lifeless body landing in a grotesque heap at his pony's hind legs.

The dead man's companions had seen enough. They were clearly on the road for rich pickings, and had neither the weapons nor the stomach for a fight with trained soldiers. They wrenched at their reins, forcing the ponies to wheel about, hoping to smash through the closing ring of scarlet-coated demons and flee with what loot they had taken. But the fight had come to them, whether they wished it or not, and two of the men with Skellen took aim. The first ball hit its mark, cracking through the back of the footpad's head in a fountain of red spray. The man died instantly, slumping forward in the saddle to loll across the horse's chestnut neck. The beast, enraged by the musket fire and terrified by the stench of his master's blood, bolted into the trees, the corpse on its back thrown wildly about like a child's doll.

The third rider, a man with heavy stubble and thick black hair cut into the shape of a bowl, had been hit too, but he had taken the bullet in the abdomen and, though such a shot would eventually prove fatal, it was not a wound that would kill outright. He screamed, snarled his fear and hatred and agony to the afternoon skies, and raked his start-ups across the pony's flanks. The animal reared, shrieked in panic and burst forth, clods of earth and stone flinging up in its wake. It powered past the pair of shooters, still obscured by their own powder clouds, and made a break for freedom, but a tall, reed-thin man stepped casually into its path.

The only indication of Sergeant William Skellen's rank was the weapon he carried. The halberd – a six-foot long shaft, reinforced with metal bands and topped by a spike, a hook and an axe blade – was an unwieldy brute in the hands of the inexperienced. But Skellen had hefted the pole-arm through countless campaigns and was an expert in its application. He swept it downwards at the last moment, avoiding the chestnut's head, and pinioning the bandit's thigh with the vicious billhook.

The horseman was dragged from his saddle before he had even drawn breath to cry out. But his feet became tangled in the stirrups, and, as Skellen tore him down with irresistible force, the pony could not run free. Instead it faltered, lost its own footing, flailed like a fawn on a frozen lake, and collapsed sideways, crashing down upon its rider in a cacophony of clanging metal, thudding flesh and screams.

Skellen wrenched the halberd free and stepped back as Stryker came to stand over the felled horseman.

'Who are you?' Stryker snapped.

'Who?' the wounded man, trapped under his horse's thrashing bulk, hissed through teeth stained brown by tobacco. 'No one! A needy man's all!' The pony made a move to stand, but, between its still tangled burden and a damaged ankle, it faltered, falling back on to its master, who renewed his pain-wracked bellowing.

Stryker signalled to one of his musketeers. The redcoat stepped up to the horse, hefted his firearm, and put a ball between the injured beast's eyes. When the shot's echo had drifted away on the breeze, the road was suddenly, eerily silent, save for the low keening of the gut-shot robber.

'Check the coach,' Stryker ordered to no one in particular, and several men immediately converged on the vehicle.

'You've killed me, you fuckin' whoreson,' the wounded man suddenly wailed. 'Killed me proper!' The dead horse twitched, causing its trapped owner to scream again.

Stryker didn't doubt it. The man had a lump of lead lodged somewhere in his pulped midriff, a cavernous hole in his thigh, and in all likelihood a pair of legs crushed beyond repair. He glanced back at the coach, at the corpses of its driver and passenger. 'Repaid in kind, sir.'

The brigand howled again as a new surge of pain went through him. 'You blind, hog-swiving bastard!'

'Half blind.'

Stryker turned away. The looming figure of his sergeant had appeared at his right shoulder. Except for the heat of battle, it was always the right shoulder, for to approach from the other side would keep a man invisible to the captain. In battle, Skellen would switch sides, becoming a shield against his perennial weakness. Stryker reminded himself how fortunate he was to have a sergeant who knew him so well.

'Think you'd better 'ave a gander at this, sir,' Skellen said, his leathery face dour as ever, though Stryker detected a hint of something like amusement in the droning voice.

'Oh?'

Skellen's long stride took him back to the inert coach, Stryker walking briskly in his wake. They were on the north side of the road now, the opposite side to where Stryker had led the initial assault, and immediately he realized there had been more than one passenger in the vehicle's plush inner sanctum. A man, seemingly unhurt, was gingerly climbing down from the open doorway. He was of a similar height to Stryker, with long, tightly curled black hair, a thin black moustache, and a beard that was no more than a sharp triangle of hair jutting forth from his bottom lip. He was dressed in a fine blue doublet, slashed at sleeve and chest to reveal the bright red lining beneath, and wore an ostentatiously wide-brimmed hat, topped with a single blue feather to match, Stryker presumed, the rest of the suit. A scabbard clanged at his thigh.

'I thank you, sir,' the man said when his expensive-looking bucket-top boots touched the ground. He offered his hand. 'Otilwell Broom at your service.'

'Captain Stryker, sir,' Stryker replied, noting the firmness in the handshake. 'Mowbray's Foot.'

'King's men,' Broom said.

'You know the regiment, sir?'

Broom shook his head, curled locks flapping about his shoulders like the ears of a spaniel. 'Heard you invoke the blessed king's name when you told these vile knaves to surrender.'

Stryker eyed Broom warily. The man might be dressed as the archetypal Cavalier peacock, but he had long since learned that looks could be deceiving. 'You are Royalist, sir?'

'Aye, sir, I am.' Broom patted the hilt of his sword. 'Though I am not in His Gracious Majesty's service, so to speak.' He looked away, suddenly crestfallen. 'After today I am in no one's service, truth be known.'

'Sir?'

With that, Broom cast a miserable gaze back at the coach. 'I am—I *was*, Sir Alfred's bodyguard. His protector. Much good that did him.'

For the first time, Stryker peered into the interior of the carriage. What he saw surprised him, for it appeared that the fellow seated inside was taking a nap. He looked to be a man of perhaps fifty, with thinning, grey hair and gigantic red nose. He was dressed in a silver doublet that made even Broom appear dowdy. His eyes were closed, and he seemed utterly peaceful, slumped back against the cushions at his shoulders. But almost immediately Stryker knew that the gentleman was not asleep, for the fuggy air in the coach still wreaked with the stench of fresh blood.

Stryker looked back at Broom. 'Sir Alfred?'

'Cade,' Broom replied. 'Sir Alfred Cade. The ball went under his armpit.'

Hence the lack of obvious wound, thought Stryker. 'And you were his bodyguard?'

Broom patted the wrinkles in his blue doublet. 'Me and McCubbin there.'

Stryker peered into the gloomy interior again, seeing the upturned boots of the dead man he had first spotted as they had reached the coach. 'And who was he?' he asked, nodding at the body, the upper part of which remained slumped face up on the road.

'Sir Alfred's other retainer,' Broom replied gloomily. 'They shot him first.'

'What were they after?'

Broom shrugged. 'Money. Jewels. How would I know?'

'You were a bit lucky,' William Skellen, still beside Stryker, muttered sardonically. 'Seeing as your mate, your master, and your driver all got snuffed. What was you doin'? Cowerin' on the floor?'

A rush of blood rose like a water fountain from Broom's lace collar, up his slim neck and across his face. 'How dare you!' he spluttered, a hand dropping to his sword. 'How dare you address me in such a manner, you insolent swine!' He glared at Stryker, fingers slipping around his sword-hilt. 'Will you not place this man on a charge?'

Stryker shook his head. 'And if you draw that,' he flicked his grey eye down at Broom's scabbard, 'I'll run you through myself. Answer the question.'

Before Broom could reply the coach began to rock slightly, and, over the incensed bodyguard's shoulder, Stryker caught sight of movement within. It seemed there had been a fourth person in the carriage; a person who, until now, had been concealed by the great bulk of Cade's corpse. Apparently the venerable Sir Alfred had had a maid, or mistress, for the face that peered back at him was fresh, pale-skinned and bright-eyed.

'Christ, I could light a match in them peepers,' Sergeant William Skellen muttered.

Stryker wondered if Skellen had acquired a talent for mind-reading, for he was thinking the same thing. Those eyes – huge green ovals, mottled with swirling specks of auburn – seemed bright as gems, though he read real sadness in their depths and wondered if the glint was the sheen of tears. Either way, she was a rare beauty. He simply stared in astonishment as the woman, who, he guessed, was in her early twenties, carefully climbed down to stand beside Broom. She briefly smoothed the folds of her saffron dress, swept a ringlet of ink-black hair from her temple, and offered a tiny curtsy. 'Otilwell was not cowering, sir. He was protecting me.'

Osmyn Hogg watched the candles gutter in their placings and wondered what foul spirits had come to torment him this evening. It was prime territory for them. A dark night, made darker still by the swollen thunder clouds scudding through Okehampton's skies. He could well imagine the grinning, cackling imps that circled the town, closing in to prevent him from doing the Lord's work. Perhaps they were already here, shrouded by the shadows dancing along the room's walls and the food-piled platters. He stared hard at the tablecloth, muttered a short, protective prayer.

'The war has turned, gentlemen,' Major-General Erasmus Collings declared, raising his glass of claret in a delicate hand. 'We bloodied Hopton's nose at Sourton, and now we'll strike him down for good.' He smiled at the growled cheers that his words had elicited, but pursed his lips inquisitively when his little eyes fell on Hogg. 'You do not share the assertion, sir?'

Hogg looked up from his meditation. He had been invited to take supper in the major-general's quarters – the rooms directly above his own – that evening, sharing the impressive spread of victuals with some of the most senior staff to be found across Okehampton's transient martial population. Most of the army, Collings had earlier explained, had ridden or marched north, to Torrington, where the Earl of Stamford was mustering Parliament's western forces. Tonight the major-general's big rectangular slab of polished chestnut was surrounded by an eclectic group. In addition to Collings and Hogg, there were two colonels of foot, a cavalry major and a quartermaster, all attired in their most gallant garb, and each as obsequious as the next. Hogg had also insisted that his assistant, José Ventura, join them, and, though the distaste for sharing a meal with a Spaniard was far from subtle, the assembled officers were polite enough.

'I share your optimism, General, naturally,' Hogg replied, feeling the eyes of the guests bore into him. 'But, alas, I do not partake of strong drink.'

The cavalry officer, a squash-nosed man named Matheson, furrowed his bushy, grey-specked brow. 'Puritan, sir? Can't say I hold with it, m'self.'

It was Hogg's turn to frown. 'Hold with it, Major? I was told the Puritan persuasion carries great sway in the rebellion.'

'It does, sir,' Matheson replied, scratching gnarled fingers at the armpit of his russet doublet. 'There are a great many Puritans in our ranks. Pym, of course, and Hampden, Cromwell, Holles, the list seems endless. But not I, sir. Not on your life. I am a man of tradition. The High Church of Queen Bess, and proud to declare it. But Charles Stuart is a tyrant. Must be stopped at all costs.'

'Men join our cause for divers reasons, Master Hogg,' Collings interjected smoothly, spindly fingers still wrapped around the glass. 'I, for instance, would have Parliament all the stronger.' He leaned back, taking another small sip of his wine. 'Give power to those who would govern with intelligence. Reason. I am not opposed to monarchy but, by God, if one should rule with a corrupt heart – paying heed to the viperous whispers of his favourites – then let's be rid of him.'

'I see,' Hogg responded, wondering to what kind of England he had returned.

'Master Hogg,' Collings went on, looking at each of his officers as he spoke, 'has been in the New World these past years.' Finally his hard gaze came back to Hogg. 'Is that not right, sir?'

Hogg nodded. 'Right enough, General. Señor Ventura and I have dedicated our lives to fighting mankind's greatest foe.'

'The Papacy?' growled another of the guests through a mouth crammed full of cheese and bread. He had been introduced as Quartermaster Timothy Ayres, and Hogg was certain he had never set eyes upon a more grossly fat man in all his life. The chair holding Ayres's immense backside groaned even as he spoke, and bits of food sprayed out across his purple doublet. 'That is surely our most fearsome enemy,' he said, his vastly layered neck bunching as he looked down to unfasten the buttons at his midriff in order to allow for expansion of his girth with the prodigious intake of food.

Hogg dearly wanted to berate the quartermaster for the sin of gluttony, but managed to bite his tongue. 'Greater still than that, sir,' he said levelly.

'None other than Satan himself, gentlemen!'

It was Major-General Collings who had spoken, and the amusement in his voice was not lost on Hogg. Not for the first time he found himself wondering why the clearly sceptical Parliamentarian had asked him to come to Devon. He tore his gaze away from Collings, meeting some of the other faces at the table as he spoke. 'I am a witch-hunter, as you are no doubt aware. Therefore my enemy is not the natural, but the supernatural.'

'Are the dark arts prevalent in the Americas, sir?' one of the infantry colonels asked. He was a slim man with hollow, deeply pock-pitted cheeks and bulbous eyes that looked as though they might pop out of his skull at any moment.

Hogg stabbed a small piece of venison with his knife. 'It is the red man, Colonel Stockley. The native. He worships all manner of false idols, every one of them a demon, of course.' With his long teeth he picked the meat from the point of the knife and chewed it for a few moments before continuing. 'The God-fearing folk of Europe fled persecution at home, only to find themselves in a land veritably flooded with evil. It is only natural those of a weaker disposition are ultimately seduced by it.'

'Tell me, sir,' Major Matheson said in his seemingly permanent gruff tone, 'which part of the New World were you at work?'

'We travelled extensively around New England, Major,' Hogg responded. 'Boston and all along the Mystic River, Salem, Charlestown, Plymouth.'

'Later Providence Plantation,' José Ventura spoke for the first time.

Hogg met the Spaniard's brown eyes, buried in two deep pits of flesh, noting wryly that, for once, Ventura was not the fattest man in the room. 'Aye, there too. And Saybrook.' A thought struck him, and he looked to Collings. 'You will know that last settlement was founded by the Lord Brooke. I hear he is one of the rebellion's foremost leaders now.'

Collings shook his head and quaffed the rest of his wine. 'Alas, no. My Lord Brooke was killed at Lichfield, near two months back. Shot through the eye, so says the story.'

'By a deaf mute, would you believe?' Major Matheson added with a face full of triumph. 'Punishment for his Puritan ways, I'd wager.'

Hogg turned cool eyes on the major, not wishing to waste valuable breath on such an imbecile, but knowing he must respond. 'Brooke's murderer was clearly empowered by Beelzebub, sir. The powers of evil are strong with the King's Army. That is why they must be driven into the sea.'

'A tragic loss, either way,' Major-General Collings muttered.

'A tragic loss indeed,' Hogg said genuinely. Brooke had been one of the more prominent reformers in both New and Old England. His death would surely prove a major blow to the gathering Puritan power base. He sucked briefly at his long teeth. 'Still, we shall not let that setback turn us from the Lord's work, eh Ventura?'

The big Spaniard swept a chubby hand through his slick hair. 'No, señor. Ours is an unending fight.'

Hogg nodded sharply. 'Amen to that.' He noticed the sceptical expressions around the table. 'You must understand, gentlemen, that Satan strives against mankind with every passing moment. He sends his minions to work towards our downfall, as he himself worked his way with Eve.'

'I saw the old woman dance the morris yesterday, Master Hogg,' Colonel Stockley said, his tone uneasy. 'Was she truly a witch?'

Hogg thought of the widow. She had denied the accusation with her dying breath, but he knew a witch when he saw one. 'Without doubt, sir,' he said, tone deliberately forthright. 'If you saw the execution, then you bore witness to her witch's teat. The very abomination with which she suckled her imps. There can be no question.'

'I suppose,' Stockley replied, pausing as a serving-boy appeared beside him to refill his glass from a large stoneware bottle. 'I have never seen such a thing on a pure woman.'

'And I saw the familiars, do not forget,' José Ventura said in heavily accented English.

'Proof, if any were truly needed,' Hogg added. He did not enjoy adding such embellishments, but, over the years, experience had taught him that folk were reluctant to hang their own, so an extra lever was often required. No imps had crept into the crone's chambers, no warty toad that had clamped its slimy mouth over her ugly third nipple. But that nipple had been there, sure enough, and its presence alone had convinced Hogg of her guilt. If the truth required a certain amount of embroidery to expedite God's work, then so be it. He chewed a small hunk of bread, gathering his thoughts. 'I say again, Colonel Stockley. Demons are the real threat to mankind. As real as any pike or musket or cannon. But more dangerous, for they would destroy a man's very soul.'

'They take the form of everyday animals,' Ventura spoke now. 'Rabbit, polecat, dog, cat. Perhaps even a frog or a mouse. Any such creature as the imp sees fit to imitate.'

Stockley's bulbous eyeballs seemed even more swollen than before. 'And it is the presence of these imps, these familiars, that marks a witch for what she is?'

Hogg and Ventura nodded in tandem, though it was the

Englishman who replied. 'Not exclusively. Often, as with the woman in the town, the final sign comes as an unholy mark upon the accused's body.'

'A Devil's teat,' Quartermaster Ayres said with a huge belch that shook his jowls. The sweat glistening on his face made it look as though he had marched all evening rather than gorged, and he mopped his brow with a bunched kerchief.

'Aye,' confirmed Hogg, trying in vain to ignore the repugnant display of gluttony. 'And in many cases they simply make confession.'

Erasmus Collings picked at a piece of food that had evidently lodged between two molars. 'And those confessions are given freely, I presume?'

Hogg ignored the hint of sarcasm. 'Sometimes.'

'And other times?' Collings pushed.

'Most confessions,' Ventura retorted hotly, 'must be extracted.'

Hogg held up a staying hand. He understood that his assistant, finally detecting the major-general's goading tone, was merely coming to his master's defence, but it irked that men should think Hogg would need such protection. He fixed Collings with a level gaze. 'I have, on occasion, been forced to compel a witch or warlock to confess. The methods are sound, I assure you.'

'Oh?' Collings replied, smirking slightly.

Hogg bit back a caustic comment. He had been summoned to Devon on the premise that the county was in the tightening grip of witchcraft, only to discover that the very man who had summoned him was as sceptical as the rest. Indeed, his first meeting with Erasmus Collings had told him that the major-general was a man of politics over principles. No matter, he thought. He was here now. God had commanded him to sniff out evil-doers, and that was what he would do. 'In some cases, I would have them walk.'

'Walk?' echoed the globe-eyed Stockley.

Hogg leant back in his chair and nodded. 'Through the night. Thoroughly tire them, Colonel, so that their minds are too befuddled to maintain the lies. It is a remarkably effective treatment.'

'But tiring for God's men,' Ventura added.

Hogg bobbed his head in agreement. 'What good is a confession, if those who would hear it are exhausted too?' He leaned in to pick at some more food. 'So, over the years I have found a better, more effective technique.'

'Do enlighten us,' said Collings.

Hogg looked at him levelly. 'I would swim them.'

'But that is no longer legal, sir,' replied the only man not to have spoken thus far. He was Colonel Thomas Last, and had been introduced by Collings as the commanding officer of a regiment of firelocks, infantrymen armed with muskets that relied upon a flint-induced spark to ignite the charge rather than the perpetual glow of a match. He was a tall, heavily built man, with blond hair that he wore just beyond his ears.

Osmyn Hogg merely offered a tired shrug, for he had given the explanation a hundred times over the years. 'What is legal in the earthly realm has no bearing on what is legal in God's sight.'

Colonel Last peered at the witch-finder with blue, watery eyes. 'God approves of binding a person's wrists to their ankles?' he said belligerently. 'God approves of toss-ing the poor wretch into a river to see if they float or sink?'

'It is a providential miracle,' Hogg argued, struggling to keep his temper in check. 'The purest of elements – water – rejects those who have renounced their baptism.'

'Put simply,' Major-General Collings added, leaning on elbows covered in pristine blue satin, 'evil men float.'

'The old king wrote of it in his revered tract,' Hogg replied swiftly, cutting short the mockery he sensed.

'I have heard of it,' Collings said, his voice cool. He tilted his head to one side, like a curious dog. '*Daemonologie*, yes?'

Hogg was impressed, and said as much.

'A curious tract for a Parliamentarian to revere, Master Hogg,' the enormous quartermaster Timothy Ayres spluttered through mouthfuls of meat and wine. He cursed as a rich dribble of rusty-coloured saliva traced its way down his many chins to stain his white shirt collar.

Hogg shuddered at the profanity. 'You are mistook, sir. Not a Parliamentarian per se. But a man who would have this island adhere to the true faith. If the current monarch held the same values, then I would love him as I did his father.'

'Values?' Colonel Last echoed. 'You mean a love of Puritanism, or of the study of witchcraft?'

'Both,' replied Hogg honestly.

The ever-watchful Collings leant back in his big chair, clicking those long, brittle-looking fingers for the serving-boy to return with the decanter of wine. 'James fell away in the end. Doubted the things he wrote in *Daemonologie*.'

'His weakness,' Hogg said. He closed his eyes. 'Praise God, I do not share it.' When he opened them again, Collings was sipping from a newly replenished glass. 'So I am here, at your service. Or rather, at God's service, praying that He will guide your hand as He sees fit. Where would you have me visit next, sir?'

Collings's small eyes darted about the room like that of a magpie as he considered the question. 'There is plenty of trouble hereabouts, Hogg. The locals band together, clubmen they call themselves, stirring up discontent. It is the Devil's workers who fan the flames, I am certain. North Tawton, Winkleigh, Crediton. The choice is yours. I merely wish to keep Devon safe for God-fearing folk.'

Colonel Last, the firelock commander, had been packing a large, ornately crafted pipe, and he glanced up at the last name. 'Crediton? We had some restlessness there a while back, sir. Clubmen up in arms. Griped like a pack o' hungry hounds, it's true, but Colonel Wild's troop rode in and chased 'em back to their damnable hovels sharp enough.'

'A grand job he did too,' Major Matheson growled, tapping thick fingers on the tablecloth. 'A fine officer indeed. Might I ask where the colonel is now, sir?'

Collings turned to look at Matheson. 'He rode out this very morn.'

'Oh? For Torrington?'

'Actually, no, Major,' Collings replied. 'Took a hundred men south, into Dartmoor, on an errand for me.' He looked at Osmyn Hogg, face split in a half-smile. 'He has become a hunter, like you.'

Hogg met the little black eyes, politeness dictating that he must show at least a semblance of interest. 'A hunter, General?'

Collings nodded. 'Very much so. Though he tracks a man, not a demon. A man of flesh and blood. A man soon to be dead. What was his name?' he muttered

98

quietly, wracking his brain for the recollection. Eventually he smiled, white teeth seeming all the more brilliant against the ethereal whiteness of his skin. 'I have it! A captain of foot.'

'You hunt a mere captain, sir?' Quartermaster Ayres said, his voice muffled by a mouth full of sugar-plums. 'Begging your pardon, General, but is such a man not rather—' he had grabbed another of the confections, and waved it before him as he searched for the right word, '— *beneath* you?'

Collings smiled, though the expression did not reach his eyes. 'I have no interest in the man himself, sir. Only what he has stolen from me. For Wild, however, it is a matter of honour.'

Witch-finder Osmyn Hogg cared not a jot for the machinations of a faceless cavalry officer, and he sat back, feeling contentment in a full belly and comfortable billet. The journey across the Atlantic had been long and torrid, and it was good to be back on dry land. His eyelids suddenly felt heavy, and he allowed them to fall. In the darkness he let his mind drift to the sound of the soldiers' voices and the heady scent of wine, rich food, and tobacco smoke.

The word punched Hogg like a fist to the guts, jolting him from his daydream in a swift, heart-pounding instant. Instinctively he gripped the table and sat upright as if a fire had been lit behind him, eyes snapping open, mind dagger-sharp. 'General?'

Major-General Collings had been speaking to Ayres, and he broke off his sentence with an acidic glance at Hogg. 'Master Hogg?'

'My apologies, General, but that name. The name you spoke.'

Collings's hairless brow creased as he frowned. 'Colonel Wild?'

Hogg leaned in, unable to keep the earnestness from his voice. 'No, sir, not he. The other name. The man Wild hunts. The *captain*, sir.' His guts churned as spoke. He could not believe it. Dared not. And yet he had heard it, clear as a Connecticut stream. 'What did you say he was called?'

Major-General Erasmus Collings folded his arms, though his face spoke of intrigue rather than irritation. 'Stryker, sir. The thieving dog's name is Captain Stryker.'

CHAPTER 5

The forest was dark and deep, lit by the ethereal emerald glow of tremulous firelight against moss-clothed rocks. Those fires, near a dozen small blazes around which the men of Captain Stryker's Company of Foot huddled, spat and crackled as the last of the provisions of salted meat were roasted above the dancing flames.

'We made land at Exmouth,' Otilwell Broom said as he came to sit at his place on a rock beside one of the fires.

Along with his officers, sergeants, and his newest recruit, Simeon Barkworth, Stryker had invited the survivors of the coach to warm themselves at his fire. It was a natural courtesy, he told himself, for a man and woman of good birth would expect to dine – if that was the right word in such rough circumstances – with the most senior officer present. But all too often that still evening, and, indeed, during the earlier march, he had found himself staring at the girl. Now, as his single eye studied her across the flickering flames, he considered what a beauty she was. Inwardly he conceded that he'd have asked her to sit at his fire even if she were the daughter of a gong farmer.

'Sir Alfred had an estate outside Tavistock,' Broom went on, fastening his expensive doublet against the night air. 'That was where we were headed.' There had not been a great deal of discussion in the hours since Stryker's men had found the coach, but Broom had, at least, explained that Sir Alfred Cade had been an extremely wealthy man. A member of the landed elite, with property in both Sussex and Cornwall. Fearing the rebellion's burgeoning grip on the counties to the east, Sir Alfred, a declared Royalist, had decided to take his only daughter to the relative safety of his western dominions.

That daughter, Cecily Cade, had not uttered a word since joining the company, but now she gave a chuckle that was near heartbreaking in its melancholy. 'But the war caught up with us anyway.'

Broom gave a snort. 'We ran into those villains, I grant you, but they were simple highwaymen. Grubby brigands.'

Cecily Cade was perched on a big stone next to Broom, and she turned her face up to look at him. 'Were they not looting us to feed their families, Otilwell?' She stared back at the flames. 'The armies pillage the land, take victuals where they find them, and leave the common folk to starve. Those men attacked us, yes, and I hate them for it, but is it not ultimately the fault of this war that drives men to such wickedness?'

'You're right, miss,' Stryker spoke now, 'but they did not need to fire upon you.'

Cecily glanced up. Her skin was as white as the lace at Broom's fancy collar, and her hair as black as coal. He noticed that her eyes, bright but sad, seemed to flicker from the good side of his face to the ravaged part, alive with intrigue, and he felt the urge to cover the scarring with a hand. But then, dispelling his embarrassment, that same, drill-like gaze began to fill with moisture. She shrugged. 'Now they're all dead.'

Dead and long since left to rot, Stryker thought. They had left the road as soon as the fighting was over, for Stryker had no way of knowing which towns, if any, were garrisoned by Parliament men. The surprise arrival of the large force at Bovey Tracey had been warning enough, but after Marcus Bailey's ominous words about the defeat at Sourton Down and the subsequent enemy push westward, he found it difficult to trust anything more than the understated farmers' tracks, known only to Bailey, and Bailey's local knowledge. Otilwell Broom had informed him that Sir Alfred Cade's party had travelled through Moretonhampstead and Postbridge and, though the former was alive with Roundhead troops, the latter was so far empty. That, at least, was reassuring, but it did not mean the high moor would remain devoid of danger.

Thus, with dusk rapidly descending, they had dragged the coach and bodies into the woodland to the north of the road, and spent a full two hours digging six shallow graves. Six, because the third bandit had swooned the moment the dead pony had been dragged away from his crushed legs. He never regained consciousness. Otilwell Broom complained bitterly about the situation, for the mere thought of burying a man of Sir Alfred's standing in an unmarked woodland pit was offensive to him in the extreme, but Stryker had insisted that he could not afford to carry a decaying corpse across Dartmoor. Cecily had seemed to understand, mutely nodding her assent, thus guaranteeing Broom's grudging compliance.

Once the burials had been completed, and the coach hauled unceremoniously into a particularly dense thicket, they had pushed northwards for a time, plunging back into woodland, until Bailey located another of his lesser-known routes that swung away to the left. It was a track that seemed to become narrower with each pace, impenetrable forest swallowing them whole, its branches whipping and clawing at the ammunition wagon's sides, darkening the already gloomy evening. Bailey informed them confidently that the track traced the path of the main thoroughfare, running south-west in parallel to the road but never glimpsed by its traffic. Stryker had questioned the wisdom of this, but, when urged to review his tattered map by the carter, he quickly understood that a march directly northward, in the direction of Launceston, would have taken them up on to the very highest part of the moor. Bleak, near impassable terrain, that was wind-seared and boggy.

'We must go round, Captain,' Bailey had explained, his natural nervousness beginning to diminish now that he knew Stryker posed him no threat. 'There is a reason the road runs thither.'

'To avoid the high moor,' Stryker had replied.

Bailey's response had been an enthusiastic nod. 'We must come this way a few more miles, only turning north again when we pass Great Mis Tor at our right hand.'

Now, with night's cloak fully drawn, Stryker had decided to make camp in the shelter of the ancient Wistman's Wood. The name, Bailey had said, was derived from *wise man*, perhaps a throwback to the pagan druids of old, and Stryker found himself wondering whether there had been anything wise in his decision to capture Colonel Wild's ammunition wagon. He looked to his right, instinctively checking the vehicle and its bounty were safe beyond the nearest trees. There it was, a large black mass against the flame-illuminated green of moss and lichen, and he chided himself for the display of uncharacteristic edginess. After all, the wood seemed so silent that they must surely be the only humans in its eerie interior. But, he told himself, the wagon's muskets and grenades, its lead balls and its black powder, were so vital to the Royalist war effort that it was natural to feel concerned for its safety.

'Tell me, Mister Broom,' Lieutenant Burton was speaking, and Stryker turned his thoughts away from the wagon to look at him, 'was it not a treacherous route to take?'

Broom brushed a speck of something from one of the fashionable slashes in his doublet. 'How so, sir?'

'To come through the moor,' Burton replied.

'The shortest route between any two points is a straight line,' Broom said patronisingly.

'I understand, sir,' Burton said with what Stryker thought was admirable patience. 'But would it not have been a safer bet to take the coast road? Or even the northern route, via Okehampton? You are not soldiers, so Parliament men would likely have let you through peaceably enough.'

'We did not know there would be bandits on the moor road, young man,' Broom retorted sharply, and placed a comforting hand on Cecily's shoulder when she began to sob quietly.

'I am sorry,' was all a shamefaced Burton could say.

Stryker looked on with interest. Burton was evidently mortified to have upset the girl, but it had been a reasonable enough question. The road through Dartmoor was wild and unprotected. A veritable heaven for footpads and the like. It did seem strange that Sir Alfred, apparently so keen to protect his daughter, had chosen such a course.

'No matter,' Broom muttered when Cecily had wiped her eyes with the sleeve of her yellow dress. A shadow suddenly fell across his handsome face. 'The truth is, McCubbin and I were employed as Sir Alfred's protectors. He felt safe with us. Safe enough to take the shortest route to Tavistock.' He swallowed thickly. 'A mistake.'

'Well, now you travel with us,' Burton said gently. 'We'll see you home.'

'We'll see you to Launceston,' Stryker corrected firmly.

Broom shot him an unpleasant glance. 'You will not provide safe passage to Tavistock, sir?'

Stryker met the challenging gaze and held it. 'I go to Launceston, sir. I give you safe passage there, upon my honour, but others will convey you to Sir Alfred's estates.'

Broom considered the statement for a moment. 'Forgive me, Captain, but is Tavistock not on the way?'

'Not on *my* way,' Stryker said firmly. 'We'll be out of the wood tomorrow, on to the open moor.'

'Cross country,' Sergeant Skellen murmured. 'Dangerous.'

Stryker looked at him and nodded. 'Aye, dangerous enough. But the track rises through hills, so we shan't be visible to anyone on the road.'

'Hills?' echoed Skellen glumly. 'It's hard enough draggin' that bleedin' wagon on the flat.' He glanced at Cecily. 'Beggin' your pardon, miss.'

Cecily offered a sad smile to show she took no offence at the leather-faced sergeant's profanity.

'We'll alternate the horses so that they remain fresh,' Stryker said. In addition to Bailey's old animals and Wild's chargers, he now had the two beasts ridden by Sir Alfred Cade's killers, and the pair that had pulled his coach.

'And, if necessary, we'll push. Whatever happens, we must stay on the track, keep away from the roads until we reach one of the tors Bailey told us about.'

The meat was ready now, and he leaned over to the makeshift spit of knotted twigs, slicing some of the sizzling flesh free with his long dirk. 'Then we'll join a bridleway running north.'

'Bypassing Tavistock altogether,' Lieutenant Burton added.

Stryker nodded as he fished a wooden bowl from his snapsack and dropped the meat on to its scarred surface. He took several more pieces and handed the bowl to Cecily. 'Here. You must eat something, miss.'

Cecily's smile was wan but sincere as she took the bowl. 'Thank you, Captain.'

'But we cannot be more than five or six miles from Tavistock now, Stryker,' Broom cut in indignantly. 'Surely you can allow us to press for the town from here?'

Stryker shook his head. 'I'll not risk our lives for it, sir.'

'You'll not risk your damned wagon, sir,' Broom muttered bitterly.

That was true, Stryker thought, and he offered a small shrug. 'It is vital to the King's cause. It would be remiss of me to risk it by marching into a town that, like as not, is swarming with rebels.'

Simeon Barkworth scratched at the ruined skin swathing his neck. 'So we head north tomorrow, sir. Where will we find this track?'

Stryker looked at Barkworth. The Scots Brigade veteran appeared almost demonic across the flames, his sharp teeth, yellow eyes and noose-burned scar all highlighted by the flickering orange light. 'A place called Merrivale.'

'Merrivale?' It was Cecily who'd spoken, and all eyes descended upon her.

'You know it?' Stryker asked carefully.

At once she shook her head, though Stryker did not miss the flicker of a glance she stole with Broom. 'Not really. But I have been to our Tavistock estate many times and know the name.'

The girl looked down abruptly, and Stryker wondered if the name had meant more to her than she claimed.

'And then what, Captain?' Otilwell Broom broke the silence, his tone more conciliatory this time. 'Where does this bridleway take us, if not to Tavistock?'

'Lydford, I'm told,' Stryker replied. 'And from there we'll make a break for Cornwall.'

'Easy,' Skellen muttered.

WIDECOMBE-IN-THE-MOOR, DARTMOOR, 29 APRIL 1643

The line of mounted men thundered along the main road through the village, thick gobbets of mud flinging up in their wake. They were a proud troop, all jutting chins and straight backs, but they knew that such a bearing was their unalienable right. For they were harquebusiers, cavalrymen of the deadliest kind, and they owned this land. Ruled it with their terrifying horses, their glinting plate and their keen swords. Daring a challenge. Willing it.

The troop rode four abreast, so that any other traffic would be forced to retreat to the gutters for fear of being crushed. They cantered behind a small black flag affixed to a pole and held aloft by a young cornet. On their heads the cavalrymen wore steel helmets with lobster-tail neck-guards and hinged peaks, from which hung a trio of vertical bars to protect the face. And atop each of those helmets, perched there like the bird from which it had been plucked, was a feather. A curved affair as long as a man's forearm and black as midnight. It was the sign of their commander, their leader, and a symbol of terror for those who gazed upon it.

Colonel Gabriel Wild cantered at the very head of his troop. They might have been just one hundred strong this day – and God rot Major-General Erasmus Collings for it – but he revelled in the power at his back all the same, at the force of arms his single word could bring. His regiment of horse was good, and he knew it. Equipped at great expense from his own deep pockets, the men had been trained by the best veterans money could buy. They were a fearless, ruthless fighting force. And that would not only secure victory upon victory for Parliament, but would allow Wild's reputation to blossom, as he so prayed it would.

The simple fact was that Parliament needed decent cavalry. They already had most of the navy, the ports, the forges of the Sussex Weald and rapidly improving brigades of foot, but the Royalists were blessed with the best mounted fighters in the realm. It was those men, Wild reckoned, those flying, charging, scything, brutal men that would decide the war. Prince Rupert's saddled peacocks, as skilful as they were reckless, and as deadly as they were dissolute, had so far not met their equal in the field, and it was in that inequality that Colonel Gabriel Wild saw his opportunity. He had heard tell of other cavalry commanders attempting to turn their ragtag formations into something serious. Something that might, at last, pose a real threat to the Rome-loving popinjays who galloped across bloody fields with utter impunity. But those men – up-and-coming young bucks like Ireton and Cromwell – were far away to the east, not embroiled in the dirty fight that had consumed this far-flung corner of England. Here, the war was bitter and merciless, the ideal proving ground for an ambitious man. Once Wild had blooded his black-plumed killers on the obstinate Cornish, he would have the best fighting force in the land, honed in fire and blood, and ready to face the finest the king had to offer. Parliament needed a warrior, thought Wild, a modern-day Alexander who would cut a cruel swathe from Truro to York. He could be that man, was certain of it, just as soon as the current matter was resolved.

The matter in question, the one he and his hundred men now undertook, was an irritation. An issue to be resolved with an ambush, a capture, and a swift, exquisitely painful death. And yet, until it had been dealt with, Wild knew that it would consume him. The colonel's stomach churned as he thought upon Stryker. A man, he presumed, who might have been handsome once, tall and dark as he was, though mutilated now by that repulsive mess of swirling scar tissue. Wild had a short temper, he knew that about himself, never denied it, but the hatred he felt for the malignant, one-eyed fiend astonished even him. Stryker had surprised him, tricked him, robbed, mocked, and humiliated him, and that was enough to ensure Gabriel Wild's need for revenge. But the scorn poured forth from the dead-eyed, pasty-faced Collings had simply been too much to bear. Stryker would have to die, Wild had promised himself, because he could not live out his days knowing that the smug bastard's heart still beat.

The alehouse came quickly into view at the end of the street, and Wild led his steel-clad column towards it, turning left into its large courtyard without regard for the four or five drink-addled sots stumbling across the filthy cobblestones. The clatter of hooves was deafening, like a prolonged thunderclap or the cannon fire from a mighty seaward fort, and wide-eyed faces immediately appeared at the windows of the complex of taphouse and stables.

'Dismount!' Wild commanded when the last of the troopers had drawn up in the rectangular yard. He swung a leg across his horse's back to plummet on to the squelching ground. It hadn't rained all day, but the sheer amount of mud, straw, and horse dung that had collected over the time since the area had last been cleaned meant the uneven cobbles were swathed in an ankle-deep carpet of muck.

He glanced at one of his officers. 'Give the men liberty, Captain.'

The captain, a squinty-eyed fellow with grey stubble and a flat nose, lifted his hinged visor. 'Will do, sir.'

'But no more than small beer,' Wild added as his men began to chatter and laugh. 'I want 'em sober and fit to ride.'

At the captain's sharp nod, Wild handed another trooper his reins, spun on his heels and marched towards the tavern's studded door.

Inside, the taproom was a dingy affair, the night's darkness barely repelled by a handful of candles, and positively exacerbated by the fuggy clouds of tobacco smoke billowing around almost every patron. Wild released the hook at the bottom of his visor, unbuckled his chin strap and lifted his helmet free. He shook his head briefly, like a dog in a rain shower, letting his badger-striped auburn hair flow freely about his shoulders.

Wild stepped slowly up to the water-ringed counter, deliberately allowing every gaze to fall on him, intending the locals to get a good look at the armoured killer in their midst. He needed them to fear him, and for that fear to loosen tongues and slacken jaws, so that the unwelcome foray into this grimy peasants' lair would be worth the trouble. Placing his pot carefully on the counter, he peered into the gloom. It was a simple enough place; a single large room with a rush-scattered floor, half a dozen low tables, and a score of rickety-looking stools. The walls and ceiling, stained by the smoke of wood, tallow, and tobacco were nearly as black as the night sky. In one wall a substantial hearth blazed. A small cauldron hung above the flames, some kind of pottage bubbling within. The solid mantelpiece held a row of pewter plates and jugs, a wooden cup full of old pipe stems, a handful of desiccated onions, and a rusty old dagger that he supposed must have held some kind of sentimental attachment for the tapster, for it had long since ceased to be lethal.

The men at the tables still gawped at him like cattle, as he knew they would, and he found their dull stares irritating in the extreme. These were low folk. The kind Wild would employ to clean his jakes or muck out his horses. Drove-boys, probably, and farmhands, ostlers, or even simple vagrants. And yet he needed them, their information and their gossip, if he was to achieve his goal.

'Stryker.'

The dull expressions did not twitch at the name.

'I am looking for a man named Captain Stryker,' Wild tried again. 'A king's man, he leads a company of redcoats.' Still nothing. 'He has scars where his eye should be.' Wild placed a gauntleted hand across the left side of his face. 'Like so. His second, a slim youth, has no use of his right arm.'

'What'll it be, General?'

Wild spun round to face the man standing on the opposite side of the sticky counter. 'Be?'

The tapster, a silver-haired fellow well drawn in his years, rested stubby paws on his potbelly. 'To drink, sir.'

A handful of Wild's troopers had filtered through the low doorway now, chattering and laughing as they crossed the rushes in their colonel's wake. Wild raised his voice to reiterate his earlier order. 'Small beer.'

The tapster went to work, filling a battered pewter cup from one of his casks. He slid the drink across the counter, peering at Wild through rheumy eyes. 'They won't talk.'

Wild had already put the cup to his lips, but held his arm at the man's words. 'Oh?'

The tapster's face cracked in a half-smile, brandishing a set of chipped and crooked teeth, all black at the gums. 'The folk hereabouts.'

'Royalists?'

'No, sir, not a bit of it!' the tapster responded as though Wild had made a raucous jest. 'But they're 'fraid, sir. There's been so many o' yon soldiers marchin' and ridin' through Widdy these past months not a single man can call 'imself safe. The answer?' He leant across the counter conspiratorially. 'Keep your bliddy pie-hole clamped and pray the likes o' yourself don't come a knockin'. Beggin' your pardon, sir.'

Wild took a swig of ale, wiped his mouth with his gloved wrist, and examined the room. Yes, he thought, the tapster was right. He had relied on fear and intimidation to cow the locals into speaking, but the strategy had had the opposite effect. He set the cup down hard, chiding himself inwardly and considering his next move, when the tapster folded his arms and winked.

'But I'd be right willin' to whisper a few words if you and your men saw fit to buy a few more throat wetters.' He grinned again, a note of triumph in the expression. 'What say you, General?'

'Get him up,' Colonel Gabriel Wild snapped, stepping back to allow a couple of his troopers to haul the hapless man to his feet. 'He's had long enough to sleep.'

The tapster, it transpired, went by the name of John Bray, and when Wild had dragged him over the ale-stained counter, the confidence had flowed out of him almost as quickly as the stream of piss down his leg.

That had irked Wild, the piss, for it had somehow found its way on to the upturned thigh protectors of his long boots, and though it would probably scrub clean, the mere sight of the liquid infuriated him. And he had hit Bray.

He had always intended to, naturally, for the man had had the temerity to attempt to extort money for what morsels of information he possessed. But the sight of the dark urine mark, and Bray's sweaty jowls and the way his filthy fat hands grabbed at the colonel's gorgeous cloth-ing, had made something snap in Gabriel Wild's mind. So Wild used his left fist for the punch. Instead of the stinging reprimand a gloved backhand might have been, Wild had employed his armour-clad hand, the one encased within the articulated steel gauntlet, rendering it more like a medieval mace than bone and flesh. John Bray did not even cry out. The blow had almost certainly broken his jaw, snapped his head back, and sent him sprawling in a heap amongst the mouldering threshings.

Now, as his men bolstered the lolling Bray, slapping him sharply back into consciousness, Wild inspected the blood spatters on his gauntlet, wrinkled his nose in disgust, and stared about the room. It had already emptied, save his own men. 'Welch.'

One of the cavalrymen near the door met his eye. He was a tall young man with a curved nose and strawberry-blond hair. 'Sir?'

'Let's wake this swine up.' He jerked his chin in the direction of the counter. 'Get back there and find a bucket.'

In a matter of moments, Trooper Welch reappeared carrying a wooden pail, water slopping over the rim in time with his loping step. He skirted round the side of the counter and strode directly up to Bray, though he addressed Wild. 'Shall I, sir?'

Wild nodded silently.

John Bray woke with a start, his mouth flapping quietly at first, like a landed carp, before he let fly a great scream of pain and terror. He tried to raise a hand to his already hideously swollen jaw, but the pinioning grasp of the men at his flanks prevented any movement. He began to weep.

Wild stalked up to the frightened tapster. He knew the weeping was really a plea. A last ditch appeal for mercy, the high-pitched keening of a broken man. But instead the sound grated on him. Made his teeth itch and his spine tingle. For this was a man akin to Stryker. A gutter-born, grubby peasant of few scruples and even less grace. The mere sight of the pathetic toad, hanging limp from the troopers' vice-like grip, seemed to make the colonel furious, and the stench of him made Wild positively enraged.

'Now, sir,' Wild said, and the mere sound of his voice seemed to make Bray wince. When he drew his broadbladed sword, an acrid, eye-burning stink seemed to rise into his nostrils.

'He's pissed 'is fuckin' britches again, Colonel!' one of the troopers exclaimed in disgust.

Wild ignored the man, choosing simply to lift his sword, turning the glinting point in the air between his face and Bray's. The wretched captive began to wail, and, interspersed with wracking sobs, a stream of panicked words tumbled from his ruined face.

Wild let the sword drop to the space just beneath Bray's engorged chin. The tapster fell instantly silent.

'As I was about to say,' said Wild slowly, 'I have neither the time nor the inclination to play silly games of cat and mouse. You will not *barter* information, Master Tapster. You will not offer me titbits as though I were your dog, and expect me to wag my damned tail. And I will not waste my time and energies battering the words out of you.' He glanced at the troopers. 'Turn him round.'

Bray screamed again, sensing some impending horror, but the soldiers were far too strong for his feeble attempts to squirm free. They forced him to bend over the counter and yanked Bray's sopping breeches down to his pudgy ankles, and then, with direction from Wild, they kicked apart his thick legs so that he was utterly exposed.

Colonel Gabriel Wild stared down at Bray's huge, trembling, lily-white buttocks. The repulsive man was babbling now, shrieking like a hamstrung cat, last shred of dignity long since vanished. Wild took no joy from the deed. He already had the stain of another man's urine on his obscenely expensive boots, and the last thing he had wanted was to become spattered in the vile tavern-keeper's blood – or worse – but it was the only means to a crucial end.

'Now, Master Tapster,' he began quietly, 'you will cease your noise. The only time you will speak is when you are spoken to. Is that clear?'

The wounded man muttered something unintelligible. Wild raised his sword so that it scraped along the skin between Bray's buttocks, the wobbling mounds of flesh tightening immediately at the touch.

Wild spoke again, his voice soft. 'Please be aware, sir, that if you do anything other than that which I instruct,' he applied some pressure to the blade, 'I will thrust this tuck so far up your backside, it will knock out those rotten teeth.'

John Bray did as he was ordered after that. His jaw throbbed and his legs trembled, but he told Colonel Wild all he knew.

TWO MILES WEST OF MERRIVALE, DARTMOOR,
29 APRIL 1643

The man was an unassuming fellow to look at. Probably in his late twenties, of average height and plain features, with brown hair to match his brown coat and breeches.

And yet, as he scampered out of the darkness, the eyes of thirty-seven red-coated infantrymen, a handful of Cornish soldiers, a plump, sandy-haired officer and a giant were fixed upon him as though he brought news of Christ's second coming.

'He bain't there, sir,' the man rasped breathlessly when he had reached the expectant crowd.

'Who?' Captain Lancelot Forrester asked, nonplussed. He might have been the senior officer present, but the messenger, a member of Anthony Payne's small unit of Cornishmen, had addressed the giant. Forrester glared up at Payne instead.

'S'blood, Mister Payne! Who were we due to meet? I have a right to know!'

The Royalist task force had covered the short but rugged journey between Peter Tavy and Merrivale during the last hours of the day and now, as midnight fast approached, they had reached the spot outside the little village that Payne had told him would serve as the rendezvous point. Except the person they were expecting to meet had not arrived.

Anthony Payne – all seven feet and four inches of him – loomed over Forrester like a great oak in the blackness, his silhouette cutting out what little moonlight there had been. 'Come with me if you would, sir.' He looked at the messenger. 'You too.'

Before Forrester could respond, Payne strode further away from the road towards a nearby copse. The rendezvous was to be beside a vast, gnarled elm that climbed almost horizontally out of the roadside just west of Merrivale. The elm was centuries old, the keeper of a thousand secrets, and Forrester had to admit that it was a good place for a clandestine meeting. He left his shrunken company beneath its twisted boughs and, with the messenger in tow, scuttled after Payne.

The giant waited for them amongst the dark trunks of the copse, only speaking when they were well within its dominion. 'Treloar?'

The messenger plucked the Monmouth cap from his head, revealing lank mousy hair that had thinned so much on the top of his skull that it looked like a monk's tonsure. 'Aye, sir.'

'Tell us again. You saw nothing?'

Treloar twisted the woollen cap in spidery hands. 'Went into the village, like you told me, Mister Payne, sir.' He shrugged, almost embarrassed. 'Not a soul there. All tucked a'bed an' not so much as a dog out sniffin'.'

'You saw no one? Not a horseman, or pony and trap, perhaps?'

Treloar shook his head again. 'Nothin', sir.'

Payne exhaled through his nose. 'Well done, regardless.' He indicated that Treloar could take his leave and waited a few moments while the man crammed the Monmouth back atop his head and scrambled out of the copse. Then he looked down at Forrester, huge hand rubbing his lantern jaw. 'We were due to meet a man this night, Captain. A man of vital importance to our cause here in the south-west. Indeed, of vital importance to the King's armies up and down the land.'

'His name?'

'All I am at liberty to say,' Payne replied, 'is that we were to find him beneath the great elm, turn around, and take him back to Launceston. He has information only to be divulged to General Hopton.'

'And now?' Forrester asked after an awkwardly long silence. 'Should we head home? Were you given leave to wait for this man? Perhaps he is merely delayed.'

Payne interrupted with a swift shake of his head. 'There were no further orders.'

Forrester felt his eyes widen. 'You mean to say there was no contingency? Nothing to direct us should this very circumstance arise?'

'The order was singular, Captain Forrester,' Payne replied in his thunder-roll tone. 'We must find our man and see him safe to the general.'

Forrester spread his palms in a gesture of helplessness. 'Where would you begin, Mister Payne? Do tell me, please, for I am at a loss. Searching for a vanished man on Dartmoor would be akin to sniffing out a ball of sotweed in a cartload of manure.'

Payne held Forrester's stare, and not for the first time the captain wondered whether it had been a mistake to antagonize the gargantuan man. But there was no malice in those huge eyes, only a steely thread of determination.

'We should wait another day,' Payne said eventually.

'This is your mission, my friend,' Forrester replied, 'and I am resigned to seeing it done.'

Payne nodded his thanks. 'We'll camp out here in the trees.'

Forrester's gaze flickered across to the stream at the field's far end. 'We have water in abundance, I suppose. How long?'

'Tonight,' Payne replied, sucking in his cheeks as he mulled over their options. 'Perhaps tomorrow night as well. We'll remain here, watch the road and wait for him to arrive.'

'That would take us into the new month. If there is still no sign by then?'

'We continue eastward. Follow the road until we find him.'

'Or until we run into Cropheads seeking trouble.'

Payne grinned at that, his small white teeth glowing in the blackness. 'Aye, perhaps.' He stole a rapid glance over his shoulder, instinctively wary of eavesdroppers however unlikely they might have been, and lowered his voice to a soft rumble.

'I am sorry I cannot discuss this matter in more detail, Captain, sincerely I am. But it is of such great import that I am to trust no man with any more knowledge than he truly requires. Just know that our task is vital.'

'You believe that?' Forrester replied, hearing the incredulity in his own voice. 'If I had a groat for every time a senior officer described a mission as vital, I'd be riding at the head of Colonel Lancelot Forrester's Regiment of Extremely Well-Equipped Foot.'

Payne smiled again, but the seriousness had not left his gaze. 'I believe it, Captain. Please trust me. The man we are to meet will change the very course of the war.'

Lancelot Forrester sighed. 'Then so be it.'

CHAPTER 6

NORTH-EAST OF TWO BRIDGES, DARTMOOR, 30 APRIL 1643

Progress as dawn carved its first chinks of light was better than Stryker could have hoped for. It had been a struggle to negotiate the last furlongs of Wistman's Wood – it had not been easy to free themselves from the clawing branches and sucking mud – but after the best part of an hour they had emerged on to coarse, flat heathland that was a far more negotiable proposition. The bridleway, promised by the carter, Marcus Bailey, had proved to be little more than a narrow strip of land where the footfall of man and beast had made the tangled heather flatter than the rest of the heath, but it was still passable for their march.

Stryker had roused the men when it was still dark, ensuring kit was ready, weapons clean and fires fully doused. And as the sun had made its first cracks across the eastern horizon he had woken the company's newest members, Otilwell Broom and Cecily Cade, shared with them what scarce victuals he could muster, and shown them to their horses. Broom had complained that, as guests, he and the girl should ride on the cart, but his griping ended abruptly when Stryker put a hand over the vehicle's side and patted one of the small kegs. 'Black powder, Mister Broom. Dry as a bone. You may ride in here, certainly, but should a spark somehow find its way on board,' he whistled, 'they'll be scraping bits of you off the thatches in Plymouth.'

The ammunition cart again trundled at the head of the column. It was cumbersome, brimful of weaponry as it was, but the heath was simple enough terrain for its broad-rimmed wheels, fresh, regularly alternated horses, and experienced driver. Behind the cart rode Broom and Cecily, perched on a couple of the fine mounts captured from Colonel Wild, and beside them walked Stryker, Burton, and Chase, the captain's big red-and-white standard propped on the stocky ensign's shoulder. In the wake of the flag trudged Stryker's two drummers, followed by the bulk of the company, divided into smaller squads of pike-men and musketeers. Before long they were well away from the dense woodland, with open plain stretching away before them and the forbidding outlines of several large hills rising in the distance.

'Great Mis Tor,' Bailey called back from the wagon. 'And the Great Staple. Couple of others I ain't sure of, but I'm thinkin' it'll be Roos Tor and Cox Tor beyond.'

Stryker studied the hills. At each summit rocky out-crops looked for all the world like small castles. He stared at those vast granite boulders, framed by white wisps of cloud, the soldier in him wondering whether such places were defensible.

After an hour the column reached a river meandering down from a flat-topped tor climbing out of the bleak terrain about two miles to the north. Mercifully the water-way was narrow and shallow enough to cross with ease, but Stryker ordered the company to rest a while so that they might water the horses and refill drinking flasks. The tight formation dissolved as soon as the word was given, pikes thrown down and bandoliers dumped in heaps on the heather like so many coiled serpents.

Stryker felt suddenly weary, as though the very wilderness of the moor had formed a weight on his shoulders, and he went to sit on a rotting log beside the gurgling water. He unhooked his scabbard, laying it on the grass at his feet, took the dagger from his belt, and began scraping at the stubborn layer of mud that had become ingrained on the sides of his boots.

'I hope I am not intruding, sir.'

Stryker stood up, startled. The voice had been that of a woman. 'Of course not, miss. How might I help?'

Cecily Cade fixed Stryker with her sad green eyes. 'I wanted to thank you for saving us, sir.' She glanced at the vacant end of Stryker's makeshift bench. 'May I?'

Stryker considered the wood's damp, pitted surface. 'It'll ruin your dress.'

The corners of her mouth twitched as she instinctively smoothed down the folds of yellow material that covered her hips. 'I think perhaps it is a little too late to worry about such things, Captain Stryker.'

He could not help running his eye over the garment, from the mud-darkened hem, up the pale yellow folds that hung about her legs, and past the trellis of lace struggling to hold the bodice together. *Christ*, he thought, what a vision she was. Part of him wanted to tell her, but he bit back the urge, feeling guilty as an image of Lisette assailed him. Suddenly feeling awkward, as if his thoughts were as etched on his face as his scars, he cleared his throat, nodded at the end of the mouldering log, and waited for her to sit. 'I am sorry about your father, Miss Cade.'

'Cecily, please,' she replied gently.

'Miss Cecily.'

She laughed for the first time since they had found the stricken coach. 'Just Cecily.'

He laughed too, unable to break contact with her mesmerizing emerald eyes. 'I am sorry about your father.' His smile drooped suddenly. 'It must have been a frightening experience.'

Cecily's expression darkened to match his as the memory of the attack struck her. 'They came out of nowhere,' she said, staring at the river now, her eyes glazed and distant. 'All swords and threats. They shouted at Father. Told him to empty his pockets.'

'But he refused?'

'Sheer folly,' she muttered. A fat teardrop welled up like a sudden spring and tumbled down her cheek. 'Foolish, foolish man.' She looked up at Stryker. 'He commanded the coachman to drive through them. He always was pig-headed.'

She smiled – a rueful, knowing smile – that told Stryker of her affection for Sir Alfred Cade, despite the harsh words.

'And they shot at you?' he prompted, though he knew the answer well enough.

She nodded. 'At the driver first, then, after the coach had stopped, they aimed at us. Father and poor Richard.'

'McCubbin?' Stryker repeated the name Broom had previously mentioned.

'Yes,' Cecily confirmed. 'Richard McCubbin was my father's bodyguard for many years. His friend really.'

Stryker eased himself to his feet, taking a leather flask from his snapsack, and walked towards the river-bank. 'And Broom?' he asked as he knelt to dunk the flask beneath the icy flow.

'Otilwell came to us a year or so ago,' Cecily replied. 'He was an old comrade of Richard's, I think.'

Stryker stood, staring up at the tor with its strangely flat summit. A dark cluster of rock crowned the pinnacle like a black cloud. 'Why did your father feel the need to keep another retainer?'

She shrugged. 'Times are dangerous, Captain Stryker.'

It was a good enough answer, thought Stryker, and he strode back to the log. As he took his seat again he noticed Cecily regarding him closely. 'What is it?'

She pursed her lips as if deciding whether to ask what-ever question had entered her mind. After a few moments she spoke, 'May I ask your Christian name, Captain?'

'I answer to Stryker, Miss Cade.' Stryker immediately regretted the hasty and rather taciturn response. Seeing her colour, he held up his water flask, wiped the rim with the hem of his coat, and offered it to her.

She smiled at the gesture, clumsy though it was, but waved the flask away. 'I'm not thirsty, Captain, but thank you.'

They sat in awkward silence a while longer, Stryker's abrasive answer to the girl's perfectly reasonable question grating at him with every passing moment. She had taken the rebuff in good nature, but that had almost made his embarrassment worse. Lisette, he thought, would have bitten his head off. Then he remembered the previous night by the fire. The way Cecily had stared at the ruined part of his face, her intrigue obvious.

'Some years ago,' he said, hoping in some way to make

up for refusing to discuss his name, 'I was attacked by two men. Eli Makepeace and Malachi Bain. They put a bag of gunpowder to my face.'

Cecily's jaw dropped. 'My goodness, Captain. I—I am sorry.'

'No matter,' he said, waving her apologies away. 'It is all dealt with now.'

'Dealt with?'

Stryker stayed silent, not willing to discuss the demise of the two villains during Brentford Fight, for the wounds he had suffered there were not long healed. He pushed himself off the log and hooked on his scabbard. 'I must be away. It is time to shake the men into life.'

Cecily nodded. 'I hope they do as they're told, Captain.'

He grinned. 'They'd better.'

In half an hour the company were on the move again. They successfully forded the meandering river at a point where it was both narrow and shallow, and emerged on to the west bank amid cheerful chatter and a bright old Cornish ditty sung by Corporal Tresick. It was a windy day, vengeful gusts whipping down from the tors to scream across the open plain, but mercifully it remained dry.

Stryker stared at the empty horizon, wondering if the improved weather was responsible for the lifted spirits. Perhaps, he thought, it was the fact that with another waterway crossed, they had also surmounted an emotional barrier. They simply felt closer to home.

The column trundled past a small hillock, a gorse-blanketed knoll the size of a small house, and Stryker jogged up to its summit where a single picket, Harry Trowbridge, was standing.

'Clear?' he asked.

Trowbridge nodded, though his blue eyes, narrowed to slits against the wind, stayed fixed on the western horizon. 'Quiet as a dry taphouse, sir.'

'Good,' Stryker said. Harry was one half of the Trowbridge twins, the company's sharpest lookouts, and he trusted the report. He glanced to the right where the land fell away in a gentle slope, at the foot of which, some two hundred paces beyond, a dense cluster of oaks blotted the otherwise open terrain. 'Might put your brother over there.'

'Aye, sir,' Trowbridge replied. 'Can't see into them trees, even from up 'ere.'

Stryker turned back to gaze westward. 'Back home in Launceston in a couple of days, eh?'

Trowbridge paused as a wailing gust lashed at them, then shook his head. 'Hayling's home for Jack and me, sir.'

'Hayling Island?' A Hampshire man himself, Stryker knew the small community well. 'Are your kinsmen panners?'

'For salt? No, sir. Fishermen. Well, oyster catchers.'

'Used to like them stewed with a few herbs.'

Trowbridge glanced at Stryker for the first time. 'Can't stand 'em m'self, sir.' He grinned. 'Good money, though. Inland towns'll pay a pretty penny for 'em pickled.'

'I believe they're supposedly an aphrodisiac.'

Trowbridge shrugged. 'A what, sir? I don't know what that is, but they're certainly meant to help keep your pizzle hard.'

Stryker laughed into the wind, but immediately fell silent.

'Captain,' Trowbridge said urgently, but Stryker was already running down the side of the knoll.

'I saw them!' he called over his shoulder.

Trowbridge stared back towards the oak copse. 'God help us,' he mouthed. On their northern flank, emerging from the tree line in a silver wave, were cavalry.

Stryker reached his long, red-coated line and turned northwards to stare across the sloping heath. There, at the place where the land vanished into the dark copse, he saw the glinting ranks of the horsemen. Jelyan Mookes, one of his veterans, was nearby. He had already registered the threat, for a horrified expression had stricken the corporal's sallow face, but his words were muffled by the gale. And then the wind dropped. Suddenly, surprisingly, there were no howling gusts to whip away all other sounds. Ears were liberated, attention was hooked, and Mookes's cry carried to the company. Shrill and desperate.

'Horse!'

They all heard the hoofbeats at the same moment. Distant thunder, growing instead of dying. Collectively heads turned to the right, northwards, gazing down the gentle slope. What they saw was a wide, glinting line of killers, silhouetted against the dark wood beyond. They spanned the near horizon like avenging angels, standing tall in stirrups, grinding wicked spurs into their mounts' flesh for ever more speed, bearing down on their quarry with hard faces and glittering eyes. Harquebusiers, light cavalrymen, armour-plated warriors with drawn swords and levelled pistols.

Stryker sprinted along the line, making for the ammunition wagon at the front of the column but all the while looking at the charging horsemen, unable to tear his gaze away from the metallic hunters. He had faced many such men before, from agile harquebusiers to heavily armoured cuirassiers, and even the fabled winged lancers of Poland. But this new enemy was different from the rest. The men now sweeping towards his company bore a field sign he knew all too well. One that told him he had brought this upon his men; for his willingness to pick a fight when a more sensible man might have marched on by, and for the humiliation of the horsemen that had followed. Because the men on the slope each wore a feather fixed into the plate of their helmet tail. A long, black feather that, Stryker knew, had been plucked from the body of a Great Cormorant.

Colonel Gabriel Wild was coming for him.

For a second Stryker hesitated. It was a bad place to be caught, open ground in front, river at their backs, and he did not know what to do for the best. But if there was one thing his years of soldiering had taught him, it was that a decisive officer, even a bad one, was better than a ditherer. 'Charge for horse!' he bellowed, hearing the command echo up and down the line. When he drilled his men, he would form them into a tight, sharp-angled square, but this was not drill, and time allowed only the simplest of movements. 'Charge for horse!' he shouted again. 'Form circle! Protect the cart! Protect the cart, God damn you!'

The column contracted like a vast snake coiling inwards when disturbed by a predator, musketeers instinctively shrinking behind the screen of spines formed by the pikemen. It seemed to take an age, but as the cavalry closed the distance between them with startling rapidity, the red-coated infantrymen finally formed a crude circle, pikes on the outermost fringe, wagon at the very centre.

Each pikeman jammed the butt end of his long, tapering stave into the instep of his right foot, angling the weapon upwards so that the leaf-shaped blade at its tip could be held rigidly in line with a horse's chest or face. Behind them the musketeers hurriedly rammed lead balls into their iron barrels and tipped black powder into firing pans. Mercifully, a handful of weapons were already primed and ready to fire, and the men blew carefully on their slow-burning cords of match, caressing the glowing embers into life.

Stryker, orchestrating matters from outside the formation, saw Cecily Cade atop her mount, jaw lolling open as she stared in stunned silence at the black-plumed horsemen. He ran to her, reached up to take her arm, and almost dragged her from the saddle. She yelped, more out of surprise than pain, and Otilwell Broom, riding beside her, gave a sharp bark of protest.

Stryker turned on him. 'Get off that fucking horse if you want to live!'

Broom, taken aback by the infantryman's coarse ferocity, held Stryker's gaze for a moment before sliding from the saddle and coaxing his mount to where Stryker waited, still holding Cecily.

'Follow me,' Stryker snapped, and paced quickly into the hastily forming circle. Cecily, leading the horse in her wake, cried out again at his iron grip, but he ignored her, shouldering men aside and releasing her only when they were safely at the rear of the last rank.

'Stay here!'

Though he could see she tried to keep the fear from her voice, her left eye was twitching slightly and the colour had drained from her cheeks. 'What should I do?'

Stryker wanted to laugh at the question, but resisted the urge. 'Get behind your horse,' he offered simply. 'Crouch low and pray.' He looked quickly over his shoulder and saw that Broom had followed them. 'Stay with her.'

The bodyguard glanced longingly at the cart, which sat at the epicentre of the formation. 'May we not take shelter there?'

Stryker followed his gaze, but shook his head. 'No!' he ordered sharply. 'If a spark catches it, you'll be blown to pieces. You stay here!'

Broom nodded curtly, and coaxed his own horse into position next to Cecily's. Both then took shelter behind the beasts.

Stryker turned to push his way out of the circle. When he reached the outermost rank he looked up at the great tide of crowing rebels in black-feathered, lobster-tailed helmets. Stryker could not yet see Wild, though he knew the colonel would be there, close to the front, scenting the kill. Stryker's eye caught the enemy standard, a small flag of black and white fluttering at the end of a pole hefted by a young cornet. An ominous smudge against the blue sky. Instinctively he turned back to catch sight of his own flag. The red taffeta flapped high and proud above the ragged circle.

'Charge your pikes!' he heard Skellen snarl. 'And load those shitting muskets!'

Time was running out. The enemy would be upon them in moments, but at least they would present a united front. He thanked God that his men were experienced, for an attack of such shocking speed would have set many of the king's greener troops to flight. His men, he knew, would stand firm.

The redcoats set their faces into grim masks as the Parliamentarians reached them. They feared the slashing blades of cavalry, but trusted that the horses would not charge their lethal hedge of pikes.

Sure enough, the attackers came to within twenty paces of the defensive formation, marginally out of pike range, and began to wheel away, curling back down the slope from whence they came.

'Fire!' Lieutenant Burton's voice barked above the hoof-beats, and those musketeers who were able to fire did so. Six or seven shots cracked out across the bleak field. Four men were punched from their saddles, staining the heath red where they lay.

The Royalists roused a jeer, but almost immediately their whistles and calls began to die away. The cavalry-men, it seemed, had been formed into two squadrons of perhaps fifty troopers apiece, the second group galloping a short distance behind the first. Even Stryker had failed to notice the division initially, but now it was rapidly becoming clear. For though that first squad were peeling away, the second squad were not.

'Christ,' Stryker said simply.

'Clever bugger's used that charge to see how many muskets we can bring to bear,' Simeon Barkworth's voice croaked at his side.

Stryker looked down at him. 'Clever or lucky.'

Barkworth shrugged. 'Either way, he's won his wager.'

That, Stryker knew, was all too true. Only a handful of his forty-nine musketeers were so far ready to fire, and Wild's first charge – a feint, it now seemed – had been designed to prove that fact.

The second phalanx of horsemen reached Stryker's

position, but instead of charging home or wheeling away, they drew up alongside the infantrymen and began firing pistols and carbines into the Royalist ranks, walking their mounts around the front of Stryker's formation like a warship firing a broadside. The great circle convulsed as men shrank from the searing barrage of lead.

Stryker watched in horror as a man to his left pitched backwards, a carbine ball tearing straight through his throat. He ran a gloved hand across his face, wiping away the blood that had sprayed him. 'Where are those damned muskets?' he screamed, and knew he had been outwitted. Ordinarily infantrymen would view the short-arm fire of mounted troops with utter disdain, such was the wasteful inaccuracy of the weapons. But here, in open country, aimed at a mass of men who could not offer anything in reply, they could not miss. There was not even a need to take aim. They could simply point their pieces at one, vast, fleshy target and squeeze the trigger. Eventually gaps would open in the circle as men died, like small breaches in a castle wall, and the pike barrier would fracture. And into those gaps would ride the victorious Parliamentarians.

Colonel Gabriel Wild was exultant. Finally, after the loss of the arms cache and resulting humiliation, he had run his quarry to ground. A memory flashed into his mind as he wallowed in this moment of triumph. The image of a poor, stricken, broken-jawed tapster, bent across his own ale-slick counter, a sword tickling the cleft between his flabby buttocks. That had been the turning point. The moment when wild goose chase had become exciting hunt. The second when hound had sniffed fox. Bray had whimpered and sobbed and wailed as Wild pressed the blade against his most private parts, and loosed his bowels when the tip had broken flesh. And then he had told Wild of the rumours that spoke of a one-eyed king's man who led a company of redcoats and a wagon packed full of weaponry. Those whispers said the Royalist fugitives were travelling westward, which Wild had already guessed, but, crucially, they also told of a circuitous route through open plains and ancient forests. With each village Wild had visited through his manic night ride, more questions were answered and more sightings reported. Stryker might have stayed well clear of the major roads, but a hundred or so men, several horses, and a wagon were difficult to hide altogether.

And then, in the grey dawn, Colonel Gabriel Wild had spotted the telltale glint of pike tips on the horizon, and he had sensed immediately that this was his fox.

But this fox, he thought with exquisite relish, had nowhere to go. No hole in which to hide. Stryker would die a most horrible death – if he was unlucky enough to survive this assault – and the thought made Wild's skin tingle with delicious anticipation.

Standing high in his stirrups, Wild surveyed the scene. To his right, the desolate plain stretched for at least another two miles, offering no shred of shelter, while to the left, at the Royalists' backs, the river formed a natural barrier. In short, there was nowhere for the enemy to go. No hope for Stryker and his company.

The redcoats had formed a ragged circle in a desperate attempt to stave off Wild's horsemen, but that had been almost as dangerous a move as remaining in a column, for now they had presented a concentrated mass of bodies for Wild's men to shoot. Things might have been different, he reflected, had Stryker's musketeers been ready for the attack, for muskets had a longer range than Wild's carbines and were vastly more accurate, but he had taken the gamble that they would not have marched with primed weapons, and that gamble had paid off.

'Shoot 'em!' Wild bellowed above the din of small-arms fire. 'You cannot miss, boys! Shoot the malignant bastards down! No prisoners, you hear me? No goddamned prisoners!' Captives were slow, cumbersome creatures that would impinge his glorious ride back to Okehampton. Besides, he wanted every last one of Stryker's motley band dead and rotting by sundown. He turned to one of his officers. 'Truth told, Grantham, I'm a little disappointed.'

Grantham stared at his colonel in surprise. 'Sir?'

'In a strange way, I had hoped that one-eyed fiend would put up more of a fight.'

The Royalist circle, entirely surrounded now, shuddered again as three pikemen went down under the hail of lead. Men in the second rank shifted forwards to plug the gap before it was filled by Roundhead horsemen.

'It ain't over yet, sir,' Grantham warned.

'Nonsense, man!' Wild called over his shoulder as he kicked at his mount. 'Come! Let us spill some Royalist blood!'

Stryker could see that his company was about to shatter. The first group of horsemen, those who had retreated after the initial feint, were returning now, sweeping back across the gorse and heather to encircle Stryker's tattered force. They maintained their distance, for they rightly feared the outstretched pikes, but their own weapons were being brought to the fight with devastating effect.

The Royalists were on the brink of destruction.

'Stay clear o' that wagon, you pribblin' bloody pizzle-lickers!' The shout reached him from somewhere on Stryker's blind left side, and he might have thought it had come from one of the exultant attackers, had it not been a voice he knew almost as well as his own. 'You want to blow us to kingdom come?'

The words hit Stryker in a moment of sheer epiphany, stabbing him like a white-hot blade.

The wagon.

He spun on his heel, pushing his way back towards the centre of the beleaguered formation, forced to step across the contorted bodies that had been dragged from the front rank. There, beside a group of musketeers hurriedly working to reload their weapons amid the chaotic terror, he caught sight of Skellen, still berating the men for lighting their match-cords too near to the powder-laden wagon.

'Grenados!' Stryker shouted.

Skellen's eyes, ordinarily so small within hooded sockets, widened at the word, and he immediately ran to his captain's side.

Stryker and Skellen vaulted over the side of the wagon, wincing as pistol and carbine balls whistled around their ears, and desperately rifled through the cloth sacks. After the longest few seconds of his life, Stryker finally laid hands upon a sack bulging with a dozen or so fist-sized spheres. '*Here*!'

Skellen clambered across the sword stacks and bushels and thrust his long arms into the bag, held open by his captain, drawing out a metal casting in each hand. '*Match here*!' he shouted as Stryker took a couple of explosives for himself.

As the pair leapt down from the vehicle, one of the musketeers from the rearmost rank scuttled across the blood-shadowed heath to meet them. He held out his musket, on which a glowing length of match was fixed.

'Good lad,' Skellen grunted, placing the grenado's fuse against the orange tip. Almost immediately the short tube packed full of black powder sprang into manic life.

Colonel Gabriel Wild drew his long blade. It was a poor thing, a standard cavalry backsword he had taken from a store at Okehampton to replace the fine weapon that had been stolen from him. Stolen by a man who, he presumed, was cowering somewhere within the heaving mass of dying redcoats. Today he would take back his beautiful blade. Today he would take back his honour. He had once heard that the old Scottish savage, Wallace, had made a scabbard from the skins of the men he had killed. Perhaps that should be Stryker's fate. Or maybe the victory would be even sweeter if he could present the thieving villain's head to Erasmus Collings. That would wipe the supercilious smirk off the effeminate major-general's pallid face.

Wild's aide, Grantham, caught the colonel's eye, jolting him from the beautiful dream. 'I fear it is taking too long, sir. They'll be ready to give volley fire soon, and our moment will be lost.'

Wild nodded. He enjoyed witnessing the slow convulsions of Stryker's company as it died, struggling to replace the men falling so rapidly about them, but Grantham was right. To delay would only gift the enemy time to load their muskets. It was now or never. He held his sword aloft. 'Charge!'

Colonel Wild was blinded at first. A sheet of white

– pure and pristine as new snow – covered his vision, wiping out the land, the sky, the distant pinnacles of tors, the frayed circle of enemy troops, and even his own proud horsemen. In its wake came the sound. An overwhelming, ear-splitting crescendo of explosions that combined high pitch with low grumble.

And then, as his eyes and ears recovered, he heard the screams.

Stryker and Skellen had shoved and bullied their way to the very front rank of the company and lobbed their grenados with as much force as could be mustered. The fizzing spheres had touched ground several paces in front of the charging horses. They had rolled for a second, quickly over-run by the foremost cavalrymen, and Stryker's heart sank because he feared the thrashing hooves had surely snuffed the bright fuses out. But at the last moment, just as the redcoats braced themselves to be smashed by the tidal wave of man and horse, the little cases of black powder erupted.

It might have taken longer than Stryker had anticipated, but, when the explosions finally came, the iron casings had been blown into the very midst of Wild's troop. Like a flock of starlings evading a hawk, the horsemen turned as one, reeling instinctively away from the thundering, blinding, burning danger, wrenching savagely on reins and raking bloody lines along their mounts' heaving flanks. Those riders on the opposite side of the beleaguered circle did manage to strike home, but their efforts were aborted as soon as they realized what had happened to their comrades. In a matter of seconds the Roundhead grip had been released, Wild's black-feathered harquebusiers galloping pell-mell down the slope from whence they came.

Stryker gazed at the carnage left behind, and was put in mind of the shambles at Smithfield. A mess of meat and bone, hair and sinew. Twisted, bleeding and unrecognizable, strewn in haphazard array amongst lumps of torn muscle and gelatinous entrails. But this butchery had been done by gunpowder, and the stench of scorched flesh hung ripe and nauseating in the air.

'Make ready!' someone shouted from within the circle. Stryker could not discern the voice, for his ears were ringing uncontrollably. 'Make ready, you idle buggers!' the voice bawled again, and this time he knew it had been Sergeant William Skellen. With that repeated order his confidence finally began to build, for he understood that his musketeers must have finally loaded and primed enough guns to make a meaningful fist of defence.

He stepped back from the outermost rank and took up position in the very centre of the formation. He saw Cecily there, curled tight against the turf, Otilwell Broom at her side with his arm across her shoulders. Marcus Bailey was with them too, shivering like a dog in a rainstorm, muttering what Stryker presumed were desperate prayers for survival. The sight of Bailey made him glance across at the wagon. Its timbers were speckled with white patches where Wild's pistol shots had hit home, splintering the wood.

'Get the wounded back here!' Stryker bellowed, forcing the terrible thought from his mind. 'Get them out of the line, damn your hides! Be quick about it!'

For a time it seemed as though the order had been ignored, for he could not see through the close-packed scarlet coats, but eventually the rear ranks began to shift as bodies were dragged clear. There were plenty of them, more than Stryker had imagined, and he took a vast breath to steady himself. Once the defensive lines had been closed, the dead and dying hauled into the centre, and all gaps filled to present a complete and sturdy front to the enemy, Stryker ran round to the far side of the circle.

Burton, commanding the men on this side, caught his eye. 'We're ready for 'em this time, sir.'

'I'm glad of it, Andrew,' Stryker responded breathlessly, before turning quickly on his heel. An urgent shout of warning had carried to him from the part of the circle facing the slope. The Roundheads were coming back for more.

Colonel Gabriel Wild felt like crying. His men had travelled halfway across this God-forsaken moor, demeaning themselves by speaking to dull-witted yokels and persevering through some of the least cavalry-friendly terrain he had ever encountered, but, for all that, they had finally run their quarry to ground. They had outflanked Stryker's infantrymen, ambushed the captain as he had ambushed them, and been no more than a heartbeat from crushing the life from the red-coated horde. But the grenados had changed everything. The explosions' roar had been enough to force the horses into hasty flight, but the fire and the wicked, scything shards of iron had truly turned organized attack into a maelstrom of chaos. A dozen of his men had been cruelly cut from their saddles in the blasts, torn and seared by the grenados and their unseen throwers, and, as if with one mind, he and his men had instinctively retreated.

Wild, at the head of his regrouped force, stared up at the Royalist formation. Obscuring their feet and hose were the remains of his men. The troopers caught in the blasts that shattered so many limbs and pierced so much flesh. Christ, he thought, but some of those flying shards had come perilously close to hitting his own mount. Enough was enough.

'More treachery!' Wild shouted left and right as his steel-clad line eased into a canter. 'They cannot defeat us by strength or valour, but by tricks alone!'

'Colonel,' it was Grantham, at his left side, who spoke. 'They will be ready with volley fire.'

Wild shot him a brutal glance. 'The time for timidity is over, by God! We must put them down!'

A huzzah greeted his words. They would go again. Shatter the enemy and leave them to bleed out on this desolate heath. He squinted at the faces of the king's men. Wondered which of them was the one-eyed captain. He knew Stryker was in there, somewhere hidden behind his forest of pikes, sheltering like the most despicable kind of coward. No matter, they would charge again. Weed the bastard out.

Wild waved his sword high, circled the tip so that all eyes could see, and led his men on once more.

Once more.

'Wait!' screamed Sergeant William Skellen. 'Wait you fuckers!'

His musketeers were eager. They shuffled forward, pulling right up to the shoulders of their pike-wielding compatriots, trigger fingers itching to unleash bloody chaos.

Stryker was in the front rank, hand raised, poised to give the signal. He heard the belaying cries of Lieutenant

Burton, his other sergeant Moses Heel, and his two corporals, all struggling to keep the formation tight and prepared to fire.

The cavalry drew closer, cormorant feathers hovering above them like so many black standards. This time they did not split apart, did not attempt to encircle the infantry island, but advanced on a single, wide front, relying on sheer weight of numbers to break the Royalist line.

Fifty paces. The land began to tremble, shivering up into knees and hips.

Forty paces. The sound of the Roundheads' snarls carried to them above the thunder of hooves. Stryker's pikemen charged their pikes, angling the lethal spears upwards.

Thirty paces. Stryker took a last deep breath.

Twenty. He brought his arm down in a snapping arc.

'*Fire!*' the sergeants bawled.

The first rank of musketeers fired, perhaps twenty shots in all. Stryker felt the air pulse either side of his neck, his ears clanged as though filled with church bells, and the leading Roundhead saddles were immediately emptied. The relief that washed over the beleaguered defenders was almost palpable, for the blast had done its work.

'Good lads!' Stryker bellowed above the din. A surge of pride bolted through him as the bulk of the harquebusiers wheeled rapidly away. 'Empties move to the rear!'

The shooters did as they were told, shifting back into the clear space in the circle's centre to reload their weapons, and Stryker caught sight of a grey uniform within the throng to his right. 'Barkworth!'

The diminutive Scot shouldered his way through the infantrymen. 'Sir!'

Out on the slope, Wild's visor-faced riders were already regrouping to launch an immediate assault.

Stryker looked down at Barkworth. 'Find the lieutenant.'

'Aye, sir.'

'Tell him to give me a score of muskets.'

Barkworth frowned. 'Will that not leave our rear exposed?'

'They're only attacking here,' Stryker replied quickly, 'so he can spare them.'

Barkworth scampered into the centre of the ring and Stryker stared back at the approaching cavalry. They were coming again, but this time the gallop had waned to a fast canter as though the Roundheads charged into a gale. They had made a grave mistake by attacking on a single front, a sign, he thought, of desperation. Perhaps, after all, there was hope.

The thick volley had almost been enough for Colonel Gabriel Wild to call off the attack, but his men were the best the western Parliamentarian army had to offer, and he'd be damned to hell if he abandoned matters now. They had bravely faced that angry hail of lead, soaked up the Royalist barrage, and still regrouped. The toll had been heavy, but now he felt certain Stryker could bring no more musketry to bear. The volley had contained at least twenty shots, he reckoned, which meant it had involved every musketeer on this side of the circle, and Stryker was too cowardly to risk leaving his rear unguarded. Which meant Wild's brave gallopers would most certainly reach the red-coated line before the malignants had time to reload.

Wild dipped his chin, locked his eyes on the foremost

pikemen, and prepared to slam home. His horse would be reluctant to charge the waiting pikes, for those bloody spears could skewer it with ease, but he was a skilled horseman and would refuse to allow the beast its way. He would veer to the side of the great ash lance, knock down its point with his blade, and slash the neck of its handler wide open.

'Parliament!' he screamed. 'Parliament!'

'Compliments of Lieutenant Burton, sir!'

Stryker turned, seeing Barkworth approach with the fresh musketeers. 'Put them straight into the front rank and give fire when the bastards reach us, Mister Barkworth.'

'Wi' pleasure, sir!' Barkworth croaked as loud as his noose-crushed windpipe would allow. He flashed Stryker a sharp-toothed grin, eyes twinkling, and went to work.

The little Scot gave the order as soon as the horsemen were within range, and the men released by Lieutenant Burton snapped back their triggers as one, the volley rippling unevenly across this part of the circle, leaving powder smoke to drift sideways over the open moor.

Stryker took a couple of throat-singeing gulps of air to steady his nerves. The moor stank of blood and sulphur. He peered through the acrid cloud, braced for the terrible sight of horsemen emerging from the miasma. But none came. Nothing. Hooves still sounded, still rumbled on the heather and gorse, but their sound was fading with each moment. The second volley, comparatively weak though it was, had been more than the Roundheads were willing to bear. It had driven them back down the slope to count losses and lick wounds.

Stryker scanned the sooty faces of his musketeers,

seeing that the first rank were virtually ready to fire again, and a palpable sense of relief hit him, because he knew Wild had been beaten.

'Sir?'

Stryker turned to see Lieutenant Burton approach. 'Aye.'

'They'll be back, sir. We can't stay out here.'

Stryker wholeheartedly agreed. To remain on the open moor with paltry supplies and no shelter would simply invite the Parliamentarian cavalrymen to keep harrying them, blocking the western road, and chipping away at the company with impunity until the Royalists had no choice but to surrender. But surrender was not an option, for Stryker remembered Wild's vengeful oaths back at Bovey Tracey. He felt a sharp stab of guilt for bringing this fate upon them, and he stared up at the sky as if the clouds could provide the answer.

'There,' he said suddenly.

Burton's brow rose. 'Sir?'

Stryker was staring at the northern horizon, or rather the stone-cluttered hill that dominated the near distance. It was the tor he had seen earlier. The flat-topped promontory that was lower than its cousins to the west, with shallower slopes and a summit crowded with sheltering clumps of granite. 'Make ready the men, Andrew. Load the dead in the cart as best you can. That's where we're going.'

CHAPTER 7

OKEHAMPTON, DEVON, 1 MAY 1643

Witch-finder Osmyn Hogg stared about the chamber with satisfaction. 'You've done well, José. Very well indeed.'

José Ventura, Hogg's Spanish assistant, peered back at him through the gloom, dark eyes twinkling like polished orbs of jet in the firelight. 'The Lord wish everything to be just so, sir. The right cond—condish?'

'Conditions. And He has guided your hand perfectly.'

Ventura bowed and moved to warm his hands above the burning brazier at the centre of the dusty floor. 'As only He can, of course.'

Indeed, thought Hogg, the gracious Lord had certainly provided great inspiration for Ventura this time. When Hogg's request for private quarters had been met with the suggestion that they use some derelict outbuildings in the fields to the rear of the White Horse, it had seemed as though the dead-eyed Major-General Collings had once again been mocking them. But the buildings – a pair of musty old storage huts with rotten doors and sagging roof beams – were certainly well positioned, far enough away from prying eyes and ears, and, after a day of clearing out the cobwebbed debris,

Ventura had transformed the place into the perfect examination room.

'Should I fetch them?'

Hogg limped to the brazier, pulled one of the iron rods from the grill's red-white bowels, and held his free hand a few inches from its glowing tip. The air between the rod and his skin became fiercely hot in the time it took for his heart to beat but twice. 'Aye, bring them to me.'

As Ventura disappeared into the pre-dawn darkness, Hogg stared at the fire, losing himself in the searing, pulsating embers.

Stryker. That name. How long had it been?

Stryker. A word that made Osmyn Hogg both enraged and sickened.

'Stryker,' he said aloud, thrusting the iron savagely back into the brazier's depths, frantic sparks spewing out to shower the floor.

Osmyn Hogg considered himself to be a rational man. Educated, principled, and above all righteous. God's representative on Earth. He had little time for petty squabbles or the base need for revenge. And yet when he had heard that name uttered across Major-General Collings's dinner table, it was as though a lightning bolt had travelled straight through his chest. He had wanted to leave then and there. Run – no, *limp*, he corrected himself ruefully – from the room, saddle the nearest horse and ride for Colonel Wild's troop. He had said as much to Collings, pleaded with the slightly bemused – and doubtless *amused* – Parliamentarian to grant him his leave. But Collings had refused, on the grounds that he did not know where exactly Wild would be. Whether that was truly the case, or whether it had more to do with Hogg's refusal to explain his reasoning, he did not know. But ultimately, it did not matter. He had remained in Okehampton. Stuck here, in this vile little town, when Stryker – *Stryker* – was so near. The very idea made his heart ache.

The door swung open revealing three figures silhouetted against the moon.

'Welcome to the Lord's house,' said Hogg quietly. 'A place for you to cleanse your corrupt souls.'

'*In.*' The speaker was José Ventura. Hogg saw that he was standing at the rear of the trio, a round, black shape in the darkness, his chubby hands shoving at his companions' backs.

The two prisoners – a man and a woman – shuffled slowly in. Hogg glanced beyond them to Ventura. 'Are we protected?'

The Spaniard nodded, sweaty jowls shaking. 'Collings give two guards, sir. They at the door.'

'All is ready, then.' Hogg turned his attention to the subjects of the morning's work. The accused. They were of late middle age, dressed in the threadbare clothes of common folk. He met the frightened gaze of the man. 'Master Merriman?'

The man, tall and wiry with a narrow jaw and deeply pitted cheeks, nodded at the woman beside him. 'An' this is m' goodwife, Elspeth, sir.'

Hogg looked at the woman. She was a head shorter than her husband, with a stout frame and warty complexion. 'Eve to our Adam.'

'M'lord?' Elspeth replied.

Hogg smiled unpleasantly. 'No matter.' He turned, limping back towards the centre of the room, where the brazier waited. Only when he had reached a place where he knew the firelight would cast suitably sinister shadows across his features did he look back at the Merrimans. He was pleased to see the fear dance in their eyes. He stood as tall as his pains would allow, attempting not to lean on his stick, and withdrew a sheet of crinkled paper from the folds of his black cloak. 'John and Elspeth Merriman. You are accused of witchcraft.'

'That's a lie, sir,' Merriman bleated immediately.

Ventura stood on tiptoes and slapped him hard across the face. 'Shut your mouth while Master Hogg speak!' Too stunned to argue, Merriman fell silent. Elspeth began to sob.

'A man known to you both,' Hogg continued, glancing down at the paper, 'one Michael Hood of Okehampton, has testified that he did see you both abroad under cover of darkness a month since. Suspicious for what your dark business might be, this Hood did follow you to an ancient grove beyond the town limits.'

'How can this be?' Elspeth suddenly shrieked. She gripped her husband's arm. 'Tell him, John! Tell him Hood lies!'

'And there,' Hogg continued, raising his voice above the woman's shrill pleading, 'you were seen consorting with the Devil, who came to you in the form of a young man. This man was heard to promise you all your worldly desires if you would deny God and wholly trust in him.'

'Madness!' Merriman interrupted, finally finding his voice. 'Michael Hood is a low, Godless knave. He hates us!'

Hogg glanced at Ventura, who immediately cracked a

beefy fist into Merriman's stomach, causing the prisoner to double over and vomit.

Wrinkling his long nose in distaste, Hogg examined the testimony again. 'Hood claims that he heard you,' he looked at them in turn, '*both* of you, make compact with the Devil, and that thereafter his newborn son did hasten to sickness and perish.'

Elspeth stepped forward a pace. Her wide, flat face was red, her little eyes puffy. 'Please, sir, believe us when we say it is all falsehood.' She held out her hands as if grasping the air between her and Hogg. 'Michael Hood did lose his child, that is true, and it was a terrible sad time. But it turned his mind bad, I swear it. He wants rid of us, and would use that tragic thing for his own profit.'

'We quarrelled, he and I,' John Merriman wheezed, still crumpled over but craning his neck up to look into Hogg's face. 'He has let resentment brew ever since. And then his poor boy passed, and it was Elspeth and I he blamed.'

Hogg turned his attention to Elspeth. 'Witchery is a grievous thing, Goodwife Merriman.'

'But I—' she blurted.

Without a word, Ventura stepped past the still gasping Merriman and took hold of his wife's arm. She was evidently a tough woman, for she shook him free and it took the Spaniard several attempts to regain the grip. Eventually, though, he was able to snare her, the hem of her moss-green shawl bunching within his stubby fingers, and he dragged her across the room.

'No!' Merriman had straightened now, concern for his wife stiffening his resolve. But Hogg knew he would not move to her aid. He'd have seen the armed guards at the door, after all.

'Book of Micah,' Hogg intoned in his deepest, most reverential voice as Elspeth was thrust violently against the crumbling cell wall. 'Chapter 5, verses 12 and 13: "And I will cut off witchcrafts out of thine hand".'

Elspeth shrieked. Ventura belted her round the side of the skull, and drew a long, thin dirk.

'No!' Merriman screamed, terror still freezing him in place.

'He will cut off witchcraft,' Hogg went on. 'Do you not see? To make compact with Belial is not only a symptom of evil, but one of its prime causes. It must be rooted out and destroyed.' He saw Ventura look back at him, and nodded. 'Search her.'

Now John Merriman moved. He lurched forward, quicker than Hogg had anticipated, and was beyond the central brazier in a heartbeat, but Hogg had been ready with his stick, and thrust it firmly between the taller man's legs. Merriman collapsed in a tangled heap, clutching a sprained wrist and weeping for mercy.

Hogg ignored him. 'I said,' he addressed Ventura, 'search her.'

In the blink of an eye the dirk swept down the back of Elspeth's dress. The material tore easily, splitting from the nape of her broad neck to the small of her back. Ventura left the woman's skirts in place, but tugged hard at the material at her shoulders, hauling it down over her arms and torso, so that her entire body was laid bare from the waist up. She had fallen silent now, trembling slightly. Her stricken husband sobbed into the dusty floor.

Hogg leaned close to the woman so the scent of her filthy flesh made him gag, and peered carefully at her skin. Nothing.

Unwilling to touch her, he used the end of his walking stick to compel her to turn. She resisted at first, but a little extra pressure soon made her comply, and Hogg leaned in again like a doctor examining a patient. 'Usually,' he said quietly, his long nose poised just inches from her ample breasts, 'a mark will come here, near the bosom.' His gaze lingered just a little longer than was necessary, before he gestured once more with the stick, compelling her to face the wall again. He studied the side of her ribcage. 'Or here, on the flanks.'

'You'll find nothing, sir,' murmured Elspeth, voice muffled by the wall. 'This body is pure. You'll see no mark.'

Hogg checked her other side, and, with his stick, lifted her arms to examine the pits. 'So it appears. Of course, it is often the case that a witch may conjure foul spells to conceal her teat. Fortunately, Señor Ventura is rather adept at revealing them.'

Elspeth Merriman's little eyes seemed to bulge out of her head when she looked across her shoulder to see Ventura's dirk. 'No, sir!' she wailed. 'You would not use such a thing on a defenceless woman!'

Ventura picked nonchalantly at his fingernails with the tip of the thin blade. 'A witch will hide her imp-suckler beneath the skin. The place will not break. Will not bleed or cause pain.'

'So it is simply a matter,' Hogg added, not bothering to hide the relish in his voice, 'of pricking the accused until such a place is discovered.'

Now Elspeth screamed, but Ventura took a fistful of her coarse, mousy hair and ground her face against the wall. She shrieked again, a sound that grew from beseeching wail to shrill, agonized cry as Ventura slowly pressed the dirk into one of her shoulder blades. She squirmed against him, thrashed with her arms, kicking backwards at him like an enraged mule, but he did not flinch. Blood seeped from the fresh hole, making the blade gleam in the brazier's orange light.

'Not there, José,' Hogg said. 'Try another.' He looked down at John Merriman, whose pale eyes seemed large as apples in the gloom. The man was simply agog at what was happening to them. Good, thought Hogg. It would secure a quicker confession. He stooped suddenly, ignoring the pain shooting through his rump and lower back, and grabbed a handful of Merriman's grubby collar. He hauled the pathetic townsman up, so that their noses were just inches apart. Behind him, Elspeth screamed again. 'You can stop this.' He pulled Merriman's face even closer, smelling the man's rank breath. 'A confession will end it.'

Merriman glanced from Hogg to his wife, gritted his teeth, blinked once to let a fat teardrop plummet down his cheek. 'I shall not condemn her. She is no witch.'

Hogg released his grip and looked up to where Ventura was taking aim with his dirk again. 'Leave her, José. Pick up this wretch.'

Ventura sheathed the blade, backing away quickly to let the bleeding, half-naked woman slide down the wall and curl into a tight, shuddering ball. He stooped without pause, hauling Elspeth's husband to his feet with a reserve of raw strength that was belied by his blubbery physique.

Hogg went quickly to the brazier and jerked one of the irons free. The last two inches of its tapering end were a livid ruddy orange.

Merriman tensed, swallowed hard. 'Please, sirs, have mercy, I beg of you,' he whispered, eyes never leaving the iron's glowing tip.

Hogg shot Ventura a glance. 'Hand.'

The Spaniard's sweaty face cracked in a wisp of a smile and he grasped Merriman's thin wrist with a strength the latter could not begin to match. In a flash, he twisted the tall townsman's forearm roughly so that his palm faced the ceiling.

'I will ask one more time, sir,' Hogg said with deliberate slowness. 'Will you confess that you and Goody Merriman did knowingly and wilfully make vile compact with the Devil, in order to bring unnatural sickness and death to the son of Michael Hood?'

'I will not,' Merriman replied stoically.

Hogg was both surprised and impressed by the accused's stubbornness. Perhaps the Devil had given him extra reserves of courage. There was only one way to find out, he thought, and let the iron drop so that it tickled the surface of Merriman's palm. The skin immediately bubbled at the touch, Merriman howled like a man possessed, and the stench of roasting flesh filled the room. Fearing Merriman might pass out, Hogg withdrew the iron, leaving it to hover menacingly before the man's face.

'Fuck your lies, sir!' Merriman bawled. 'Fuck you both, and Hood too! I cannot! I will not condemn her!'

Hogg wielded the iron again, but this time he bypassed Merriman's blistered hand and dragged it along the brittle forearm. The skin melted at the touch, sizzled and crackled like an animal carcass on a spit, smearing the tissue beneath as though it were fresh curds, and Merriman bellowed to the rafters.

'Stop!'

It was Elspeth who screamed. Hogg thrust the iron back into its searing home and turned to look at her. She was sitting now. Rocking gently. 'You wish to speak, madam?'

'It was I, sir. I did see this man-imp like how Master Hood claims. I made a pact with him, as you say.'

Hogg's heart began to hammer. 'To follow Satan in exchange for the power to kill?'

She nodded. 'I swear it. And I swear John knew not a thing of it. Upon my life.'

It felt as though a great weight had been lifted free of Hogg's shoulders. He whispered silent thanks to God. Another one rooted out. Another condemned.

A knock at the door shook him from his private contemplation, and he jerked his chin at Ventura. The porcine Spaniard released Merriman to paw at his destroyed arm, waddling quickly across the room to yank the door back.

A man stood there, the moon above his pate like a halo, and for a moment Hogg thought it might just be the angel he had prayed so long to see. A just reward for righteous works. But then he noticed the man's breastplate and tall boots, the scabbard at his waist and the gauntlet on his left arm.

'Well?' he snapped irritably. 'This had better be good.'

The trooper took a step inside and seemed to sniff the air, evidently scenting Merriman's cooked limb. Then his interested eyes settled on the two bodies, curled like tight foetuses, and the brazier at the room's epicentre, and he rapidly backtracked, speaking only when he was well out into the fresh night air. 'You are Osmyn Hogg, the witch-catcher?'

Hogg tapped the ground impatiently with his stick. 'I am.'

'Compliments of Major-General Collings, sir. He said you'd wish to hear the news from Colonel Wild?'

The hairs on the back of Hogg's neck bristled uncontrollably. 'News?'

'The Colonel's found the man he was looking for.'

THE TOR, DARTMOOR, I MAY 1643

By first light Captain Stryker's Company of Foot had reached the summit of the natural fortress they had spotted as Wild's defeated troopers made their hasty retreat. Those horsemen, deflated and vengeful, had regrouped quickly and trotted their mounts alongside the straggling Royalist column, watching like a flock of hawks for a sign of weakness. But the redcoats had driven them away once already, and they knew better than to venture within musket range. Without the element of surprise they were rendered toothless against seasoned infantry. Thus, the two groups had passed the dusk hours eyeing each other warily as Stryker's company followed the northerly course of the river. Wild must have known they were headed for the tor, but there was little he could do to prevent it, and eventually his troop had skulked away beyond the horizon.

The tor itself was not as vast and forbidding as some of the others on the high moor. It was more hillock than mountainous crag, with slopes that, though steep, were perfectly scalable on foot. Had it been an empty mound, simply carpeted in the ubiquitous heather and gorse,

Stryker would have ignored it, for Wild's horsemen would be posed little difficulty in reaching the summit, but his eye had been taken by the jagged network of boulders strewn all over the slopes, rendering any cavalry advance treacherous at best. Moreover, he had been attracted by the far larger outcrop of granite clustered on the flat pinnacle. To Stryker, it seemed like a derelict citadel, uneven and weather-beaten but imposing nonetheless, still proud in its mouldering grandeur, guarding the river that meandered past its eastern foot. And with every step his battered charges had taken, picking their way between the scores of smaller stones littering the slopes, Stryker felt a building sense of optimism. Because it was a fort. Not one made by man, but a fort all the same. And he would defend it.

'Stone me if m' kneecaps ain't fallin' off!'

Stryker, standing at the edge of the tor's crest in order to count his company home, could not help but grin as Sergeant Skellen passed him. 'Getting old, Will?'

Skellen, finally over the sharp brow, snatched off his wide-brimmed hat and fanned himself, before putting hands to thighs and chuckling breathlessly. 'Think you're in the right of it, sir.' He looked up, revealing a leathery face and thinning scalp that gleamed with sweat. 'Dead are all a-bed, sir.'

The company had lost a total of sixteen souls in the fight. Corporal Omphrey Shepherd was the most senior man to fall, shot in the mouth by a carbine ball that had killed him instantly. He had been joined on the butcher's bill by nine pikemen and six musketeers. The loss brought bile to Stryker's mouth each time he dwelt on it, and he had to swallow hard as he considered Skellen's words. 'All properly buried?'

Skellen frowned as if hurt by the question. "Course, sir. Down on the flat, as you ordered. Lads had to watch their backs for them harky-busiers, but we got the job done. In truth we was glad to get them in the ground. I wouldn't 'ave liked tryin' to drag them up this bleedin' hill. The wagon's heavy enough as it is.' The tall sergeant's eyes drifted beyond Stryker's shoulder, and he whistled. 'Christ, but this is a snout-fair little castle you've found, sir.'

'It'll keep Wild off our backs.'

Skellen nodded. 'Aye, sir. All we need now is a roof 'case it rains, a fat powder magazine, a few cannon, plenty o' food and runnin' water. We'd be set for the rest o' the war, sir.'

Skellen's tone had been light enough, but his meaning had not been lost on Stryker. 'Do you trust me, Sergeant?'

Skellen frowned, chewed the inside of his mouth, scratched his balding pate, then grinned broadly. 'With my life, sir.'

'Set the Trowbridge twins to picket. Have them watch for Wild's approach; he's doubtless nearby. Then fetch the lieutenant and the rest of the senior men,' he pointed to the nearest granite stack, 'and meet me there.'

All around the summit's fringe were lonely stone stacks, tall and sharp like giants' teeth. If this was a fortress, then these were its turrets, forming a ragged ring around the outer walls. Within, at the very centre of the tor, were two impressive rows of clustered stacks, each as tall as a two-storey house, running diagonally parallel to one another from north-west to south-east. Between them was an avenue of rocky grassland, like the fort's courtyard, and it was into this flat, open space that Stryker took the leaders of his company.

'If we remain on the lower ground,' he said, turning to face the impromptu assembly, 'then Wild will cut us to pieces a little at a time.'

'Let him come, I say.' It was Simeon Barkworth who spoke, typical aggression shaping his opinion. With him were Burton, Skellen, Ensign Chase, Sergeant Heel, and the two drummers, Lipscombe and Boyleson. 'I'd prefer a straight scrap to hidin' up here. We'll show the bastard how proper fighting's done.'

'Aye,' replied Stryker calmly, prepared for out-and-out attack to be the Scot's first and only recourse, 'and we'd repel his charges time and again, for certain. But where will we go? He has blocked our route west. So would you have us run east, back to Parliament's lines?'

'All the while taking casualties,' Lieutenant Burton put in.

'He'll take us at his leisure,' Stryker went on remorselessly. 'Attack us by night, so that we cannot see him coming. Our musketry is only effective when we can see to aim.' He removed his hat, rearranged the grimy feathers jutting from the band, and gently patted some specks of dust clear. 'Eventually our bravery would count for nothing. He would wear us to the bone.' Barkworth's fiery gaze dimmed a touch at this, and Stryker saw that he was winning the man over. 'We need shelter. This will suffice for now. It's not the ideal place to garrison, isolated as it is, but the stony slopes will give Wild something to ponder, and these,' he indicated the formidable granite stacks towering either side of them, 'provide good protection from the wind.'

'And if it rains?' Skellen asked bluntly.

'Then we'll get wet,' Stryker replied with matching

tone. He studied the places where each stack met the earth, noticing that, here and there, small caves had been formed where the huge, irregular shaped stones touched. He pointed to the largest cave. 'But the wagon can go in there, which means our powder will stay dry.'

'Ideal for protecting against sparks as well,' Barkworth said thoughtfully.

Stryker nodded. 'Aye, but no fires up here, just to be certain. The weather's fine enough to do without.'

He led the group along the avenue while the sounds of the company settling into their new home rattled on in their wake. They had advanced to the tor from the south, and he was eager to investigate its northern approaches.

The sunlight seemed unusually bright as they moved out of the natural corridor's shadows, finding themselves on the edge of the crest. They gazed down at a landscape of wide, fallow terrain, punctuated in the same manner as the southern periphery by gorse bushes and craggy rocks. Tiny birds, chatting and singing, skittered madly along the slopes from boulder to boulder, in and out of bracken and between the wind-stripped branches of small trees. The view was expansive, affording a clear sight for several miles, with a horizon interrupted by other, grey-topped tors and patches of green forest.

'We'll see him coming,' Stryker said to himself.

'He will attack, then?' Barkworth's croaking voice responded, though it was more of a statement than a question.

Stryker nodded. 'Be certain of it, Simeon. But thanks to Master Bailey's wagon, we have plenty of shot and powder. We'll place our pikes in the gaps between the rocks,' he turned to look back at the huge stacks, 'and our muskets will fire down from up there. He'd find this no easier than taking a real fort.'

'Sir,' the short, barrel-chested Ensign Chase hailed Stryker from ten paces down the hill's northern face. He was pointing away to the north and east, where a smudge of grey and russet blotted the landscape some six hundred paces from the foot of the tor. 'Is that a barn?'

Stryker followed Chase's gaze for a moment. 'I think it is. We'll send out a party to take a look. Perhaps it stores something useful.'

'Vittles,' Skellen said hopefully.

Stryker kept his eye trained on the building. 'One never knows, Sergeant.'

'And if it's empty?' Burton asked, his voice unusually glum.

Stryker looked at the lieutenant. 'Supplies are dwindling, I accept that. But water is more vital, and the river runs right past us. We can last a few days.'

'And after that?'

'After that, Andrew,' Stryker said seriously, 'we eat the horses.'

'Sir!' a man called suddenly from further along the avenue.

'What is it?' Stryker shouted back, recognizing the voice as one of the company's twins, though unable to tell which.

After a few seconds' wait, Jack Trowbridge emerged from the grassy passageway. 'It's the enemy, sir,' he said, chest heaving from the run. 'They're back.'

As ever, Colonel Wild's cavalry troop were easily identified by their tall cormorant feathers. They filed along a track just over half a mile to the south-west of the tor, following the cornet and his fluttering black and white flag.

Stryker, having jogged back through the avenue to stand on the southern edge of the tor's summit, peered down at the horses and their silver masters, wondering which of the lobster pots concealed the face of Colonel Gabriel Wild. The obvious guess was that Wild would be at the head of that glinting serpent, the rider in place beside the standard bearer, but from this distance he could not tell for certain. At least up here, on this new-found bastion, Stryker could feel some semblance of security. The Roundheads could circle the hill like a shoal of hungry sharks for all he cared, but they would be tempting death if they came within musket range.

'Just having a look,' Stryker said when Lieutenant Burton appeared next to him.

Burton adjusted his shoulder strap, as he tended to do when he was agitated. 'They can't attack us here, can they, sir?'

Stryker looked at his second-in-command. 'They'll try, Andrew. By God they'll try. But we have the advantage now. They can no longer catch us unawares.' He glanced at a lonely granite obelisk that stood tall and jagged a little way down the slope. 'Keep an eye on them, Pikeman Clegg!'

A man, perched at the very top of the stone, raised a hand in acknowledgement. 'I will that, sir!'

Stryker turned back to Burton. 'We'll have to forget the barn for the time being. Have the men sleep on the upper slopes. I want them in amongst the stones near the crest.' He pointed to the distant cavalry troop. 'No easy pickings for those whoresons, understand?'

163

'Sir.' Burton glanced back at the interior, where the sprawling jumble of building-sized stones dominated the hill. 'The wagon is to be kept in there?'

'As I said, Lieutenant, we keep it in the big cave.' It seemed strange giving a rickety old vehicle pride of place in their new fort, but too much blood had already nourished Dartmoor's heather in its protection, and Stryker was damned if it would be lost to them now.

'And what of the girl?'

Stryker caught the almost imperceptible twitch in Burton's cheek as the young man spoke, and realized that he would naturally be interested in such a beauty. He nodded warily. 'She stays on the crest too, with Broom and Bailey.'

Burton turned on his heel, leaving Stryker to stare after him. In all the turmoil of recent days he had not given enough consideration to the impact Cecily Cade would doubtless have on a large group of soldiers. And now they were all trapped together on a small hill.

Quietly, he swore.

TWO MILES WEST OF MERRIVALE, DARTMOOR,
I MAY 1643

The horseman's arrival was greeted with a level of excitement that spoke more of the soldiers' boredom than of his innate importance. The men, redcoats of Captain Lancelot Forrester's Company of Foot in the main, had spent the better part of two days camped in the same field, making do with dried biscuit and gritty stream water, and the arrival of a newcomer was accompanied with great interest.

The outlying pickets let the lone rider approach their commanders, for he had given the field word of General Hopton. He galloped expertly along the bridleway tracing the corrugated stream, confident and stern atop his sleek-flanked, froth-mouthed bay; a creature that would have set most of the infantrymen back more than a year's pay to purchase. The men, at liberty beside the water or under the broad trees, immediately rose to their feet, wondering what news he might be carrying.

Forrester and Payne had been puffing on tobacco and discussing the merits of Shakespeare's *King Richard the Third* when they saw him, and abruptly tapped their clay pipe bowls clear, pacing quickly into the rider's path.

'Ho there, friend!' Forrester called up to the newcomer. 'What news?'

With a deft tug of his reins, the horseman brought his muscular bay to a juddering stop, and greeted them with a wave of his buff-gloved hand. 'Captain Forrester?'

Forrester took off his hat. ''Tis I, sir.'

The rider gave a curt nod and dismounted. He wore civilian dress; tall, spurred boots, green breeches and russet coat, with a dishevelled falling band collar and grey hat. Every inch the costume of a gentleman's outdoor servant, which, Forrester presumed, was exactly what he had been before the war had changed everything. 'My name is Richardson, aide to Sir Ralph Hopton.'

'Well met, sir,' Forrester replied, sensing a huge shadow appearing at his side. 'May I present to you Mister Anthony Payne.'

Richardson's eyes drifted away from Forrester and rose, widening as they went, until they settled on Payne's face. He removed his own hat in salute, revealing a head of close-cropped brown hair that gave a hint of copper in the sun's rays. Forrester noticed the ribbon tied about the hat's crown. It was an old piece of material, mud-spattered from the ride, but it was, undoubtedly, red. 'Well met, Mister Payne,' he said, swallowing hard. 'If I could venture—'

'Four inches above seven feet, sir,' Payne replied in his ocean-deep voice.

'My apologies,' Richardson muttered, embarrassed. 'You must be frequently asked.'

'Every so often, sir.'

'And,' Forrester cut in, suppressing an amused snort, 'do you carry the King's commission?'

Richardson looked at the captain, hazel eyes narrowing slightly, as though he were attempting to gain Forrester's measure. 'I do, sir. But my duties are invariably—'

'Of a private nature?' Forrester suggested when the pause had lingered too long.

Richardson's thin lips lifted at the corners. 'Aye, you might say as much.'

'Then, sir,' Forrester went on, 'I can only assume you have come from General Hopton on some important matter?'

Richardson crammed his hat back on to his head and lifted a hand to smooth down his brown moustache. 'You are in the right of it, Captain, yes indeed.' His face hard-ened as his thoughts turned to business. 'We are on the move.'

'Move?' Payne rumbled.

'The army, Mister Payne. General Hopton has received intelligence of Lord Stamford's plans.'

'Stamford?' Payne's face creased into a scowl as he

echoed the name. 'What plans might that rogue be hatching now?'

'We hear he musters as many men as possible at Torrington, sir. All available garrisons in Devon and Somerset have been stripped of horse, foot and supplies.'

'He means to strike into Cornwall?' Payne asked.

'Aye, that is the fear. He is emboldened after Sourton.'

To Forrester, Payne's eyes were already as big as plums, but somehow they seemed to enlarge further. Seeing that the giant had been struck dumb by the news, he prompted, 'What is it, old man? You look as though you've lost a cannon and found a carbine.'

Payne's gaze shifted from Richardson to Forrester. 'Cornwall is my home, Captain.'

Richardson went on, more concerned with imparting his message than dealing with the feelings of those who were in receipt of it. 'Needless to say that Sir Ralph makes plans to intercept the rebels forthwith. Make hazard of a battle, if needs be.'

'But where will Stamford advance?' asked Forrester.

Richardson screwed his mouth into a grimace. 'That is our problem, sir. We do not know.'

'Which is why the army moves out from Launceston.'

'Indeed. Lord Mohun has been sent west to Liskeard, Slanning goes to Saltash, and John Trevanion is to remain at Launceston.'

Payne stepped up. 'What of Sir Bevil Grenville, sir? Where does his regiment march?'

Richardson paused in thought, then snapped his fingers. 'North. Up towards Stratton. But most importantly, Hopton advances upon Beaworthy.'

'Beaworthy?' echoed Forrester. 'Never heard of it.'

Payne looked down at him. 'A small place between Launceston and Okehampton.'

'That's it,' Richardson said brightly. 'Sir Ralph would block the road to Launceston, lest Stamford choose that route.' He offered a hand for both men to shake. 'And now I must be away.'

Forrester followed the messenger as Richardson strode briskly back to his horse. 'Wait, sir. That is not all your news, surely?'

'Why ever not?' said Richardson, turning. He leant against the saddle, gathering the looped reins in a hand. 'I understand you men are charged with bringing your—' he glanced skyward in search of the word, '*bounty* to Hopton. For his part, he will no longer be at Launceston. Does it not make plain sense that you should be alerted to this new destination?'

And that was the crux of the matter, thought Forrester. He did not know if it made sense. 'I suppose,' he muttered, unwilling to look the fool in front of Richardson.

In a flash, Richardson was back in his saddle, clicking softly in his mighty steed's ear. Without the need for brusque commands or raking spurs, the horse slipped easily into a canter. 'Then *adieu*, gentlemen!' He lifted the grey hat briefly, planted it back on his skull, and was gone.

As the hoofbeats faded, they were replaced by Payne's heavy steps, and Forrester turned sharply to face him. 'An honest tale speeds best, being plainly told.'

Payne levelly met the captain's gaze. 'More from King Richard, sir. Though something tells me you did not wish to demonstrate your impressive knowledge of theatre.'

Forrester stepped closer so that they were out of earshot

of the men. 'That man was no ordinary messenger. He was an intelligencer.'

Payne pursed his lips. 'I wouldn't know.'

'Of course you bloody would!' Forrester hissed. 'Aside from his cocksure bloody demeanour, the bugger rode a horse fit for royalty. Royalty or intrigue.' He waited for a response, persevering when none came. 'So Hopton sends a spy simply to tell us that he's no longer in Launceston.' He paused for a moment, thinking. 'This man we're to meet. He really is as important as you say, isn't he?'

Payne nodded sombrely. 'The general would have us take him direct to Beaworthy, if that is where he will soon be. He must speak with him with all haste.'

'Who is he, for Christ's sake?'

'I am sorry, Captain Forrester. You know I cannot—'

'And yet here we are,' Forrester muttered, staring out across the field that had become their home for the last two days, 'without the first clue where this fellow's got to.' He turned back to Payne. 'Shall we have a peek to the east on the morrow? We've waited here long enough.'

Payne considered the question for a moment, before letting out a sigh that sounded like a gale through oak branches. 'East.'

CHAPTER 8

THE TOR, DARTMOOR, 2 MAY 1643

The large square of red taffeta flapped in the breeze. It had a Cross of St George in one corner and two white diamonds in the field, telling all who cared to look that the tor was garrisoned by Captain Stryker's Regiment of Foot.

Stryker, standing on the lip of the crest to greet the breaking dawn, gnawed a stale biscuit and stared up at his flag. Its colour was bleached and its edges frayed, here and there were patches where it had been so often repaired, and he noticed a couple of small holes that had doubtless been rent by recent pistol fire. He snorted with laughter.

'What amuses you so?'

Stryker turned abruptly to see Cecily Cade. He swallowed his mouthful of the gritty biscuit, watching her as she approached. She still wore the pale yellow dress, and it was becoming increasingly dishevelled. But, for all that, Stryker found her utterly beguiling. 'I was thinking how alike my ensign and I are.'

'Mister Chase?' She walked to his side, pushing a stray lock of black hair behind her ear. 'Really? He is shorter and has a beard.'

He smiled. 'Not that ensign, Miss Cade.' He pointed

up at the flag with his half-eaten biscuit. '*That* ensign. Weather-beaten and oft stitched back together.'

She returned the smile, though her cheeks reddened slightly.

'No matter, Miss Cade.'

'I told you,' she chided, tapping his arm gently, 'you must call me Cecily.'

Stryker looked back to a horizon rapidly flooding with orange light. In the near distance, where the tor's steep flank ended, the terrain still gently sloped for the best part of a mile, interrupted only by the river. Further off, the undulating pattern of tors and ridges was undeniably spectacular, though it served only to compound his feeling of isolation. They really were alone out in this wilderness. Alone in the cause of King Charles, at least, for the dawn was steadily revealing glinting armour in the distance, the signal that Wild had placed pickets at regular intervals all around the tor. They were constantly watching, waiting for Stryker's next move.

'I must say,' Cecily ventured, 'you've made a fine job of this place.'

'Oh?'

'Turning a bleak tor into a little castle, I mean.'

Stryker shrugged. 'The walls were already here, and most are thicker than anything you'd find built by man.'

She nodded. 'Still, I'm a tad surprised you've kept the horses up on the hillside.'

Stryker frowned. 'They can hardly be kept down there,' he said, pointing to the flat heathland stretching endlessly in front of them. 'Aside from the threat from the enemy, there'd be nowhere to tie them.'

It was Cecily's turn to point, but her finger stretched

slightly to their right, south-east of the tor. 'But they might have been stabled in the village simply enough.'

Stryker followed the direction of her arm until his eye settled on a place some two hundred and fifty paces away, perhaps fifty strides beyond the glistening river. He had seen it before, of course, but paid no real attention, for it had appeared at first glance to be no more than a wild area of meshed gorse, tangling bilberry bushes, and boulders. But as he studied the messy outcrop shapes began to form. Clear lines were discernible within the rubble. The more he stared, the more he understood that it was all that remained of a settlement; ancient, certainly, and crumbled to near invisibility where nature had reclaimed it for her own, but a settlement all the same. As Cecily said, it had, at one time, been a village.

'You're right,' Stryker muttered, still amazed that the place had lain hidden from them until now. 'Those walls are waist height.'

'Higher in places,' Cecily added.

'Aye, so they are. We could certainly keep the horses penned there.' Immediately he stepped back from the brow and hailed the nearest man. 'Gather a party of half a dozen lads. Get down to that patch of rubble and see what's there.'

The soldier nodded, turning on his heel to carry out the order, and Stryker looked at the grinning Cecily. He stole a glance at her inviting lips, and felt the sudden impulse to kiss them.

'Will you give me one of the horses?' Cecily asked abruptly.

The question threw Stryker at first and he simply stared into her eyes as he absorbed her words. 'I do not follow,' he replied eventually.

She moved closer, her voice becoming a whisper. 'I must leave here, Captain Stryker. It is important. I have given you the village. Now will you help me?'

Stryker half expected her to smirk then, admit that it was all in jest, but all he saw was the rigid set of her jaw as determination shadowed her expression. 'Leave? I understand it is frightening up here, and I know you wished to reach your father's estates, but you saw what happened. I had no choice.' He looked down at the river. 'We'll fight our way out of here before long.'

Cecily laughed bitterly. 'I am not stupid, Captain. You spin your brave tale, but cannot look me in the eye when you do it.' She bit her upper lip, moving a hand to grip his elbow. He noticed she was trembling slightly. 'I *must* be away from here, sir. Please, I beg you, there is precious little time—'

'For what?' Stryker cut across her. He held her gaze. 'Time for what, Miss Cade?'

'Captain!' The voice of William Skellen jolted them like the crack of a pistol.

'This isn't over,' Stryker whispered, before looking up at the sergeant. 'What is it?'

Skellen scratched his stubbly chin. 'Not really sure, if truth be told, sir.'

'Spit it out man!' Stryker snapped.

'Apologies, sir,' Skellen replied, 'but seein's believin', ain't it?'

The sergeant was not given to unnecessary dramatics. 'Very well,' Stryker sighed, turning back to Cecily, but she was gone.

Stryker's first impression was of a vagrant. A man probably in his sixties, skinny as a weasel, with filthy, matted grey hair and a beard, also grey, that stretched all the way to his concave belly. His breeches were brown, though they might have begun life a lighter colour, and his shirt and doeskin singlet were darkened by a network of old stains.

'Found 'im sniffin' around one o' the stone piles to the sou'west,' Sergeant William Skellen said.

Stryker turned back to the newcomer, who was standing between a pair of burly redcoats. 'Who are you?'

The bearded man, whose dishevelled appearance was exacerbated by a slight stoop, glared up at him with eyes that were a surprisingly clear shade of blue. 'The Lord God Almighty's representative in this shit stinkin' country,' he said in an accent that reminded Stryker of the soldiers from Sir Thomas Salusbury's regiment he had encountered at Brentford Fight.

'A Welshman?'

The man did not shift his eyes from Stryker, or blink even once. 'You don't call a man from Wales Welsh, my boy!' he exclaimed in a shrill cry. 'You calls him *sir*!'

On another day Stryker might have been amused, but he was still irked by the strange conversation with Cecily, and the newcomer's antics irritated him further. 'I've no time for this.' He glanced at Skellen. 'Get rid of him, Sergeant.'

'*Ha!*' the old man shrieked, blue eyes darting like some feral creature. 'You'd have me killed off here and now, would you?' He craned his head up to the wispy clouds. 'You hear that, Almighty? Have me sent to meet you before my time, he would! Can you fathom it?'

Stryker shook his head in bewilderment. 'Of course not, you old fool. See that he is fed and watered, Sergeant

Skellen, then take him across the river and get yourselves back here.'

'Across my river?' the old man exclaimed. He looked heavenward again. 'Now why would he want me to cross my own river, eh, when it is he who sits pretty in my home?'

Stryker ground his jaw. 'Your home?'

The Welshman grinned, exposing little stubs of blackened teeth, and seemed to dance from side to side as though his bare feet were touching hot coals. 'This here hill's my house, isn't it, boy? My house and my home and my fucking castle all in one. Gardner's Tor, the good Lord calls it. God-given, it is.'

'This is Gardner's Tor?'

The old man nodded violently, twisting the point of his beard about a talon-tipped forefinger. 'That's me, it is. An' this is my house. So it is Gardner's Tor.'

'You're this Gardner?' Stryker asked incredulously.

The man ran a flickering tongue over cracked lips and suddenly bent into a low bow. 'You have it, my boy. Seek Wisdom and Fear the Lord Gardner, to be precise and exact!'

'Christ, that's a mouthful,' Skellen muttered.

Gardner rounded on the tall soldier, seemingly unconcerned with the formidable halberd in Skellen's hand. 'Thou shalt not take the Lord's name in vain, you fucking English moldwarp!' He reached up to thrust a bony finger into Skellen's chest. 'I'll not have it in my castle, no, no, no, I shan't!' Then, as suddenly as his anger had boiled up, Gardner's face creased into a broad grin and he cackled madly once more.

Skellen whistled softly. 'He's crazed, sir. Frantic as a tyke in a rat's nest.'

'Frantic?' Gardner hissed, gently slapping his own cheeks. 'You call a man frantic when it is you who scuttle up here like a fistful o' frightened beetles?' He licked his lips again, like a frog catching a fly. 'Your guns could best those feather-headed bastards.'

That piqued Stryker's interest, and he waved a hand so that Gardner would acknowledge him. 'What do you know of Colonel Wild's troop?'

'That's him, is it, boy?' Gardner asked, piercing eyes seemingly frozen open. 'The black-feathered bugger with a badger's hair? He lurks around my castle like a virgin outside a bawdy-house.'

'You what?' Skellen asked, nonplussed.

Stryker held up a staying hand. 'Aye, that's him. Colonel Gabriel Wild has a silver stripe running through his hair, like a badger. You've seen them?'

Gardner nodded. 'I've watched 'em gallop about like they own the place, aye.' He glanced skywards. 'But they don't, do they, God, eh?' Looking back to Stryker, he winked. 'They're camped out to the west, so as you little beetles don't make a run for it. The badger's based himself in the big barn.'

'The barn?' Stryker said in surprise, glad he had not sent a reconnaissance party to check what was inside.

'As God is my witness,' the old man replied, 'and He is, boy, He is! The badger makes plans. He wants to capture a fat stash o' powder, so they say, and he wants to skin the man who stole it from him. A fellow with only one eye. Any idea who that might be, boy?'

'How can you possibly know this?'

Gardner smirked. 'I come and go. Been into the badger's set, haven't I, boy!'

176

'Bollocks,' said Skellen.

Gardner looked up at him. 'They don't notice me, see. You didn't till I bloody let you!'

Skellen made to protest, but Stryker interjected, 'You've been to Wild's camp?'

Gardner tilted back his grimy head and beamed at the clouds. 'He can be taught, Lord, you were right!' Looking back at Stryker, he added, 'As ever, eh?'

'Master Gardner—'

'Seek Wisdom.'

'Very well,' replied Stryker. 'Seek Wisdom, you claim to have been into their camp. Tell me more, I ask you.' He rubbed a hand across his ever-lengthening stubble. 'If you assist me now, sir, you will be free to remain here, on the tor.'

'You hear that, God?' Gardner yelled. 'He thought to keep Gardner away from Gardner's Tor! Have you ever heard the like?'

'Get this man vittles,' Stryker ordered one of his men, before turning back to Gardner and pulling an apologetic grimace. 'We have only dried meat and biscuits, but there is plenty.'

Gardner grinned. 'You're a good sort, boy. God told me.' His voice dropped conspiratorially. 'Though he hadn't warned me how bloody ugly you were.'

Stryker cracked a smile. 'I need to know of Colonel Wild,' he pressed. 'What say you?'

Seek Wisdom and Fear the Lord Gardner leaned close, so that Stryker could smell the foul stench of decay wafting from his gums. 'Your feather-headed badger.' His blue eyes seemed to glint with mischief as he spoke. 'He'll come tonight.'

Terrence Richardson paced quickly along the corridors of the mazelike town house until he approached a large studded door, paused for a moment to flick some of the more conspicuous specks of mud from his russet coat, and rapped loudly on the thick timbers.

'Come!' boomed the order from inside.

Richardson twisted the black hoop of iron, gave the door a gentle nudge with his shoulder, and strode in. The room was large but dingy, its windows too few and too small to allow in enough light to make an impact; walls, furnishings, and faces appearing greyer than he had expected. But then these were grey men, he supposed. The abstemious, dour, sober-headed Parliamentarians he had always loathed. The very reason he had enlisted with the king's men down at Liskeard back in the autumn. As he gazed upon them, four sour-looking gentlemen poring over a long, deep table scattered with paper, he found it hard to reconcile his change of heart. Indeed, men such as these littered the warren-like building's many chambers. He had already been made to endure the suspicious glares of those familiar with his background, glares he might have expected had he brandished a pair of horns and a trident. But then it was not for these people he had turned his coat.

'Hopton's portmanteau,' said one of the four men. The only man seated, he was soberly attired in a suit of black, with a large white collar and orange sash. The vein of silver thread zigzagging down the front of his doublet gave a suggestion of his status, though Richardson did not require the hint.

'Aye, my lord Stamford,' Richardson replied respectfully, snatching the grey hat from his head, 'he lamented its loss at Sourton Down.'

Henry Grey, First Earl of Stamford, leader of the Parliamentarian faction in the south-west, was a short, slim-faced man in his mid forties, with brown eyes and straight, black hair that fell in lank strands about his shoulders. He worried at the fibres of his neat black beard and allowed himself a smirk. 'I bet he did. When first I laid eyes upon this veritable treasure trove,' he nodded at the assortment of papers on the table, 'I was trapped down in Exeter.'

'Trapped, my lord?'

'By the gout, d'you see?' There was a walking cane on the table, and Stamford grasped it, tapping it gently against his ankle. 'Excruciating, I can tell you. But I verily leapt from my chair when first I read the Somerset communiqué.'

Richardson nodded. 'I do not doubt it, my lord.' He had been party to Hopton's angry tirade when the Royalist general had discovered that his portmanteau – carrying scores of vital items of correspondence – had been captured. That cache of intelligence had included a letter from the king's secretary of state ordering Sir Ralph to march into Somerset in order to link up with the forces of the Marquis of Hertford. 'And that is why you muster here, my lord? To cut him off before he makes his move?'

'Indeed it is,' Stamford replied triumphantly. 'This is to be the deciding contest for the war in the south-west, and I have assumed personal command.'

'He knows you gather here, my lord,' Richardson said, letting a note of caution colour his words.

One of the men standing at Stamford's right hand gave a short grunt of derision. 'But he knows not where we shall strike.'

'No, sir,' Richardson commented dutifully. He did not wish to become embroiled in a discussion with the earl's black-suited lackeys, gathered at his shoulders like so many cawing jackdaws. Let them bluster about their invasion plans. That was not any of his concern.

'What news?' Stamford said suddenly.

Now we come to the nub of it, Richardson thought with relief. 'It is done, my lord.'

Stamford eased back in his rigid armchair. 'You did well to discover Hopton's plans, Richardson.'

'He trusts me.'

One of the jackdaws cleared his throat and scratched his sharp nose. 'You were a well-known Cavalier, sir. Hopton trusted you, so why should we?'

With deliberate nonchalance, Richardson looked down at his hat and began to flick bits of dried mud from its new tawny ribbon. The old red one had been replaced upon entering Devon. 'Because I have good reason to see the Parliament win this conflict, sir. I am no bowl-headed Puritan whipping the Commons along like a pack of musty old mules.'

The intimation was clear, and the jackdaw bristled. 'How dare—'

'I believe in trade, sir,' Richardson cut through the older man's protest while he still had momentum. 'Enterprise. I was naturally for the King when war broke, sir, but I have been—*enlightened* these last weeks. I have a passion for commerce. The King's cause would stifle that passion.'

'And Parliament,' the Earl of Stamford added, 'would

not.' He glanced left and right at his wary aides. 'Mister Richardson, here, has the ear of General Hopton himself. I initially asked him to keep an eye on the malignants. Forewarn me of any strike against us. Indeed, he was instrumental in our victory at Sourton Down.'

The black-suited aide eyed Richardson for a long moment. 'My compliments, sir,' he muttered grudgingly.

'Thank you, sir,' Richardson replied with his most dazzling grin. 'And may you see that I deserve your faith.'

'You said initially?' another of the aides prompted.

'Ah yes,' Stamford said. 'Well it appears Mister Richardson is a great deal more than a mere pair of eyes.'

'If I may, sir,' Richardson interjected, observing a prime opportunity to prove his worth to this gaggle of Doubting Thomases. 'I discovered some unwelcome news while in Hopton's service, and passed that news to my lord Stamford.'

The earl nodded. 'News, gentlemen, that, with swift and direct action, can be turned into the most welcome kind.' He drummed his fingers on the edge of the table. 'What it required was a minor stitch in truth. A subtle lie that will turn matters in our favour. Is it done?'

The last question had been for Richardson, and the spy offered a tiny bow. 'Aye, sir. They will take him to Beaworthy, as we agreed. There they will be intercepted.'

'You had better be right in this, Richardson.'

'My men watch the road.'

Stamford shifted in his chair, wincing at the evident pain in his gouty leg, but when he had settled he smiled. 'And we will have him.'

'Who?' It was the first aide who spoke, looming above the earl. 'Who will we have, my lord?'

Stamford interlinked his fingers across the paunch of his belly, studying his knuckles for a moment. 'A man who will change everything.' When he glanced up, his look was one of supreme satisfaction. 'Everything.'

GARDNER'S TOR, DARTMOOR, 2 MAY 1643

Stryker called a council of war at noon. The sun was high above the bleak plain, and, though the temperature was no greater than usual for early May, the tor's exposed nature made the new afternoon uncomfortable. The company's most senior men, therefore, were gathered in a circle in the looming shadow of one of the granite stacks, hats and coats lying in bundles on the trampled grass.

'If only we had a stash o' faggots in the wagon,' Sergeant Skellen muttered when thoughts turned to how they would repel a night attack.

Stryker nodded. Faggots, bundles of brushwood, could be set alight and rolled into a breach – or, in this case, down a hillside – in order to shed light on potential attackers. 'No such luck.'

'Grenados?' Lieutenant Burton said. 'Plenty of those.'

'The flame would be too short-lived,' Stryker replied. 'And then we'd be left with a great cloud of smoke.'

'Making visibility worse,' Burton conceded.

'Better think of something, hadn't they, God?' the barefooted hermit, Seek Wisdom and Fear the Lord Gardner, jabbered up at the sky. He was scuttling around the edge of the group, unable to keep still.

'*If* that old palliard speaks true,' Simeon Barkworth grumbled. 'Pay him no heed, sir, his head's full of bees.'

'Lord!' Seek Wisdom Gardner exclaimed suddenly, startling the soldiers. 'This nibbler of ankles doubts us! I ask for your forgiveness on his behalf.'

Barkworth was on his feet in a flash, knife in hand. 'You seem friendly with God. How about I send you to meet Him now, you Taff-bathing bastard?'

'Hold,' Stryker said calmly enough, though Barkworth knew to obey.

The Scot slipped the blade back into his boot and fixed his yellow glare upon Gardner. 'You'll get yours, fellow. Better watch your back, eh?'

Gardner brandished his black mouth in an amused grimace. 'Kill a priest, would you?' As ever, he leant back to stare straight up at the sky. 'Hear that, God? The dwarf would murder one of your own. How'd you like that?'

'You're a priest?' Barkworth said, stepping back involuntarily.

Gardner's tongue flicked across his lips. 'Aye, little man. Was once upon a time, leastwise.'

'No longer?'

Gardner's tongue flickered again. 'A follower of John Calvin, I was.'

'Bloody Puritan, then,' Skellen droned. 'Brilliant. We're surrounded by Roun'heads, only to find we're cooped up with one an' all.'

'I didn't say I was one o' them, now did I, boy?' the old man replied, voice softer than before.

Stryker stood. 'What happened to you, Seek Wisdom?'

Gardner's pale eyes looked at Stryker, then seemed to drift beyond him, fixed on some distant point known only to the skeletal Welshman. 'Laud.'

'Zounds, man, speak to *me*, just this once!' Stryker snapped.

Gardner's lips curled upwards in a sad smile. 'Not *the* Lord,' he said. 'Laud. William Laud.'

Stryker frowned. 'The Archbishop?'

Gardner nodded, though this time it was a slow, deliberate movement. His eyes stayed mesmerized on the near distance, glassy with memory. 'The very same, boy. I should have been on the *Griffin* in '34.'

'The *Griffin*?' Stryker asked, wishing Lancelot Forrester had been there to explain.

To Stryker's surprise, it was Lieutenant Burton who replied. 'The ship carrying the Independents to the New World?'

Gardner beamed. 'Aye, the very same.'

'Father told me about them,' Burton said defensively when several gazes fell upon him. He addressed Gardner: 'Those who would have each church free and independent to govern itself.'

'This one's good and keen, Lord, yes!' Gardner bellowed up at the blue ether, before jerking his chin down to glare at Skellen. 'You sneer at me, boy. Call me Puritan. I'm a reformer, of course, for it is God's very will, but I am not one of your joyless bloody apprentices who see righteousness in a splintered altar rail, and salvation in a smashed window.'

'Then what have you against Archbishop Laud?' asked Stryker.

Gardner looked at the captain as though he were witless. 'Laud hounded the Independents. Imprisoned many of us. Branded the cheeks of some with the letters S and L.'

'Seditious liar,' Burton said. 'Because you spoke out against the episcopy?'

'You have it again, boy. We advocated congregational control rather than bowing and scraping to some bloody bishop.' He smiled ruefully. 'The result was enmity from all quarters. Anglicans, Catholics, Presbyterians. They all feared us, for we stood for the dissolution of their power. In '34 the *Griffin* carried many people of my thinking to the New World, where they might avoid Laud's vile persecution.'

'Why were you not aboard?' asked Stryker.

Gardner shrugged. 'Arrogance. Pride. I would not be chased out by that prim little villain. Lost my home for it, mind. My whole life really.' He did a sudden manic jig, like some drunken April Fool. 'But I made it across the Severn, and here I am, eh God?'

Stryker regarded the frenzied old man for a few moments. 'You may not be in love with the hardliners in Parliament, but, if you hate Laud, you can hardly be for the King.'

'And there you have it, my one-eyed friend,' Gardner said, flashing a blue wink. 'I take no sides in this buffle-headed war, so neither side can harm me.'

'Or both will,' Stryker replied bluntly.

Gardner grinned again. 'I like you, one-eye.' He looked up. 'God does too, you blessed bastard!'

'I don't know about that,' Stryker said, 'but thank you for the word on our enemies down in the barn. We'll be ready for Wild when he comes.'

Gardner turned on his filthy heels and scuttled over to the edge of summit. 'Now I'm off, boy.'

'I offered you protection, sir!' Stryker shouted at his back.

The old man turned. 'Protection, he says!' He smoothed down his greasy beard with both hands. 'Who'll protect you while you're protecting me? Ha! I'm off to the hills where God and I will keep ourselves to ourselves. And it's a shame about the faggots. You'll all be cut down like dogs come midnight, I shouldn't wonder. Better get busy with musket drill!' With a final grin the old man disappeared down the slope, but after a second his head popped up above the brow once more. 'Stay away from the dry gorse, mind. That stuff'll take a spark like one o' your powder kegs.'

Stryker opened his mouth to speak, but the former priest had vanished. He looked at the men in turn, and saw that some of them were smiling. When his gaze fell on Skellen, the sergeant stood, stretching his long limbs like a cat.

'Better get harvesting, sir,' Skellen said.

Seek Wisdom and Fear the Lord Gardner had offered them a lifeline.

It was dark, the night sky clear and crisp, as Stryker walked with Cecily Cade down to the remains of the village she had spotted earlier in the day. They had taken the first few steps in silence, but the tension had eased as soon as Cecily realized Stryker was not inclined to resurrect their earlier discussion. For Stryker's part, he was more concerned with the threat from Wild than with Cecily's demand for a horse.

Up on the tor the men rested. They had passed the afternoon making preparations for whatever the night would bring, and Stryker had given them liberty to chatter and dice, gnaw at what few provisions they had left, or puff what secret stashes of sotweed they had left. It was a crowded place to garrison, for, though the hill was more than five hundred paces across, from foot to foot, the sense of imminent danger meant that most of the eighty soldiers and three civilians were keen to remain as near to the summit as possible.

'Who was that man?' Cecily asked as they passed a red-coated sentry, carefully scrutinizing the land to the east.

Stryker acknowledged his subordinate with a brief nod and looked down at the girl. He had asked her to accompany him, ostensibly in order to inspect the new horse pens, which, of course, had been her idea, though secretly he knew that he simply wished to spend time with her. The thought gave him a pang of guilt, but he stifled it harshly. Lisette Gaillard had left him again, gone off to God knew where on some clandestine mission that would doubtless require the seduction of some unsuspecting fool. 'Seek Wisdom Gardner. A former priest, or so he says.'

'You did not believe him?'

He thought for a moment. 'Actually, I think I did.'

'He seemed mad.'

'Aye, but he was driven to it. He has been wronged in his life, so he protects himself by playing at madness. When he spoke of Archbishop Laud, his eyes were still, his words calm. I think he is sane when it suits him.'

They cleared the highest area of the tor, where the terrain was mostly empty grass, and moved down to the point where gorse and rock began to dominate. Mossy granite and blanched animal bones cluttered the slope, and as they slowly made their way to the lower ground, careful of their footing in the darkness, brown patches of bracken and the thin claws of bilberry bushes became dominant.

'Look,' Cecily said, indicating the black smear of a hill perhaps a mile away.

Stryker stared at the hill. It appeared darker than the sky where it blocked out the stars. Almost immediately he noticed movement on the crest, shapes slowly stirring, silhouetted by the moonlight. Horses.

At first Stryker's heart began to accelerate, for he thought they were the vanguard of an attacking force, but quickly realized the animals were riderless.

'That's what I like to see.'

She cocked her head inquisitively. 'Oh?'

'They're wild, not Wild.'

She gave a small snort of amusement. 'Terrible!'

The ruins of the abandoned village stood out starkly from the rest of the undergrowth, the pale, wind-whipped stones seeming to gently glow in the darkness. Gaps where doorways had once been were clearly visible in the walls, while the odd hearthstone, flat and wide, still poked out from the soil. The walls themselves were predominantly waist high, pushing up between grasping bushes, though some were higher in places and some lower, stripped by time and plunder. Not ideal, Stryker had conceded, for corralling the company's horses, but better than leaving them to roam free on the already crowded tor. Wild's sleek chargers – powerful, proud, and skittish – were kept together in the largest compound, tightly tethered to some of the more robust overhanging trees, while the rest – Bailey's emaciated nags, the two workhorses captured from the brigands, and the brace that had drawn Sir Alfred Cade's ill-fated coach – were left loose in one of the smaller structures.

Stryker sat on one of the walls, feeling strangely relieved by the eerie silence, and listened to the skittering wing beats of bats and the crackle of decaying, dew-laden bracken.

'What do you think happened here?' Cecily asked after a short while.

Stryker stared at her. Her lily-white skin that seemed to smoulder in the moon's glow. 'Plague, famine, it's anyone's guess.' He tapped the wall with his boot heel, noticing a tiny hunter spider scurrying between two grey stones. 'But these homes have long since gone to ruin. Maybe hundreds of years.' He shrugged. 'They may yet prove useful.'

'Oh?'

'This place is too low lying to defend against cavalry,' he said, studying the various walls thoughtfully. The former buildings seemed to be rectangular in shape, though varying in size, and were aligned lengthways down the hillside, terraced into the foot of the tor. 'If Wild attacks from the east, we can place musketeers down here. It is a maze of breastworks. We'd cut them down as they picked their way through the bushes and stones.'

Cecily looked at him. 'Do you always think of ways you might kill people?'

'Only when they're trying to kill me first.'

For a time Cecily stared out at the distant hills, watching them darken in the gathering gloom, while Stryker paced about the ruins, kicking the walls in places to test their integrity and occasionally stopping to pat the whickering horses.

'Stryker,' Cecily said eventually, 'how will we ever escape?'

Stryker was several paces away from her, standing on a

thick wall of coarse rubble some four feet high. He looked down at her, thinking to dissemble, but no suitable words would come. 'I don't know,' he said simply. 'We've all seen the glint of plate on the horizon. They're watching us. Wild has enough men to surround us at intervals, in pairs and threes. They're all on horseback, which means they can communicate very quickly. He'd have his men gathered and at our backs before we could put any distance between us.'

'Perhaps he will lose interest,' she said hopefully.

Stryker shook his head. 'He wants the wagon.' He felt bad for the lie, for he knew in his heart that Wild sought revenge above all else, but the guilt was too great to utter. 'Our only hope lies with a messenger. A man who'll ride direct to Launceston and beg help from General Hopton.'

'I will go,' Cecily replied hopefully.

'No. Absolutely not.'

'I—' Cecily began, struggling with the words. 'I really must be away from here.'

'So must I, Miss Cade.' He pointed back at the tor, the vast outcrop of granite appearing more like an ancient fortress than ever. 'You think any one of us relishes being trapped up here?'

Pursing her lips in frustration, she said, 'That is not what I meant.' She shook her head, voice weary. 'You cannot understand.'

Stryker leapt down from the wall and went to her. Cecily shrank back, startled by his sudden movement, but halted her retreat when he pinned her by the shoulders. He stared at her, close enough to feel her warm breath in the chill night air. 'Then make me.'

Cecily returned his gaze, bit her bottom lip as if mulling over what she might say next, and drew breath to speak.

And then the guns fired.

CHAPTER 9

Cecily returned his gaze, but her bottom lip as if mulling over what she might say next, and drew breath to speak.

And then th.

BESIDE THE ROAD WEST OF TWO BRIDGES,
DARTMOOR, 2 MAY 1643

Lancelot Forrester ran the whetstone across the edge of his sword in smooth, practised movements. 'What a beauty, eh?'

'Captain?' the deep voice of Anthony Payne rolled across the flames.

The evening was a sullen one for the men of Forrester's company and their Cornish allies. They had moved east during the course of the day, scouring the road, searching for any sign of the enigmatic man known only to Payne. And they had found nothing. All the while they had been aware that the main Royalist army was far away to the west, making plans to defend the king's stronghold on the other side of the River Tamar. Now they were camped at the edge of a little field near Two Bridges, the farthest either of their commanders was willing to travel into enemy territory.

Forrester caught Payne's gaze on the far side of their little fire, and lifted the blade. 'Picked it up after Hopton Fight.' He stared lovingly at the weapon. 'Had to prise it from a dead lieutenant's fingers. Note the hilt. The swirling pattern is Venetian, I believe.'

'Schiavona style,' the gigantic Cornishman replied.

'Quite so,' Forrester said in surprise. 'You know your blades, Mister Payne.' He glanced back at the flames, venturing, 'Not so unusual in such a warlike people, I suppose.'

Payne, his massive backside perched on a fallen tree trunk, raised his brow slightly. 'If you refer to the rebellions of the last century, Captain, I tell you that we are loyal to the King. Be certain of that.'

Forrester could not tell whether he had caused offence or amusement, so decided to err on the side of caution. 'Your Cornishman,' he said warily, 'has a keen sense of independence.'

At last Payne smiled. 'Aye, perhaps.' He rubbed broad fingers against his clean chin, shaven pale by his knife not an hour before. 'We lead a strange existence down here, sir. We are part of the realm and yet we are our own nation.' Payne's big, twinkling eyes seemed to drink in the dancing flames. 'An ancient nation. Proud and set apart.' He glanced up. 'And that makes us conservative in our nature.'

'How so?' Forrester said, setting back to work on the blade.

'We naturally favour the monarch.'

Forrester considered the statement for a moment. 'Most Cornish remain tenants of the Duchy, do they not?' The Crown owned most of the land in the shire through the Duchy of Cornwall.

'Aye,' Payne agreed, 'but in other ways too. Politics, industry, even religion.'

Forrester narrowed his eyes in mock suspicion. 'The old faith?'

Payne's big head shook. 'Not Papism, Captain, but traditional church. Anglican. We perhaps see Puritanism as peculiar to the rest of this island. An English matter, if you will. Ultimately, though, it is this love of tradition that drives us to support the King. The rebellion will change much, and such a thought sits ill west of the Tamar.'

'Is Devonshire so different?'

'Aye, strange as that must sound. More so than you'd imagine, I think. They have a larger Puritan element for a start. And they fear Catholicism more, for any invasion from Ireland would likely make landfall on the north Devon coast. But most of all,' he grinned then, exposing his neat white teeth, which shone in the firelight, 'they're more English.'

Forrester laughed. 'Well I'm glad the Cornish are on my side, sir, and that's God's truth.'

Anthony Payne stretched out his legs, like twin mortars aimed at a breach, and unfastened his boots. He quickly tugged them free, wiggling toes the size of potatoes before the fire. 'I think we have reached the end of the road, so to speak, Captain.'

Forrester looked at the giant sadly. 'I am sorry we could not locate this man.'

'Not so sorry as I, Captain.' He picked up a gnarled branch, though it seemed more like a mere twig in his hand, and stabbed at the flames. Manic cinders burst up and out, whirling and skittering into the gaping sky above. 'Why, if you knew—'

The bark of a fox screeched across the field, cutting across Payne's words. It barked twice more, the shrill sound somehow chilling in the blackness. Out across the field men impulsively hunkered closer to their fires, seeking comfort in the flames and the stories they each told. Payne leant forward again to disturb the glowing embers with his charred stick.

'If I knew what?' Forrester prompted.

Payne glanced up at him. 'Pay my ramblings no heed, sir. It is tiredness speaks for me.'

That was it, thought Forrester ruefully. The opportunity was gone. He sighed. 'What now for us then? We have not succeeded in our task, and we are dangerously isolated so far east.'

Payne considered the words for a short time, and Forrester knew well the turmoil that must have afflicted the big man. 'You're right, Captain,' he muttered eventually. 'We're of no use out here. Back to Cornwall.'

'Or rather, to Beaworthy?'

Payne shrugged. 'I suppose. Though it hardly matters now. Hopton ordered us direct to him so that he might speak with our bounty, as Richardson put it. But without that bounty, we must surely return to our regiments. I to Grenville, and you to Mowbray. I will arrange for a rider to make a report to General Hopton.'

'Abject failure, eh?' Forrester said, giving his blade one last scrape. He set the whetstone down on the leaves at his side and flicked the cutting edges gingerly with his thumb, revelling in the lethal zing the motion produced. 'Still, I should be glad to return to the army, nevertheless.'

It was then that the silence of the night was shattered by musketry. It came from somewhere up in the hills of the high moor, faint, yet distinct. Like a far-off thunderclap, but sharper and more sporadic. The rattle and cough of dozens of firearms discharging in the darkness.

Dozens of heads jerked up from around the company's

fires. Men gritted teeth, sniffed the air and cocked ears, sensing some unknown danger. 'Two or three miles off,' Payne said to Forrester.

The captain nodded. 'To the nor'-west. Sounds a fair old scrap too. What the devil are that many men doing out here?'

'I know not,' replied Payne, 'and I care not.'

Forrester stared at him in amazement. 'You cannot be serious, Mister Payne.'

'It is a couple of patrols only, sir. They have become lost, like as not, and stumbled across one another in the darkness. But it is not our man, and I would sooner return to my master than waste my men on another fool's errand.'

'You think much of Sir Bevil, don't you?'

Payne nodded. 'I was born into his household, Captain. We grew up together. I have always been there to protect him. If we must abandon this mission, then I should return to his side forthwith.' He tossed the stick into the fire, a shower of sparks kicking up in its wake, and delved a hand into his snapsack to retrieve a stale biscuit. 'But do not mistake me, sir. Sir Bevil Grenville needs no nannying. He is the best commander my county can offer.'

'A great man.'

'Aye, the greatest fighter Hopton has.'

Forrester allowed himself a small smile. He, perhaps, knew one better. 'Then we are agreed. We leave whoever that is,' he waved a hand in the direction of the distant skirmish, 'to resolve their own differences, and make direct for the army.' He glanced at the dried biscuit still clamped between Payne's massive fingers. 'Besides, supplies are too short to linger out here.'

Payne grinned, took a tentative bite of what Forrester

knew was a rather gritty concoction, and swallowed it down with theatrical disgust. 'Quite right.'

Forrester leant to one side, retrieving his scabbard. After a final glance at his now keen blade, he thrust the weapon home, stopping only when hilt slammed into throat. 'Launceston, then?'

'Stratton for me, sir.'

'Of course,' Forrester replied, remembering the spy Richardson's words. 'That is where Grenville's regiment have been stationed.' He wrinkled his nose as he thought. 'I know not where Sir Edmund has taken our lads, so it is perhaps to Launceston for us.'

'Someone there will know where you should go.'

'Right enough.'

Forrester reached down again, fumbling amongst the pile of belongings he had placed beside his sword. Eventually his fingers touched upon a small leather flask, and he pulled out the stopper with his most rakish grin. 'Spiced mead,' he whispered conspiratorially. 'Liberated from my colonel's billet at Launceston. Do not worry, Mister Payne, he practically declared his antipathy for the stuff, so it shan't be missed.'

Payne offered a resigned smile. 'And what do we drink to?'

Forrester held up the flask and shrugged. 'To failed missions.'

'How about to new-found comrades?'

Captain Lancelot Forrester grinned broadly. 'Aye, Mister Payne.' He took a hefty swig, jammed the stopper home, and tossed the flask to the Cornish giant. 'New-found comrades.'

Stryker grabbed Cecily's arm and bolted back up the slope.

They passed a score of soldiers on their way, though this time the redcoats were in a state of high agitation, strapping on bandoliers and lighting match-cord. Stryker continually looked back and to the sides, anxious lest the attack be coming from this flank, but the crackle of firearms seemed concentrated on the far side of the hill. 'They're coming from the west,' he rasped.

'Could it not be drill?'

'No,' he replied without slowing, 'the higher-pitched shots are small arms. Pistols and carbines. We don't carry those.'

When they reached the tight mass of granite topping the tor, Stryker took a spare musket that had been loaded and primed for him by one of the men, and then halted. 'In there!' He pointed to the lawn corridor between the two largest stone piles. He saw the carter, Marcus Bailey, and Sir Alfred Cade's bodyguard, Otilwell Broom, shrinking down against one of the lone standing stones. 'You too! Get inside!'

The group made their way into the interior, Stryker in the lead, until they reached one of the small caves formed by the coming together of irregular-shaped boulders. 'In there!'

Cecily and Bailey went first, stooping into the pitch blackness, with Broom at the rear.

'Not you!' Stryker snapped.

The bodyguard turned in surprise, the red inner lining of his slashed doublet flashing in the moonlight as he moved. 'Not me?' he spluttered. 'Why the devil not?'

'No hiding tonight,' Stryker replied, a little more harshly than he had meant. He had allowed Broom to keep within the defensive circle when Wild first attacked, but that had been for Cecily's protection, not his. This time she could keep safe within the tor, flanked on all sides by granite thicker than castle walls, and Broom was needed elsewhere. 'Can you ride?'

'Of course I can bloody ride,' Broom snapped waspishly.

'Then I have a task for you.'

'What about him?' Broom thrust an accusatory hand at the mouth of the cave, causing Bailey's wan face to reappear.

Stryker looked at the carter. Even in the darkness he could see that the man was trembling violently. 'He's in no state, Mister Broom. With a musket in hand he'd kill one of *us*, like as not. And I'd wager he is no horseman. Bailey?'

'C—Cap—Captain?' the skinny man replied falteringly.

'Stay in there. I'm trusting you to see Miss Cade is protected.'

The last comment seemed to put some renewed steel into Bailey's demeanour, for he nodded stoically. 'Aye, sir, you may rely upon me.'

Stryker looked back at Broom. 'Take one of Wild's horses from the pen. Ride south to the road, and then strike westward.'

Broom swallowed thickly. 'To what end?'

'Find our people, Mister Broom. Bring them back. We cannot lift this siege of our own accord.'

Broom's eyes darted nervously left and right as though seeking some unlikely escape. 'Can you not send one of your men?'

Stryker nodded. 'I could. But you're a gentleman, Mister Broom. I'd wager you're the superior horseman.' He stepped closer, seizing Broom's finely upholstered elbow. 'We need you tonight, sir. One way or the other. Pick up the reins or pick up a musket. The choice is yours.'

Stryker was both surprised and impressed when Otilwell Broom nodded. The man he had taken for a weak-hearted dandy took his hand in a firm shake, and disappeared into the night, their hopes resting on him.

Without further discussion Stryker turned, grinding the earth beneath his heels, and, gathering men as he went, dashed further along the avenue to the cave where the wagon was kept. 'Fetch what you need,' he ordered, not wishing to approach the vehicle himself in case a spark from his match-cord drifted free. 'Then meet me on the west slope.'

Leaving the group to gather arms, he ran to the westernmost fringe of the tor, took a few knee-jarring paces down the slope until he reached a stout-looking boulder, waited a moment, and edged out to scan the scene. Many of his men were already in place. The hillside was awash with granite lumps, some as big as a large dog, others the size of Sir Alfred's coach, and all ideal for defence. The redcoats had placed themselves at regular intervals behind those stones, and resting their long musket barrels on the smooth tops they were pouring fire down on to the lower ground. In amongst them were pikemen, holding out their huge spears to present a steel-tipped barrier.

But who were they fighting? At first it was only Stryker's own men that he saw, for the glowing matches and long pikes were conspicuous all around him. Moreover, there was no thunderous rumble of hooves, no shrill whinnying or gleaming sabres. But then a shot burst forth from fifty paces away, near the very foot of the tor, and its bright fleeting flare briefly lit up the man who had pulled the trigger. A man on foot but dressed in tall cavalry boots, buff-coat, back and breast plates, and lobster-pot helmet with hinged visor. As his eye adjusted to the scene, Stryker gradually noticed more of the metallic forms advancing up the west slope.

'Keep them back!' he bawled. 'Make your shots count!'

The game had suddenly changed. Colonel Wild, clearly realizing that a mounted assault against such a treacherous position would be difficult in the extreme, had plumped for an attack on foot. His men would not be comfortable on *terra firma*, cavalrymen were ever thus in Stryker's experience, but this tactic would at least negate the granite-strewn approach and, to some extent, nullify the threat of the pikes.

'They match our numbers, sir!' Lieutenant Burton barked. He had scuttled from a large stone somewhere to the left, and now slammed his back against Stryker's granite shield. With his useless right arm, Burton could not wield a musket, but had his sword drawn and ready in his good hand. 'I count at least eighty of the bastards.'

'He means to punch a hole right the way to the top,' Stryker responded. He had assumed Wild would surround the tor, make his ascent on all sides, but the colonel had evidently chosen not to spread his force too thin. He would throw all his men into one all-out thrust, an iron-fisted blow that would take him all the way to the summit. 'But they're shooting uphill, have hardly any protection, and our muskets have greater range and accuracy. Tell the lads,' he fixed Burton with a hard glare, 'I'll personally tan the hide of any man who wastes his shot.'

'But we can't see the buggers well enough,' Burton protested. 'Only when they give fire or their plate catches the moonlight.'

Stryker twisted from behind the boulder to peer down the slope. He could see the enemy right enough, but as his second-in-command had bemoaned, they were cloaked by the night, moving like half-solid wraiths. Conversely, the Royalist defenders would have to stay close to their rocks, keep behind the protective screens as best they could, for their muskets made them vulnerable in a night engagement. Stryker generally favoured the matchlock over the firelock, because the latter was useless if its flint was knocked free, whereas should a matchlock's firing mechanism become damaged, a man could simply dip the smouldering match into his pan and the weapon would still fire. Under cover of darkness, however, flint-sparking weapons came into their own, simply because they did not present a constantly glowing light to the enemy. The cavalrymen carried such weapons, and that was a problem.

He turned to Burton. 'Is Barkworth ready?'

'Sir.'

A bright tongue of flame leapt forth from lower down the slope, and Stryker instinctively flinched. The sound of splintering granite cracked somewhere behind. He peered down, eyes straining for the blue gout of smoke that must be rising in the spent pistol's wake. There it was. He stepped clear of the rock, shouldered the musket and fired, but heard no yelp of pain, and knew the shooter must have already moved.

More shots rang out from the advancing Parliamentarians, weaving in and out of the rocks and gorse bushes like a horde of ghosts. A pikeman, waiting impotently with his steel-pointed pole for a cavalry assault that had never materialized, was thrown violently back, a carbine ball hitting his chest. Like all Stryker's pikemen, he wore a steel breastplate, and that seemed to have saved him, for he sat upright and vomited, but when he looked up a second ball hit him, blasting away a chunk of his jaw. He bellowed like a gelded bullock, the sound sickeningly muffled through the carnage of his mouth, black blood jetting freely over his metal-clad torso. The musketeer closest to him darted out from behind a rock, dropping his weapon and hooking hands beneath the wounded man's arms to drag him out of the open, but another spatter of shots peppered the earth all around.

'Get back!' Stryker shouted across at the flailing musketeer.

After one last heave on the dying pikeman's inert body, the musketeer did as he was told and let his friend slump. As he turned, a bullet screamed close. He flinched, but the lead shot had flown wide, slamming into earth somewhere in the darkness. He looked up at Stryker, catching his captain's eye with an expression of sheer relief. But even as the soldier offered a tight smile, his eyes seemed to glaze, his head lolled, and he slumped on to his knees. In the gloom Stryker could see the long shard of stone, kicked up by the ball, jutting from the back of the man's skull.

Stryker turned quickly back to the slope. The swarming Parliamentarians were making slow but steady progress. This was not good. They would be in amongst the higher boulders before his men could properly pinpoint them, and then it might be too late.

Stryker put his back to the granite and shouted up to the summit. 'Now, Mister Barkworth! Light the bastards up!'

Immediately a dozen redcoats appeared on the ridge above him. They were arranged in pairs, one man in each pair holding a large black sphere on the outermost lip of land. Stryker watched as the second man in each pair produced a glowing length of match, touched it to his partner's sphere, and stood back. The balls, a yard in height and depth, came fizzing to life, first consumed with blinding white flame, then settling into roaring oranges and reds.

A second later, a tiny, childlike figure, dressed in grey madder wool and brandishing a short sword, emerged on the brow. Simeon Barkworth, the smallest yet most fearsome man Stryker knew, jerked his blade sharply upwards, and brought it down in a sweeping arc.

The flaming gorse faggots tumbled down the slope, brushing against rocks as they went, often coming dangerously close to the red-coated defenders. But Barkworth had chosen each one's course well, and the tightly packed gorse, collected during the day, dried in the sun, and sprinkled liberally with black powder, plummeted rapidly down the slope, the little Scot's obscenities screaming in their wake.

And the tide had suddenly turned. The lower part of the hillside was now bathed in warm, clear light, transforming wraiths to men, and the Royalists could see their targets.

'Shoot them! *Fire*! *Fire*! *Fire*!' Stryker bellowed, his order echoed all along the slope by Burton and Skellen, Chase and Heel, corporals and drummers and pikemen.

The musketeers, emboldened now, emerged from their hiding places. They rummaged in bullet bags, blew on match-cords – both ends, lest one glowing tip be snuffed out – and adjusted the bandoliers that ran across their bodies from shoulder to hip. From those bandoliers hung a dozen wooden pots, each one carrying enough black powder to prime a single shot.

Stryker involuntarily glanced back up at the biggest stacks, to where he knew the wagon waited, protected within its granite cave, and felt a wave of relief that it carried such a plentiful supply of powder and shot. Remembering his own weapon was spent, he crouched low, scuttling across to the rock where the musketeer lay dead, the splinter of stone still lodged deep in his skull. Stryker forced the disgust from his mind and jerked the shard free so that he could turn the corpse on to its back. Quickly he set about unfastening the man's bullet bag and priming flask, dumping them on the ground at his feet before going to work on the bandolier. But his fingers fumbled unsuccessfully with the buckle and he hissed a savage curse, unsheathing his long dirk and slicing straight through the leather, allowing him to yank the belt free. Checking the first couple of powder pots, he found that they were empty, but the third was reassuringly heavy. The majority of officers in the King's Army were unused to wielding the long-arm – at least during the panicking heat of battle – but Stryker had grown up on the killing fields of Europe where life was cruel and cheap. A place where a man became expert in as many weapons as possible, if he wanted to survive.

Moving by sheer instinct, he up-ended the musket, thumbed open the lid of the full pot, and tipped the powder into the cold barrel. As soon as the pot left his hand, his fingers were grasping a lead ball and a piece of wadding from the bag of ammunition, popping them into the muzzle. Taking the scouring stick, Stryker rammed the ingredients home, making sure they were as compacted as possible against the charge. He levelled the musket, blew on his match to keep the embers bright, and pulled the trigger gently to bring the glowing cord down on to the closed pan. Satisfied with the positioning of the match, he flicked back the pan cover, poured in a small charge of the finely grained gunpowder that the musketeer kept in his horn, and took aim.

Now, with the makeshift faggots still blazing at the foot of the slope, the horseless cavalrymen were clearly visible. Indeed, their breastplates and helmets gleamed brightly in the flame light, and it was an easy thing to pick out a man. Stryker selected one of the Roundheads who had climbed highest, sighting the black cormorant feather along the barrel, then inching the muzzle down so that it was level with the target's midriff. He pulled the trigger smoothly, this time with the pan exposed, and the orange match-tip plunged into the powder, in turn igniting the charge in the barrel, and the musket kicked like a donkey as the ball blasted free. The harquebusier screamed as he was snatched back, tumbling down the slope from whence he came.

Stryker did not stop to see whether his victim still lived. He sucked in a sulphurous breath that stung his throat. '*Charge!*'

Like a legion of ghosts rising from the earth, the Royalist defenders left the shelter of the rocky outcrops and bolted down the slope. Some had loaded muskets, and they emptied them first, but most either carried spent firearms or swords, and they knew what their captain expected of them. Further down, the steel-encased Roundheads fired what few shots they had left, holstered their pistols and drew swords. This was to be a fight of the bitterest kind. Hand to hand, and face to face.

'King Charles!' Stryker roared as he pelted down the slope, boots thudding into the soft earth, heart clanging in his chest, blood rushing at his ears. He leapt a small boulder, dodged a dense gorse thicket and ducked beneath the slicing blade of the first Roundhead he met. He ran on, leaving the man to flail in his wake, and dropped his shoulder, bowling into the chest of the next enemy in line. The Parliamentarian's broad tuck was poised for the attack, but Stryker's sheer speed beat its arc, and the pair smashed to the ground in a tangle of limbs and metal. In a flash both men were up, and, to Stryker's alarm, the cavalryman had kept a grip on his sword during the fall. That sword now scythed the air at his face in a blow that would have cleaved his skull in two, had he not raised the empty musket to meet it. The sword hammered into the outstretched barrel, bounced clear, and Stryker brought the heavy wooden stock across to crunch into one of the trio of bars that made up the Roundhead's visor. The thin strip of metal, hanging vertically from the helmet's hinged peak, was no match for the bludgeoning stock, and it crumpled inwards, mangling the flesh it was supposed to protect. The cavalryman staggered back, blinded by his own blood, and dropped his sword. Stryker hit him again, this time stabbing the musket butt straight ahead in a blow that destroyed another of the bars and pulverized the recoiling man's nose.

He moved on quickly, parrying the next man's sword thrust with the improvised club. The blade snapped under the jarring hit, and its owner tossed the useless hilt away. But he was a tall man with a remarkably long reach, and he surprised Stryker by lurching forward while the Royalist was off balance and grasping him in a bone-cracking bear hug. Stryker felt the wind explode out of his chest as though he were a giant set of bellows, the pain of the crush amplified by the big man's plate armour, and the strength left his arms, forcing the musket to drop to the ground. Feeling himself getting weaker with every heart-beat, he desperately searched for an escape. The only weapons he could bring to bear were his teeth, and he yearned to clamp them on to the huge enemy's nose, but the visor was fully down. So Stryker spat. He drew up as much phlegm as his powder-dry mouth could muster and sprayed it into the Roundhead's eyes. Just for a moment, the man's grip faltered, and Stryker worked an arm free to reach for his belt. He jammed the dirk upwards at an angle, trying to slide it between the Roundhead's ribs, but, even though the area was not protected by plate, he could not penetrate the thick coat of buff-leather. He reversed the blade, plunging it low, slashing down at the cavalry-man's thigh. That worked, for the grip was suddenly released, and Stryker staggered backwards, heaving air into his throttled lungs as though he were half-drowned. He realized he had found flesh when the huge Parliamentarian came at him again, for he was disabled by an exaggerated limp, one hand clamped tight over a spurt-ing knife wound on his upper leg. Stryker lunged, ducked a wild punch, and kicked the big man on the place where the blade had entered. The cavalryman roared in pain, and Stryker kicked him again, this time in the balls. When the injured man doubled over, both hands now clutched at his lower regions, Stryker released his own ornate broadsword and plunged it deep into the Roundhead's neck, showering them both in a fine crimson spray.

Save for the few men on both sides who had hung back to keep firing from a distance, the shooting had all but died away. Muskets and pistols had been emptied in those first exchanges, but, since the Royalists' charge, there had been precious little time to reload the awkward pieces. And yet all around him the fight raged. Stryker's pikemen had led the charge, finally able to ply their trade, and Stryker could see at least three skewered Parliamentarians on the slope. Most, of course, had dropped their cumbersome ash shafts after first coming together with the black-plumed assailants, instead drawing swords for the close-quarters melee. Alongside them many of the musketeers still brandished the butt ends of their muskets, preferring the heavy clubs to thin steel. It was hot, dirty, cruel fighting, where technique and training gave way to tenacity and the will to stay alive. It was the kind of fight Stryker's men relished, and as he watched the individual duels play out all along the tor's north-west face, he knew that they would win. Cavalrymen were not, after all, cavalrymen because they enjoyed fighting on foot. They had had the advantage of surprise and the cover of darkness, but both of those had vanished now, and they had found themselves in a pitched gutter-brawl still too far from their target.

'King Charles!' Stryker bellowed at the top of his hoarse lungs.

'Stryker's!' another man shouted, and his call was repeated all across the tor.

They were winning, edging the Parliamentarians on to the back foot with each bloody second. Stryker saw one of the enemy plunge his sword into a pikeman's eye, gore and fluid shooting in a stream all the way along the blade's fuller. He ran to engage his comrade's killer, hurdling a stone and sweeping his ornate sword sideways at the man's head. The cavalryman turned at the last moment, his lobster-pot helmet taking the brunt of the blow, causing Stryker's weapon to glance away. Stryker was forced to duck below the Roundhead's own thrust now, and only just managed to bring his blade up to meet the second stab. The pair separated, circled, both blades red and glistening, hovering before one another like fighting snakes.

The Roundhead moved first, lunging forth, making a powerful play for the artery at Stryker's groin, but the Royalist was equal to it, blocking the blade in a snapping parry and shunting it to the side. As he forced the sword away, he let his own steel slide all the way along his opponent's until the guards met in a wrist-numbing clang. He flicked his wrist in a savage jerk that twisted the hilt from his opponent's grasp, the weapon clattering noisily against one of the big stones, and he immediately stumbled rearward, desperate to be out of range of the scarlet blade.

And Stryker let him go, because a new order was echoing throughout the lower part of the slope, and down on to the flat. It was the order for the Parliamentarians to withdraw. Retreat.

He stood and watched the silver-backed troopers dash pell-mell down the hillside and away from the tor, exultant redcoats crowing in their wake. They disappeared as quickly as they had come, swallowed whole by the blackness of the night, gone, no doubt, to rejoin their mounts left somewhere out in the wilderness. They would be back, that much was certain. But for now it did not matter.

The Royalists had won.

CHAPTER 10

Not a single person on the tor slept for the remaining hours of darkness. The night's tribulations had been exhausting in the extreme, but the sudden carnage on the tor's north-west face had put the survivors on edge, fraying nerves and keeping eyes pinned wide and watchful.

As dawn came, a new scar stood out on the lower ground to the south and east, adjacent to the ruined village. A brown blemish on the green landscape, freshly dug soil conspicuous against the carpet of heather, bracken, and grass. It was a pit, deep and wide, carved out amongst the stones and bushes of the tor. The final resting place for twenty men. Eleven had been Wild's harquebusiers, stripped of their weapons and armour, dumped side by side in the mass grave, while the remaining nine were Stryker's, five pikemen and four musketeers.

'Never gets easier, sir,' Sergeant William Skellen said as he came to stand beside Stryker. His face was gaunt, deep eye sockets sepulchral.

'Never,' Stryker agreed.

'Still, could've been worse. If it weren't for those burning faggots we'd have all been rotting.'

Stryker was staring absently into the pit while a team of

grunting redcoats used swords, stones and feet to backfill the huge hole. 'We have Seek Wisdom for that,' he said without looking up. 'What a goddamned failure.'

'Failure, sir? We won didn't we?'

Now Stryker met the taller man's hooded gaze. 'Won? We're still trapped here like rats in a barrel, Will. Wild will replenish his forces, his supplies, his weapons. He'll change his bloody horses and send the buggers in again. And again and again, until there's no one left to defend this grand pile of rocks. It's a failure, Sergeant, because it was my ambition that led us here.'

'But, sir—'

'But nothing,' Stryker said, rounding on Skellen. 'You think a fine troop of horse spends their days and nights in the middle of this bloody moor for the freshness of the air? They're here because we've got their ammunition cart, and they want it back. Add to that Wild's oath to personally geld me, and you can appreciate the situation. They will never leave.' He turned to look up at the tor and its limp red and white flag. 'Not while my colour flies.'

Skellen followed his gaze. 'They'll have a rough old time takin' it down, sir.'

'I know,' said Stryker, appreciating his old friend's stoicism. 'In the meantime, we must hope Otilwell Broom made it past Wild's pickets.'

They walked on, intending to inspect the entire perimeter of the tor in an effort to identify some way of strengthening their defences. But the reality blew away any vestige of hope Stryker might have harboured. The night's violence had left him with thirty-nine musketeers and just twenty-two pikemen, not nearly enough to hold off another concerted assault.

'Difficult to man the whole hill,' Skellen muttered behind Stryker, anticipating his captain's thoughts. 'Still, least we won't run out o' shot or powder.'

They moved up to the flat summit, weaving slowly between a couple of jagged obelisks and up to the grassy, granite-flanked avenue that had offered such vital protection during their time on the tor. Cecily Cade was there, slumped against the wall of grey, eyes red-rimmed from powder smoke and exhaustion. To his credit, Marcus Bailey, the perpetually terrified wagon driver, was with her, still at her side as Stryker had ordered. Stryker lifted his hat to them as he and Skellen strode past. They went to the far side of the tor, acknowledging pikemen and musketeers alike, stopping briefly to offer words of encouragement to the wounded.

Lieutenant Burton stood on the north-west lip of the crest. His face was dark, a layer of soot mingling with the wispy hairs of his beard. He had removed the leather strap that pinned his withered right arm to his body, instead cradling it with his left, rubbing the chafed skin with blackened fingers. 'Strange to think the bastard's just down there,' he said, nodding at the grey building half a mile away.

Stryker went to stand beside the younger man, studying the barn and the little figures that moved around it. There seemed to be a deal more activity than usual and he squinted in a futile effort to pick out the Parliamentarians more clearly, but soon gave up. 'Plotting our downfall.'

'Aye,' Burton agreed. He looked up at Stryker then. 'We're not going get out of this one, are we, sir?'

Stryker shook his head. 'Supplies are running short.' He felt thankful that they still had access to fresh water, but that would not fill their bellies or give them the strength to fight.

Skellen cleared his throat noisily. 'Beg pardon, sirs, but I should see to the lads.'

'Carry on, Sergeant,' Stryker replied. When he looked back at Burton, he saw that his second-in-command had turned to face the tor's interior, staring intently at the entrance to the avenue.

'Should a soldier marry, sir?'

Stryker was momentarily taken aback. 'Marry? I—er—I suppose. Women follow the armies up and down this bloody land.'

'Oh, I wouldn't want her following,' Burton responded tartly. 'She'd be set in a house where it is safe.'

'Safe?' Stryker mused. 'And where might that be?'

'Perhaps down in Cornwall,' Burton said with a nonchalant shrug, though it was clear that he had put some thought into such a union.

Stryker watched the young man carefully for a moment, noticing that Burton's eyes kept flicking back to the avenue. 'Christ,' he said suddenly, 'you already have a woman in mind, don't you?'

'And what if I have?'

'Easy, Andrew,' Stryker said, shocked by his subordinate's combative tone.

Burton cast his gaze to his boots, a crimson tide flooding his hollow cheeks. 'Forgive me, sir. I—I lost my mind for a moment.'

'No matter,' Stryker replied, and was surprised to find that, far from anger, he was assailed by his own wave of embarrassment, for he too had secretly coveted Cecily Cade. It stood to reason that the lieutenant would also find the girl attractive. She was a singular beauty, well educated and forthright, and far closer in age to Burton than Stryker. He forced himself to keep his eye on the barn, in case his awkwardness was etched across his face. 'She would be quite a catch.'

Burton patted his useless arm. 'Too great a catch for one such as me?'

'No,' Stryker said, wondering if he had responded too quickly, 'of course not.'

'I feel,' Burton began self-consciously. 'I feel if we are to die here, then I should cast aside my damnable timidity.' He stared at Stryker until the latter was forced to meet his gaze. 'What have I to lose?'

Stryker's heart felt like a culverin shot weighing against his ribs, because he feared his own reaction. But when he finally cast his eye down upon the lieutenant, he did not see a rival but the young man who had become the nearest thing he had to a son. What he felt was not jealousy but pride. 'You have nothing to lose, Andrew. You're a fine soldier and a good man.'

Burton visibly coloured. 'Thank you, sir.' Then he frowned, because he had seen something down amongst the bullet-chipped stones and churned earth of the west slope. 'Sir?'

Stryker searched the terrain for himself. There, standing on a small boulder, immediately accosted by a pair of musket-toting redcoats, was a pike-thin, filthily clothed man with bare feet, black gums, and long, silver beard. Seek Wisdom and Fear the Lord Gardner had returned.

'See, God?' Gardner barked at the sky when Stryker had ordered he be allowed up to the summit. 'He is not an imbecile, just as you said.'

'Enough, Gardner.' Stryker did not feel inclined to trade insults, however good-natured they might have been, with the enigmatic hermit. Instead he jerked his angular chin at a pair of rocks a little way along the edge of the crest. 'Come, I would speak with you.'

'Now then,' Gardner said happily when he had placed his bony rump on one of the stones, 'what might you have to say to an old priest, who knows for a fact that the English are the good Lord's least favourite creations?'

Stryker went to take the stone opposite, but his long scabbard made sitting difficult. He removed it and, realizing he had not thought to inspect the sword since the fight, drew the double-edged blade. 'I would offer you my thanks.'

'Funny way to thank a man,' Gardner replied, blue eyes transfixed by the darkly stained steel. 'A fine beast, if ever I saw one.'

Stryker discovered a perverse pleasure in unsettling the loud-mouthed old man, and he found it hard to stifle a smile. 'A gift from the Queen.'

Gardner ran his gaze over the rutted blade, the ornate basket hilt and the heavy pommel set with a huge red garnet. 'Fit for a king.' He looked up finally. 'You would thank me?'

Stryker nodded. 'For forewarning us of Wild's intention to attack.' He thought of the gorse faggots that had proved so vital. 'And giving us the means to fight him off.'

'No matter,' Gardner shrugged.

'And secondly,' Stryker went on, running a finger along one of the pockmarked edges of his sword.

'Secondly?'

'I would ask you what it is you're doing here.'

'I live here, boy, have I not already told you?' The old man glanced heavenward. 'Are his ears made entirely of cloth, Lord?'

Stryker abandoned his inspection of the blade and stared into Gardner's weather-beaten face. 'What are you doing here now? Why did you come to us yesterday?'

Gardner smiled wryly. 'I was having a little peek at you fellows, and some of your men in red surrounded me.'

'You said before that you let Skellen capture you.'

'Aye, well. I wanted to see who it was that had evicted me from old Seek Wisdom's hill.' He scratched at some unseen parasite within the filthy beard at his chin. 'I helped you because you looked like you needed it. You'd have been annihilated without me, boy, and I couldn't live with that.'

'Why? You're hardly for the King.'

'No, but I'm hardly for the Parliament either, boy. Old Seek Wisdom won't care a rat's ballock which side wins this war, long as I'm left alone, but you were kind to me. I repaid the kindness.'

Stryker drove the point of his sword into the earth between his tall boots and leant forward, resting his chin on the pommel. 'Seek Wisdom and Fear the Lord,' he mused, 'what kind of name is that?'

'A good, Christian name,' Gardner retorted sharply, before offering a sly wink. 'And one not too far removed from your own first name, I'd guess, *Stryker*.'

That was a shrewd thrust, Stryker had to concede, and the corners of his mouth rose in a sardonic smile. 'You're not so mad.'

'Mad?' Gardner glared at the white smears of cloud crowning distant tors. 'Mad he calls me, God.'

'Seek Wisdom,' Stryker prompted evenly.

Gardner let his gaze drift back to the soldier. 'It is a hard existence out here, boy. Bleak and unforgiving. If a man may not converse – with his creator, or the moor, or the hills – then he truly sinks into madness.'

Stryker watched the former priest for a minute or so. Watched his reptilian tongue flicker across cracked lips, watched spindly fingers fiddle with the strands of his grime-ingrained beard, and stole a glance at the red-raw toes of his naked feet. Stryker knew Gardner was not insane, for he read intelligence in those wide, unblinking eyes. Indeed, Gardner had often spoken with a presence of mind that belied his frantic demeanour. Yet somehow he had been reduced to this waif. This shadow of a man. 'Laud did this to you?'

Gardner nodded, a staccato gesture putting Stryker in mind of a woodpecker. 'And his lackeys, aye. So I have hidden myself away on the moor these past years. Not many live hereabouts, Captain, and those who do tend to steer a wide berth. I have grown accustomed to it.'

Stryker straightened, leaving the sword jutting vertically from the soil, the hilt quivering gently. He took off his hat, rearranged the dishevelled feathers, and propped it on the rock at his side. Then he took the black ribbon from his blacker hair and ran his fingers roughly across his scalp, shaking out the soot-clogged knots. 'It must be difficult, nevertheless. Nothing could be farther from the clergy.'

Gardner's mouth cracked open in a smile that brandished some of the most decayed gums he had ever seen. 'Oh, you'd be surprised, my boy. The priesthood gave me a life of prayer, contemplation, and fasting, and so does this!' His grin broadened. 'Though the fasting is generally not of my choice!'

'You still pray?'

'Aye, why wouldn't I?'

'Forgive me, Seek Wisdom, but you do not sound like a priest.'

Gardner cackled. 'Do not let my occasional Celtic oath fool you, boy.'

Stryker was still unconvinced. 'You keep your faith? After all that's happened?'

Gardner tapped the side of his pointed nose. 'Ah, now there speaks a damaged man. Your faith took flight long ago, yes?'

'Well, I—' Stryker hesitated.

'Ah, fret not, boy,' intervened the Welshman cheerfully, slapping Stryker on the shoulder. 'I'm not one o' your Banbury hot-gospellers, about to stick a finger in your face and cry heretic.'

Not that the old man's condemnation would have been a problem, reflected Stryker, up here on an isolated hill in the middle of a vast wildness, but admitting a crisis of belief was still something that did not come easily to him. Such confessions were dangerous affairs, and he had long since decided to keep his thoughts on the matter hidden. In public he would bow his head if a prayer was spoken, or nod obediently when the regimental preachers brewed up a rant, for to articulate his inner feelings would be tantamount to suicide.

'I believed once,' Stryker replied tentatively, 'but I suppose life has steadily chipped it away.' In actuality, he had always regarded religion with a degree of scepticism. The Roman church seemed all too elaborate and ritualistic. A faith where mysticism and obfuscation were wielded as tools to awe and confuse. Conversely, Protestantism, especially the increasingly powerful Puritan element, appeared a dour and joyless business. A system designed to drive any last vestige of happiness from the human soul. Both sides of the spectrum, it seemed to Stryker, were intent on one thing: keeping the common man obedient.

'You hear that, God?' Gardner asked the sky. 'Chipped away, he says! Ever heard such buffle-brained swine slop?'

Stryker sighed heavily. 'You cannot begin to imagine what I've seen. What I've witnessed.'

'Half of what everyone else sees, I'd wager,' Gardner replied with a quick wink.

Stryker ignored the impish barb. 'In the Low Countries death was an everyday thing.'

Gardner shrugged. 'War, disease, it was ever thus, boy.'

'More than that,' Stryker shook his head, staring directly at his sword, long buried images suddenly swirling in his mind. 'More than war. There was a cruelty I have seen nowhere else.' He had witnessed a good deal of barbarity in England this last year, clambered across bodies, waded through red-stained rivers, seen men hacked, sliced, hanged, and shot to pieces. But nothing had come remotely close to the horrors of Germany. 'A depravity and a—an evil that showed me once and for all that the world is—'

'Is?'

Stryker lifted his head, fixing his grey eye on Gardner. 'Godless.'

'But you are a man,' Gardner replied, his tone uncharacteristically soft. 'You see a rich, pink horizon. The stars on a clear night. You cannot believe it is all one giant accident. It is the will of the Lord, boy.'

Stryker snorted a short burst of mirthless laughter. 'I have also seen men mutilate one another for sport.' He leaned further forward. 'Rape for pleasure, Seek Wisdom. Massacre for God.' At once, Stryker's right hand darted out, snatching the sword from its earthy scabbard and casting his eye across the steel. 'You're right. There are many wondrous things in this world. Things I cannot readily explain. But I find it hard to believe in the God you speak of – a God of love – when His creation is so drenched in wickedness.'

'But, Captain—'

Stryker was glaring now, and he knew he would look a fearsome sight, but he could not, *would* not relent. 'Were you at Magdeburg?'

Gardner shook his head mutely.

Stryker knew the memory of that doomed city would never leave him. 'I was. Caught up in that damned siege. Trapped inside for near six months, half starved. And then they came.'

Gardner's wild blue eyes had ceased their habitual darting. 'The Imperial troops?'

'Aye.' Stryker wondered if his face reflected the severity of his mood. 'They were mad, frantic-eyed bastards.'

'Like me?' The Welshman's lips twitched at the corners.

'No,' was all Stryker could think to say.

'Famished too, boy, I should wager.'

Stryker nodded. 'Plundered the place, butchered everyone – every*thing* – they saw, and burnt it to the ground.' He chose not to reveal how he still sometimes woke during the darkest nights hearing the screams. 'The stench of scorched flesh never leaves my cursed nostrils.'

Gardner waited a while, waiting as Stryker's thoughts

dallied far from this Devon hillside. 'I heard the tales,' he ventured at last. 'They said twenty thousand souls.'

'More,' Stryker replied grimly. 'So many more than that. Little children. Carved up and tossed in the Elbe. If that river is still poisoned to this day, I would not be surprised.' This time the former priest did not respond. He let his gaze glide beyond Stryker's shoulder, to the horizon of heath, forest, and tor. 'The world is decaying,' Stryker went on remorselessly. 'A blood-drenched mess. If that is the will of your God, then I can live without Him.'

Seek Wisdom and Fear the Lord Gardner took his long beard in both hands and smoothed it down, twisting the tip into a sharp, greasy point at his sternum. 'It is not God who wills these things, Stryker.'

Stryker laughed, a deliberately harsh sound, like the rasp of an iron file. 'Ah, free will!'

'Of course.'

'How many times have I heard those two little words explain away the world's evils?'

'I do not know, boy.'

'More than I care to count, that's for damned certain.'

'Then what do you believe?' Gardner asked calmly, in a tone that Stryker could finally associate with a man who must once have ministered to scores of souls. 'In what do you put your trust?'

'I believe what my ears and nose and eye report.' Stryker turned his face to look up at the tor. His redcoats milled about on the flat, granite-cluttered crest, honing blades, repairing clothes or simply resting after a night of such trauma. 'I trust those men up there,' he said, before pointing a finger at his own chest, 'and this man here. And this.'

Gardner nodded as Stryker tapped the tip of his long

sword against the stone beneath his backside. 'Well I hope your trust is not misplaced, boy, for I'd wager it'll soon be tested again.'

'Oh?'

The old man's eyes drifted to a point beyond Stryker's shoulder, and Stryker twisted his neck to gaze down upon the big barn that rose like an ominous grey storm cloud from the trees to the north-west. There was movement all around the squat building, men and horses, but this was not the usual evolutions practised by Wild's harquebusiers. Something was different this time.

Stryker squinted, forcing the detail to sharpen. And then it hit him, and he was on his feet shouting up at the men on the tor, roaring orders to any within earshot. Because the men he saw, though mounted, wore coats of brown rather than steel plates and helmets, giving them the appearance of mounted infantrymen. Which meant they were dragoons.

'Sir?' It was Sergeant Skellen, cantering awkwardly down the slope, long limbs jarring on the treacherous gradient.

Stryker thrust his sword towards the north-west. 'Look to the barn, Will. The bastard's got dragooners.'

Skellen stared at the distant figures, screwed up his leathery face, then hissed the filthiest curse he could think of.

After all they had been through. All the courage they had shown to turn back the enemy tide in the hell of the previous night's fight, it was all for nothing. Because Wild had been reinforced.

Colonel Gabriel Wild was angry. Furious.

He had been humiliated yet again by the ugly infantryman who had become the object of his vengeance. The
plan to send nearly all his men against a single point on
the hill, overwhelming the enemy and reaching the top
under cover of darkness, had failed dramatically and
bloodily. Somehow Stryker had found blazing faggots to
illuminate the attackers, and then his peasant musketeers
had gone to work.

And yet that terrible defeat was not the hottest spark to
his current rage. That dubious honour was reserved for
the column of horsemen that now cantered down from
the hills, mustering noisily in the barn's courtyard.

'This is it?' Wild snarled as he strode out to meet the
newcomers. 'This is all that bastard sends?' He spat on
the hoof-churned mud. 'Goddamned dragooners?'

The lead dragoon, a sour-faced fellow of sharp nose,
bloodshot eyes, and a thin-lipped mouth that seemed
perpetually pursed, lifted his wide-brimmed hat in salute.
'Compliments o' Major-General Collings, sir.'

Wild felt himself redden. 'Unless you are a fucking
general yourself, sir, I suggest you get off that tumbledown
nag and address me properly!'

The dragoon commander did as he was told. 'Beggin'
your pardon, Colonel, sir. Name's Welch. Cap'n out o'
Chudleigh's force.'

'That errant knave James?'

Welch shook his head, pinched face twitching slightly
at the left cheek. 'No, sir. Sir George Chudleigh, his father.'

'Little better,' Wild sneered. He examined the new arrivals. They looked for all the world as though they had been freshly plucked from one of Stamford's regiments of foot. Short brown coats, grey breeches, and brown montero caps, firelocks slung at their backs and bandoliers at their chests. Indeed, the only concession to their real trade, save the tu'penny mares beneath them, were their long riding boots.

They were the usual sort, he mused. The army's expendable ragamuffins. Dragoons, he had always felt, were an admirable experiment gone wrong. A perfectly reasonable attempt to deploy infantrymen across battlefields quickly, their ranks, more often than not, ended up populated by those men not fit to stand in a tertio of pike and not skilled enough to control a proper horse. 'How many do you have?'

'Sixty, sir,' Welch said sheepishly as he handed his reins to a subordinate.

It was all Wild could do to stop himself throttling the dragoon where he stood. 'Sixty? Christ on His cross, but Collings mocks me!' He glared at one of his own officers. 'Mocks me!'

Now Wild did make for the dragoon captain, but instead of throttling Welch, he took the skeletal officer by the scruff of his brown coat. Welch instinctively resisted, but Wild, bigger and stronger than the weasel-faced officer, lifted him on to the tips of his toes and dragged him round the corner of the barn, only halting when they could see the high tor that loomed over the quicksilver river.

'How am I supposed to dig out that whoreson?' Wild snarled. 'How, by Christ, would the all powerful Erasmus Collings have me chase that one-eyed Pope's turd from his lair, when all he sends is a detachment of fucking dragoon-ers? Tell me, damn you!' He let go suddenly, thrusting Welch to the seat of his breeches. The dragoon scrambled backwards desperately, terrified of the big, metal-plated cavalryman and his volcanic fury.

'Firstly,' came a new voice at Wild's back, 'he would ask you how you have so far failed in your task, when you have had ample time and resource with which to execute it.'

Wild forgot the sprawling dragoon and turned to see a face he could not immediately place, but one that was familiar nevertheless. The man, mounted atop a piebald beast, was swathed in a long, hooded cloak the blackness of coal. He had a remarkably sharp chin, shaven utterly clean, a prominent hooked nose, huge teeth that seemed too large for his mouth, and, when he drew back the cowl, he exposed shoulder-length auburn hair, speckled with dashes of grey.

'Hogg,' Wild said eventually.

'And secondly,' witch-finder Osmyn Hogg announced in a steady, confident voice that seemed to bore into Wild's skull, 'he would tell you that you no longer require force of arms.'

Wild looked up at Hogg incredulously. 'Oh?'

Hogg slid down from his saddle, boots sucked by the cloying mud, and took a long, gnarled stick that was almost as black as tar from a strap at his saddle. He used it to limp uneasily to where Wild stood. 'Now, Colonel, you have *me*.'

The barn was a musty old structure that had not been put to use for anything agrarian in a good deal of time. It was windowless, had a single, large door on its north-western side, and a high, rotten-beamed ceiling. The floor was made of compacted earth, carpeted in an ancient layer of droppings and feathers donated by the generations of cawing birds that roosted in the lofty roof. That filth had been further deepened in recent days as the barn was employed to stable Colonel Gabriel Wild's horses.

Witch-finder Osmyn Hogg struggled not to curse as his boot sank into the mire. 'Charming.'

Wild was behind him. 'It is not the White Hart, I grant you, but we were fortunate to have found this place so far from the towns.'

Hogg wrinkled his long nose. 'No matter.'

'Is this truly all Collings sends me?' Wild asked abruptly, unwilling to let the matter of reinforcements drop. 'When I sent the message back to Okehampton, I requested a full troop of cavalry or at least a half-regiment of foot. Not these ragtag bloody dragooners.'

Hogg wanted to smile, not because Wild's request had been so swiftly denied, but because Major-General Collings had had the good sense to inform him that the colonel had successfully run his quarry to ground. 'It is as I have said, sir,' he replied, forcing his face to remain impassive, 'Stamford requires all available forces. Collings cannot spare any more men for your personal crusade.'

Wild's heavy jaw twitched as he ground his teeth. 'And the ordnance?'

Hogg could not help but smirk then, as the memory of Collings's caustic tirade leapt into his mind. Cannon to catch a single infantry company? Collings had been positively incandescent at the suggestion. 'I'm afraid the general did not feel your appeal worthy of artillery, Colonel.'

'A pox on that—'

'Hold, sir,' Hogg held up a staying hand. 'He did, however, dispatch a pair of falconets. They'll be here in a day or two.'

'A pair, you say?' The falconet was only a small field-piece, the type used against personnel rather than for siege work, but a brace would be a fearsome thing for the tor's defenders to face at such close range.

Hogg smiled urbanely. 'I thought that might lift the spirits somewhat. They might not have the range or calibre to blast that tor to smithereens, but I'd wager you could shower the stubborn malignants in lead well enough.' He turned back to the barn's gloomy interior, leaving Wild to ponder his words. 'Now, shall we get to work?'

'Where is prisoner?' A new, taciturn voice broke between them.

Colonel Wild, a head taller than both of his guests, glared down at Hogg's corpulent assistant. The Spaniard's hard, dark eyes were belligerent, his fleshy face coated in sweat, his lank hair oily, and the cavalryman's own expression seemed to tighten. 'Mind your tongue, Diego.'

José Ventura crinkled his upper lip in a gesture that demonstrated his evident lack of concern. 'We sent from Collings. Let us work.'

'Why, you insolent churl! I'll—'

'Hold, Colonel!' Hogg interjected quickly, palms raised in an effort to pacify the bigger man's bubbling indignation. 'Hold, sir, please. José meant nothing by it, I assure you. It is a matter of language, only. Of translation.'

Wild still glared at the Spaniard, his throat emitting a low growl.

'Now, please, I ask you,' Hogg continued, seizing his opportunity, 'may we proceed?'

Without hesitation, he led the small party under the worm-eaten lintel and into the barn. There was no fire inside, lest the dry beams catch a deadly ember, but it was still stifling, and he removed his thick cloak, handing it to Ventura.

Wild stepped to his side, pointed to one of the room's far corners. 'Over there.'

Hogg led the way, limping tentatively across the slimy floor towards the corner in question, stick sliding hazardously in the mulch. He could see nothing at first, the murkiness positively oppressive in such a large space with only the doors left open for daylight, but with each faltering pace the irregular lines of a man began to resolve.

'One of my patrols took him a couple of miles out,' Wild explained. 'Refuses to speak.'

'Have you—' Hogg took a lingering breath, '—encouraged him?'

Wild shook his head. 'Not yet.'

'Then how do you know he is one of them?'

'Because he had no provisions,' Wild replied. 'No supplies, no snapsack, nothing. He is either a messenger or a deserter.'

Hogg was unconvinced. 'Could he not have come from elsewhere? One of the villages, perhaps?'

'No.'

'How can you be so sure, Colonel?'

'Because he was riding one of my goddamned horses, Mister Hogg.'

Hogg stepped closer to examine the captive, who was slumped against the rough stone wall, arms wrapped tight about his knees. He might have been a tall man, though it was hard to tell in his current predicament, and had long, tightly curled hair that was nearly as dark as Ventura's, a thin moustache, and a small, fashionably sharp beard. He had been handled roughly, Hogg supposed, for his slashed doublet, once an extremely fine garment, had become dishevelled, and the huge falling band collar was now more brown than white.

'What is your name, sir?' Hogg said, his voice echoing deeply around the cavernous barn.

The captive looked up, revealing a right eye that was swollen and deeply blackened. 'No business of yours, crook-leg.'

Hogg sighed heavily, ignoring Wild, whose lips, he noticed, twitched slightly. 'I have been sent here by the Parliament, sir. Upon matters of the utmost gravity.'

The battered man offered a weak shrug and slouched, dropping his gaze to the floor. 'I am of no consequence to Parliament.'

Hogg leaned in, lifting the walking stick so that its filthy tip touched the underside of the prisoner's chin, and gently eased the man's narrow face upwards again. 'Oh, but you are, sir. You mistake me, for I am no military man. I transcend such petty ideals.'

That hooked the prisoner's attention, for the lids of his eyes seemed to widen a touch, despite the swelling.

'I have matters to attend,' Colonel Wild muttered abruptly.

Hogg let the captive's head drop again, glancing up at the cavalryman. He nodded, understanding that this business was not to every man's taste. 'Ventura and I will take care of proceedings, sir, have no fear.'

Wild frowned. 'You are certain that your *methods*,' the last word was almost spat out as though the officer's mouth had filled with acid, 'can smoke Stryker from his den?'

Hogg's heart beat faster at the mention of the name. He nodded, finding himself unable to speak, and simply watched Wild as he paced purposefully out of the barn.

'Now, you sin-drenched leech,' José Ventura's voice boomed in the darkness. 'I would see about your marks.' The Spaniard seized the cowering prisoner by the wrists and hauled him to his feet. The captive, who was, as Hogg had imagined, fairly tall, seemed to swoon, but Ventura left a pudgy hand on his sleeve so as to keep him still.

'M—marks?' the man said, sudden panic helping him find his tongue.

'*Si*,' Ventura grunted. 'All witches have marks.' Before the man could resist, the fat Spaniard slammed a meaty fist into his belly, punching the man double. Even as his victim desperately dragged air into his lungs in ragged gasps, Ventura drew a small knife and whipped it efficiently across the stitches at the sides of the expensive doublet. At first it seemed merely that the garment had been given more fashionable slashes, for Ventura's handiwork served only to expose several new smears of red lining beneath the blue wool. But, with a hearty wrench from his thick fingers, he soon tore it to frayed shreds, ripping it clear of the reeling prisoner's willowy frame. The man yelped, more from shock than any pain, but Ventura slapped him hard. 'Shut mouth, devil turd!'

The baggy shirt beneath was off in a trice, leaving the man's upper body exposed, his pale skin almost luminescent in the barn's murkiness.

Osmyn Hogg sidled up to the half-naked captive as

Ventura forced the winded man to straighten. 'Name,' he said quietly.

Something in Hogg's tone must have struck a chord, because the man's shoulders suddenly sagged in acquiescence. 'Broom.'

'Well now, Mister Broom, that wasn't so difficult, was it? Please answer me this; what is your relationship to a man named Stryker?'

Broom peered into his face. 'Who are you?'

'My name is Osmyn Hogg, Mister Broom.' Hogg casually examined the polished knot at the top of his stick. 'And I am a catcher of witches and warlocks.'

Broom's angular jaw fell open. 'But I am no witch, sir.' He lifted his arms out straight. 'See? Inspect me, sirs, and witness a body devoid of marks.'

'I see that,' replied Hogg, glancing up from his stick. He shot a well-exercised look at Ventura, and the Spaniard immediately produced a long, needle-like implement from his belt. 'But Satan is a sly fiend. A foe never to be underestimated. He has ways to hide his marks. To conceal the teats that would surely betray his followers.'

Ventura stepped forward, brandishing the needle before him, the wan light from the doorway glinting at its keen point. Broom began to shake, his legs losing their solidity, and a shrill mewing sound escaped from his throat.

In the more contemplative moments since leaving Okehampton, Osmyn Hogg had wondered at the morality of this task, at Collings's idea that a small amount of torture and a hanging or two might expedite an end to the stand-off. He knew the task had nothing to do with witchcraft and everything to do with instilling fear into the tor's defenders. Ordinarily, of course, the scheme would have been anathema to him, but this time things were different. This time his prize would not be spiritual, but in the shape of a man. The man he despised more than any other. He had been forced to agree to ply his trade on behalf of the Parliamentarians in return for riding into the moor with the fresh dragoons. It was, he reflected, the only way to get to Stryker. And it was eminently worth the trade.

'Pricking is a difficult skill to acquire,' Hogg intoned slowly. 'One must thrust the point deep,' he said, aping the described motions in the air with his stick, 'twisting it as hard as is possible, levering flesh from muscle, and muscle from bone. But eventually the mark will be exposed.'

'Eventually,' Ventura repeated the word with chilling relish.

Hogg planted the stick hard into the stinking bird shit and leaned forward to press his point. 'You will tell me what I wish to know, sir, or Señor Ventura will prick the very skin from your skeleton. Do you understand?'

Broom took a rearward step, slipped, and slammed into the wall behind. His legs shook, his eyes seemed like glass sceptres in the dark, and yet still he shook his head defiantly.

Witch-finder Osmyn Hogg shrugged. 'Be about your business, José.'

CHAPTER 11

It was an hour past midnight, and Captain Lancelot Forrester was ready to turn in. It had been a hard day's march, made slow by the interminable terrain and the word, from a local drover, that a reasonable Roundhead force was stalking the area east of Tavistock. He had seen nothing during the day, and wondered whether the frightened man had cooked the tale somewhat, assuming the juicier – and, by turns, more useful – his information, the less hostile the soldiers would be. Nevertheless, it had been a painstaking march west, made all the more sullen by the failure of their task. At least, Forrester thought as he ground grubby palms into tired, stinging eyes, they had found the tavern, so that a decent repast could be enjoyed prior to their journey's final leg.

Forrester placed his hands on the table and pushed himself up off the creaking bench. His head swooned a little, though that was down to exhaustion rather than drink, for he had only imbibed small ale this evening. The reports regarding enemy activity had disquieted him, and he had taken it upon himself to stay up late in order to keep an eye over the building. His men, however, had been allowed free rein. They had first shared a tremendous meal that earned many a hearty handshake for the landlord and his goodwife. Rose-watered loaves of soft manchet had been torn eagerly, shared about the grasping, grit-nailed fingers. Heavenly salted gammon had followed, with barley pottage and even a fresh batch of custard pies. In short, it had been a veritable feast, and the men had decamped in boosted spirits to smoke, dice, or regale their comrades with ribald stories at the big hearth.

Now, though, most were enjoying their dreams of women and home. The tavern was not big enough to support so many bodies, so they huddled in corners, slumped against the rough-hewn walls, reclined on and under the sticky tables, and snored at the tobacco-blackened ceiling beams.

'Into Cornwall 'pon the morrow.'

Forrester peered through bleary eyes at Anthony Payne, who stood hunched in a doorway leading to one of the tavern's rear rooms. 'Aye, and a good thing too. It is not safe in this cursed county.'

'For king's men, leastwise.' Payne stepped through to the taproom, forced to stoop to clear the lintel. He went to the counter, peered into several large blackjacks, and lifted the first one he found to be full. 'Let us drink to Cornwall, Captain.'

Forrester rubbed his stinging eyes, and smiled. 'To Kernow.'

The musket shot seemed to shake the very timbers of the sleepy tavern. Its ball, fired from somewhere out on the street, blasted through the window shutters in a spray of splinters that had Forrester flattening himself face down on the table. When he glanced up, he saw Payne

236

still standing where he was, but now his meaty paw was empty and his head and chest glistened with ale. The blackjack, it seemed, had taken the bullet's ire, plucked clean from Payne's grasp to twirl away to the wall beyond.

'*Down*!' Forrester barked.

Payne ignored him, running nimbly over to the inn's main entrance with a speed that belied his colossal frame. He wrenched the heavy door back quickly, snatching a risky look outside, before slamming it shut again. 'Foot, sir, judgin' by the matches.'

'Numbers?'

'Least a score, I'd guess. P'raps more.'

'Whose are they?'

'Can't tell. Greycoats, by the looks of them.'

'Ensign?'

'Can't see one.'

'God's wounds, man, where are the damned sentries?'

The men of Captain Forrester's Company of Foot were stirring now, heaving themselves upright, grinding the dregs of sleep from their eyes with grimy fingers. More shots came, four or five in quick succession, cracking against the stone front wall. Another came through the thin wood of a shutter, annihilating a pewter jug that perched on a shelf above the counter.

Forrester crouched as low as he could and scuttled across to the opposite corner of the tavern. Here, farthest away from the dangerous embers of the hearth, were half a dozen muskets, loaded for emergencies and ready to kill. He snatched two up, tossing them – stock-down so that the ball stayed against its charge – to the nearest men, then turned back to take the next pair, allocating them as well. The final two he kept, dashing to the front wall, flattening his back against the cold stone to the side of a shutter. Further along the wall Anthony Payne hefted a stout length of timber into place to bar the door and shuffled along to take position on the opposite side of Forrester's window. The captain handed one of his muskets to Payne and the big man immediately used its heavy stock to smash the shutter to kindling. An incoming shot cracked the stone a yard or so away, and they both shrank back, but a second later Forrester thrust his weapon through the remnants of the splintered wood and pulled the trigger. Everything immediately vanished in the powder smoke, the familiar stink of sulphur filling his nostrils. He had no hope of telling if his shot flew true, but at least the men in the tavern were returning fire, forcing their attackers to think twice before approaching.

'Who are they, for Christ's sake?' Forrester hissed, glaring up at Payne.

Payne bent down to shove his own firearm through the hole, flicked back its pan cover and sent the leaden ball racing through the darkness beyond. 'Buggered if I know, sir. Must've jumped the pickets.'

'Clearly,' Forrester muttered laconically as he feverishly reloaded his musket with the spare powder and shot he kept in his snapsack. To his relief the shots coming from outside seemed to be steadily more sporadic, a symptom of the attackers' sudden need to find shelter, compounded by the fact that they now had to reload their own weapons. 'One hopes they ain't ours!'

'Parliament!' a lone voice rose up from the lull outside. It was shrill, pitched high, and Forrester wondered if they had been engaged by a force of women and children. 'Jesus Christ and the Parliament!'

'There's your answer, sir,' Payne said with a twitch of a smile. 'I think we're free to shoot them.'

Even before the Cornishman had closed his mouth, the first of Forrester's redcoats began to give fire. They ran quickly to the tavern wall, either side of the twin commanders, and smashed through any window they could find, jabbing muskets out into the chill night air. The crash of so many shots let loose in such a confined space was near deafening, and Forrester could barely hear his own voice as he bellowed to the rest of his men – those bigger, stronger street brawlers who specialized in hefting the great pikes into battle – to exit the tavern via the rear door and make haste round the building's flanks. It was dangerous, for they did not know how many enemy guns waited for them out in the darkness, but to stay cooped inside the tavern was to invite the Roundheads to simply take their time wearing the Royalist defenders down, whittling their numbers and gnawing their morale. They were stuck here, trapped and forced on to the back foot, and all Forrester's instincts told him that it was a bad place to be.

A bullet found its way through Forrester's window, hissing past his nose to smack into the wall beyond. His musket was finally ready to fire, and he thrust it out to face the enemy and jerked back the trigger, only vaguely taking aim at the grey figures some twenty or so paces away. Payne, still at his side, had reloaded too, and his shot immediately followed the captain's. More musketry crackled all along the tavern's face as his redcoats took turns at pumping lead out into the night, hoping against hope that some of their shots would find flesh.

'That's it, my lads!' Forrester screamed, voice straining above the din of gunfire.

Another bullet somehow found its way through one of the windows further along the wall. It sped whip-quick through the room, cuffing the side of a musketeer's head, taking a big chunk of skull as it went. The man brayed like a gut-stabbed ox, reeled backwards into one of the tables, and collapsed on to his back. Forrester ran back into the room, dropped his weapon and knelt beside the man. 'Johnny,' he said gently. 'I'm here, Johnny.'

The musketeer peered up at him through eyes that seemed to have turned to glass. 'Mammy?'

'Aye, lad, it's your mammy,' Forrester replied, a lump forming tight in his throat. 'I'm here for you.'

A single tear welled at the wounded man's right eye, fattening until the lids could not contain it, and tumbling down to his ear. 'Is it bad, Mammy?'

Forrester looked at the musketeer's damaged head. A huge, ragged, hair-fringed hole had been torn open by the passing ball. A wide, gaping mouth of glistening blood and bone, speckled with gelatinous grey lumps beyond. 'No, son,' he murmured. 'You'll be right as rain.'

The musketeer lurched then, his torso curving upwards as though God Himself pulled at his sternum. He opened his mouth wide, lips peeled back in a grotesque mask of agony, preparing to let loose the worst cry of pain a man could muster. But no sound came. Johnny's body suddenly sagged, thumping back on to the hard table, and all that seeped from his mouth was a pathetic stream of air.

Forrester ran his blackened fingers over Johnny's eyes and retrieved his empty musket, returning rapidly to the window.

'Ready, sir!' a shout came from outside.

Forrester recognized the voice instantly and risked

240

leaning through the window. One of Payne's cannon-barrel arms shot out to haul him back, but not before the captain had bellowed, 'Now, Sergeant Briggs!'

A great cheer went up outside, growing from a breeze to a gale in less than a heartbeat, and the enemy musketry suddenly ceased. Still Forrester could not make out any detail in the Roundhead ranks, but he could well imagine the scene that was unfolding out in the street. Orders would be barked by frantic corporals and sergeants, muzzles would be swivelling away from the tavern to face this new and unexpected threat, and those whose muskets were empty would be desperately reversing the heavy weapons to brandish their wooden butt ends like clubs. Because Forrester's pikemen would soon be upon them.

'Reload!' Forrester bellowed, desperate to be ready in support of his pikemen. 'Reload, damn your sluggish hides!'

Without the incoming fire, the Royalists inside the tavern felt free to hang their heads out of the windows, craning necks to the left in order to see the charge of their pike-wielding comrades. Those comrades emerged out of the gloom like a huge leviathan. A fearsome creature of flesh and muscle, topped with glinting scales and rows of lethal spines. The red-coated monster snarled oaths to the black sky with its score of voices, and then, with its phalanx of ashen shafts levelled as one, it slammed into the Roundhead flank, sweeping men asunder like pebbles dashed by a wave.

Forrester, watching the sudden carnage from inside the tavern, ran across to the heavy door. 'Get that cursed thing open!'

Immediately Anthony Payne was there, prising the bar

from its slots as though it were nothing weightier than a dry bulrush. He tossed the chunky length of timber away and kicked the door wide open, Forrester and the musketeers swarming past him on both sides.

Outside, the air was murky with drifting smoke and the road was slick and treacherous. It had not rained, and Forrester wondered whether it was water that covered the turf or something altogether more sinister. He reached the first man, who, he could just about tell in the darkness, was kitted in a coat of dark grey, bandolier clattering at his breast. The Roundhead's face was shadowy, obscured by a thick beard that made the whites of his eyes glint all the more brightly. His teeth appeared then, exposed by a maniacal grin that told of a man ready to kill or die, and Forrester saw that the musket he held was pointing at his chest, muzzle out.

The shot burst forth. Forrester threw himself to the slippery ground, elbows crunching as he desperately fought to keep hold of his own weapon, empty though it was, and his heart felt as though it would surely explode as the racing ball whistled across the top of his head, snatching his hat clean away.

Ignoring the sudden wetness springing about his burning scalp, Forrester scrambled to his feet. The Parliamentarian, he guessed, would still be squinting through his own gun smoke, eagerly awaiting the prone form that would tell him of a successful shot. There was no room for delay, and he stepped into the roiling cloud, screwing his eyes into slits so that they would not water, reversing his musket as he went. Even before he could see his opponent, the Royalist captain slapped the brutish stock upwards in a speculative blow and sure enough the heavy wooden club crunched into something solid and metallic. It was the greycoat's black muzzle, wisps still meandering from its gaping mouth, and its owner staggered backwards in shock. Forrester gave him no respite, bringing the stock to bear once more, hammering it down against the bearded man's own musket with as much force as he could muster. The weapon jolted free of the Roundhead's numb-fingered grip, clattering on to the bloody ground between them, and Forrester stepped in again, merciless, ruthless, jabbing the butt end into the Roundhead's face. Lips and teeth smashed together, blood sprayed darkly over the stricken man's beard and neck, and Forrester tossed the musket at him, one last barrage to keep him on the back foot. As the greycoat held up clawing hands to protect his face, Forrester whipped the long dirk from his belt and stepped in one final time. The musketeer wore no plate or buff leather, and the blade slipped easily through the wool of his coat. Forrester felt fleeting resistance as the honed point skittered off a rib, but he drove it onwards, forcing it through the flesh and into the chest beyond.

Forrester stepped past his victim's body as it went to its knees, air gushing from the holed lung like giant bellows, and waded into the chaos. He still had no clue who the greycoats were. It was enough that they were the enemy. What mattered was their strength. It had been a surprise that the attackers had not surrounded the tavern and approached from all sides. They seemed to have simply disposed of his pickets and launched into a frontal assault. Perhaps that was reasonable, he considered, given the logical assumption that the Royalists were sleeping and unprepared, but now the plan had tumbled like a blazing thatch. Forrester had a sizeable force, and the greycoats had clearly hoped to pin them inside the building. But now the vengeful redcoats were out in the open, bringing their charging pikes to bear against ill-armoured musketeers, and the attacking force was shattering like a glass goblet.

Still, though, the Parliament men were putting up quite a fight, and Forrester was keen to finish it before he took any more casualties. He moved further into the fray, ducking a scything blow from a singing tuck and driving his dirk deep into his assailant's belly. The man, a craggy-faced fellow of around forty, doubled over, clasping hands to his opened guts, desperate to hold in the slippery entrails as they snaked between his fingers. Forrester kicked him hard on the knee-cap, sending the greycoat to the rapidly blood-washed ground, and strode on, seeking the man whose death he knew would end this fight.

There he was; a slight figure, grey coat, glinting gorget and broad tawny sash giving his status away despite the night's shroud. Forrester wiped the dirk on his sleeve, sheathed it, and drew his sword, revelling in the extra range and power it brought. He moved on through the melee, eyes never leaving the Parliamentarian officer, but a heavy-set sergeant with short arms, stumpy legs, and no neck stepped into his way, brandishing a formidable halberd.

The sergeant brought the weapon – a full foot taller than himself – crashing down in a blow that might have cleaved a bullock in two. Forrester dodged the lethal blade, feeling the air cut like butter at his right shoulder, and brought his sword across in a horizontal riposte. But as he planted his boot in the soft terrain it lost traction, slipping wildly. He slewed forward, balance all but vanished, and took a knee, stabbing at the sergeant's ankles in a puny stroke that simply glanced off the man's leather-clad ankle. The sergeant crowed, spittle showering Forrester's bare, bleeding head, and raised the halberd once more.

It was then that the night went from dark to utter pitch. For a moment Forrester wondered if the fatal blow had come and he was already heading to the afterlife, but a deep, rumbling snarl, like the lions he had once seen at the Tower Menagerie, rushed into his ears and shook his ribcage. He stared upwards at the black figure that had obscured the victorious sergeant, only to see a face he knew well. Anthony Payne had swatted the sergeant's halberd aside with the butt end of a musket and smashed his gigantic fist into the grinning Roundhead's face. It seemed to Forrester as though the sergeant's features had been wiped clean from his skull, such was the devastation left in the fist's wake, and the battered man disappeared from view.

Payne stooped to help Forrester to his feet, and the captain felt a surge of relief; victory was assured, for a real, breathing, terrifying giant fought at his side. In seconds the two men were a sword's length from the Parliamentarian commander. They were close enough now for Forrester to see that the officer was merely a stripling, a man certainly not beyond his teens and perhaps not a great distance into them. Now he understood why that first warning call had seemed so shrill, and, moreover, why the enemy had launched such a rash assault.

He levelled his blade, aiming its tip directly at the young man's throat. 'You are beaten, sir. Do you yield?'

The youngster's face scrunched in a defiant grimace. 'Never, sir! We shall never yield to base Cavalier rogues!'

Forrester almost laughed. He glanced at the sword that twitched in the Roundhead's gloved hand. 'Lay down your weapon, sir.'

'Never!'

'Christ, boy, do as you're damn well told!'

The tone of voice seemed to have more effect on the youngster than the martial odds now firmly stacked against his beleaguered men. It was as though, Forrester later reflected, the enemy officer were a naughty lad scolded by his tutor. 'I—I—'

Forrester waved his sword at the scene around them. 'Enough, sir. No more should die this night.'

GARDNER'S TOR, DARTMOOR, 4 MAY 1643

The tor's defenders had not slept. It was not the elements that kept them awake, for the breeze had been weak and the weather clement. Nor was it the impending threat of attack, for they knew Wild, though recently reinforced, would be compelled to spend time regrouping after his defeat. It had been the screams. The blood-freezing, bone-grating banshee wail of a man taken to – and beyond – what he could bear. A sound that would stay with them, seared on to the memory, for as long as they each lived. They did not know whose screams had torn the night apart, nor why such apparent horrors had been inflicted upon him, but they knew well enough from whence the sound came.

Stryker had watched the barn all night. The building, near a mile to the north and west, was obscured by the undulating terrain, the surrounding trees, and sheer distance, yet he had sat, perched on the very peak of a lone granite stack, and stared at it, guessing what terrors lay within. And then, just after dawn, he had noticed activity. It was impossible to tell what exactly was happening at first, but there were figures scuttling about the grey walls like so many ants at a rotten carcass, and his instincts told him the rising commotion meant trouble.

Now, two hours later, he still remained on his high vantage point, like a lookout in a ship's crow's nest, and watched the procession moving out on to the barren plain. There were twenty cavalrymen, or thereabouts. All plated in metal, all protected by shining helmets with articulated neck guards – the lobster tails – and decorated with flamboyant cormorant feathers. The small column were not bent on attack, he felt sure, for they walked their mounts with deliberate slowness, ambling from the tree line to the heath that would lead them south-eastward to the tor. Nevertheless, he had ordered his men to stand ready, taking up positions behind rock and gorse all the way down to the foot of the slope.

Once the Parliamentarians, snaking along a narrow track to avoid pot-holes, tangled brush, and treacherous bogs, were fully out in the open, Stryker was startled to realize that they were not alone. They were Wild's men right enough, for, aside from the telltale feathers, the head of the serpent had sprouted a black pennant that left no doubt as to the identity of their commander. And yet there were three new figures, two dressed in black, one in a doublet of red and white, mounted at the rear of the column.

Skellen and Barkworth were standing immediately below Stryker's stone platform. The tall sergeant spat a thick ball of phlegm between his boots. 'What they playin' at, sir?'

'I don't know,' Stryker replied cautiously, squinting at the oncoming force.

'What you wouldn't give for Dyott's telescope now, eh, sir?' Barkworth reflected.

Stryker nodded without looking down at the Scot. Sir Richard Dyott had been one of the Royalist notables trapped with Stryker and his men in Lichfield Cathedral Close during the siege the previous March. His telescope had been a true godsend, allowing them to foil a particularly dangerous ambush.

The red-coated ranks waited and watched for ten minutes more as the procession traipsed ever closer. Soon they were near enough for the whinnying and snorts of the horses to be audible from the very summit of the hill, and a little while later the Royalists could even hear the lead officer barking his orders. The horsemen eventually reached a crooked tree, wind-stripped and ancient, some hundred paces from the foremost of Stryker's musketeers, at which point the rider at the very head of the serpent called for his men to wheel round and form a long line running across the face of the tor. By the voice, the physique, and the bearing, Stryker knew that the officer was Colonel Wild himself.

'What the fuck are they about?' the company's shortest man, Simeon Barkworth, muttered in his croaking voice.

'My thoughts precisely,' Lieutenant Burton said as he came to stand beside the Scot.

'Summink to do wi' them cloaked buggers,' Skellen grunted from Barkworth's other side. 'I don't like the look of 'em.'

Nor did Stryker, his sense of unease building rapidly. 'They're not Wild's men.'

Burton adjusted his arm strap. 'Dragoons?'

Stryker glanced down at his lieutenant. 'In heavy cowls?'

'Does seem strange, but who else could they be?'

By way of an answer, one of the hooded riders lurched from the line. He walked his horse slowly across the flat ground, halting near the foot of the slope. He was well within range of Stryker's outermost muskets, and matches were given encouraging breath by their eager owners, though none would shoot without an order. The rider seemed to be relying on this, for he did not appear intimidated by the proximity of the weapons as he lifted a gloved hand to draw back his voluminous hood.

From his high stack, Stryker felt a strange feeling of familiarity as the man's face was finally exposed. It was not a particularly remarkable countenance; plain skin, dark eyes, hair falling straight to his shoulders. But that long nose, hooked like a beak, seemed oddly memorable.

'My name,' the cloaked rider shouted suddenly, addressing the tor, 'is Osmyn Hogg.'

More peculiar resonance, thought Stryker. The name meant nothing to him, but the powerful voice, and those huge, jutting teeth, seemed as familiar as the nose. He shook his head to rid himself of the disquiet, and drew breath to return the introduction. 'Stryker. Captain, Mowbray's Regiment of Foot.'

The man named Hogg tilted his head up to stare directly at Stryker. 'I know who you are, Satan's servant!'

For a moment, Stryker was utterly taken aback. 'A strange choice of words, sir,' he called back, 'for I know you not.'

'Oh, but you do!'

Stryker leaned over the edge of his stack to look at his senior officers. 'Have any of you met him before?' The resounding response was in the negative, and he turned back to Hogg. 'I think you have me mistook for another, sir.'

The beak-nosed man shook his head. 'Nay, sir. There has been no mistake.' Before Stryker could reply, he stood in his stirrups. 'Now, I command all here, in the name of the Lord Jehovah, to bear witness to His judgement!'

With that, Hogg took to his saddle again, wrenched on his mount's reins, and cantered back to the line. It was only then as Hogg rejoined his two companions that Stryker's eye fell upon the third figure in the trio. He had first presumed that man to be dressed in a white doublet striped with scarlet thread, but now, shockingly, he saw the truth. The third rider, slumped across his horse's neck, was not clothed from the waist up at all. The paleness was simply his own skin, showing white in the sunlight, and the red . . .

'Shite on a pole,' Sergeant Skellen droned suddenly. 'That poor bastard's been flayed alive.'

Stryker said nothing, for it needed no confirmation. They all saw the blood that had dried in long, vertical stripes all across the naked man's torso. It was dark, caked, and crusty, but it was blood without doubt.

'Well we know who did all that screaming,' Simeon Barkworth said.

'Aye,' Burton agreed grimly. 'I wonder who he is.'

The scream that went up then was almost as heart-shivering as the ones that had rent the previous night. High, shrill, agonized, grief-stricken. All eyes turned back to the tor's flat summit to catch sight of a woman, red-eyed, ashen-cheeked, and utterly beside herself. She screamed again, slumped to her knees, and buried her weeping head in Burton's chest when he ran to comfort her. The men waited, watched, no one daring to speak, until Burton turned back from her racking sobs and looked up at Stryker.

'Cecily recognized him immediately.'

Stryker frowned. 'Who?'

But the question needed no answer, for suddenly, gut-wrenchingly, he understood. The broken, tortured man down on the plain was Otilwell Broom.

'You're certain this will work?' Colonel Gabriel Wild said gruffly.

'Have faith, sir,' Hogg replied, jerking his chin at José Ventura in an indication that he should follow. 'After today, they will scuttle down from their hiding places like mice from a blazing thatch.'

Wild glowered, watching the corpulent Spaniard gather up the reins for both his horse and the one carrying Broom. 'I am not comfortable with this.' He leaned forward, saddle creaking beneath his rump. 'There are rules.'

Hogg paused, and gave a short sniff of derision. 'The *rules*,' he sneered, 'are that witches should be dealt with once confession is secured. Have we secured confession, señor?'

That last was addressed to Ventura, who nodded sagely. '*Si*.'

'There you have it, Colonel. A confession is all I need for this to be legal. You have failed to prise this man from his hill, and Major-General Collings requires your

251

strength for the army's push into Cornwall. To expedite the situation, you are therefore ordered to defer to my techniques.'

Wild straightened, plucked his gleaming helmet from his head, and ruffled the sweaty hair brushing his shoulders in sweaty clumps. The silver stripe shone in the sunlight. 'What's in this for you?'

Hogg frowned. 'Colonel?'

'You do not report to the Parliament. *Ergo*, you are no more obliged to obey Collings than those Christ-abandoned brigands up on the hill.'

'Your point?'

Wild drew his carbine from its snug holster, inspected the firing mechanism, and thrust it home. 'I understand why Collings would wish to employ your—*expertise*—to smoke the malignants from their nest, but why do you so readily acquiesce, when there are no witches here?'

Hogg turned away from Wild to stare with narrow eyes at the craggy, sun-dappled tor. 'Oh, but there are, Colonel. There most certainly are. Broom named his accomplices.'

'A man with one eye, his wench, and the halfling?' Wild asked incredulously. 'Easy targets for a man stabbed to near death.'

'Pricking is a legitimate device, Colonel,' Hogg retorted acidly. 'Besides, Stryker *is* evil. The others are irrelevant. If the rest must be sacrificed to expose the true devil amongst them, so be it. *He* is the one we want.' He shot Ventura a quick glance. 'Bring Mister Broom, José.'

Stryker watched with impotent rage as Hogg and the second cloaked figure led Broom's horse across the face of the assembled cavalrymen. He could hardly believe what he was seeing. Every fibre of his body yearned to bolt down the slope and prise the forlorn prisoner from his captors. But the Parliamentarian procession remained just out of musket range, and the harquebusiers would cut his redcoats down the moment they ventured away from the tor's protection. They could but watch.

Otilwell Broom did not look up as his mount was led to the ancient tree. His broken body simply lurched from left to right with the horse's loping stride, head lolling like a broken-necked sparrow. He did not respond when the mount was halted and held beneath the biggest of the tree's gnarled boughs, nor when Hogg's companion, a hugely fat, dark-skinned fellow, produced a thick length of rope and slung it across the branch. The end dangling above Broom's bare head had been fashioned into a noose. The fat man dropped to the ground, tying the opposite end to the base of the trunk, before clambering awkwardly back into his saddle.

On the turf below Stryker, Cecily Cade wept. Burton was still with her, his single good arm braced about her trembling shoulders. Stryker lent over the side of the stack. 'Take her back to the avenue, Andrew.'

To his astonishment, the words, intended for comfort, seemed to have the opposite effect. She shrugged Burton's arm away violently, glaring up at Stryker, big eyes wide and bright with fury. 'How dare you, sir!'

'Miss Cade?' Stryker spluttered.

'How dare you presume to *remove* me,' she thrust an accusatory finger up at Stryker, 'when it was you who sent Otilwell to his death!'

Stryker drew breath to argue, but the words would not

form, for he knew she was right. It had been his order that sent Broom from the tor. Sir Alfred Cade's bodyguard had been reluctant to leave, but Stryker had insisted it should be he who took the message. He sagged, letting his chin rest on the cold granite, wondering what to say next.

'This man!' The hard tones of Osmyn Hogg jarred across his thoughts suddenly. 'This evil-doer has entered into solemn league with the Devil!'

Stryker lifted himself up again, peering down at the cloaked man who now sat in his saddle some twenty or so paces in front of the twisted tree. 'What is this game, Hogg?'

Hogg stared up at him. 'No game, Stryker. I am a witchfinder. Charged by God and by His blessed Parliament to seek out and eliminate witchcraft and sorcery where I discover it.'

Stryker's eye flicked along the line of cavalry to the man – now without a helmet – he knew to be Gabriel Wild. 'What is this madness, Colonel? You want the wagon, I understand that, but who is this antick?'

Wild did not flinch.

'This warlock has confessed!' Osmyn Hogg bellowed up at the tor. He rummaged briefly in his saddlebag, eventually producing a small sheet of paper and holding it up like a trophy. 'See here, the man's confession. Signed in his own hand, and witnessed by the honourable Colonel Wild and his men.'

'Confessed?' Cecily squawked. 'He has confessed to nothing!' She bolted down the slope then, stopping only when her toes clipped a large stone, sending her tumbling in a heap. When she sat upright, her head twisted back to stare up at the tor's summit, eyes fixed upon Stryker, pleading. 'He is no witch, Captain!'

'Ah, the woman!' Hogg's mocking voice rose up from the lower ground. 'The second in our coven of devilry!'

Cecily's green eyes became huge, and she turned immediately back to Hogg. 'Devilry?'

Hogg kicked his mount forward another few yards to be certain his voice would carry. 'The condemned spoke much of you, harridan. Names you as his vile confederate!'

He waved the confession again, raking his gaze from the men at the very foot of the tor all the way up to those guarding its summit.

'I implore all you God-fearing men; hear this! The warlock known to you as Otilwell Broom has given up his secrets. Three others among you have suckled Satan's imps!' With his free hand Hogg pointed directly at Cecily Cade. 'The girl you harbour. She is a witch of the foulest kind!'

'What?' It was Cecily, glancing uneasily at the men all around her. Her voice was barely more than a whisper. 'I—I am a Godly woman.'

'She and Broom are known witches, cavorting with demons, suckling the Dark One's imps, working magic upon those who would pray to the Holiest of Holies. And the third and fourth spokes in this wheel of hell are none other than your leader, Captain Stryker, and his familiar, the dwarf, Barkworth!'

The tor erupted in laughter. Stryker was glad of it. 'I have known Broom not six days!'

'But Broom has confessed,' Hogg went on, unperturbed. 'He claims, as God is his witness, that he and the witch travelled to Dartmoor in order to commune with you.'

He urged his horse on again, slid down from its muscular back, and drew a long stick of polished, dark timber from a loop in his saddle. Planting it firmly in the soft earth, Hogg lent heavily against it, limping several more paces towards the looming hill. He raised his voice further, beseeching the red-coated garrison.

'Witchcraft, sorcery, contrived by the power of Beelzebub against the Church and the law of Almighty God, shall cease to thrive. The Lord most high has charged His people, His most righteous witch-catchers, with the Godliness and zeal to ensure that foul devilry is done only in vain.'

Hogg twisted the upper part of his torso back to stare at the tree, pointing his crutch at Broom. 'Today you will see justice done to one part of this coven. Señor Ventura!'

With that, the dark-skinned man, waiting patiently beside the still silent Broom, stretched across to grasp the noose, slipping it quickly over his captive's head.

Stryker watched in stunned silence. He knew he should say something – *do* something – but he was frozen as solid as his granite perch. Because he had remembered Osmyn Hogg. The name and face had meant nothing to him, but the maniacal voice and blazing eyes had stabbed at him from a time long since past.

Down at the tree the man called Ventura dropped Broom's horse's reins and slapped the beast's rump sharply. The horse skittered forwards. Broom, pinioned by the noose, stayed in position, the saddle sliding away beneath him. And then his booted feet slipped from the stirrups, and, for a second, it seemed as though his body hovered in mid air, almost horizontal. But the rope snapped taut, jerked him backwards, snatching him violently in the opposite direction as if it would smash his bloody body into the tree.

And that, Stryker thought, would have been a mercy, for it might have crushed the life out of him quickly. The reality, of course, was painfully different. Broom simply swung there, dangling from the end of the rope, feet tantalizingly close to the ground, but not close enough to make a connection. And his body, so inert and lifeless until now, seemed to lurch sickeningly, abruptly awakened like a puppet having its strings roughly jangled. He could not cry out, for the air was being steadily strangled from his throat by the tightening noose, but there had been no drop, no snapping fall to break his neck and spare his struggles. This was to be a hanging the hard way.

Broom danced. His arms, bound at the wrists behind his back, jolted left and right in a desperate struggle to become free, the muscles of the shoulders rippling, flexing, and tearing as they fought uselessly against secure bonds. His legs, though, were free to kick, and kick they did. They jerked and flung and writhed, knees thrusting high as they might, toes clawing at an invisible ledge out in front. Broom's eyes bulged, his tongue gradually poked through swollen lips like a small snake venturing out of its cave. Even from this distance, Stryker could see the piss drip in a steady flow from the dying man's boot heels.

And then, finally, the thrashing began to slow to a series of sporadic jerks as the life finally eased out of Otilwell Broom's body. Stryker wanted to look away, but he could not. Instead he let a heavy, juddering sigh escape, realizing as he did that he had been holding his own breath.

'Thou shalt not suffer a witch to live!' witch-finder Osmyn Hogg suddenly boomed from below the tree.

'Exodus, chapter 22, verse 18. Praise the Lord that His righteous work is now done!'

Stryker hauled himself to stand on the stack's high crest. 'I remember you, Hogg! I remember your cowardly face and your screams! That's what this is about, isn't it? Not witchcraft, but vengeance!'

Hogg ignored him, limping back to his horse and clambering into the saddle.

It was then that Colonel Wild spurred forth, coming within range of the foremost muskets but aware that the distance would render any shot feeble against his robust plate. 'You have two nights!' he bellowed, addressing the entire Royalist contingent. 'Give up Stryker, his half-man and his witch, and you will walk from here unhindered! If you refuse, all will swing!'

Without further words, the Parliamentarian colonel wheeled his mount round and led the procession back towards the distant barn, leaving Otilwell Broom's half-naked, blood-crusted corpse to sway gently in the breeze.

CHAPTER 12

Cecily Cade found Stryker down at the ruined village. He was patting one of the horses, leaning across the waist-high wall of an ancient building to whisper soothingly into the skittish beast's pricked ear. He straightened when he caught sight of her approach.

'I would apologize for the way I spoke to you yesterday,' Cecily said when she had successfully negotiated the stones that pushed up from the narrow river. 'I know you were trying to protect me.'

Stryker nodded awkwardly. 'I had no right to try and send you away. Broom was your friend.'

Cecily offered a tiny shrug. 'Not really. That is to say, he was a faithful servant to my father, but I did not know him well. It was simply a shock.'

'It is always a terrible thing to watch a man die.' He thought of the hanging tree, happy to be on the other side of the hill to those sinister branches. At least, he supposed, Broom was no longer swinging from its creaking bough. A party of musketeers had crept warily from the tor as dusk had lengthened the shadows around the granite stacks. They had cut down Broom's body, stiff and reeking of blood, and carried it back to be buried with the rest of the dead. He looked up at Cecily suddenly. 'It is my fault, all of it.'

Cecily gave a sad smile and shook her head gently. 'I am no fool, Captain. I understand that you were compelled to take Wild's powder wagon. It was your duty. And I have not forgotten how we came to be with your company. Without you, Otilwell and I would be dead already.'

'You do not understand,' Stryker said obstinately. 'Broom was not hanged as a witch.'

'He signed a confession. Albeit one tortured out of him, but a confession nevertheless.'

Stryker left the wall and went to Cecily, taking her shoulders in his hands. 'Hogg is after me, and me alone.'

The image of Osmyn Hogg came into his mind. He was older now, of course, and his face, if anything, was even sourer than Stryker remembered. But the hard eyes and hooked nose, the deep voice and those prominent, almost equine teeth were the same as they had been so long ago. 'Our paths crossed many years back. I had near forgotten him, truth be told, and I never knew his name, but he has not forgotten me.'

'What happened?' Cecily asked.

'He tried to hurt someone—someone dear to me. I stopped him.'

'A woman?'

Stryker nodded, retracing the explanation he had earlier given to his senior men. 'Aye. Though she died soon after.'

'And now Hogg wants revenge?'

'I think so.'

'Do you have a woman now?'

Stryker looked up sharply, so unexpected was the question. 'Yes—no—I don't know. She is often

260

overseas.' He knew the answer was inadequate, but in truth he did not know how to describe his relationship with Lisette Gaillard. He loved her, that was for certain, and would have long since married her, had she felt the same about him. But her first love was duty. Duty to Queen Henrietta Maria. And that love, that diamond-hard loyalty, meant that Lisette would spend most of her time away from Stryker. Away, indeed, from England altogether.

Stryker drew breath to speak, hoping to offer a better explanation, when he noticed Cecily's distant expression. 'What is it?'

She peered back at him, brow furrowed, tense. 'He told them.'

'He?'

'Otilwell. He told that vile man about me.'

'They could see you, Miss Cade. Your presence was hardly a secret.'

She gnawed at her bottom lip. 'But if he talked, what else might he have said?'

'What do you mean?' Stryker replied cautiously. 'What might he have said that is worse than naming you a witch?'

She looked past his shoulder, eyes suddenly fixing on something beyond. 'It does not matter.'

Stryker turned, letting his hands fall away from Cecily, to see Lieutenant Burton ambling down the slope towards them. 'What is it, Andrew?'

The younger man's gaze had been set firmly on Cecily, and it seemed to take some effort to acknowledge Stryker. 'Simeon is in a rare stupor, sir,' he said eventually. 'He's dangerous. Made to stick Fallon with his dirk. Skellen had to bully the fight out of him with his halberd.'

Stryker sighed, unsurprised. 'I'll speak to him.' He saw Cecily's look of surprise. 'He was once hanged as a witch.'

Cecily's jaw dropped. 'Hanged?' She covered her open mouth with a hand. 'That is how he came by his scar?'

'Aye,' confirmed Stryker. 'Folk took pity on him, cut him down before he died, but he is haunted still. To be accused again is difficult for him.'

'Go, sir,' Burton said, moving to stand close to Cecily. 'I will take care of Miss Cade.'

Stryker bade Cecily farewell and left her with the lieutenant, and jogged nimbly up the tor's eastern face. When he looked back, Burton was still staring up at him.

'I want to kill that witch-catcher, sir,' Simeon Barkworth rasped.

Stryker had found him on the tor's summit, leaning against one of the largest stacks and staring away to the north-east. A dirk glinted in his hand. 'Then you'll need to get in line.'

Barkworth's little eyes, so catlike in their gleaming depths, darted across at the captain. 'It was a hard thing to watch.'

'I understand.' Stryker stepped closer, noticing Barkworth's knuckles whiten around the knife's hilt. 'But there's talk you threatened Pikeman Fallon.'

'A matter of regret, sir,' Barkworth croaked, still examining the north-eastern hills. 'He made to jest—'

'But not about the hanging.'

Barkworth looked round at him. 'I know that now. I heard laughter, Fallon's high bloody chirp. I mistook him.'

Stryker glanced at the dirk. 'Nearly a fatal mistake.'

Barkworth offered a wan smile. 'For us both. Skellen

might be a gangling piece o' piss, but he's mighty fearsome wi' that pole-arm in hand.'

'Just as well he was there.'

The Scot nodded. 'Aye.' His eyes widened then, and he stared down at the dirk in his fist, as if realizing for the first time that he still gripped it. He immediately sheathed the thankfully unbloodied weapon. 'I will apologize to Fallon.'

'Yes, Simeon, you will.' Stryker took a small step closer. 'This siege is taking a heavy toll.'

'That it is,' Barkworth said heavily. 'When I think back on Lichfield, I know we were no better off there. At least we're not starved this time. But here,' he swallowed thickly, 'we are utterly alone. There'll be no aid, no chance of reinforcements. And still I might have dealt with it better.'

'But the hanging changed things.'

Barkworth closed his eyes, rubbed them hard with the palms of his little hands. 'It was a thrust too deep, sir. It has filled my head with old memories. Poisoned me, like digging up a rotting corpse.'

'You will make your peace with Pikeman Fallon,' Stryker said after a moment's silence. 'Then you will make the best of this situation as the rest of us must. When the time comes, I need you ready and willing to kill the enemy.'

'To kill Osmyn Hogg.'

Barkworth pulled a puzzled expression. 'Did you really give him that limp?'

Stryker thought back to the day he had encountered the hanging party in a Saxon forest. 'I shot him.'

'In the leg?'

'In the arse.'

Barkworth snorted with laughter. 'Money or girl?'

263

'The latter.'

'Ach, the best fights always come back to some wench. Was she worth it?'

Stryker let Beth Lipscombe's face come to him. He remembered whisking her away from those hypocritical Puritans, caring for nothing but the girl. They had plummeted from the horse into a pile of leaves, and there, in the sun-dappled wood, they had made frantic love. He remembered unpicking the lace of her bodice, freeing those warm brown breasts, and remembered rifling in her voluminous skirts like a man possessed. Beth had died of a fever just months later, but, by God, it had been worth it. 'Aye, without doubt.'

'But now you have a witch-hunter after your neck,' Barkworth said with a weak smile.

Stryker thought of Broom's piss-drenched body. 'We'll flay the bastard together.'

'I look forward to it, sir.'

'But mark me well, Simeon. If you kill any of *my* men, I will flay you myself. Do you believe me?'

Barkworth's mottled neck convulsed as he swallowed. 'I do, sir.'

That would suffice as far as Stryker was concerned. He had had to deal with his own demons more times than he cared to consider, and would not condemn Barkworth for one lapse. Offering his hand for the diminutive Scot to shake, he went to Barkworth's side, watching the dark hills. He ran his single eye from the craggy summits, down beyond the gorse-blotted slopes and on to the bleak plain that stretched all around. The river cut through the plain, running north to south, and he tracked its rushing progress for several hundred paces, until something caught his eye.

Movement; a white flash, darting in and out of view amongst bracken, rocks, gorse, and trees. He squinted hard, trying to add definition to the elusive shape. There it was again, a bright smear against the dark earth, and he realized that it was a man, pale and bearded, scampering stealthily along the western bank in the direction of the tor. Seek Wisdom and Fear the Lord Gardner had returned.

'I saw what they did to your man,' the former priest said as he knelt by the river. Filling cupped hands with the clear water, he splashed his face and hair.

'Hidden away somewhere, were you?' Stryker, standing behind Gardner, replied bitterly. 'Having a grand cackle at Broom's expense?'

Gardner turned, beads of river water dripping off his long, matted beard. 'No, boy. I prayed for him.'

The pleasantness of the reply seemed to puncture Stryker's bluster. He sighed. 'Forgive me, I am easily vexed.'

'I was out in the trees near their bloody barn,' Gardner went on, shrugging off the apology. 'Saw it all. A sad and terrible thing to witness the life throttled from a fellow.' His face creased impishly. 'They're saying you're a witch, boy.'

'A lie.'

'The girl too,' Gardner added with relish, turning back to the river, 'and even your firebrand Pict.'

Stryker knelt beside him, taking a leather flask from his snapsack and plunging it into the finger-numbing depths. 'You're a man of the cloth, Seek Wisdom,' he said, watching the bubbles of air escape from the vessel's throat. 'Why are you here, if you believe I am a witch?'

Gardner stared at him, pale eyes wide with surprise. 'I don't, boy! Not all priests are that gullible.' He stood, shaking his head in bewilderment. 'I could see they'd tortured your man, plain as day.'

Flask now heavy, Stryker took a long draught of the cold liquid, topped it up with a last dunk, and stood. An image of Broom's bloody torso came to him. 'Cut him to pieces.'

Gardner met his strained gaze. 'It is called pricking, boy. An abominable practice.' He extended a thin, gnarled forefinger and jabbed the air between them. 'They stick the flesh with sharp pokers till they find a spot that don't bleed. And that's your witch's mark.'

'Christ,' Stryker whispered.

'There's no commandment for filthy words, boy, but number three's quite clear about blasphemy, so mind your fucking language.' Before Stryker could respond Gardner had strolled to a nearby hawthorn bush, and busily set about stripping the skinny branches, cramming the green leaves past his black gums. 'Trouble is,' he went on, lips dyed emerald, 'in my experience a man'll tell you whatever you want to hear, just to make the pricking stop. Imagine that bed-pressing Spaniard jabbing you again and again.'

'Spaniard?' Stryker interjected. 'The darker man?'

'Aye, or so I can gather. I heard one o' the tin-heads call him Señor. He's the witch-finder's lackey. The matross to Hogg's gun captain, if you will.' He popped a handful of leaves into his mouth, a trickle of dark juice welling at the corner of his lips and tumbling down the coarse grey hairs of his beard.

'As I say,' he mumbled through the pulp, 'imagine that

sweaty pottage-guzzler stickin' you with his wicked little poniard. You'd confess to any amount o' sorcery if it meant the pain would stop. If I were that poor bugger, I'd finger a few of you too, just to make the tale that bit juicier. And who better than a beautiful girl, a man with only half his face, and a midget?' The Welshman cackled madly, greatly amused by his own words.

'Ha! You're the perfect coven!' The silver fibres of his bushy brow ruffled. 'Come to think on it, I might turn you in myself.'

Stryker shook his head. 'I don't believe it was Broom's intention to name me. They want me dead, Hogg and Wild.'

Gardner was incredulous. 'The badger wants you for taking his wagon, boy, I understand. But that horse-faced warlock sniffer?'

'Hogg and I have unfinished business from the Low Countries.'

The former priest tilted his head to the sky. 'Hear that, God? Our friendly Cyclops truly requires your grace, for his enemies verily converge upon him!'

Stryker smiled ruefully. 'Aye, it appears that way.'

'So our witch-finder is here for you, boy.' Gardner's face became serious. 'Will the men betray you?'

'No.'

The blue eyes narrowed. 'The suggestion of witchery is a powerful brew, boy.'

Stryker thought of his company. The men that had fought alongside him for so long, endured so many hardships, spilled so much blood. 'They will not turn me in.'

Gardner nodded, his attention returning to the hawthorn. 'Then there'll be more fighting. Except this time you'll lose.'

'I know what you'll say,' Stryker responded quickly. 'They have dragooners now, meaning we're sore outnumbered.' He stared up at the high tor, the natural fortress squatting on its flat summit. 'But they will struggle to chase us off this hill, nevertheless. Our supplies are good for another few days, and they cannot keep us from the river, lest they wish to brave a hail of lead.'

'No no no, boy,' Seek Wisdom Gardner retorted, 'I wasn't about to say anythin' o' the sort. Not about dragooners, leastwise.'

'Oh?'

The old man scratched at a blob of green paste that had congealed on his beard, and leaned close. 'Guns, boy. They got cannon comin'.'

It was as though Stryker had been punched in the guts. 'You jest.'

'Why would I?'

'You're certain?'

Gardner winked. 'Certain as I am that Archbishop Laud used to suck——'

Stryker held up a staying hand. 'If you say witch's teats, I'll——'

'I was going to say Strafford's balls.'

Stryker could not prevent a smile, though the news was dire. 'Do you know what kind?'

Gardner pursed his lips as he considered the question. 'The usual kind, boy. Low hangin', I shouldn't wonder, and shrivelled like a couple of dried plums.'

Stryker glowered. 'The cannon, Seek Wisdom!'

The Welshman shook his head rapidly. 'No, boy, I couldn't discover that particular morsel. But they're expected in a short while.'

Stryker thought about that. The terrain was treacherous all across the moor. Hills one mile, woodland the next, interspersed by valley and bog. It had been difficult enough dragging a cart across the inhospitable land, let alone a piece of ordnance. 'Which means they're probably smaller pieces.'

'That's what I thought,' Gardner agreed.

'Again you help us, Seek Wisdom.'

The bony man shrugged. 'Like I said before; I don't hold with either side in this scrap. But I like you, boy.' He looked directly upwards. 'Isn't that right, Lord?'

'Then you have my gratitude once again.'

'Besides, the badger is in league with a witch-catcher now.'

That surprised Stryker. 'In my experience, priests are ever too eager to hunt witches.'

Gardner's big blue eyes fixed on a point some distance away. 'I dislike zealots, boy. You know that. It is zeal that chased me here, chased my friends to the New World. Witch hunts are merely another form of zeal. A way for powerful men to control the weak by stupefying them with fear.'

'Thou shalt not suffer a witch to live,' Stryker replied, quoting Hogg.

'Thou shalt not suffer a witch to live,' Gardner repeated. 'I'm sure God meant it. But let Him point the evil-doers out. Witch-finders are but men, and they must be seen to be proficient in their work, boy. So they accuse the most vulnerable. Those easily blamed, and never missed. They are the worst kind of men; mean, merciless, and cruel. If the badger and his tin-heads are allied to such a fellow, then I am allied to you.'

Stryker nodded his thanks just as a thought struck him. 'We have food here, Seek Wisdom. Not much, but something to fill your belly better than leaves. Thankfully plenty was taken from Ilsington.'

'Poor Ilsington,' Gardner replied wryly.

'Aye, well,' said Stryker, embarrassed by Gardner's sharp thrust. 'Would you take victuals? Stay?'

'I'll eat, my boy, certainly.' Gardner patted his inwardly curved midriff. 'This stomach's been growlin' all too much of late. But stay? When I've just told you there's ordnance on its way?' He tutted theatrically. 'I might be mad, boy, but I'm not insane.'

Stryker nodded his assent. The enigmatic former priest would leave again, melt back into the Dartmoor terrain like a dusk wraith. An idea came to him then, and he chided himself for not thinking of it sooner. 'Will you take a message out, Seek Wisdom? Broom was my only hope of rescue.'

'And Broom had his skin flensed,' Gardner replied, quick as a pistol shot. 'And then his neck was wrung like a quarrelsome bloody hen. No fear, boy, I'd rather stay unpricked and short-necked, if it's all the same to you.'

'But they would not see you, Seek Wisdom,' Stryker pushed again. 'Broom was on the road, but you would move in the shadows.'

Gardner's head shook firmly. 'I said no, boy, and that'll be an end to it. Besides, I am too old to traipse off into Cornwall. I was a sprightly lad once,' he chuckled ruefully, 'but time is the ultimate traitor.'

There was an uncomfortable silence as a frustrated Stryker paced away, slumping down on a lichen-bright log a short distance along the riverbank. He watched the water meander past, aware of the company's hopeless isolation.

'But do you have a man willing to run the badger's gauntlet?' Gardner's voice interrupted his thoughts after a while.

He looked across at the wizened hermit. 'No, but I would have no difficulty finding such a man.'

Gardner's eye twitched in his conspiratorial wink. 'I said I would not take your message myself, boy. I never said I would not help another.'

PETER TAVY, DARTMOOR, 5 MAY 1643

Forrester had ordered the dead buried quickly, eager to have the matter dealt with before the red kites could swoop to feast. They were interred in a lonely corner of the village churchyard. The local vicar had attended the cere-mony, joined by a smattering of curious locals, and all had watched in solemn silence as soil was shovelled on to the eighteen waxen bodies. They had been enemies in life, only to share a grave in death.

Neither Forrester nor Payne had welcomed the delay, but such matters were entirely appropriate after so lethal a fight, and they had encouraged the men to take refresh-ment from the river and food from any local folk kind enough to offer.

'What'll become of me?' the defeated Parliamentarian commander uttered meekly after the grim funeral. Lieutenant Reginald Jays had spent the night locked with his remaining dozen men in one of the rickety outbuild-ings of the Peter Tavy Inn. He had only been given the chance of sunlight for the burials, and that had been under the kestrel gaze of a squad of Forrester's musketeers.

'All depends how willingly you answer my questions,' Forrester replied, strolling away from the burial site with the grey-coated officer on one flank and Payne on the other.

'I'll endeavour to do my best, sir.'

Forrester stopped. 'Good. Well firstly, I should like to know why in Hades' name you did not encircle the inn.'

Jays lifted a gloved hand to smooth his tiny moustache. 'I don't follow, sir.'

'And therein lies my question. Why did you blunder straight into our front, where we could easily make a stand?' He was pleased, of course, not to have faced a more able foe, but men had died for the man's incompetence, and that fact irked him.

Jays flushed, swallowed thickly, inspected his hose. 'I—I cannot—'

Anthony Payne, looming over both officers, cleared his throat thunderously. 'How old are you, Mister Jays?'

Lieutenant Jays peered up at Payne as a rabbit might stare at an eagle. 'Near fifteen, sir.'

Payne looked at Forrester. 'Seek no further for explanation, sir. It was no deliberate tactic.'

Jays was crestfallen. 'It is my first command.'

'Christ on His Cross,' Forrester hissed angrily. 'They send boys against us.' He fixed the lieutenant with a caustic glare. 'Which regiment?'

'Merrick's,' Jays replied, sounding more like a rebuked child than a leader of men.

'You've cost me dear, Mister Jays.'

Jays managed to meet the Royalist's eyes. 'But, sir, did you not win?'

Despite the prevailing sourness of his mood, Forrester felt his face crack in a reluctant smile. 'Impertinent whelp,' he said, though without conviction. 'You are now my prisoner, sir. As are your twelve disciples, and that causes me a problem, for I have neither the time nor vigour to waste on your keeping.'

'You'll free us?' Jays asked hopefully.

Payne snorted his amusement.

Forrester shook his head. 'I'll do no such thing, Lieutenant. You'll stay with me until you're able to secure funds.'

'Funds, sir?'

Forrester plucked the wide-brimmed hat from his head and fingered the bullet hole in its crown. 'You owe me a new hat.' He placed the damaged item back on his head, wincing as the hair moved around his scalped pate. He thanked God the musket-ball had not been a fraction lower.

'Where do we march, Captain?' Lieutenant Jays ventured.

'West to Launceston,' Forrester replied. There was no need to explain Payne's imminent departure north to Stratton. 'Where you will be clapped in irons, I do not doubt.' He noticed Jays's bottom lip quiver slightly. 'But you are a gentleman, so have no fear.'

'You'll likely be offered the king's commission,' Anthony Payne put in.

Forrester nodded. 'We need ever more men, Lieutenant Jays. Your best chance of liberty is to switch allegiance.'

Jays was taken aback. 'But my honour, sir—'

Forrester dismissed the protest with a wave of his hand. 'There is no honour in war, young man. The quicker you learn that, the longer you'll live. But enough of this. You'll

273

come back to Launceston as my prisoner, and there you will be dealt with accordingly. Your presence will necessarily hinder our progress, so I would warn you that any trouble from you or your men will not be tolerated.'

With that, Forrester looked pointedly from Jays to Payne. The Parliamentarian stared up at the colossal Cornishman with dumbstruck awe. 'Good,' Forrester added, satisfied that his intimation had been understood.

'Best get moving,' Anthony Payne muttered. 'Dusk soon.'

'Right enough,' Forrester agreed. 'Let us cover a mile or two before dark, eh?'

GARDNER'S TOR, DARTMOOR, 5 MAY 1643

Twilight saw the now established routine play out. Stryker's pikemen – pots, breastplates, and pikes stacked in the avenue – set about taking their familiar positions all around the higher parts of the tor. Some stood on the vast stacks at the very summit, others on the obelisks fringing the crest, and many on the smaller granite heaps further down the slopes. They were the lookouts, the men who would raise the alarm if an enemy advance was spotted. Down on the lowest climbs, and, to the south-east, around the breastworks made by the tumbledown village, Stryker's musketeers stood in wait, staring out into the grey ether, occasionally blowing on cords of match to keep the crucial embers alive.

Yet, on the plain to the west of the tor there was new activity. Five men snaked, single file and silent, through the network of bushes and stone that pocked the area at the foot of the hill. Four of them were soldiers, boots thudding and weapons clinking in the deathly silence, but they were led by a cadaverous figure with the hair and beard of a pagan druid, the clothes of a beggar, and the name of a Puritan.

Seek Wisdom and Fear the Lord Gardner had promised to show Stryker the secret of his ability to approach the tor unseen, for it would prove, he claimed, the way a message might be carried to the Royalist high command. Stryker had been incredulous, but he, Skellen, Burton, and Barkworth had followed the former priest into the darkness nevertheless.

After several minutes picking their way slowly over the perfidious terrain, Gardner came to a halt at a dense thicket of bracken. He glared, wide-eyed, at the four men in turn, raising a spindly finger to his lips to urge a complete hush. Thus satisfied, he eased his way into the undergrowth, parting the bracken at his waist. The rustle of foliage seemed unnaturally loud in the still night, and every man winced as he followed the path cut by the Welshman.

Stryker was last through the bracken, coming to a standstill at the thicket's epicentre. To his surprise the ground here was cluttered with flat, pale stones. They were set in a wide circle, and he realized that this was no accident of nature. 'What is this?'

Gardner's blue eyes twinkled in the wan moonlight. 'An ancient place,' he whispered softly. 'A secret of the old Britons, the ones the cursed English chased all the way into Wales and Scotland, and across the Tamar, of course.'

Burton was staring down at the stone circle. 'Some kind of tomb?'

Gardner clicked his fingers. 'You have it, boy. They call it a cist in these parts. But this is more than a tomb, I can assure you.' With that, the hermit paced to the cist's heart and dropped to a crouch, digging fingertips beneath a stone that was larger than the rest. In a flash he had prized the flat tablet of granite away from the earth, revealing a gaping patch of blackness. 'Much more.'

Sergeant Skellen moved to take a look. 'Well I'll be a Tom O'Bedlam.' He looked back at Stryker. 'A tunnel.'

'Goes off west,' Gardner elaborated, pointing to the woodland that concealed Wild's large barn. 'Its twin hides in those trees. I'll lead your man through.'

Stryker moved to take a look for himself. The mouth of the tunnel was less than a man's pace across. 'It's narrow.'

Gardner nodded. 'See now why I said your man would have to be a littl'un?' The Welshman had been adamant that whoever was chosen would have to be slight of frame. Stryker had been bewildered by the request, but had acquiesced all the same. 'On land your brawn keeps you alive. Down there it'll see you dead.' Gardner glanced up at Skellen. 'Imagine old spider-limbs crawlin' down there, boy.'

'P'raps not, eh?' Skellen grunted.

'I am to go,' Barkworth's voice, ordinarily a virtual whisper, croaked from the edge of the cist. 'I am the smallest,' he looked at Skellen, 'and the bravest. Besides, I cannot stay on this fucking tor any longer.'

Gardner beckoned him to the centre of the stone circle. 'I'll take you as far as the woods, then you are on your own. It'll be risky once you're out in the open, boy, for the badger's eyes are everywhere, but if you move with guile you might just make it beyond the hills.'

'Shall we?' Barkworth said quickly, perhaps before he could think too deeply upon the matter. He moved around the cist, shaking the hand of each of his comrades, before returning to the tunnel's entrance and following the hermit to his knees. 'Launceston, then.'

Stryker stared down at him through the gloom, even as Gardner vanished from view. 'Aye. Head due west, but beware of Tavistock. We cannot know which side holds it.'

'I'll have a care, sir.'

'All's well, then. Pick up the road west of Tavistock. It will take you all the way home. Find Colonel Mowbray. Get some men out here with all haste.'

Barkworth began to slide into the tunnel. 'And if Mowbray refuses?'

'Then fetch Captain Forrester.'

Simeon Barkworth flashed a final, sharp-toothed grin, and was gone.

CHAPTER 13

THE BARN NEAR GARDNER'S TOR, DARTMOOR,
6 MAY 1643

Witch-finder Osmyn Hogg slurped steaming pottage from his wooden spoon. Some of it dripped on to his cloak, congealing in a mealy blob, and he hurriedly rubbed at it with a sleeve.

'Here, sir,' José Ventura leapt up from his place at the little fire outside the building's double doors. 'I have cloth.'

Hogg waved the Spaniard away. 'No matter, José. Sit.'

Ventura did as he was told, returning to his cross-legged position on the rotten log, but his face spoke of confusion. Hogg was not surprised, for Ventura had seen him fly into a rage for less than spilt pottage, but today he did not mind. Did not care for such trivialities. 'I am sanguine, señor. Sit and finish your breakfast.'

Indeed, today Osmyn Hogg was in a positively buoyant mood.

The hanging had gone almost to plan. Not perfectly, he had to admit, for part of him had expected Stryker to be handed over as soon as Broom's body ceased its thrashing, but some vestige of loyalty from his men was to be expected, he supposed. One thing that was not in doubt, however, was the imminent delivery of the fiend into

Wild's – and, by turns, Hogg's – hands. Soldiers were rough men, hard and inured to fear, but, in Hogg's experience, they were often remarkably Godly creatures. As if a life of fighting and killing, of plundering and whoring, made such men more sensitive than most to their lot in the afterlife. These were the kind of men who would not wish to harbour a witch.

It had been Hogg, of course, who had suggested Stryker as a potential collaborator to Otilwell Broom. The man had bled that night, screamed as Ventura and his needle had sought a witch's mark Hogg knew would never be found, and, eventually, he had talked. He had admitted of his involvement with the men on the little tor. Had blurted information about their strength, their provisions, their strategy. He had even muttered something about a girl being trapped up there with the malignants. Stryker's bitch, no doubt. And, simply to get the pain to stop, Broom had signed a piece of blood-spattered vellum that declared his compact with Lucifer. When Hogg had initially put his quill to the confession, Stryker's was the only name he had thought to scratch, but Ventura had suggested they include the girl, and Colonel Wild had mentioned that a dwarflike beast marched with the king's men. Both, Hogg had decided, would be worth adding to the pot, if only to bring a note of authenticity to the charge.

It was a shame, Osmyn Hogg inwardly accepted, that Broom should have to die in such a manner. Judging by the man's hair and clothes, he had doubtless been a Godless rakehell, but he was no witch. The death, as with Hogg's every thought since that fateful meal in Okehampton, came down to one thing only. One person.

'Stryker.'

José Ventura glanced up from his piping bowl. 'Señor?'

Hogg shook his head as though it were full of wasps. 'Nothing.' It had been a surprise even to him that he had uttered the word out loud. Such was the power the knave's very name had over him, he supposed. He took another tentative sip of pottage, pushed the beads of barley about his mouth with his tongue, and swallowed slowly. 'I said Stryker.'

Ventura looked at him, fleshy jowls tremulous as he nodded. 'What of him, señor?'

'He is an evil man, José.'

Ventura nodded again. 'I know this, señor. You tell me of his cavort with witches.'

Hogg closed his eyes, throwing his mind back a decade to an unassuming little place called Podelwitz. 'One witch in particular.'

Ventura sniffed derisively. 'Germany full of such wenches.'

'This one was English, José. She followed the armies as did we.'

'You were priest then?'

'I was,' confirmed Hogg. 'And I know what you must think. A whore, and nothing more. But she was so much more. A consummate seductress. Luring men to sin with her wiles.' And what wiles, he thought, guiltily. He remembered catching her with the young novice, Jerome. Remembered walking into the lad's chamber to see him thrusting and grunting at her naked, glistening behind. Remembered that he had grown instantly hard, unable to tear his gaze from her exquisite buttocks. And she had looked back at him then, glancing over her slender

280

shoulder with the most coquettish of smiles, and shot him a wink that told him she could read his very mind.

Hogg swallowed thickly, though there was no pottage in his mouth. 'She brought one of my novices to sin. To ruin in the eyes of God. Would have done the same to me had I not been strong in faith.'

Ventura peered at Hogg for a short time, expression contemplative. 'He give you your limp?'

Hogg subconsciously put a hand to his hip, rubbing the area that still ached after all these years. Stryker, the witch-helping, faithless obstructer of justice, had shot him in the rump without so much as a second thought. The memory, the hatred, the need for vengeance rankled within the witch-finder even now. 'Aye,' was all he managed to say.

'We will get him,' José Ventura said matter-of-factly. 'We will get him and he will swing.'

'I pray so,' Hogg said, and that was all too true. He had prayed for Stryker's demise every night for eleven years. And now, on this bleak plain in a far-flung corner of England, justice would finally be done.

Inside the barn Colonel Gabriel Wild spoke soothing words to his big stallion. The troop's horses had been stabled in here since the prisoner's execution, and, though the place was now empty for them, the stench of old blood had clearly unsettled the flighty beasts.

Christ, he thought, but there had been a lot of blood. Broom had squealed like a stuck boar, the blubbery Spaniard had grinned like a hideous ghoul, Hogg had kept a face of stone, and the floor and walls had been stained crimson. But at least Broom had talked. He had signed Hogg's damned confession, pleasing the witch-hunter, and, more importantly, he had confirmed that morale in Stryker's camp was at a low ebb.

'We'll go in soon,' Wild said.

Welch, the dragoon captain sent by Collings, was seeing to his own mount nearby. He left the beast and went to stand at Wild's flank. 'Sir?'

Wild stared at the pinch-faced dragoon. 'I said we will attack soon, Captain.'

Welch frowned. 'Mister Hogg believes they will surrender of their own accord.'

'Then Mister Hogg is a fool,' Wild sneered. 'He believes they'll stroll down that bloody slope like reproached children.' He chuckled at the thought. 'But he forgets that I have faced Stryker before. He is a swash-and-buckler out of the classic mould, as are the men at his command. Mark me well, Captain, there will be a fight before this is done.'

'Then—' Welch began, but his words trailed off to nothing.

'Then what? Speak plain, sir.'

'Then why did you allow him to hang the prisoner, sir?'

Wild considered the question for a moment. 'Because the prisoner signed a confession stating that he is a witch, and that puts him under Hogg's justice.'

'But surely you do not believe—'

Wild held up a hand for silence. 'Hogg carries Collings's authority, Captain, which means he may act as he wishes within reason. I have no idea why he is so bent on smoking Stryker from his lair, but his methods can only aid my cause. Broom confessed to being a messenger for the malignants. He was to ride to Launceston for help. Which means?'

'Which means they are desperate,' Welch replied. 'They do not believe they can hold out much longer.'

'Precisely,' Wild said cheerfully, leaving one hand on his mount's thick neck and resting the other on the hilt of his sword. 'Hogg believes they will capitulate. I do not. But I do suspect the presence of a witch-catcher will weave disquiet into their ranks, and that, in turn, can only soften their resolve.'

'And soon we will have ordnance,' Captain Welch added, understanding.

Wild nodded firmly. 'And soon we will have ordnance. And those guns will pound Stryker's nest till there is nothing left, forcing him out into the open, where we will cut down that bastardly gullion and his motley followers and take back the wagon.'

The horse, a big, skewbald gelding, announced its entrance with a thunderous snort through flared nostrils spattered in foam. Its rider, a man of perhaps twenty years of age, with a wispy blond beard and pale eyes that seemed too close together, was not a typical soldier, for his clothes were nondescript and he bore nothing to betray his allegiance. Yet as he cantered along the once narrow forest path, now beaten broad by the comings and goings of Wild's cavalry, the words he bellowed secured his safe approach.

'Parliament! General Collings!'

Gabriel Wild had only just stepped into the clearing outside the barn. He was secretly pleased for the commotion, for it excused him from exchanging pleasantries with Hogg and Ventura, who squatted by their small fire, and thrust his way through the gathering men to greet the newcomer. 'What news?'

The rider drew up amid a spatter of mulch, snatching off his hat. 'I come from Major-General Collings, sir.'

'So I gather,' Wild responded dryly.

'Or rather,' the rider said, sliding briskly from the saddle and handing his reins to one of Wild's troopers, 'I am with the ordnance train. My name is Penny, Colonel. Lieutenant Thomas Penny.'

Wild felt his pulse quicken. 'The guns are close?'

Penny nodded. 'Not a day hence, sir. Gun Captain Laws bade me warn you of his impending arrival.'

'I was told you had two pieces.'

'Aye, sir. A pair of solid falconets. Small but steady, sir.'

Wild sucked at his top teeth. A falconet was hardly ideal. They were small fieldpieces, requiring a crew of just two, with a two-inch bore and shot weighing no more than one and a quarter pounds. But, for all that, he did not face castle walls here. The obstinate tor might appear fortress-like, but there was no real keep, nor moat, or cannon. All that was required of his new artillery was that it cow the Royalists into submission. Keep them hemmed in at the summit or drive them on to the plain, he did not care which. 'All to the good,' he said after a short time. 'My compliments to Mister Laws, and can you not ask him to make more haste?'

Penny pursed his thin lips. 'They're still heavy old things, sir. A team of dray horses draws each gun.' He shrugged apologetically. 'Gun Captain Laws would have it here in a trice if he could, but it takes time to negotiate this damnable moor.'

Wild grunted his disapproval. 'Then tell him I anxiously await his safe arrival, Lieutenant.'

'Naturally, sir.' With that, Lieutenant Penny clambered

back on to his mount. The skewbald gave a huge whicker that sounded more like a roar and scraped at the churned earth with a filthy-fetlocked front hoof. Penny lifted his hat, dipping his head in a tight bow. 'Till the morrow, Colonel.'

GARDNER'S TOR, DARTMOOR, 6 MAY 1643

'He can swive 'imself, sir.'

Stryker's rather informal council of war sat along the edge of the tor, facing the woods to the north-west and the enemy camp within. The big barn was heavily obscured by a forest canopy that seemed to grow more dense with each passing day, but the grey smudge of its stone walls was still visible, as were the figures in silver and brown who milled about its edges.

'Well I appreciate the sentiment, William,' replied Stryker, responding to Skellen's proposed answer to Colonel Wild's ultimatum, 'but I cannot be held responsible for your deaths.'

'But, sir—' Skellen protested.

'Why are we here, Sergeant?' Stryker cut across him.

Skellen, sat on his captain's right side, long legs stretched out in front, scratched a spot on his rough chin. ''Cause old badger ballocks wants our wagon.'

Stryker raised a hand to his own chin, noting how the unkempt stubble had now become a short beard. 'He wants the wagon *we* took from him.'

'That's war, sir,' Skellen retorted firmly.

'Aye, but we took it on my orders. We kicked the hornet's nest on my word, and they've chased us up this damned tor.' He thought of Hogg then, and of Broom's pathetic corpse swaying in the breeze, and of Cecily Cade's juddering sobs as the witch-finder accused her of witchcraft. 'And now Osmyn Hogg and his Spaniard are here, threatening all with the noose. And that is most certainly not war.'

'Well, like I said,' Skellen persisted doggedly, 'Wild and Hogg and their bloody diego chum can go and stick their noose where the breeze don't reach.'

'Well said, William!' exclaimed Stryker's other sergeant, Moses Heel. He leaned across to slap Skellen on the shoulder, but looked at Stryker. 'The men are with you, sir.'

Stryker nodded his thanks, only to turn and catch sight of Andrew Burton for the first time. His second-in-command had been sitting on his blind left hand, and out of Stryker's field of vision until now. Burton's expression was stony in the extreme, pallid and tight, his eyes fixed on the woods. 'Something vexes?'

Burton turned to face his captain. 'It is no matter, sir.'

'Andrew?' Stryker pushed, unconvinced.

Burton chewed the inside of his mouth for a second, screwed up his face as he considered his next words, then gazed off into the middle distance. 'May we speak later?'

Stryker nodded, suddenly feeling a strange sense of disquiet. 'Of course, Lieutenant. Come and find me when the time is right.'

'I will, sir, thank you.'

'We'll face Wild's guns, then,' Skellen said suddenly, tone artificially jovial.

Stryker blew out his cheeks. 'Aye. Seek Wisdom warns they come soon.'

'Where is he?' Skellen asked. 'Ain't seen him since he led Barkworth down that coney hole.'

The intimation was stark, and Stryker had a hard time masking his own concerns. 'The old palliard made it very clear he wouldn't be back with Wild's cannon on their way. And Barkworth will be free and on his way to Launceston.' He studied the woodland where Gardner had said the tunnel ended. 'I'm certain of it.'

RUSHFORD, DEVON, 6 MAY 1643

'Get yer bliddy arses movin', damn yer pox'n eyeballs!' the burly sergeant bawled, spittle flecking the wiry bristles of his auburn beard. He levelled his vicious halberd, prodding the long-staffed weapon's blade – point at the centre, axe on one side, and billhook on the other – at the air close to the prisoners' backs in undisguised threat. The dozen grey-coats, marching in front of their Royalist captors, picked up the pace in bovine obedience.

'They move so damnably slow,' Captain Lancelot Forrester growled as he watched the snaking column at the roadside. 'We have made dire progress. It is like herding bloody elephants.' Angrily he tamped his pipe. 'What was it the Bard said about delays?'

There was a giant at Forrester's side. A man almost two feet taller than the sandy-haired captain, with limbs like the masts of a man-o'-war. 'Delays have dangerous ends,' he replied in a tone that made Forrester's chest vibrate.

Forrester craned his neck to glance up at Anthony Payne. 'Quite right, sir.' He shook his head, irritated by his own slip in knowledge. 'This damned task has my mind fogged, I swear it. *Henry VI,* Part II, eh?'

'Part 1,' Payne corrected.

Forrester's tamping became quicker. 'Damned mission.' In truth, the mission to locate an important man on Dartmoor had not been his mission at all, but Payne's. But that did not stop Forrester's feeling of irritation, of anger, at its failure.

'But you are in the right of it, sir.'

'Oh?' Forrester grunted as he thrust the clay pipe stem into his mouth.

'The delay is not ideal.' Payne dipped a vast hand into his snapsack and drew out a desiccated piece of meat, tearing a piece off with his front teeth.

Forrester located his tinderbox as Payne chewed, and lit the pipe. The tobacco was cheap sotweed, not the kind he would normally favour, but it was all he had left. Nevertheless, when the smoke billowed into his lungs, it was a welcome feeling. 'You'd rather be away to Stratton,' he said on his cloudy out-breath.

Payne swallowed the meat. 'I would, sir.'

Forrester nodded. Of course the big Cornishman would prefer his home to traipsing back to Launceston with the red-coated men of Mowbray's Regiment of Foot, but Forrester had insisted that he and his six men remain with the larger force. Forrester had less than forty under his command after the bloody scrap at Peter Tavy, and, now that he had a significant number of surly prisoners to escort, it was imperative that he maintained as strong a unit as possible. He had agreed to head south and west, pushing back towards the main road to Cornwall now that they were beyond the dangers of Tavistock, but that would be his only concession. He sucked on the pipe again. 'You'll be free to head north as soon as we find a garrison capable to taking this raggedy bunch.'

Payne was clearly unhappy, but, now that their original mission had ended in abject failure, any power he had held was now forfeit. Forrester was the sole officer here. 'Understood, sir.'

The final rank of redcoats filed past them, followed by Payne's half-dozen. Forrester upturned his pipe, tapped the bowl so that the contents scattered over the muddy road, and thrust it into his snapsack. 'Let's see if we can't pick up this snailish pace.'

'Just fucking go round, you buffle-'eaded lummox!' a voice boomed from further along the column.

'What now?' Forrester muttered, leading Payne up the road, striding rapidly past the ranks that had suddenly come to a complete halt. He eventually came to the head of the marching force, where the sullen greycoats, stripped of weapons, coin, and food, were milling uncertainly before a massive tree that had fallen across the road. The bearded sergeant, eyes bulging with ire, was still screaming at them to walk around the wide spread of branches, but the sides of the road were almost entirely smothered in wicked thorny gorse, and the Parliamentarians were not inclined to negotiate such an unforgiving gauntlet.

'Cap'n, sir,' the sergeant said as he saw Forrester, snatching off his hat in quick salute. 'Road's blocked.'

'I can see that, Briggs, thank you.'

Sergeant Briggs planted the hat back atop his thinning pate and pointed at the gorse hedge with his halberd. 'Bambry buggers won't go through, sir.'

A young man, barely more than a child, pushed his way to the front of the down-trodden Roundheads. 'Have you no shred of honour, sir?'

'Have a care, Lieutenant Jays,' Forrester said.

'You cannot ask my men to wade through these needles,' Jays went on indignantly. 'I really must protest.'

Forrester wagged a reproachful finger. 'Hold, Reginald, or I will toss you in there myself.' Sergeant Briggs smirked, and Forrester turned to him. 'Get some of our lads over here.'

Briggs's jaw slackened in consternation. 'But, sir, you don't mean to—'

'So that they might cut through this wretched barricade with their tucks, you dull witted oaf!' Forrester snapped.

Briggs blushed, nodded, and set sharply to work.

Forrester drew his own blade and, along with the men Briggs had corralled, began to slash at the vicious foliage. A gap rapidly began to open, a breach in the armoured bush that soon deepened, becoming a passageway the width of three men. The air was alive with the sounds of scything steel, grunting men, and rustling undergrowth.

But suddenly a strange new sound could be heard. It was a low, guttural growl, like an ale barrel being dragged across gravel. Forrester ignored it at first, determined as he was to make inroads into the dense gorse, then unexpected movement caught his eye. The redcoats must have noticed it too, for, as one, they stopped, straightened, and turned to stare at the road.

The toppled tree, vast, sprawling, and ancient, was moving. Its massive branches shook, leaves fluttering on to the road in their droves, and as though a great miracle occurred before their very eyes, the soldiers saw light emerge between the broad trunk and the road.

Lancelot Forrester stared goggle-eyed at the scene. He watched as the tree slowly rose into the air, hovering at the height of a man's waist. Vacantly he sheathed his sword and sketched the sign of the cross over his chest. 'God's blood,' he heard himself say.

It was then that he saw the man. Stooped as he was, straining against the huge trunk around which his arms were hooked, the figure was still a colossus. He trembled with the weight, face scarlet and etched deeply by lines carved from the strain, yet the tree kept rising. And then he roared, a visceral, pain-wracked explosion that sounded more lion than man.

'Help him!' Forrester shouted suddenly, startled into action by Payne's scream. 'Get in there and help him, damn you!'

Ten redcoats dropped their blades and shoved their way through the clawing branches to thrust palms beneath the trunk. Alone they could never have hoped to budge the tree, but together, with Anthony Payne at the very centre, the once immovable bar slowly started to shift. It moved just a fraction at first, stubbornly refusing to shift, but then, amid much howling and straining, backs slammed against the bark and heels dug deep in the earth, it began to swing away from the road.

The men had to run with it, for the sheer momentum of the huge object would certainly have crushed any who might have thought to rest, and finally, with one last bellow from Payne, it had moved sufficiently to unblock the thoroughfare.

The ten redcoats scuttled clear of the trunk and branches, the rest crowed their delight and, with a crash that might have woken the hounds of hell, Anthony Payne let the tree smash to the ground.

The Royalist infantrymen applauded. They raised muskets and swords in salute to the unmatched power of

Anthony Payne. He was immense, terrifying, but he was theirs, and they knew the war would be won with men like him in the king's ranks.

Forrester shook his head in disbelief, joining the applause and grinning with his men. 'Glad I kept you!'

Payne, bent low with hands on knees, heaving air into his huge chest, glanced up at Forrester with a wry smile. 'Glad I could help, sir.'

The shot rent the air with a shocking crack. Forrester spun instinctively away from Payne to face the greycoats, drawing his sword once more. He fully expected to see the Parliament men in open revolt, having snatched muskets from their guards as the Royalists cheered their Herculean champion. But there they stood, huddled nervously together, as mesmerized by the enormous Cornishman as their captors had been.

'Down there!' a voice called from somewhere to the rear of the column.

The men near the tree turned as one at the alarm, seeing a wispy pall of smoke drift clear of a musket barrel, its shooter pointing into a stand of trees further back along the road. Another musketeer, evidently the one to have issued the warning, was pointing at those same trees. 'He's there!' he shouted again. 'I seen 'im!'

The man who had fired lowered his weapon, looking at his mate. 'Did I get the bugger?'

'Dunno, Clem. Diff'cult a'tell.'

'Report!' Forrester barked as he reached the rearguard.

The shooter stood rigid, staring at a point somewhere beyond his captain's shoulder. 'Bein' tailed, sir.'

'By?' Forrester snapped. 'Colours? Numbers?'

'Dunno, sir.'

The second musketeer cleared his throat nervously. 'Didn't see, sir. There's someone down in them oaks though, sir. I saw 'im move back when Clem shot.'

Forrester angrily shook his head, hoping his over-eager men hadn't just holed an innocent local. 'Get half a dozen of the boys together, Musketeer Pett. Get down in that copse and flush this fellow out.'

'That's six lads you'll be buryin' then, Captain!' came a shout from within the trees.

The musketeers immediately twitched their weapons level, muzzles wavering out in front, searching for the target.

But Lancelot Forrester stepped in front of his men, presented the formidable broadsword, and ordered them to hold their fire. He marched a little way down the slope towards the copse. 'You really think you could take all six?' he called in the direction of the dense canopy.

The voice came back, loud but hoarse. 'Don't you?'

And Captain Lancelot Forrester beamed, because he knew that voice as well as any. Harsh, constricted, and in a broad Scots brogue. 'What the devil are you doing here, man? Come out and show yourself.'

The low-slung branches of the copse began to rustle, eventually parting like a pair of leafy drapes. And from beyond the tree line stepped a tiny figure. An adult, certainly, dressed in the grey wool of the Scots Brigade, but a fellow whose head would not have reached Anthony Payne's waist.

Simeon Barkworth grinned, bearing small, sharp teeth and eyes that were a deep yellow hue. 'Well met, sir.'

Stryker was checking on the ammunition wagon when Burton found him. He was standing on the tips of his toes, leaning across the side-slats performing a rapid inventory of the arms and powder, but turned when the lieutenant cleared his throat.

'Something of a millstone about our necks, eh?'

Burton shrugged as he stepped into the gloom of the little cave. 'None blame you, sir. We all would have taken it had we the chance.' He removed his hat, propping it in the crook of his inert arm, and ruffled his long, mousy hair. It was a relatively muggy evening, and the strands at his forehead were matted and dark. 'And at least we'll never exhaust our shot and powder.'

Stryker chuckled ruefully. 'That's true. If only the Roundheads had been transporting food as well.' He leant against the wagon, suddenly tired, shoulder blades digging into the timbers. He felt his stomach rumble, and a thought struck him. 'Slaughter one of the horses.'

Burton's brow rose. 'Sir?'

'Wild is coming. We will not surrender to him, and Hogg's threats have failed, so they will come as soon as their cannons arrive. The men cannot fight on parched beef and berries alone.'

'But to cook the meat—'

'If an ember strikes our cache,' he patted the side of the wagon, 'would that be so bad?' Even as the words left his mouth, Stryker regretted the fatalistic sentiment. He was glad only Burton had heard. He shook his head angrily. 'I am sorry, Andrew. That was wrong of me.'

'No harm done, sir,' the lieutenant replied stoically.

'But now I come to think on it, perhaps the men *should* eat well. The cart is nicely protected in this cave, after all.'

'Then we're agreed. Have Skellen pick one of Wild's destriers.'

'I will, sir. The men'll be pleased.' A shadow crossed Burton's face suddenly, as though a terrible thought had stabbed at him. 'I confessed my feelings to Miss Cade.'

The words had been blurted so unexpectedly that it took Stryker several moments to absorb what his second-in-command had said. 'You did what?'

Burton grimaced. 'Confessed my feelings, sir. You advised me to—'

'Wait,' Stryker ordered, stepping away from the wagon. '*I* advised you?'

'Aye, sir,' Burton retorted defensively. 'There was nothing for me to lose, you said.'

Stryker struggled to recall the detail of their earlier conversation. 'I—I did.' He scratched a sudden itch at his neck. 'But I meant further down the way, perhaps. Not days after the deaths of her father and protector.'

'But that's just it, sir,' Burton protested, the words becoming shrill as they tumbled from his mouth. 'I should wait until we're away from here? Safe at Launceston or Oxford or wherever? We're never getting off this damned hill. I decided to seize the moment. *Carpe diem*, as Captain Forrester would say.'

Stryker drew in a huge breath and blew out his cheeks, feeling the scar tissue on the left of his face pull against the movement. 'Christ, Andrew, what did she say?'

Burton sighed. 'She was her usual polite, radiant self.'

'But?'

'But she said this was not the time for such matters.'

295

'Hardly surprising,' Stryker said without thinking. A pang of wretchedness twisted his guts when he saw his friend's crestfallen expression. 'I am sorry, though, Andrew. Truly.'

'I—' Burton began tentatively, staring hard at the ground.

'Go on.'

The lieutenant's gaze finally drifted up from the floor to fix on Stryker's lonely eye. 'I had thought, perchance, that you and her—'

Stryker remembered the strange, almost hostile looks Burton had given him these past days, and realized with shock that they must have been borne of jealousy. 'Miss Cade and I?' he spluttered, desperately hoping that the guilt would not be etched on his face. He might never have acted on his attraction for Cecily, but attraction there most certainly had been. 'S'blood, Lieutenant, no! What gave you that—?' He remembered the moment when Burton had seen him with his hands on Cecily's shoulders. 'The other evening?'

Burton nodded, but already his challenging expression was transforming into a look of embarrassment. 'Aye, sir. It was silly of me. My mind playing tricks, evidently.'

'Evidently.'

Burton looked at the wagon suddenly, his face cracking in a sad smile. 'Perhaps it would be a good thing if that lot were to go up. It would save my blushes.'

Stryker moved back to the vehicle, peering in at the powder barrels and bags of shot. 'What a sight it would make. I can imagine old Seek Wisdom would be a tad vexed if we were to blow up his castle, though.'

And then a thought came to Stryker. It hit him like one

of the huge mortar shells he had faced at Lichfield. Screaming, blazing, and awesome. He spun on his heel. 'Fetch ten men, Lieutenant.'

'Sir?' Burton, still crestfallen, muttered in a hollow voice.

'Fetch ten men,' Stryker repeated, 'and be quick about it.' Burton and his worries would have to wait.

Because Stryker had had an idea, an epiphany, and the game would change once again.

CHAPTER 14

Stryker was glad he had risked a fire the previous night, for the garrison's bellies were full, their strength and spirits high, when the first ashen light began to lift night's shawl. He was glad because out on the grey plains from which the tor sprang there were cannon.

The dread alarm had been cried out from the lookouts on the very highest crags. The hawk-eyed Trowbridge twins, Jack and Harry, had reported movement out on the flat ground to the east during the darkest hours, but they could not tell exactly what transpired. Encroaching daylight had gradually illuminated the hills and the woods, the river and the abandoned village, and, ominously for the beleaguered Royalists, a pair of gleaming black tubes, each mounted on large wheels and drawn by a pair of horses.

Musketry splintered the still morn as soon as the ordnance was spotted, for Stryker immediately dispatched a squad from the summit to harass the gunners and matrosses.

'He means to drive us out,' he had said to Lieutenant Burton as the officer, still sullen from Cecily Cade's rejection, led the redcoats down towards the shimmering waterway and the crumbling village beyond. 'They hope to push us on to the open ground before the barn.'

'Where they'll shred us,' Burton replied bluntly.

'Aye, so get as close as you can. Don't let the bastards fire.'

Burton had done well, for his red-coated squad were able to take shelter within the ruined longhouses, propping their weapons on the rough-hewn walls and spitting shots at the men gathered about the black-mouthed guns. The range was too great to be effective, but their bullets still whipped close enough to make the crews flinch and falter, and the Royalists jeered at them from up high.

But the victory was small mercy, for, by midday, Colonel Wild, conspicuous with his stark stripe of grey hair, had ridden out to personally assess the dismal progress. The crews were redeployed almost immediately, one sent south and the other circling all the way round the hill to take up position on the western plain, a squad of Wild's fearsome harquebusiers left in their wake to guard any potential escape eastwards.

Stryker suspected that this was not an ideal situation for Wild, but the compromise would allow the colonel's gunners to come close enough to do certain damage without the fear of vengeful musket fire. He ordered his men to keep up the harrying shots, but, with the squads now forced to shoot from back on the tor, the range was far too great. The crackle of flying lead served only to irritate the Parliamentarian crews as a swarm of flies might pester a horse, but they stuck to their work in the knowledge that, even if a lucky ball were to hit home, its speed would be pathetic.

The falconets quickly began their barrage. The

opening shots came in together, one from the south and the other from the west, twin reports echoing like distant thunder across the high moor. The screaming iron spheres missed, flying well above the granite crest, passing each other in the still air, but the cheer from the Royalist garrison was desultory at best. They all knew that, eventually, the gunners would find their range.

Stryker barked orders for his men to seek shelter. They moved to the higher ground, huddling behind the jagged standing stones, the smooth, broad boulders, and the vast stacks. Stryker himself took up position on the crest, moving quickly to the wide avenue between the largest two stacks. There, secreted in one of the little caves, he caught sight of Cecily Cade. Her eyes were wide orbs, tear-reddened and glistening. The carter, Marcus Bailey, was with her, thin hands trembling in his lap. He nodded to them both, hoping his show of confidence would provide some solace.

The next shots exploded from down on the plain, first from the south and then the west. Falconets were not siege pieces, their missiles tiny by comparison, but here, firing with impunity at the isolated hill, they might have been a brace of demi-cannon. The shots missed again, but their screaming sound was louder this time, closer, and even the hardest of Stryker's veterans involuntarily flinched.

'No riders, sir,' Sergeant Skellen's droning voice reached him in the aftermath of the volley.

Stryker turned to look up at his old ally. 'They mean to soften us up a while.'

Skellen nodded. 'Aye, I think you're right, sir. Mash our wits afore they strike.'

'That's what I'd do. Still, we must be thankful they do not have lanthorne, eh?'

Skellen whistled softly. 'Jesu, sir, that'd sting a bit.'

'More than sting, Will.' Lanthorne shot consisted of a closed cylindrical case, packed with smaller lead balls, that would disintegrate when fired, spraying its lethal projectiles in a wide area. The weapon might have been extremely useful against the men trapped on the tor, and Stryker was thankful Wild's falconets were too small to fire such ammunition.

The air filled with an ear-splitting crescendo as the next shot came in. It was the gun to the south that had fired, and, though Stryker could not see where it had struck, a call from one of his men on the south-facing ridge confirmed that the ball had hit the slope, pounding into the earth. He imagined the huge clump of soil and grass driven up before it.

The cannon to the west fired almost immediately. Stryker shrunk as low as he could, feeling the turf on his cheek. This time the gunners had found their range, and the careening round shot ricocheted off the side of a tall stack to his right, smashing noisily into another. A shard of rock twirled away, scything frighteningly close to a crouching musketeer's face.

Even as Stryker breathed a sigh of relief, a shrill scream cut across the cannon's echo, and he saw that another man had been sitting behind the first musketeer. The vicious stone splinter had cleaved sickeningly into his groin, its wider end still jutting from the redcoat's inner thigh in a macabre parody of his genitals. Blood jetted steaming and unyielding from the wound to drench the ground. His face seemed to become blue, then faded to a deathly white, and he slumped back in silence.

'Jesu,' Skellen whispered.

Stryker might have been thankful that the pieces were too small to fire lanthorne, but now, faced with a brace of falconets working in tandem, he realized the situation was nevertheless dire. Yes, his men could seek shelter in the avenue at the tor's summit, protected by the impenetrable granite stacks that jutted skyward like a giant's crown, but then who would defend the hill? Their survival thus far had been the ability to man the slopes with pike and musket. The jagged stones littering the hillside negated any horse-borne assault, and the muskets, fired from behind those stones, had been enough to keep men on foot at bay.

But now things had changed, dramatically and fatefully. The cannon would set to work on the once safe slopes, pounding great chunks out of the lesser rocks and forcing the Royalists to seek solace higher up. Which meant Wild's men, his dismounted cavalry and dragoons, could charge up the tor unhindered, overwhelming the men on the crest with their superior numbers.

Stryker caught Skellen's hooded gaze. 'It's not riders we should watch for, but infantry.'

Out on the plain to the west, Colonel Gabriel Wild bent low to direct one of the falconets. He was not a gunner, of course, and had no real experience with ordnance, but this fight was personal, and he'd be damned if he was not spearheading the bombardment.

'A little higher,' he snapped at the matross.

The gunner's assistant rolled his eyes, but sullenly did what he was told.

'Truly, Colonel,' the gun captain insisted, 'I do know my business.'

Wild straightened and fixed the gunner with a baleful

look. 'I dare say you do, sir, but I have overall command here, and you'll take my direction or you'll be this cannon's next target. Understand?'

The gunner nodded stiffly. 'Sir.'

'Good.' Wild wound a strand of hair about his forefinger, silver stripe mixing helter-skelter with brown. 'Now keep pounding the Romish malignants.'

'We will, sir,' confirmed the gun captain. 'Though they're safe enough up on the crest.'

Wild frowned as he stared up at the grey tor. 'You'll hit it, though.'

The gunner nodded frantically, aware that the words had been meant as a statement rather than a question. 'One more shot, Colonel, and we'll have them locked in sight. There'll be no missing after that.' He wrung gloved hands nervously. 'But we shan't penetrate it, d'you see? 'Tis granite, sir. Thick and sturdy. Good as any castle wall.' He patted the falconet's big wheel affectionately. 'And she'd be no use 'gainst a castle.'

'It will suffice,' Wild grunted. 'All I want is to keep the buggers up on the high ground. If you can do that for me, my lads will do the rest.'

The gunner wiped his sooty brow, smearing the stain with more filth and sweat. 'Oh, that'll be simple enough, sir. They won't want to come a pace b'yon' those biggest stacks. Give me an hour, and the whole place'll be empty as a slut wi' punk's evil.'

'Quite,' Wild said, the corner of his lip upturning in distaste. 'But do not rush to it so. I would attack on the morrow.'

The gunner gawped up at the big cavalryman. 'The morrow, sir?'

'You were too damned late in preparation,' Wild said irritably. 'I would escalade in daylight.' In truth, Wild did not relish the prospect of another night assault, given the failure of the last attempt. If they attacked now and things went wrong, he would soon find himself running short of light.

'You will find your shots now, sir. Pound the very wits out of the knaves for the rest of the day, and wear them down to shadows. Rest only with nightfall, and begin again at dawn. By the time we attack, they will be begging to surrender.'

Just then the matross signalled that the gun had been scoured to eradicate any debris from the previous shot. 'She's ready?' the gun captain asked.

'Aye, sir, that she is.'

'Then load her up and let her fly, Jed, eh?'

Wild watched the gunner pace over to the cannon as the matross, Jed, reloaded and primed it. He turned away just as the crew were about to fire, fixing his sharp eyes on the high tor, praying for the round shot to somehow find a chink in that deep stand of rock and pluck Stryker's head from his shoulders.

The falconet roared, muzzle flashing, and the whole scorching unit reeled back on its groaning wheels. Smoke billowed all around in a stinking cloud, and Wild had to screw up his face to prevent his eyeballs from blurring with moisture. He saw the ball strike home, slamming with a cacophonous crash into the granite face, shards of iron and stone flung far and wide. Up on the tor, the redcoats jeered defiantly, but Wild did not care.

'Well done,' he said simply, catching the gunner's eye.

Stryker and his men could crow all they liked, he

thought, for the falconets had found their range, and now they would turn the stubborn hill into a place of nightmare.

NEAR TORRINGTON, DEVON, 7 MAY 1643

Henry Grey, First Earl of Stamford, had to be carried off his horse when he arrived at the River Torridge, for his gouty leg was as bad as ever. He swore when the aides set him on the mangled earth, shards of pain shooting through his feet and up to his knees, and the men froze, fearful of his temper. He waved them away, insisting that he could walk so long as one of them brought him a robust cane. When it had been fetched, Stamford took a huge breath, gritted his teeth against the pain, and limped slowly towards the river. Because it was there, crammed along the west bank of the rushing Torridge, that a large part of his army had gathered.

There were tents as far as the eye could see. Grimy ranks of off-white awnings, ordered in rough lines, narrow corridors of dead grass between. Men practised sword-play in those corridors, bare-chested and grunting behind their blades, while some sang songs of home and others darned clothes or puffed smoke. The camp followers – whores, goodwives and their multitude of filthy urchins – sat around the black remains of long-cold fires, calling to one another with coarse voices and bawdy humour. Some fished in the bone-chilling river, others stood knee-deep in the corrugated flow, dunking, scrubbing, and wringing garments for their menfolk.

As Stamford walked with his lurching gait into the

camp, a pair of sentries, faces wreathed in tobacco smoke, clambered to their feet from rickety stools and doffed caps respectfully. He acknowledged them with a curt nod, glancing sideways at one of the officers who had accompanied him from the town. 'Which are these, Major Lewendon?'

Lewendon, a sharp-featured fellow of average height, wrinkled his pointed nose like a rat sniffing the breeze. 'Northcote's, my lord. Devon men all. No room left in the town for them, I'm afraid.'

'Good, good,' Stamford replied absently, more concerned with the agonies in his limbs. He paused for a rest, swollen ankles screaming at the unwanted exercise. 'How many?'

Lewendon thought for a moment, removing his hat and sweeping a long-nailed hand across a head of slicked-back auburn hair that smelled strongly of lavender. 'Twelve hundred or so, sir.'

Stamford pursed his lips as he calculated his strength. 'Which brings us just shy of four thousand foot, does it not?'

Lewendon's head twitched in a minute nod. 'Thereabouts, my lord, aye. A healthy number, what with the horse reaching more'n a thousand.'

'Not healthy enough, Major,' Stamford said. In truth, he was pleased with the results of the rapid muster. He had spared no effort in raising the largest field army possible to deliver a fatal blow to the region's Royalists. Yet he would never be entirely happy. The Cornish might have been villains to a man, but they were tougher than the swords they carried, and he knew their destruction would be a difficult task indeed. 'Still, we must net this flock of Cornish choughs before they're allowed to fly to Hertford.'

'That is their plan?'

Stamford nodded. 'Aye, Major, we know it.' He thought of one of the paper sheets found in General Hopton's portmanteau. The scrawling lines of ink had ordered the Cornish army into Somerset to merge with Royalist forces from Oxford, under the command of the Marquis of Hertford, the King's Lieutenant-General for the West. 'It is a matter of certainty.'

Lewendon's nose wrinkled again. 'Might we wait a week, my lord?'

Stamford frowned deeply, irritated by Lewendon's timidity. He was a clever fellow, astute and sensible – the ideal aide – which was why the earl tolerated his company, but the man was as craven as a baby dormouse. 'We must strike as soon as is practicable, Jonathan.'

The major's little brown eyes flickered around the encampment as he evidently searched for the right words. 'There are other units en route, sir,' he said finally, fidgeting with the sash at his waist. 'A detachment comes from Somerset, and men are yet expected from Dawlish, Sidmouth, and Honiton.'

Stamford resumed his progress through the camp, wincing at his puffy legs, which seared as though gripped by hot pincers. 'Strength?' he asked through labouring lungs.

Lewendon, keeping pace at his side, held his hands at the base of his spine. 'Another thousand, I'd wager, sir.'

The Earl of Stamford clicked his tongue as he considered the impact that reserve would make. It would be quite some number to leave behind. Perhaps even the difference between victory and defeat. He passed a pair of bare-chested sergeants locked in private duel, each

307

wielding a huge halberd in knotted hands. They immediately broke away when they spotted him, standing straight-backed, embarrassed that their commander had found them in such an undignified state. But Stamford offered a smile, waved them on, for he was pleased that his men took time to perfect their craft. Soon they would face a formidable foe.

'Another thousand such fighters would be valuable,' he said to no one in particular, tugging gently at the black hair of his moustache.

'Aye, they would, sir,' Major Lewendon replied. 'Invaluable.'

Stamford sighed. 'So be it. We linger here a little longer, then. Hopton will still have to guess at the focus of our thrust.' He halted again, this time to point a threatening finger at his advisor. 'Not a week, mind, but a matter of days, understand?'

Lewendon nodded rapidly, again putting the earl in mind of a rodent. 'Aye, my lord.'

They walked a while in silence, each immersed in his own thoughts. Eventually the major glanced up, his pinched face creased in concern. 'The Cornish will not receive us kindly, my lord.'

'Ha!' Stamford bellowed heartily. 'You truly are the master of understatement, Major Lewendon!' He shook his head, the smile still present. 'No they damn well won't receive us kindly. Not a bit of it. They're king's men through and through. Near as bad as the bloody Welsh. The county will require an amount of persuasion before they bow to the Parliament.'

Lewendon searched his commander's face. 'Persuasion?'

Henry Grey, First Earl of Stamford, set his jaw, leant

heavily against his stick, and rested his free hand on the hilt of his sword. 'Rough wooing, I believe it is called, Major.'

Major Jonathan Lewendon gnawed his lean bottom lip, swallowed hard, and stared down at the sword. 'Rough wooing, my lord.'

GARDNER'S TOR, DARTMOOR, 7 MAY 1643

It was just before midnight, and Stryker decided to make a sweep of the tor. He began at the village, where the horses were tethered and bright-eyed pickets searched the blackness, then made his way carefully about the periphery of the hill, acknowledging his men as he went. Some gambled, eyes straining to see the dice in the gloom, others enjoyed the meat they had cooked the previous night. Some kept careful watch, one or two cleaned and honed weapons, but most snatched much needed sleep.

They needed sleep, because none had been free to them during daylight. The bombardment from the pair of small cannon had been relentless, ceasing only when darkness fell. The round shot were just small things, meant for tearing flesh on the battlefield, not hammering holes in stone, but the noise and the flying, lethal debris had forced the Royalists to huddle in tightly packed groups behind the biggest granite shelters, wondering with each shot whether a land attack was being launched as they impotently cowered. None came, although the lack of rest, the cramped conditions, and the merciless volleys took a serious toll. Darkness had not come soon enough.

Stryker, finally free to roam, walked the avenue as soon

as he reached the flat top, nodding to the lookouts positioned on the pinnacles of the core, cannon-pocked stacks. His boot clanged against something hard, and he had to quickly leap to avoid a pile of discarded pikes, cursing softly as he went.

The noise must have reached the caves further along the passage, for a figure emerged from one of the larger ones.

'Is everything as it should be, Miss Cade?' Stryker asked as Cecily, near luminescent in the darkness, approached him.

He could not see her face clearly yet, even though her voice rang smooth and clear from the night. 'Just so, Captain, thank you.'

Stryker tried to see past her to the other small caves. 'Bailey?'

'He sleeps, sir. His snoring wakes me, even through our stone curtain.' She began to turn away. 'May we speak privately, sir?'

Stryker nodded, padding quietly in her wake. She returned to the cavern set in the foot of the granite stack, and he stooped to follow her inside. Not for the first time, Stryker was impressed by the thickness of the walls. It might have been the lowest form of abode in which the girl had ever stayed, but at least it would keep her perfectly safe from the falconets out on the plain.

'You have spoken with Andrew?' Cecily's voice emanated from the very rear of the chamber.

'Lieutenant Burton?' Stryker, only a pace inside the low entrance, could barely see her, so he aimed his voice at the place where he thought she stood. 'Aye. He is—' he searched quickly for the right word, '—disappointed.'

'And I am sorry for that, truly. He's a kind man.'

'That he is.' It seemed strange to speak about his comrade, and Stryker felt suddenly awkward. 'I do not wish to be rude, Miss Cade, but is there something you want?'

With that, Cecily emerged from the back of the cave, features coming into focus as she stepped nearer to Stryker and the moonlit entrance. 'I want to leave this place.'

Stryker barely stifled a laugh, such was his surprise. 'You still sail that course? Have you seen what is out there?'

The girl's face was almost silver in the feeble glow, and beautiful as ever, but he noticed a tension in the eyes and mouth. It was not an expression of fear, he thought, but one of determination. 'Aye, sir. We are surrounded, they have cannon, and we are all going to die.' She shrugged. 'Hence my need to be away.'

Stryker was taken aback. The terrified, trembling, orphaned child seemed to have been overthrown by a resolute, single-minded woman. The tear-puffed eyes were wide as ever, but now the glisten of moisture had hardened into a glint of steel. 'Did you not see what they did to Otilwell Broom?'

She nodded firmly. 'I did, sir, and it cut me to the quick.'

'But?'

'But that changes nothing.' She stepped closer, eyes boring into his. 'I must leave. It is imperative.'

'Why?' Stryker asked, baffled. 'It is dangerous here, I freely admit, but you are safer with my men than out there alone. And there'll be no clemency for you. They have condemned you as a witch.'

'I will take my chances, Captain.'

He shook his head. 'No, miss, you will not.'

Her pale face lifted in a tight smile. 'I know how a man's mind turns, Captain. I have seen the way you look at me.'

She approached him then, slowly, silently. Stryker held her gaze, and saw that the green eyes were unblinking, huge, and intense. Her fragile hands rose into view, thin fingertips fumbling at the lace that fastened the plunging neckline of her saffron bodice.

'Cecily,' was all Stryker could say, his voice low and thick. He knew the protest was pathetic, even reluctant, but no other words would come. Still he stared, still her dextrous hands worked, and then the string was free, the ends hanging slack, and Stryker felt himself stir as she grasped the detached halves and eased them apart. Gradually the uppermost parts of her breasts were exposed to the midnight air, pure white and swelling gently with her measured breath. Stryker stared at them, and at the dark cleft between, imagining what else would soon be free. It was not a hot night, but he felt sweat prickle at his neck.

'We will trade,' Cecily whispered. 'You will give me a horse and free passage. And I will give you—' Gently, she began to pull the bodice down further, revealing more and more flesh.

Stryker knew he should tear his gaze away, but, in that silent moment, he found that he did not want to. She was truly something to behold. A vision of pure, breathtaking, heart-jolting beauty in this place of loneliness and death.

And then he thought of Lisette.

'Cecily,' he said finally, some clarity falteringly restored. 'Miss Cade. This is insane.'

Cecily moved closer, so that there was less than an arm's length between them. 'What have you to lose, sir?'

'No,' Stryker said with a resolve that startled even him. He took her wrists in his hands and drew them away from her chest. 'This is wrong. I have a woman.' He took the ends of the lace and refastened the bodice. 'And you are in my care, Miss Cade.'

Suddenly Cecily's eyes seemed to dim. The temptress was gone, chased away by the frightened girl. 'But—' she stammered, 'but I thought—'

Stryker smiled as he finished tying. 'You are a rare beauty, Miss Cade, and I confess that I am a weak enough man. But my affections are elsewhere.'

'But I am desperate, sir,' Cecily pleaded, hands grasping his to her sternum. 'I have important—'

'What?' Stryker snapped. 'Important what?'

She shook her head in mute defeat.

Stryker sighed. 'Then you will stay with the company.'

'Now I understand,' a man's voice echoed suddenly about the low chamber.

Stryker had to turn to see the newcomer, but he recognized the voice well enough. 'Andrew,' he said, pulling his hands from Cecily's grasp.

Lieutenant Andrew Burton was a young man. Yes, he was a veteran of many a fight, battle-hewn and tough as rawhide, but he was still just a stripling in Stryker's paternal eye. Still the nervous boy packed off to war not even a year since by a proud father and clucking mother. Yet now, here, in this dingy recess on an isolated Devonshire hill, his face bore all the marks of a man who had lived ten lifetimes. It was a mask of sorrow, etched and furrowed by deep despair. 'I sensed it.'

'Hold,' Stryker began, raising palms as if trying to calm a skittish colt. 'You have it wrong.'

Burton's gaze, harder than Stryker had ever seen it, flicked from his captain to Cecily and back again. 'You encouraged me.' He seemed to swallow hard suddenly, as if bile had spewed into his throat. 'When all the while you knew she would not—'

Abruptly the stunned lieutenant turned away, stooping to leave the cave as if the air within was poisoned.

'Wait, Andrew,' Stryker tried again, following Burton out into the night. 'It is not—'

Burton twisted back, thrusting a finger forcefully into his captain's chest. 'Damn you, sir.' And then he was walking again, striding away down the grey-walled avenue towards the south-east edge of the crest. Stryker followed, keeping pace but maintaining the distance, not wishing to confront his subordinate until they were beyond the range of prying eyes and ears.

'Lieutenant,' Stryker near growled when Burton had come to a standstill at an outcrop of shoulder-height rock part way down the slope. 'Have a care.'

Burton rounded on him, hissing angrily, 'Do not bring rank to bear here, sir. It demeans us both. I am young, but I am not stupid.'

Stryker was taken aback by the savagery in the younger man's tone. He lifted placating hands. 'Mark me well, Andrew. She is not all she seems.'

But it was as though he had addressed one of the boulders, for Burton's expression did not flinch or soften. 'Damn you, Captain,' he muttered in the lowest of voices, a look of utter hatred in his eyes. 'God damn you.'

'I did nothing,' Stryker protested forlornly. 'Mark me well, Andrew, she is hiding something. She meant to seduce me in order that I should allow her to leave.'

But even as he uttered the words Stryker knew how ridiculous they sounded, and it was no surprise to see Burton's look of bitter incredulity. 'You have Lisette, sir.'

He shook his head in disbelief. 'How many more women do you want?'

Stryker had had enough of his junior officer's attitude and gritted his teeth, stepping close so that Burton would see the dangerous glint of quicksilver in his eye. 'Rein in your manners, Lieutenant.'

But Burton simply gave a rueful sneer. 'A pox on your threats, sir.' To Stryker's amazement, he spat on the ground between them. 'And a pox on your false words, and on your greed and on your lust and on your goddamned treachery.'

'But—'

Burton turned away then, swift and abrupt, breaking through Stryker's sentence and stalking into the darkness. Stryker wanted to follow, to chase his protégé through the granite gauntlet of the tor's steep face and shake some sense into him. But he knew it would do no good. The younger man was in an incandescent rage, a fire burning so bright in his jealous heart that no amount of discussion would dowse it. And Stryker did not wish to give Burton the opportunity to turn the matter physical, for that could lead nowhere good. Instead he slumped back against the nearest stone and watched him go.

CHAPTER 15

Colonel Gabriel Wild strode out from the shit-carpeted building just as the falconets resumed their barrage. It was a new dawn, one that would finally see Stryker prised from his hill like a flea trapped between thumb and forefinger. Wild filled his lungs with the bracing air, revelling in the faint smell of sulphur it carried from the powder smoke, hawked up a gritty clump of saliva and despatched it on to the earth some yards away. He dug filthy fingertips into his bleary eyes, rubbed clear the last dregs of tiredness, and shook his head to untangle the long hair that had become so knotted during a fitful night's sleep.

'Spare me the rhetoric, Mister Hogg,' Wild growled as he noticed the witch-finder hobble into his field of vision. 'Your efforts have come to nothing. They will never surrender Stryker or his wench.'

The enormous Spaniard, José Ventura, waddled up behind Hogg, a sweaty sheen already glimmering across his blubbery face. He swept a tendril of oily hair from his forehead. 'His men must be greater devils than he.'

Wild smirked. 'Undoubtedly. Though I'm hardly shocked that they protect the girl. I would.'

Ventura looked aghast. 'But she is a witch, Co-lo-nel.'

'A witch with a young face and a snout-fair pair of tits, from what I could make out.'

Hogg held up his walking cane when his assistant made to argue. 'I would still see him hang.'

Wild looked at the witch-finder, his face becoming serious. 'Oh, the captain will die, sir, have no fear.' He bent down to pull the folded bucket-top boots up to his groin. 'Though I shall cut off his stones before he so much as sees a noose.' He straightened, scratched an itch at his stubbly chin and fastened the string at the top of his shirt. 'If he does not bleed out, then he's yours to dangle.'

Hogg nodded reluctant agreement. 'The man is a God-forgotten follower of Satan, Colonel. Señor Ventura and I have made it our life's work to seek out and destroy such men. Stryker is the worst of them. He *must* hang. And I must do it.'

'You have my word,' Wild said, clicking his fingers at a nearby trooper. 'But I get the girl.'

'So be it,' Hogg agreed.

The rapidity of the reply surprised Wild, and he raised an eyebrow. 'You do not want her neck stretched?'

Hogg bit the inside of his lip. 'I would see her hang, of course, Colonel. But she is irrelevant when compared with Stryker.'

The trooper had scuttled up to Wild with a sack full of kit, and he was busily laying out the colonel's gloves, gauntlet, and armour. Wild watched him carefully, braced to give the man a swift kick should he drop an item in the mud, but when he spoke it was to Hogg. 'Stryker means that much to you?'

'He does.' He paused as the twin cannon blasts

shattered the morning. 'God tells me that he, above all others, must be sent to hell.'

'Then you're in luck, sir, for I would attack this very morn.'

'Not luck,' Ventura muttered.

Wild glanced at him. 'As you like, señor.'

'You attack?' Hogg asked. 'It will succeed this time?'

Wild nodded confidently. 'We have cannon now, so they cannot man the lower slope, which, in turn, means we can send in our men without fear of those bloody muskets.' He shrugged. 'At least until our advance is well underway. Without the falconets that one-eyed Pope-swiver would place his musketeers down on the flat, and we wouldn't get close. But if the gunners keep up steady fire till the last moment, forcing Stryker on to the highest ground, we'll get a storming party to the slopes before he can respond. And once we can get enough men on that damned tor, we will overwhelm them.'

'But last time—' Hogg began.

'Last time,' Wild retorted sharply, 'we had only short-arm fire. Their muskets had the greater range. I had hoped that a night assault would hinder them, but they set the gorse alight and turned night to day.'

'What different?' José Ventura said belligerently.

Wild gritted his teeth, angered by the fat man's insolent tone. 'What is different, señor, is that this time we have dragoons. And though they are an inadequate bastard breed of foot and horse, they have decent muskets.'

The trooper had taken a large garment of buff leather from the cloth sack. He held it up for Wild to put on, and the colonel eased his arms into the sleeves, revelling in the feel and smell of his beloved coat. It smelled of war, of victory.

'It means,' Wild added, 'that this time when my men are climbing the slopes and Stryker's whoresons poke up their heads and start shooting, we can shoot back.' He let his aide fasten the ties of the buff-coat, noticing Ventura's inquisitive stare. 'What?'

Ventura's black eyes shot up. 'Why do you not wear armour?'

'I do,' Wild replied, nodding at the breastplate that lay at his feet.

Ventura shook his head, chins quivering in unison. 'I see men covered,' he said, running a hand from head to toe, 'like this.'

'Heavy cavalry, señor. Cuirassiers.' Wild thumped a fist against his leather-bound chest. 'But I am a harquebusier. The buff-coat may not protect me from pike thrusts or guns, but it offers robust protection against sword cuts. It is lighter than the full-body casing you've seen worn by the cuirassiers. *Ergo*, it gives me a good deal more manoeuvrability. Allows me to hunt even the most fleet-footed quarry.' He tapped the breastplate with his toe. 'And when worn with the simple plate, I am well protected from bullets too.'

The aide continued to fasten pieces of clothing and equipment on to Wild's body, and he tingled with the usual feeling of strength, of invincibility. 'We will batter the vipers from their nest,' he said, tugging his gloves over his fingers. One of the falconets boomed out on the plain, quickly followed by its sister to the south. He smiled as the echo faded. 'By Christ, we will batter them.'

'It's them dragooners we saw,' Sergeant William Skellen grunted as he squinted at the approaching force. 'Wondered when he'd get 'em on to us.'

From the western fringe of the tor's summit the Royalists watched the column of horsemen break from the tree line around the barn. They moved in good order, cantering in double file towards the waiting defenders. But these were not the destrier-mounted men of Wild's elite force. These men trotted to battle on smaller, poorer-looking beasts. They wore no plate, but coats of brown wool, breeches of grey, and simple montero caps. And most strikingly of all, the advancing horsemen brought with them the long-barrelled weapons of infantrymen.

'Aye,' agreed Stryker. 'He was giving Hogg a chance to scare us out.'

'Balls-up, that was.'

Stryker glanced across at his tall sergeant, who was crouched at his side behind a hefty boulder. 'And I'm grateful.'

Skellen sniffed derisively. 'If I 'ad a groat for every time some bugger called you a devil, I'd be harvestin' me own sotweed in the Chezzypeake, sir.'

Stryker laughed. 'I believe you would.'

They ducked when the falconets coughed their iron round shot once more. The ball coming from the west whipped in with a hellish scream, slamming hard into the rock to their right. Wicked splinters spun in all directions, and all across the crest Stryker caught sight of red-coated bodies shrinking back lest they be filleted by the deadly hailstorm.

'The delay,' Lieutenant Burton's grim voice reached him from further along the ridge, 'was due to the ordnance. Wild wished to give those falconets time to soften us up.'

And that, thought Stryker, had worked. He might have lost only one man, but the continual barrage could not go on forever. They were too exposed on the tor, too easy a target and with little hope of rescue. Wild could bombard from a distance or advance on foot, alternating the attacks until eventually the Royalists could stand no more.

Stryker peered beyond his sergeant's long-limbed frame to catch sight of Burton. 'He means to throw them at us.'

Burton ignored him as he had since the pair had resumed their vigil at dawn. Burton was still the company's second-in-command, and there was never any question as to whether he would do his duty, but the young officer had refused to look his captain in the eye even once. It was as though the bond between them had been utterly and irreparably severed.

Skellen chuckled blackly. 'Don't he remember what 'appened to the last lot what took a stroll up this hill?'

Stryker, still smarting from Burton's snub, peered gingerly above the boulder, studying the approaching dragoons. 'These are ones he can afford to lose.'

Burton clambered to his knees to watch the column. 'He'll use the dragooners and cannon to force us off the tor,' he said, pointedly addressing Skellen, 'and save his feather-heads for the chase.'

That was the size of it, thought Stryker. The chase. Those fearsome, brooding, glinting harquebusiers would hold back, letting the expendable dragoons weed the Royalists out, and then, when Stryker's force was out on the plain and with nowhere to run or hide, they would go to work.

The next shot exploded to the south. Shouts rang out across the summit to confirm that none were harmed, but even Stryker inwardly admitted that his nerves were beginning to fray. Part of him would rather have taken his chances out in the open, and he considered making a break for the slopes. But that, of course, was what his enemies wanted.

'Hold!' he bellowed as loudly as his parched mouth would allow. 'Hold, I say, or you'll deal with me!'

The falconet to the west bolted backwards as its black mouth spewed fire and smoke. A dread silence reigned for a second as the defenders awaited the inevitable, and then, like a thunder clap immediately at their heads, the little projectile struck home, taking a sizeable chunk of rock from the tallest obelisk. Stryker winced, Skellen cursed, and somewhere back within the safety of the avenue Cecily Cade screamed.

Cecily Cade. The image of her in that moonlit cave came to Stryker's mind. The woman who was so desperate to leave the tor that she had attempted to seduce him. He had chosen Lisette, the woman he loved and hated in equal measure, yet would never admit how close Cecily had come to succeeding. But why had she done it? He had not spoken to her since those surreal hours of darkness, and now, as the enemy approached once more, he wondered if her reasons would ever be revealed. Instinctively he looked across at Burton, and found that the lieutenant was staring at him. The young man's gaze was steady, unblinking, and malevolent.

A cry of alarm went up before Stryker could think of something to say, and he inched his head above the natural barricade, only to see the dragoons spurring into a gallop.

They had spread out, near threescore of them, dividing into two sections, one maintaining its course, the other veering away to the south.

'Here they come!' someone bellowed away to the rear.

'Muskets!' Stryker barked. 'Muskets down on the slope! Pikes go with them!'

In that moment he had understood that the dragoons were mounting their attack, and the ordnance, for now at least, would be forced to keep silent, lest they shot at their comrades' backs.

'Lieutenant! With me!' Stryker barked, and scrambled to his feet.

Keeping as low as possible in case his assumption proved wrong, he scrambled quickly back to the tor's epicentre. He straightened when he reached the avenue, protected now from any round shot, and sprinted along its length until he was on the southern periphery of the hill. There, crouching low again, he observed the advance of the detachment of dragoons. They swept past the smoking falconet, kicking their mounts on, desperate to reach the foot of the tor while the Royalists were gathered at the summit and hence too far away to bring their muskets to bear.

'*Muskets*!' he bawled again. It was then that he turned back, relieved to see that Burton had obeyed the order to follow. He had half expected the lieutenant to ignore him. 'Andrew, you command here. Get the musketeers down on the lower ground and shoot the buggers as they come in.'

Burton's surly nod annoyed Stryker, and he considered slapping some sense into his subordinate there and then, but this was not the time. Leaving the southern face in Burton's capable hands, he ran to check on the eastward slope. The squad of harquebusiers, stationed there when the first cannon position had been abandoned, were already advancing, safe in the knowledge that the redcoats were fully occupied with the dragoons. The first of them had crossed the river, and three or four, dismounted and with blades drawn, were cutting the tethers of the white-eyed destriers. Colonel Wild had his horses back.

When Stryker returned to the western face he was pleased to see that Skellen and Heel had organized the musketeers and pikemen into pairs, placing them at intervals all the way down to the flat plain. They were giving sporadic fire from the advanced positions, desperate to turn back the charging dragoons. But those horsemen, far from abandoning their assault, slewed to a mud-flinging halt at the foot of the tor and dismounted, moving quickly behind the bodies of their snorting mounts. Thus protected, they unslung their own muskets, propped them across the terrified horses' spines, and returned fire.

This was what Stryker had feared. The far greater range and accuracy of the dragoons' muskets made them a deadlier force than Wild's pistol-wielding cavalry. It was as though the Parliamentarians deployed infantrymen against the tor, except these men brought their own living, breathing shields to battle.

For a time it seemed as if the fight had reached an impasse. The Royalists, freed by the lack of artillery fire, were far enough advanced to make their shots meaningful, while the dragoons, evidently hard-bitten men of experience, held their positions stubbornly.

And then the falconets fired.

It was as if time stood still in those first moments. The

cannon out on the west plain coughed, recoiled, and, to Stryker at least, it seemed as though every man at the tor, Royalist and Parliamentarian alike, froze in utter horror. Every pair of eyes flickered skyward, every man prayed that it would not be him picked out by the hurled lump of iron.

The round shot roared in above the shocked dragoons, missing their heads and impacting midway up the slope. It took one of Stryker's pikemen in the shoulder, tearing away skin, muscle, and bone as though the man were made of water. The pikeman screamed for his mother, fell back on the turf, and vanished amid the fine spray of his own blood as it pumped wildly from his shattered torso. He kicked suddenly, flailed as Otilwell Broom had flailed, and then fell still.

All at once the fight changed. Stryker's redcoats began to retreat, albeit falteringly and in good order, and the dragoons, suddenly emboldened, emerged from behind their horses and ran to the slope's first granite outcrops. They had a foothold now, and it would be harder to repel the new invaders. Stryker's veterans had done it before, of course, for Wild's first attack in the dead of night had penetrated this far, but crucially those men had carried inferior weapons. The dragoons were not so hamstrung.

A runner from the southern edge drew up beside Stryker, breathlessly recounting a similar tale from Burton's position. The enemy were on the hill. 'Tell the lieutenant to move on my mark. He'll know what to do.'

'Aye, sir,' the messenger nodded, scampering up the hillside like a fallow deer.

The first dragoons began to break free, scuttling up to the next boulder, shrinking back to load their muskets, giving fire and moving on. Again they began to stall as Stryker's men dug in, the foremost pikemen dashing down the slope to jab with their vast spears in order to disrupt them as they prepared their weapons. But the artillery rent the air once more, another ball sent speeding towards the tor, and the redcoats were forced to fall back, scrambling behind the rocks that littered the slopes. This time the advancing dragoons were caught in the line of fire, and one of their men was cut near in two by the merciless iron, guts exploding forth as the ball hit him in the small of his back.

Now the dragoons understood. They would bear the brunt of the fight from both sides. Wild would keep his cannon to their bloody work, and Stryker would shoot down at them from on high. Their only hope was to purge the tor of the enemy once and for all. With a banshee scream, their captain brandished his sword, whirled it like a pirate's cutlass about his head, and roared his men on. The Roundheads clawed their way up the hill, hand over hand, past stone, bracken, and bush, desperate to reach the summit before the falconets were ready to fire again. Their young cornet was out in front, using his flagpole to jab at the defenders. Half a dozen musket-balls flurried past him in a sudden squall, shredding the colour, but, amazingly, sparing him.

Stryker was on the summit now, staring down at the raging torrent of brown coats that surged towards his men. He went to find Cecily Cade. As ever, she was in the little cave, curled in a tight ball and shrouded by the tremulous arm of Marcus Bailey. He stooped to get inside. '*Up! Up!*'

The frightened pair stared at him, orb-eyed and

326

shaking. Stryker strode quickly over to them, grasping Cecily's shoulder a little more roughly than was necessary, and dragged her to her feet. He twisted to look at Bailey. 'You too. *Out!*'

'What?' Cecily shrieked. 'I am sorry for my actions, sir, but do not offer me to them, I beg you!'

Stryker slapped her. 'Enough! You wanted to leave; we're leaving!' He dragged her into the avenue.

'What about the wagon?' Bailey's high-pitched voice came from a few paces behind them.

Stryker ignored him. They could not save it now.

He led them to a point on the west side of the tor that was equidistant between the two dragoon assaults. From here he could see both squads of brown-coated Parliamentarians and both sets of defenders. He turned to his drummers, who had come, as prearranged, to stand behind him. 'Give the order!'

The drums beat out their call, echoing about the slopes and the granite and into the clouds above and the hills beyond. At once men began to gather. They swarmed to Stryker's position from the east, where Wild's cavalry were waiting, from the south, where Burton led the defence, and from the north and west; muskets, pikes and swords brandished, lungs heaving, faces caked in soot and sweat. The dragoons seemed to falter at the sudden retreat, wondering at the reasoning after such a stoic defence, and they peered up at the summit in bewilderment.

Cecily met his gaze. 'What is happening, sir?'

Stryker drew his sword. 'Wild believes we will flee to the east, to the village and its walls, for we would be mad to take our chances on the open ground.'

Her eyes widened. 'But we *are* to take our chances?'

Stryker turned away, releasing his grip on her arm and raising his sword. 'Follow me! Fight your way through the dragooners and follow me! Don't look back! Do *not* look back!'

And then he ran. He leapt over the brow of the hill, stumbled as he hit the first sloping turf, and bolted down the slope. The dragoons to the south and west, still mystified from the sudden disengagement, were beginning to realize that the defenders were making a break for freedom, and their leaders ordered them to engage. They scuttled sideways like crabs on the hillside, the most alert managing to waylay the slowest redcoats, and the tor suddenly rang with the clanging song of swords.

But most of Stryker's company made it to the flat ground unhindered. Stryker regretted leaving Cecily and Marcus, but he needed to move quickly, to show his men where they must run. He sprinted across the heather-swathed terrain, leaping rocks and rabbit holes, sword still high, chest on fire. Then he heard the thunder, and, disobeying his own order, risked a glance over his shoulder. What he saw chilled the very pit of his stomach. Cavalry galloped in their wake. Elite cavalry with muscular chargers and razor-sharp swords, black cormorant feathers sprouting from their glinting lobster pots. A wide, snarling, thundering, metal-crested wave, dark pennant rippling at the head.

Wild and his troop had swept round from the east, where they had gathered, beyond the decrepit village, expecting to cut Stryker's fleeing men down, not imagining for a moment that the Royalists would run to the south-west. But they had seen the fugitives go and had moved to intercept them, and now he saw the mad blood-lust in the whites of their eyes and the gleam of teeth beyond savage grins as they inexorably shortened the distance. The cavalrymen had had to change tack, certainly, but a fight out here, on the exposed, flat heathland, would be like slaughtering so many lambs.

The ragtag mass of Royalists had only moments left when Stryker reached the cist. The ancient stone circle was exactly where he remembered from the night Gardner and Barkworth had vanished into the ground, and he crashed through the bracken veil, dozens of clattering footsteps hitting the stones in his wake.

He turned quickly. 'Pikes to the flanks! Pikes to the flanks!'

William Skellen was there, head and shoulders above the melee. He repeated the order, physically moving many of the men into place, shoving those wielding pikes out to the sides and hauling the rest into the centre. 'Charge fer 'orse!' he bellowed when he was happy with the formation. The pikemen jammed the butt ends of their pole-arms against the instep of a shoe and angled the bladed head upwards. The sergeant glared at the musketeers. 'Any wi' primed pieces, give 'em murder!'

Colonel Gabriel Wild was only a matter of yards from the Royalist stragglers when he saw the front rank of redcoated musketeers shoulder matchlocks. He wheeled away at the last moment, cringing as the weapons flashed, spitting deadly lead into his charging cavalrymen. Two men fell, the rest followed their leader, hauling on reins to sheer out of range.

As the Roundhead harquebusiers regrouped, Wild wondered at the sanity of this last-ditch break for freedom. They had to flee, of course, for they could not hope to ride out the destruction wrought by Wild's cannon and dragoons, but it had surprised him that they chose to run on to the wide expanse of the plain. He had waited out to the east, fully expecting to see them bolt into the tumble-down enclosures of the old village in a futile attempt to find at least nominal protection, and had been entirely bewildered to see them bolt in the opposite direction. But so be it, he thought as he brought his mount back to the troop's right flank. This would be easier.

Wild searched briefly for one of his officers. 'Captain Hound!'

One of the riders spurred from the line, lifting his visor to see Wild. 'Sir?'

'Take half the men, Captain, and chase them out o' that bloody bracken.' He never trusted such concealed terrain. One never knew what hoof-breaking horrors might lie in wait, and he had no intention of risking the whole troop until the way was clear. 'Attack their centre. You'll have to put up with one more volley, but it'll be weak enough, and you must avoid those damned pikes at all costs. Understood?'

The captain lowered his visor. 'Sir.'

Wild watched as half his troop cantered out of the line, breaking swiftly into a charge. Soon they filled the land between him and the Royalists, and he could not easily discern anything beyond their plate-covered backs, bobbing in time with the horses. But he did notice the redcoats begin to move. The pikemen at the edge of the bracken stayed rigid, their horse-killing spears angled up to pierce any mount that dared gallop close, but things seemed more fluid at the centre of Stryker's last stand. A new rank of musketeers came to the fore, shots cracked out from their malevolent muzzles, unsaddling three Parliamentarians, to be quickly replaced by the next group. But then, when that last volley had been spat into the Dartmoor air, the musketeers melted away.

'What the devil?' Wild whispered to himself as he watched the men at the very centre of the bracken run pell-mell in the opposite direction. Their fear was understandable, but he could not fathom why they had left the pikemen in place. Something in the pit of his guts twisted. He did not know why, could not understand the feeling in his moment of triumph, and yet something here was out of kilter.

'Wait!' Wild bellowed, but his voice was drowned out by the din of hooves and the cheers of his men. He stood tall in his stirrups, ignoring his churning bowels and willing his beloved horsemen on. They broke through the outermost bracken leaves, pulverizing the mouldering foliage to mulch and pouring between the flanking pike units, who quickly stepped back, intent only on bringing down the musketeers who had so suddenly abandoned their comrades.

'Why aren't they engaging?' one of Wild's inferiors muttered at his left hand. 'Sir?'

'What?' Wild snapped irritably.

'Why aren't the pikes engaging?'

'Now!' Captain Stryker roared. He had retreated some fifty paces, allowing the horsemen to funnel deep into the pike-walled corridor. 'Now!'

Ensign Matthew Chase was at Stryker's side, gloved hands gripping tightly to the huge red and white banner under which Stryker's company fought. Immediately he

331

thrust the standard aloft, waved it in a wide figure of eight, and the world erupted.

Stryker had not wanted his pikemen to engage in the fight for two reasons. Firstly, their purpose was to force the cavalry into the narrow passage that followed the course of Seek Wisdom Gardner's secret tunnel. And secondly, they needed to be free to run as soon as the explosives, packed tight along the length of the ancient vault, took the spark. In the event, those men had executed their task perfectly. The half-troop had galloped above the tunnel, the short fuse had been lit on Ensign Chase's signal, and the ground had opened, gaping and terrible, to gulp nearly forty of Colonel Wild's best men into oblivion.

Smoke choked the air, stung the eyes, burnt the throat. The stink of scorched flesh pervaded without remorse, the groans of the wounded ringing out from the huge crater. The earth seemed to hiss, steaming like a vast cauldron. For a time all was still. The pikemen, only just clear of the explosion, and many with singed eyebrows, staggered back to rejoin the rest of the company. Stryker, ears ringing, nodded his thanks before searching for the next danger. Beyond the detonated mine, beyond the ragged, torn hooves and the strewn limbs, Colonel Wild still stood in his stirrups, slack-jawed and apple-eyed. Stryker waited for him to move, but he seemed as static as one of the tor's rocks.

It was when the dragoons appeared that Stryker knew the fight's heart still beat. They drew up around Wild's remaining men, stunned faces surveying the twisted carnage.

'You see?' a nasal voice, harsh and insistent, cut through the silence like a rapier through silk. 'You see? A witch!

Look what he does, this suckler of imps! This Satanic fornicator!'

Stryker peered through the powder smoke as it drifted sideways, masking and revealing faces like a transient shroud. Then he saw the face he knew he would find. Dark eyes, huge, hooked nose, long, horselike teeth. 'Hogg.'

Osmyn Hogg still berated the Parliamentarians. Cantered on his little piebald at their backs, screaming for them to lynch the warlock who had conjured such a fate for honest, godly folk. He was red-faced as he spat his venom, hands balled to white-knuckled fists, hatred etched deep in the lines at his brow and eyes.

And finally the Roundheads moved. Wild, perhaps shaken into action by the raging witch-finder, slumped down into his saddle and shook his head. He glanced at the men at his shoulders, eyes red-rimmed and expression groggy, but Stryker could see his lips twitching as orders were spoken.

They surged forward as one. Wild's fifty or so cavalrymen and a similar number of dragoons, come to smash the stubborn Royalists once and for all. Stryker's mind raced, but no more ideas would come. He had known the mine, crammed full of explosives from the ammunition wagon, would only stall the enemy. This outcome was no surprise. And yet now, as he lifted his sword one last time amid the eruption's smouldering aftermath, he knew he would fight to his last breath. He swallowed hard, throat sore, blinked the grit from his eye, and steadied his breathing. 'Come on, you bastards!' he snarled, thrusting his left foot out to brace for the impact of the charge as his pikemen prepared a steel hedge that would at least make life difficult for the oncoming horses.

It was a surprise, then, that the impact never came. At the last moment, with only a few yards to spare, the front rank of cavalrymen peeled away in a welter of curses and snorts and whinnies and cries of alarm. The second rank followed, then the rest, and soon the entire Roundhead column were wheeling back on to the open plain like a flock of startled sparrows.

Stryker let out the breath he did not realize he'd been holding. He watched the cavalry and dragoons gallop away, wondering if this were some elaborate feint designed to fool him.

'Well I'll be a ben bowse clap'dudgeon,' William Skellen's dour tone carried to Stryker's revived ears and he turned to look at his sergeant.

But he did not need to ask the cause of Skellen's exclamation, because through the clearing smoke cloud he suddenly saw men. Not dragoons or harquebusiers but infantrymen, most dressed in the same scarlet coats as his own company. They were a formidable-looking force, somewhere between forty and fifty, all armed and fresh. At their front stood three men who looked so dissimilar that they might have been part of a circus act, had Stryker not known two of them. One was a plump man with fleshy face, rosy cheeks, and sandy hair that fell beyond a wide-brimmed hat worn at a suitably rakish angle. The second man was a tiny figure, the size of a child, clad in a suit of grey, with a small sword at his waist; while the third was simply a giant. The biggest man Stryker had ever clapped his eye upon.

The sandy-haired fellow stepped forward, offered a theatrically deep bow, and grinned. 'What would you do without me, Stryker, old man? I dread to think.'

CHAPTER 16

Stryker led his newly expanded force from the tor as soon as the bodies had been buried. That had taken longer than usual, for, though a ready-made pit awaited the rows of dead, gaping like the mouth of a smoke-wreathed volcano, the grim task had been hampered by the sheer number of charred limbs that lay scattered far and wide. But, with the extra pairs of hands at Stryker's disposal, he had seen the job done with sombre efficiency in the eerie silence of the afternoon. And silent it had been, for the enemy had gone. Vanished northward on their thrashing mounts, battered and humiliated.

Thus, with Gardner's Tor at their backs, Stryker's column – ranks suddenly swollen to well over a hundred redcoats, six grizzled Cornishmen, Forrester's dozen prisoners, and a pair of crewless falconets – marched straight into the evening sun. They had the wagon too, though its powder cache had been substantially depleted, and the twin companies walked with a confident step, suddenly a force to be reckoned with.

'I am constantly your guardian angel,' Captain Lancelot Forrester chirped happily as he paced at the head of the column with the most senior men. All except Lieutenant Burton, who chose to keep watch over the falconets at the rear.

Stryker was at Forrester's side, and he smiled ruefully before glancing at the diminutive Scot who scampered quickly in their wake. 'My guardian angel is Mister Barkworth. And Seek Wisdom and Fear the Lord Gardner.'

'Who?'

'The hermit I told you about.'

'Ah,' Forrester nodded, 'the one with the escape tunnel. What happened to our priestly friend?'

Stryker thought of the old Welshman. A man whose faith made him a natural Parliamentarian but whose moral compass steered him towards helping Stryker. 'He'll have been there somewhere. Watching. I have a lot to thank him for.'

'Stroke of genius,' Forrester exclaimed suddenly. 'Blowing up the tunnel, I mean.'

An image of Gardner stayed in Stryker's mind, though the space around him darkened with the memory of the night he had helped Barkworth escape. 'When I saw Simeon disappear into the ground, it hit me. Prince Rupert detonated a mine at Lichfield not three weeks ago. It sucked the walls into the ground, by all accounts.' He shrugged. 'Seemed we could do the same here.'

'Lichfield,' Forrester muttered wistfully.

'You said you spent some time there, sir?' a booming voice rumbled across their conversation, and both captains craned their heads to look up at Anthony Payne, his pace remarkably slow in comparison with the rest of the column. It was as though he need only take a casual stroll to match his purposeful comrades, such was the length of his vast stride.

'I did,' Forrester replied, before glancing at Stryker. 'We did.'

'I heard Sir John Gell put the place to the sword,' Payne said darkly.

Forrester wagged an admonishing finger. 'You mean you *read* it, Mister Payne. The pamphleteers made merry with the dastardly Gell's behaviour, though it was not so.'

Payne's moon-round face furrowed. 'Did he not refuse to return the Earl of Northampton's body after Hopton Fight?'

Forrester bobbed his chin. 'He did. Captain Stryker and I saw it with our own eyes.' He winked at Stryker. 'Eye.'

'But at Lichfield,' Stryker said, ignoring his friend's gentle mockery, 'he allowed most of the garrison to walk free from the Close. He was not compelled to that judgement, but chose it of his own accord. No man was put to the sword, as the pamphlets would claim.'

'But Captain Forrester told me he was like to hang you, sir,' Payne pressed.

Stryker nodded. 'Aye, that is true. And the captain, here.' He pointed rearward to where Skellen marched at the flank of the column, berating a pair of musketeers for dragging their feet. 'And Sergeant Skellen for that matter. But he considered us spies, Mister Payne. Is it such a surprise to hang a gang of intelligencers?'

'I suppose not,' Payne mused. 'Parliament hangs all intelligencers and all Irish.' He blew out his cheeks with a sound akin to a gale. 'A narrow escape, then.'

'Especially for Lisette,' Forrester said, 'Stryker's woman.'

Payne's brown eyes swivelled down to peer at Stryker. 'She was to die, sir?'

'Aye,' Forrester answered for his friend, 'though she really *was* a spy!'

Payne rubbed one of his great paws across his face. 'Zounds, sirs, but this war is a thing to tie a fellow in knots. I am glad to be a man of Kernow, where we may tell our friends and enemies apart.'

Stryker was not so sure things were that simple, even amid the Royalist fervour of the extreme south-west, but decided to let the matter rest. 'Suffice it to say, I wagered our best chance of survival would be to undermine the enemy.'

'Risky, though,' Forrester replied. 'You still had to funnel the buggers on top of the charge.'

'Aye,' Stryker agreed, 'but I knew Wild's men would not charge directly at our pikes. We left the musketeers as bait, and they took the easy route. Besides, we had no other course to take. With the cannon and dragooners, Wild had us beaten. In the event, the mine did not win the day. They'd have overwhelmed us, were it not for your timely arrival. I understand that you cannot speak of your own mission, but I'm grateful you were still on the moor.'

Forrester smiled, twisting suddenly to look back at the wagon. 'Hopton will be pleased. You've plucked him a juicy apple.'

'Though we have a deal less powder and ammunition now,' Stryker tempered his friend's optimism.

'Aye, that's true.'

'And we've lost most of the bloody horses.'

Forrester frowned. 'Well something is better than nothing, old man.'

Stryker thought about all the bodies they had committed to the Dartmoor soil. All the good men – on both sides

– who had died because of his ambition. He did not know if Forrester was right. Was all that blood worth a wagon of powder and shot and a pair of small cannon?

The bare heathland fell away to a shallow valley following the course of a trickling waterway and quickly choked with trees and bracken. The column plunged into the forest, heavily laden boughs meeting overhead to dim the world, lichen and fungi adding splashes of colour to the overriding greens and browns.

'The Roundheads are truly invading?' Stryker asked eventually.

Forrester's face was sullen. 'Aye, so we hear.'

'How many did we lose at Sourton?'

Forrester's blue gaze met the grey of Stryker's, and the latter saw a deep sorrow in their depths. 'Too many, old man. Too damned many. It was a bad business, Stryker. We were over-confident after Launceston. Arrogant. Thought we could thrust right into Devon and chase the Parliament men all the way to London. But they were ready for us. Jumped us on that bleak down just west of Okehampton.'

He shook his head at the memory. 'Jesu, but the darkness and the rain and the lightning. I began to think we were in purgatory, truly I did.'

'I'm sorry I was not there.'

Forrester offered a wan smile. 'The sentiment is appreciated, old man, but trust me when I tell you we'd have taken a beating regardless of your admittedly talismanic presence.'

Stryker ignored his friend's chiding. 'And you mentioned Mister Payne will head north?'

'Aye, as soon as we reach the high road up to the north coast.'

'I am manservant to Sir Bevil Grenville, sir,' Anthony Payne intoned. 'He defends his estates at Stratton, lest Stamford strike there. Stratton is my home too.'

'We were on our way back to Cornwall, I to Launceston and Payne to Stratton, when Simeon appeared,' Forrester explained. He chuckled suddenly, the melancholy of Sourton Down briefly alleviated. 'I truly believe Mister Payne thought a demon puckrel had pounced from the wood.'

Payne looked over his shoulder at Barkworth, speaking loudly enough for the Scot to hear. 'He is a remarkable sight.'

Barkworth glared back. 'As are you, you oak-legged bastard.'

Payne gave a burst of thunderous laughter. 'Have a care, little sir, for I would not wish to imprison you in my pocket.'

Barkworth's tiny hand slid to the bone handle of his dirk. 'Ach, I'll slice your gut open, sir, and you'll have yourself a new pocket.'

Stryker stared from the dwarf to the giant and wondered how he was to calm this storm, but Grenville's manservant boomed with a delighted chortle. 'You are a grand man, sir!' Payne slapped his thigh. 'Why, you must have Cornish blood!'

Barkworth shared the grin, but shook his head. 'Scots through and through, sir.'

'Yet both Celts!' Payne replied heartily.

'A grand fellow, Mister Barkworth,' Forrester agreed, 'though I hear you were indeed one of Satan's imps, according to your witch-finder.'

Barkworth's feral gaze glinted dangerously at the

memory. 'Aye, he'd have seen me swing for certain, sir. And the captain and Miss Cecily.'

'Osmyn Hogg,' Stryker said. 'A fiend if ever there was one.'

'Twin fiends, he and Wild,' Forrester replied.

'In truth, no,' Stryker corrected with a shake of his head. 'Wild wanted his wagon back. And wanted me dead for its capture.' He wondered what he might have done in the same situation. 'I can understand that well enough.'

'But did you not say you shot Hogg in the arse?' Forrester retorted. 'That seems motive enough for me!'

Stryker's mind drifted back to that day in the forests of Saxony. 'All was chaos in those dark days after Breitenfeld.'

Forrester plucked the hat from his head, using its wide rim to fan the flies from his sweaty face. 'I remember it well, old man.' He looked up at Payne. 'What a victory that was. We hammered the Holy Romans, the Hungarians, the Croats, and the Catholic League. But at such a cost. Ten, perhaps fifteen thousand dead. It was anarchy for weeks afterward. Stinking corpses left out in the cold, looters swarming like these damnable flies, soldiers marauding. A paradise for wicked men.'

'Hogg was one such man,' Stryker cut in. 'A black-guardly priest in those days. I shot him for the attempted hanging of the woman I loved.'

Forrester's blond brow shot up. 'Beth? She was a whore, Stryker.'

Stryker nodded. 'She was a whore, aye. A good one. And I was besotted with her.'

Forrester's thin lips twitched upwards. 'Plenty were.'

'Hogg's priestly compatriots included. He claimed she bewitched them.'

'She did,' Forrester replied.

'Aye, but she never needed Satan's help. In truth, Hogg's privy member grew hard when he clapped eyes on her. He could not reconcile the shame of it, and would happily have seen her die to salve his own conscience. I shot the bastard, and he deserved it.' He shrugged. 'I should have killed him then and there.'

William Skellen, for once not the tallest man present, had caught up with the leading group. He gargled a batch of dusty phlegm into his mouth and spat it into the tall grass at the roadside. 'Bugger sounded sane enough when he condemned you at the hill, sir. Babbled plenty o' Bible talk as poor Broom kicked 'is last.'

'The Devil can cite Scripture for his purpose, Sergeant,' Anthony Payne replied. 'That is from *The Merchant of Venice*, but it holds great truth.'

Lancelot Forrester clicked his tongue against the roof of his mouth. 'I was searching for that exact line, Anthony!' He glanced across at Stryker, perhaps catching the intrigue in his friend's face. 'He is a scholar, Stryker. He might look like a bloody philistine,' he shot Payne a mischievous wink, 'but his mind is sharp as a Toledo hanger.'

The land sloped gently downwards as high moor gave way to the first patches of pastureland a couple of miles outside Tavistock. There they found the northbound track that had conveyed Forrester's company cross-country from Peter Tavy, and it was agreed that that would be the safest route to take. The modest road took them between small copses, over pebble-banked streams, and beyond isolated farmsteads. As they marched Stryker began to feel a little more positive, his despair at the argument with Burton starting to erode as they neared the safety of Cornwall.

'And what of your new fellows?' he asked Forrester as the column drew up beside one of the narrow waterways that cut through the land.

Forrester followed his friend's gaze to where his group of prisoners had gathered at the stream's edge. 'Had something of a brabble near Tavistock. This sorry lot staggered into our camp like a herd of cupshot blind men, and we bloodied their noses.'

When Forrester removed his hat, using it to fan his rosy cheeks, Stryker noticed a crusty brown smear across the top of his scalp. 'Looks as though their noses weren't all that was bloodied.'

'Aye, well,' Forrester muttered, his forefinger appearing through the crown of his hat like a worm from its hole, 'I have informed Mister Jays that he owes me ten shillings.'

'Ten?' echoed Stryker. 'That old thing cost, what, three at most?'

Forrester tapped the crusty scalp wound. 'There is the matter of my injuries, old man. The indignity I have suffered in losing such a swathe of hair.'

To Stryker's eye Forrester's once lustrous locks had become so thin these past few years that the damage was not all that critical. He decided to keep quiet.

'In truth,' Forrester continued, waving the holed hat in the direction of the sombre-faced greycoats who now knelt to plunge cupped hands in the water, 'Reginald Jays, there, ain't a bad sort. He's a stripling. Aged fourteen, fresh of face, and foolish as a virgin in a trugging den. Speaking of which,' his gaze drifted casually to the rear of the column, where Lieutenant Burton was patting one of the falconets' horses. 'What happened between the two of you?'

343

Stryker stared at Burton for a long time, the feeling of despondency returning. He and the lieutenant had been through a great deal together, and he regarded Burton as something akin to a son. The wedge that had formed between them was near unbearable. 'Cecily Cade tried to seduce me.'

Forrester regarded him askance. 'Good Lord.' His eyes shifted along the riverbank to the place where Cecily stooped, filling a small flask with water. 'Good Lord.'

Stryker looked at the girl too. 'It was strange,' he said, thinking back to that dark night. 'She didn't even seem as though she wanted to.'

'Well lock her up in Bedlam,' Forrester exclaimed sarcastically, 'for she must be positively frantic!'

'Thank you, Forry,' Stryker said glumly, before walking over to the stream, unfastening his scabbard, and taking a seat on the ground.

Forrester joined him. 'Cecily Cade, the mysterious beauty.' It was then that a great shadow crossed overhead. They both turned, expecting rain, only to see Anthony Payne. 'Cade, Mister Payne,' Forrester said. 'What is that, a Cornish name?'

'Cade?' repeated Payne. His eyes narrowed suddenly beneath a deeply furrowed brow. 'Cade, you say?'

'Aye, sir,' Forrester nodded. 'Cecily Cade.' He leaned forward to peer along the course of the meandering river, pointing at the only female in the company. She was still absently taking refreshment some fifty paces upstream. 'The siren in our midst.'

Payne's face seemed to blanch, the colour draining clear away, and his neck convulsed as though he was trying to swallow an entire egg. '*That* is Cecily Cade?'

Forrester sighed impatiently. 'That is what I said, Mister Payne, yes. Stryker's damsel in distress.'

But Payne did not seem to be listening. Already he had turned away and was stalking along the bank.

'Mister Payne?' Stryker called to him, clambering up from the ground when the big Cornishman failed to respond. 'What is it?'

Forrester scrambled to his feet as well, disturbed by the giant's sudden change in disposition. 'Anthony?'

Now Payne seemed to register their voices, for he paused to glance round. 'Sirs, I must speak with her.' He fixed Stryker with a gaze that spoke of a man who would not be denied. 'Please, Captain. It is a matter of the utmost import. I must speak with Miss Cade this very moment.'

BEAWORTHY, DEVON, 9 MAY 1643

Terrence Richardson had made camp in fields just outside the village. Here, flanked by thick hedgerows and taunted by crows, his threescore cavalrymen had waited the best part of a week for the arrival of a Cornish giant, a foppish Cavalier, and their precious cargo. Yet none had come, Richardson's men had become increasingly agitated, and the crows seemed to jeer his failure.

It was with great fuss, then, that the pickets first spotted the lone rider on the eastern horizon. Richardson had been examining a jagged notch on his backsword's single cutting edge when the message was relayed to him. He forgot the irritating blemish all at once. Thrusting the blade back through the throat of his scabbard, he strode straight out of his tent and across the field to the tumbledown gate that served as the camp's main entrance, not even taking pause to put on his coat.

The rider was an incongruous sight, for he wore the clothes of an infantryman, and was clearly uncomfortable on the exhausted nag that snorted and whinnied its way through the gate. Richardson knew at once that this must be one of Forrester's men.

'News from Mister Payne, one hopes,' he said as casually as he could, though he sensed the tightness within his throat.

The rider took off his cap in salute. 'Aye, sir, with his compliments, and where might I find General Hopton?'

Richardson's head was bare, and he lifted a hand to ruffle his close-cropped brown hair, wincing apologetically as he did so. 'I am sorry to report, sir, that he is engaged further north with the main army.' He offered an embarrassed shrug. 'He could not linger here forever, you understand.'

One of Richardson's men sidled up to the heaving horse and took the reins as the redcoat jumped down. 'I suppose not, sir, but my report is for the general only.'

Richardson pursed his narrow lips and pulled at the brown bristles of his moustache. 'And who rode all the way out to tell you to march to Beaworthy?' he asked calmly.

The redcoat's eyes darted left and right. 'Y—You did, sir.'

Richardson smiled urbanely, and patted the infantryman on the shoulder. 'Then you may pass your news to me, good fellow, for you know that to speak with me is to speak with Hopton himself.'

Some of the cavalrymen were gathering around the pair of them now, and the messenger's shoulders seemed to sag in resignation. 'Aye, sir, I'm sure you're right.'

Richardson smiled again, flashing teeth he knew to be

bright against his whiskers. 'Good man!' He glanced at one of his men. 'Get this wise fellow a blackjack brim full of our best ale.'

'Thank you, sir,' the redcoat said, eyes still pinned open with intimidation.

'No matter,' Richardson waved away the thanks dismissively, deciding the man was now ripe for questioning. 'They have located Cade?'

The rider shook his head. 'Not exactly, sir.'

Richardson exhaled noisily, dropping the act of smooth charm in favour of something more direct. 'Well spit it out, you dissembling numbskull.'

'Cade is dead, sir.'

That stopped Richardson in his tracks. He thought for a moment that he would vomit. 'Dead?'

'Aye, sir. Ambushed and killed by brigands. But we have located his daughter. Captain Forrester and Mister Payne bring her here even now.'

'Daughter?' Richardson repeated absently. It was as though he could not see, could not think, beyond the realization that Sir Alfred Cade was dead. He felt swamped, trapped in a miasma of despair by this gut-wrenching news. 'Christ, man,' he muttered as the situation turned in his mind, 'what use is she?'

The redcoat suddenly stepped closer. 'Sir,' he said, voice falling to barely a whisper, 'she has the information.'

The miasma cleared. The painful pounding of Richardson's heart was suddenly a soft murmur, twisted bowels easing back to comfort. 'You're—you're certain?'

'Aye, sir.' He offered a non-committal shrug. 'That is what I was told to tell General Hopton, sir. I am not privy to anything further.'

'Of course not,' Richardson replied distantly, his mind already tumbling thoughts like so many acrobats.

'Sir?'

Richardson forced himself to look up. 'Hmm?'

'Might I ask,' the messenger said, staring about the encampment curiously now that his information had been imparted, 'which regiment these men are from?'

Richardson placed a hand firmly on the redcoat's shoulder and steered him back towards his waiting mount. 'I think we're finished here, are we not?'

'But, sir,' the confused infantryman spluttered, 'do I not have ale on the way?'

'I'm afraid not, good man. Time's of the essence, eh?'

'Might I not stay a little while to rest?' the redcoat complained, trying to shrug Richardson's hand away.

Richardson stopped dead, fixing the redcoat with a blistering stare. 'No, man, you may not. Be gone with you, and tell Payne and Forrester to bring Miss Cade to me forthwith.'

It was then that Richardson saw the redcoat's eyes narrow as they fixed on a point just over his shoulder. He released his grip, turning to see what the man had noticed, only to catch a smudge of tawny over in the hedge line at the other side of the field.

'Christ,' Richardson hissed angrily, 'but that man'll be on a damned charge before the day is through, by God he will.'

The redcoat gaped, eyes darting between Richardson, his surly gang of cavalrymen, and the tawny sash. 'Sir?'

Richardson sighed, rubbed his eyes in a tired manner, and stepped back. 'I had hoped to avoid this, good fellow, you must believe me.'

348

The pistol cracked before the redcoat even knew it was at his temple. Its echo reverberated around the trees and hedges, sending all manner of birds skyward in fright. The messenger slumped to his knees, swayed there a moment, and crashed on to his face, the grass about his skull stained rapidly dark.

TORRINGTON, DEVON, 9 MAY 1643

Henry Grey, First Earl of Stamford, was examining a large map of south-west England at his expansive campaign table when his second-in-command, Major-General James Chudleigh, strode beneath the doorway's high lintel.

'How do you like my new billet, General?'

Chudleigh plucked the leather gloves from his hands and stuffed them into the crown of his upturned hat. He peered about the room, the wooden panelling shining brightly in the sunlight that streamed through the large windows. 'Very much, my lord. You were on the upper floor before, were you not?'

Stamford nodded, indicating his left leg. It jutted out to the side of his chair, useless and inert. 'The gout rages again. I am utterly trapped by it.'

Chudleigh was a young man, of reedy neck and willowy frame, yet his woollen coat, leather doublet, and dark green cloak gave him a formidably martial appearance. He looked down at the leg, noticing that Stamford's pale hose were stretched tight by the swollen calf. 'My sympathies, my lord, truly. It is an agonizing affliction.'

'Jesu, but it is, James. Yet I have not summoned you to speak of such matters.'

Chudleigh ran a hand through his long hair in an effort to untangle the black curls that massed around his shoulders like shavings of jet. 'I had thought not, sir.'

'Firstly,' Stamford said through teeth gritted against a sudden wave of pain, 'I should like to know of the victuals for the men. Have the provisions been requisitioned?'

Chudleigh nodded, glancing out the window at the wisps of white cloud that drifted aimlessly above. Soon, he thought grimly, the clouds would be gritty, hot, and stinking of sulphur. 'Aye, my lord.'

'Provisions?' came a new voice from the doorway.

Chudleigh turned to see a man of similar height and build to himself, though the flowing curls that had once been as black as his own were now distinguished by silver flecks. He stretched out his hand. 'Are you well, Father?'

Sir George Chudleigh paced briskly into the room, spurred boots clomping loudly on the wooden floor. He shook his son's hand warmly. 'Well indeed, James. Well indeed. We have a fine army mustered.' He removed his hat, bowing to Stamford. 'My lord.'

Stamford smiled. 'It heartens me to see you, Sir George. You will forgive me if I do not rise to greet you.'

'Naturally, my lord,' Sir George agreed as he and his son approached the earl's table. 'And I must beg your pardon for my tardiness, sir. My horse tripped and is lame.'

'No matter,' Stamford replied, shifting his rump in the creaking chair, a tiny yelp of pain escaping his mouth as he aggravated the immobile limb. He took a moment to compose himself, patted the wrinkles from his bright blue doublet before meeting Sir George's brown eyes once more.

'Now to business. We were speaking of the provisions,

Sir George. We have ordered the garrisons hereabouts to send supplies from the towns. Some will provide meat, others milk, others bread. Barnstaple, for instance, has agreed to send biscuit, bacon, peas, and small beer.' He grasped a scrap of paper from the cluttered desk and held it out for Sir George to take. 'Here.'

Sir George studied the requisition order. 'Send to Stratton,' he read aloud, before looking up sharply. 'Our target?'

Stamford nodded. 'You have it.'

Sir George Chudleigh stared at the name on the paper once more before glancing across at his son. 'You are aware that Stratton is Grenville's heartland?'

'His estates are thereabouts, aye,' Stamford snapped hotly, clearly irked by the older man's deferral to his son, 'but the town itself shifts for the Parliament.' He jabbed a finger at the place on the map marked *Plymouth*, and tracked an irregular ink line northward with his nail. 'As you both know, the River Tamar forms the only natural barrier between Devon and Cornwall, and for many miles it is easily defended by the Cornish.'

James Chudleigh looked at his father. 'The river rises in the north. It is the simplest crossing point.'

Stamford tapped a spot on the north coast labelled with the word *Stratton*. 'This is where we must strike. We'll make our base at Stratton itself, and it is there that Hopton will have to come and face us. It is there, gentlemen, that we will trap his army by the sea.'

Sir George took a deep breath, let it out gently, and whispered, 'God be with us.'

'God be with *us*, Sir George,' Stamford corrected, pointing between himself and the younger Chudleigh.

Sir George's brow rose at the intimation. 'My lord?'

The earl propped a hand under his narrow chin. 'Hopton knows we shall attack soon. And he knows we will likely outnumber him. To that end, he plans – according to my intelligencers – to raise a posse down at Bodmin as soon as he discovers the exact nature of our thrust.'

Sir George nodded, considering the words. 'That would alleviate the disparity in numbers somewhat.'

'Thus,' Stamford went on, 'said posse must never be allowed to form. And that is where I need you, Sir George, as my Commander of Horse. How many troopers do you have at your disposal?'

'Twelve hundred, my lord,' the older man answered smartly.

'Then I want them tacked, saddled, and ready to ride for Bodmin. The moment we march upon Stratton, you will go south. You will surround that damned town and prevent High Sheriff Grylls from mustering a single man against us. Understood?'

'Of course, my lord.'

James Chudleigh cleared his throat. 'And we shall lead the main assault, my lord?'

Stamford's gaze switched to the more youthful, if higher-ranked Chudleigh. He smoothed down his moustache for a few moments, as though he needed the time to choose his words. 'The gout makes travel tedious and slow, General.'

Chudleigh dipped his head. 'I do not doubt it, my lord.'

'Consequently my presence with the army will prove only a hindrance.' Stamford straightened, collecting up the assortment of parchment scrolls and paper that littered the table and bunching them into a neat pile. When he had laid them flat he looked up into Chudleigh's expectant gaze. 'You will therefore lead the van.'

Major-General James Chudleigh had expected as much from his commander. The Devonshire men held little respect for the earl. Like the Cornish, they were loyal to their own, but cared almost nothing for men such as Stamford or the politics that would drive them to battle. It was that knowledge, rather than gout, that meant the Chudleighs would lead Parliament to battle. Without them, Stamford knew that he could not guarantee his army's loyalty. Chudleigh simply nodded quiet acceptance. 'I understand, my lord.'

'Then you have your orders, gentlemen,' Stamford said curtly. 'Sir George is to take the horse to Bodmin, while you, James, will lead our main advance towards Stratton. I will follow, naturally, and take personal command when eventually we face Hopton.'

'And we will push him into the sea,' said James Chudleigh.

Stamford smiled. 'By God, that is precisely what we shall do, General. Him, Berkeley, Grenville,' he hissed, slamming one fist into the palm of the other at the mention of each name, 'Trevanion, Godolphin, Slanning, Basset, and the rest of those popish rogues. And the three of us will ride to Westminster and make a gift of the Cornish colours to John Pym himself, eh?'

But Major-General James Chudleigh was not listening any longer because he was saying a silent prayer. The invasion of Cornwall was underway. And he was going to battle.

CHAPTER 17

Stryker's column seemed to pick up its collective step as, just an hour after dawn, they finally spotted the funnels of smoke climbing above dense woodland about a mile to the west. Anthony Payne knew the country well, and had declared that the village lay just beyond that wood, and there, he was sure, they would find General Hopton.

It had been a strange conversation that had altered their course, reflected Stryker as he kept pace at the head of the snaking force. Payne had insisted on speaking with Cecily, the pair had then spent several minutes in hushed discussion with much nodding and gesticulating, and then, to everyone's surprise they had approached Stryker together and informed him that he should lead his motley cohort not to Launceston but to Beaworthy.

'I was sent to fetch her father,' Anthony Payne, compelled by events to shed light on his shadowy mission, had explained when Stryker and Forrester took him to task beside the trickling moorland brook.

'Sir Alfred?' Stryker had asked.

Payne nodded. 'The same. He carries—carried—information vital to our cause.'

Stryker remembered being unable to hide his disdain. 'I

354

cannot tell you how many times I have heard that phrase, Mister Payne,' he had said. 'One man's vital is another man's—'

'Gold,' Payne's growl of a voice had cut across him like a shot from the demi-cannon named Roaring Meg, at Hopton Fight. 'Silver, gems, I do not know what else. I do not speak of strategic information, Captain, but of treasure.'

Stryker saw the sudden earnestness dance across the huge man's eyes like white flame. 'Come now, Mister Payne, you really believe—'

'It is not relevant whether I believe or not, sir,' Payne replied firmly. 'Only that General Hopton believes. And the King believes.'

Forrester glanced across to where Cecily Cade waited just beyond earshot. 'Sir Alfred Cade had some kind of map?'

'I had assumed as much when we were sent to meet him, Captain Forrester, aye. But, according to his daughter, it was a matter of memory. He never committed the location of the trove to paper.'

It was then that Stryker had summoned Cecily Cade. She had peered up at him through eyes that, though worried, glinted with inner steel. 'Captain?'

'You know the location of this bloody treasure?' Stryker had said, more harshly than he had intended, but he still felt angry at the way she had fractured his friendship with Burton.

Cecily nodded. 'I do.' She looked him square in the eye, setting her jaw defiantly. 'But I will not speak of it. Not to any man alive, save Sir Ralph Hopton or King Charles himself.'

355

And then the pieces had suddenly slotted together in Stryker's mind. 'You were not travelling home, were you?'

'Sir?' she had replied.

Stryker thrust a finger close to her face. 'Do not be coy with me, girl, for I've a mind to leave you on this God-forsaken moor! Now tell me,' he said when her sheepish nod had cooled his ire a little, 'where were you bound when first we encountered your party?'

Cecily's green eyes glazed a touch as she thought back to that fateful day. 'Launceston, Captain.'

'To Hopton?'

'To Hopton.' She glanced up at the vast figure of Anthony Payne. 'By way of Merrivale.'

'Where you were to rendezvous with our detachment,' Lancelot Forrester said in quiet epiphany.

Cecily had nodded confirmation. 'We were to meet an escort sent by the general, and conveyed back to Launceston, where my father was to arrange for the treasure to be retrieved.' Her eyes filled with moisture, a sudden squall welling from the green and brown depths. 'But all went wrong. So terribly wrong.'

Stryker remembered hearing the shots, remembered bursting on to the road to see the carnage wrought within the coach. 'A grand plan undone by simple brigands. Except your father imparted the information before he died.' His mind shifted to the black cave where Cecily had picked away the lace of her bodice and he had had to fight his every instinct in order to resist. 'That was why you yearned to flee the tor. Why you tried everything to convince me to give you leave.'

'Aye, Captain,' she retorted hotly. 'And I would do it again.'

356

Stryker had sighed then, unexpectedly assailed by tiredness, and scratched at his burgeoning beard. 'Why could you not have trusted me with this knowledge? I would have assisted you, had I known.'

Cecily's eyes narrowed as she studied him suspiciously. 'Or killed me and gone a gold-seekin' yourself.'

'Jesu, Miss Cade,' was all Stryker could think to say. For all his frustration, he understood her stance well enough. Why should she have trusted him above anyone else?

And so, thus presented with the compelling argument by Cecily and Payne, Stryker had turned northwards to Beaworthy, where, Forrester had verified, Sir Ralph Hopton eagerly awaited their arrival.

As they drew closer to the village's woodland fringe the ground dipped suddenly into a fallow meadow. It was bowl-shaped, speckled with the bright petals of wildflowers, and undulating with unkempt tufts of long grass. But those colours, the darker shades of the forest beyond, and even the blacker funnels of chimney smoke all rapidly vanished from sight. A white, roiling mist sat like a thick stew at the centre of the bowl, devouring everything around it, and the column were made to march virtually blind as they felt their way towards the safety of Beaworthy.

'Sir! There, sir!' It was one of the blond twins, Jack Trowbridge, who drew Stryker's attention to a shadow resolving from the mist. 'It's Ox!'

The lone man was indeed one of Stryker's, for the red of his coat and cap became suddenly visible as he staggered towards the column, a bloody smear against the white miasma. John Booth, known by the men as Ox for his square frame and lack of neck, was one of Stryker's pickets, feeling the way out in front of the column. Now, though, he was returning to his mates, but he had somehow lost his musket and tuck, and, as he weaved and tripped over the uneven terrain, Stryker could see that his face had been split diagonally from eye to jaw.

Ox, once so formidable, let out a pathetic, high-pitched keening sound, and seemed to gargle something unintelligible. He twisted back suddenly, lifting a hand to flap feebly into the dense mist, and slumped to his knees.

'Sir?' Jack Trowbridge murmured, unable to take his eyes off his wounded friend.

But Stryker was already turning. 'Charge for horse! Charge for horse!'

He had no idea what they were dealing with. It might have been horse or dragoons, infantrymen, clubmen, or mere footpads, but the pikes would be useless unless they were deployed to fend off the worst possibility. And that possibility came to him in a stark, heart-wrenching image of a fully armoured, white-eyed, snarling harquebusier with a badger stripe through his head and the coke-black feather of a Great Cormorant in his helmet.

'Charge your damned pikes!' he bellowed again furiously, taking one of the nearest drummers by the scruff of his neck. 'Beat the order!'

But it was all too late. The tired pikemen were painfully slow to react. They had thought they were home and safe, so near now to Hopton's main force. Moreover, the men further back had not seen Ox stagger from the thick mist, had not witnessed the big man collapse, his face a ruin of gore, and, though the redcoats nearest Stryker stumbled backwards to begin forming a circle around the more vulnerable elements of the column, the rearmost men were confused and inert.

And out of the mist came noise. A deep, menacing rumble that shook the ground and struck fear into the chaotic mass of redcoats. Horses. They appeared as faint shapes at first. Grey, nebulous apparitions gliding within the white fastness. But then those apparitions found form, beasts and their riders bursting from the pale wisps like a troop of demons, and they were galloping headlong towards the alarmed Royalists.

Stryker's force was terribly exposed. There were no hedgerows behind which they might hunker, no rocks to protect them, no rivers for the enemy to ford. Just open grassland, ideal for charging cavalry.

Stryker was in the thick of the panicked infantrymen, shouting orders, shoving men into ranks, knocking pikes up or down to achieve the proper killing angle. His musketeers stepped between those hastily presented spears, and the men whose weapons were already loaded gave a smattering of fire, but it was too thin to break the wave that still came forth from the mist.

Stryker squinted through the dirty powder smoke to search for Wild's field sign, finding some small sense of relief from the fact that the black feathers were not worn by this new enemy. It was not Wild.

'*Fire! Fire! Fire!*' the savage shout of Sergeant Skellen carried across the redcoats' heads. Stryker repeated the call.

The first cavalrymen slammed home, the crunch of pike and horse and armour and sword ringing loud and blood-freezing over the grassland. There were something like forty horses involved, which might, Stryker reflected, have been easy enough to fend off had the mist not given the enemy the element of surprise.

But it was just too late.

The horsemen, blue-coated chests clad in metal plate, wheeled suddenly away, unwilling to enter into a prolonged engagement, and Stryker's men closed their foremost ranks quickly, ready for the next charge. But when it came, it was like a blow from a hammer wielded by God himself, such was its devastation. For it had not come from the front, but from the rear. Ten horsemen – possibly nearer twenty, such was the concealment offered by the mist – had evidently circled round the column, and they smashed headlong into the men at the tail; men who were not prepared to receive such an assault.

The second charge did not end quickly. This time the wave went through the desperate pikemen, beyond the half-cocked musketeers and directly through to where the wagon was positioned.

Stryker watched in disbelief. *Was* this Gabriel Wild? If not him, then why would these unknown assailants pick such an innocuous vehicle as their target?

But there was no time to wonder for a new scream rent the air. It was piercing, raising the hairs on Stryker's neck and making his very teeth ache. A woman's scream. One of terror.

He ran, jumping potholes and patches of shoe-mulched earth, sprinting as fast as his feet would allow towards the origin of that scream. Some of the men went with him, for he heard their thudding footfalls and juddering breaths, but many were forced to turn back when the first horsemen came at the head of the column once again.

All was chaos. All was anarchy. Screams and whinnies, agonized bellows and snarls of violence clashed in a macabre orchestra, a din to break a man's heart. And all was shrouded in mist. Deadly, horrific, yet intangible.

Stryker hurdled a body, one of his own fallen men, and drew his sword. Already the horsemen who had battered the rear of the column were wrenching at their reins, tearing their mounts' foaming mouths about to fall away from the defenders. Again, it seemed so strange to Stryker. Infantry were no match for cavalry in so exposed a situation. Out in the open, without a hedge of stoical pikemen out front, they were easy pickings. But just as he tried to read his enemy's mind, he heard Cecily Cade scream again, and through the mist he saw her. Saw her legs kick and her fists beat, saw the harquebusier pin her easily across his saddle with one hand and steer his destrier with the other. Saw them vanish into the whiteness. With them went the rest of the horsemen, the thunder dying almost as soon as it had begun. One man was unsaddled, dragged from his mount by the billhook of Sergeant Heel's arcing halberd, and his shout of surprise and fear cut through the mist like the sun's rays, but the rest were long gone.

Stryker peered around about him, at the devastated column, in utter bemusement. He sheathed his unbloodied sword.

'What the fuckin' ballock-burners just 'appened?'

Stryker turned to see Skellen. He shook his head. 'They didn't want us, Will.' He looked back into the mist. 'They wanted Miss Cade.'

'His name is Terrence Richardson.'

Stryker stared at Forrester, though his mind was searching old acquaintances for the name. 'Richardson? Never heard of him.'

Lancelot Forrester shrugged. 'I'm not surprised, old man, the bugger's an intelligencer.'

The officers, plus Anthony Payne, were in a small, stone-built house at the edge of Beaworthy. The column had gathered up its five dead and marched straight into the village, still reeling from the cavalry attack that had vanished into the mist as quickly as it had appeared. A small party would bury the bodies, the remainder would enjoy the brief respite, and Stryker would take stock.

'And it was definitely him?' Stryker asked as he paced up and down the centre of the little building.

'Oh, aye, Stryker,' Forrester replied firmly. He was perched on a low, three-legged stool in the room's corner, busily packing his pipe bowl. 'No doubt in my mind whatsoever. Out at the very head of the charge.'

'I saw him too, Captain,' Payne added in his deep tone. 'It was Richardson.'

Stryker took a moment to absorb this news, unsure what it all meant. He stared at the huge Cornishman, who, standing against the rough stone gable end, was forced to stoop so as to avoid hitting his head on the ceiling beams. 'And he was the man who told you to come to Beaworthy?'

'Aye,' Payne answered. 'With Sir Alfred Cade. He claimed to be sent from Hopton himself.'

So this, Stryker thought, was no random attack at all. It had been an ambush, orchestrated by the mysterious Richardson. 'Your spy knew about Sir Alfred. Knew his importance. He orders you to bring Cade here—'

'Ostensibly on General Hopton's word,' Forrester interjected.

'But instead,' Stryker took up the tale again, 'he

362

ambushes you.' He took off his hat and fiddled with the dishevelled feathers. 'But was he not waiting for Sir Alfred?'

Payne straightened suddenly, muttering an oath when his forehead clipped a worm-holed beam. 'The messenger.'

'Messenger?' Stryker echoed, narrowing his grey eye as he stared up at Payne.

Payne nodded slowly, letting out a yawning sigh that seemed to Stryker as though a North Sea squall had whipped in through the open doorway. 'The rider I sent ahead when first we found you.'

'Telling Richardson that we were on our way,' Forrester said, his voice strained by the implication.

Payne looked at him, eyes glinting in the gloomy room. 'And that we had Cecily.'

Forrester swallowed thickly. 'And that Cecily was as important as her father.' He looked across at Stryker. 'Bugger.'

'All is lost,' Payne said disconsolately. He rubbed a meaty paw across his face, the scrape of stubble unnaturally loud among the roof beams. 'Damn this war, where no man can truly know his enemy.'

'Or his friends,' Stryker replied, beginning to understand Cecily's deep distrust.

'Richardson has turned his coat,' Payne went on. 'Taken Miss Cade to the enemy.'

Stryker stopped pacing to look into Payne's face. 'Then we must get her back, Mister Payne.'

'But how, sir?' Payne replied, gesticulating with an outstretched arm that reminded Stryker of a Thames waterman's oar. 'We do not know where they have gone.'

Stryker walked to the doorway, turning back only to say, 'Then let us ask.'

The man was seated on cracked mud on the main road bisecting Beaworthy. He still wore his faded blue coat, but his buff jerkin, back plate, gauntlet, breastplate, and weapons had been stripped as soon as quarter was given. His helmet had been taken too, revealing a head of thick copper curls and a face carrying several thin, white scars. He was a well-built fellow, brawny at the shoulders and thick of neck, speaking volumes of a good diet and proper training. Richardson's troop had clearly been a professional force.

Stryker stalked past the half-dozen guards to squat beside the Roundhead. 'You are in a great deal of danger, sir.'

His captive, the only man unhorsed during Richardson's raid, stared directly into Stryker's eye. 'But the battle is over and—'

The words began to tail off, any defiance he might have felt sapped clear by Stryker's hard expression. His light blue eyes seemed to dart left and right as if seeking an unlikely escape, before he seemed to sag, defeated by stark reality. 'Danger from whom, sir?'

Stryker gnawed the inside of his mouth, leaned in so that the trooper would feel the warm breath at his ear. 'From me.' He watched as the corner of the trooper's eye flickered. It was almost imperceptible, but he saw it well enough, and knew he had his man. 'Now let us speak.'

The bluecoat's broad neck convulsed as though he had swallowed a hedgehog. 'I—I do not know anything, sir, truly. Just a soldier is all. Here for conscience, not blood.'

Stryker offered his most saccharine smile. 'I am merely a soldier myself, sir. I'd set you free in a trice if things were different.' He leaned closer, the acrid stench of sweat and horse flesh filling his nostrils. 'But your friends carried someone away with them. Someone important to me. You will help me get her back.'

Evidently deciding to call Stryker's bluff, the bluecoat set his jaw. 'And if I refuse, sir?'

A rasping hiss came from behind Stryker, and both men looked back to see Forrester sucking air through his teeth in a dramatic wince, as though the Parliament man's defiance was a chilling faux pas. Beside the plump officer stood Anthony Payne, who shook his head slowly, empathizing with the captive amid his impending fate.

Stryker turned back to the seated cavalryman, casually inspecting the tip of the dirk he had quietly slipped from his belt. 'If you refuse, sir, then I will cut off your ears and feed them to Prince Rupert's hound. You have heard of the beast? Boye is its name. It will want your nose after that, and then your tongue and your fingers and your stones.'

The prisoner's face immediately drained of colour, becoming starkly ashen against the copper colouring of his hair. He looked from the dirk, up to Forrester, and back to Stryker. 'You would not, sir,' he muttered, though the challenge was weak at best.

A man's scream rent the air, shrill and piercing, lashing out from one of the buildings fronting on to the road. That did it. 'I did not know who the girl was,' the Roundhead blurted in sudden terror, 'or why she was taken.'

Stryker heard Lancelot Forrester sigh with relief. 'You have made a good choice, sir.'

The captive met Stryker's eye. 'That vile popinjay commanded.'

'Richardson?'

'Aye. He ordered the attack, sir. We had not expected so large a force.'

Stryker considered this information. Of course they had not expected to encounter Stryker's company and Forrester's as well. It must have come as quite a shock to Richardson and his troop. 'That is why your comrades retreated as soon as the girl was taken?'

The Roundhead nodded. 'We were under orders to leave none alive, sir.' He held up flat palms, gripped by the sudden need to placate the narrow-faced Royalist. 'We are a simple troop, sir, I swear. Part of Lord Stamford's army, and not commanded by Richardson until this task.'

Stryker twisted to glance at Forrester. 'You were right. An intelligencer.'

Forrester dipped his head. 'He'd have killed the lot of us to conceal his face.'

'We were not privy to his reasoning, sir,' the captive continued, the words tumbling earnestly from his trembling mouth. 'Only that he wanted you dead and the girl captured. When we discovered that your strength was far greater than expected, he ordered us to pick out the girl.'

Stryker scratched the tattered remnants of his left eye, the swirling, mottled flesh always felt irritatingly tight when he was frustrated. 'What I wish to know is Richardson's destination. Where has he taken Miss Cade?'

The Roundhead grimaced. 'I cannot say, sir—'

Another abrupt cry seemed to reverberate inside their skulls as the man concealed within Beaworthy's

366

timber-framed buildings was consumed by agony. The blue-coat shivered. 'Please, sir—'

The scream cut the morning air again, this time making his body visibly jolt. 'Christ!' he exclaimed, 'I yield, I yield. Lord forgive me. He rides for Stratton.'

'Richardson?' Stryker prompted.

The bluecoat nodded rapidly, like a starling searching for worms. 'Aye, sir. Richardson, aye.'

Stryker instinctively shot Payne a glance before addressing his petrified prisoner. 'Stratton? Why?'

The Roundhead's blue eyes were desolate, racked by the knowledge that he betrayed his own side. His shoulders sagged. 'Because Lord Stamford marches thither.'

Stryker frowned, mind spinning. He stood, paced out through the ring of watchful redcoats, and went to stand with Forrester and Payne. 'That is where the enemy attacks.'

'Would Hopton know by now?' Forrester asked.

Stryker shook his head. 'Not if he's still in Launceston.' He looked back at the Parliamentarian, still hemmed by guards, knees drawn up to his chest. 'Trooper. Have you heard tell of king's men moving against you?' When the bluecoat failed to respond, he took a step closer. 'I promise you, brave sir, that if you hold your tongue, you will soon lose it altogether.'

The disconsolate captive lifted his chin from its knee-cap perch. 'I have heard nothing, sir. When we left Torrington, your army were none the wiser, and we have heard no more.'

Stryker turned back to Forrester. 'Then we must assume Hopton has no knowledge of this, and, moreover, that he remains at Launceston awaiting just such news.'

'I believe you're in the right of it, old man,' Forrester agreed sombrely.

'Sergeant Skellen!' Stryker bellowed in the direction of the nearest houses.

A tall man in a filthy brown buff-coat emerged from the nearest building, a halberd propped in casual fashion across his right shoulder. 'Sir.' He sidled on to the road, darkly hooded eyes betraying an air of amusement as he caught sight of Forrester. 'Hope you appreciated me actin', Cap'n Forrester, sir.'

Forrester smiled wryly. 'I did indeed, William. You could play the leading man for my old Candlewick Troupe.'

Skellen brandished his amber teeth. 'Kind in you to say, sir.'

'If you weren't such an ill-spoken troglodyte, naturally,' the captain added, face set firm.

'Troggy who, sir?'

'Wait.' It was the Parliamentarian who had spoken. He peered wide-eyed through the gap between his guards at the sinewy sergeant, before glaring at Stryker. 'You played me false?'

'I do not enjoy meting out torture,' Stryker replied levelly, 'any more than I enjoy suffering it.' He pointed a gloved hand down at the captive. 'But do not be mistook, sir. Things would have gone very badly for you had you remained stubborn.'

He left the dumbfounded bluecoat to stare at the ground and addressed Forrester. 'Let us raise the alarm, Forry. Hopton must be warned of the enemy's move.'

Payne stepped forward, surprising Stryker with the unexpected movement. 'We must to Stratton, Captain. Cecily Cade cannot be brought before Lord Stamford.'

'Where's Heel?' Stryker raised his voice.

'Here, sir!' Sergeant Moses Heel had been leaning against one of the nearby doors. He approached briskly.

Stryker pointed at Heel and Skellen. 'You two get the men ready. We march immediately. Forry?'

'Aye?'

'Do you have a decent rider amongst you?'

Forrester pursed his lips briefly. 'Thornton, I'd guess. Where must he ride?'

'Launceston. Direct to General Hopton.' He indicated the bluecoat. 'Give him this fellow's mount.'

'I will go.'

Stryker turned to see Andrew Burton. The lieutenant had evidently been watching proceedings from one of the buildings to Stryker's compromised left side. Stryker walked across to him. Even now, Burton gazed straight at his captain's hat feathers, gaze blank as a fresh corpse. 'I need you here,' Stryker said as calmly as he could, though he could hear the new tension inflect his tone.

Burton's stare did not falter. 'Let me go, sir.'

Stryker wanted to throttle his second-in-command, but he could not allow himself to damage the relationship further. He paused for a moment, although he could see well enough the determination in the younger man's face. 'So be it,' he muttered eventually. 'Find Sir Ralph. Tell him of Stamford's plans.'

Burton nodded brusquely, spun on his heels, and was gone.

Anthony Payne loomed into view. 'And the rest of us, sir?'

Stryker craned his neck to look up at the Cornishman. 'Us, Mister Payne? We go to Stratton.'

369

Witch-finder Osmyn Hogg watched the surly soldier spit a wad of tobacco juice into the fire that had been lit at the back of the small cemetery. A short-lived tempest of orange sparks blew up, blasted from the red logs by the sudden disturbance, only to vanish in the chill breeze. They had found the Parliamentarian army spread out on the road running westward out of Torrington, and it had taken two whole days to locate the man to whom they knew they must explain recent events. Here, at this tiny hamlet, they had taken rest, lit fires, spread out for the night. But other regiments had taken the few buildings that were available and the tiny chapel was given over to the horses, so, much to Hogg's indignation, they had been forced to spend the night in amongst the undulating burials of the graveyard. Hogg instinctively drew his black cloak tighter around his shoulders, though at least, he thought, it was not raining.

'I am regarded unfairly, sir,' the soldier grunted when the mad sizzling had died. He had always been a gruff man in Hogg's opinion, but tonight Colonel Gabriel Wild was positively bad-tempered. It was no surprise, he supposed, for seated beside the cavalry commander, and dressed in a suit of fine reds and blues that made him seem like a giant kingfisher, was Major-General Erasmus Collings. The small eyes, fishlike in their blank stare, seemed to bore straight through any to fall beneath their gaze.

'Unfairly, Colonel?' Collings replied in a voice that seemed at once both soft and razor-edged. 'Not only did you fail to dispose of Stryker, but you did not even manage to retrieve my ammunition.'

Hogg noticed Wild's neck quiver as he swallowed. 'Sir.'

'And in the process of this abject humiliation,' Collings continued, hairless scalp wrinkling with each word, 'you lost several of your best men and several of the dragoons I sent you. You are a disgrace, man. An utter disgrace. Not fit to command a party of tipplers.' Without changing his empty expression, the general's eyes flicked across the fire to where Hogg sat. 'And you?'

Hogg frowned. 'Sir?'

'What have you to say for yourself?'

Beside him, Hogg felt José Ventura shift his rump, unable to resist the bait. 'We not 'holden to you, señor,' he levelled a fat finger at Collings, 'but to God.'

'José—' Hogg muttered in warning.

Collings startled them both by breaking into a sudden bout of shrill laughter. It was not a happy sound. 'José Ventura,' he said after a time. '*God's Toad*, they call you, did you know?' He smirked, though the movement did not reach his cheeks. 'I cannot fathom why.' The hard gaze darted to the witch-finder. 'The Hogg and the Toad,' he announced, relishing each word.

'I not—' Ventura began his riposte, but the words snagged in his throat as Collings's straw-thin forearm shot up to point at him.

'Hold that viperous tongue, señor,' Collings rasped coldly, 'or I will have it out before you can say *no!*'

That last word was inflected with an exaggerated Spanish accent, and Ventura instantly leaned forward, unable to resist biting back. Hogg quickly placed a firm hand on his assistant's shoulder. The gesture seemed to stay whatever verbal assault Ventura had been brewing, for he simply stared across the tremulous flames, regarding Collings with simmering hostility. Eventually he muttered something in his native language.

To Hogg's surprise, Collings grinned, small white teeth appearing sharklike in the hellish glow. 'Spain will do what, señor?' He chuckled as he had before, revelling in Ventura's own astonished expression. 'Shall I tell you? Spain will do absolutely nothing. Not to help you, leastwise.'

It was Collings's turn to lean close, the bright colours of his coat shimmering against the firelight. 'You are a convert to Puritanism, Ventura. An abomination in Spanish eyes. A heretic. I could burn you at Torrington market, *señor*, and Madrid would celebrate. The emperor's fire-workers would illuminate the skies above the Manzanares, even as your ashes settled on Devon soil.'

Ventura remained stone still for a second, licked huge lips with his glistening slug tongue, then sat back. Collings's thin mouth twitched and he turned to Hogg. 'You, sir, were sent on to the moor on the proviso that you aided this brainless router,' he jerked his fragile chin at the crestfallen Colonel Wild, 'in his hapless attempts to liberate my wagon.' The black eyes became slits. 'You assured me, Mister Hogg.'

Hogg was not a man easily cowed, but he felt instantly uncomfortable under the general's drilling attention. 'I did my best, Major-General, believe me. They saw one of their own swing.'

'And?'

Hogg thought back to the death of Otilwell Broom, Stryker's unfortunate messenger. He remembered the torture to which Broom had been subjected, and the condemned man's final thrashing, piss-drenched moments. 'And nothing, sir. Stryker's men remained loyal. It was—'

'Was what?' Collings prompted impatiently.

Hogg could only shrug. What more could he say? That, for the first time, he had found a man people feared more than the peril of being charged with witchcraft? More than the silent, swaying threat of a waiting noose? 'Remarkable.'

The breeze turned briefly into a strong gust, lifting the smoke towards the stars and stirring the phalanx of beech and oak that rimmed the cemetery. Then all became still again. A chorus of guffaws ruptured the silence from another of the small fires: some bawdy jest had animated a group of Wild's men. Hogg peered across at them. He noticed one stand, stretching out his back like a newly woken cat, pushing balled fists into the base of his spine. Hogg felt his own back aching in empathy. The frantic retreat in the face of Stryker's unexpected reinforcements had taken a heavy toll on his body. His backside hurt too. It always hurt. The pistol ball was still there, still lodged deep in his rump, jabbing at him, searing his leg, reminding him of the man who had pulled the trigger.

'What now, sir?' Colonel Wild said, running a hand through his long hair, the grey stripe turned to quicksilver by the moon.

Major-General Collings looked at Wild with an expression of utter disdain. 'Now that you have failed me, Colonel, we will march to Stratton. We have more men than Hopton could muster in another month, perhaps two, so our victory is not in question. We will find a defensible position,' he went on, marking each event on his fingers, 'wait for the malignant horde to come a-knocking, hold it firm until General Chudleigh's father returns from Bodmin with the bulk of our horse, and crush Hopton betwixt our combined forces.'

Wild nodded as he imagined the events so confidently relayed by Collings. 'Aye, sir. I will lead my troopers to glorious—'

Collings tutted lightly, fixing him with those dead eyes. 'You will lead no one, sir. As I said, you have proved your-self unfit for command.'

Wild's mouth lolled open. 'Sir, you cannot—'

Collings wagged a finger in Wild's face as though he was admonishing an errant schoolboy. 'Oh, but I *can*, Gabriel. Your regiment will ride for Bodmin on the morrow. They will join with the rest of the horse and aid in the suppression of the enemy militia.'

Hogg glanced from Wild to Collings and back again, wondering if the new glint in the colonel's eyes was the beginning of tears. Wild ground his teeth together, eventu-ally asking in a tiny voice, 'And me, sir?'

Collings sighed. 'Stryker has made you – and, there-fore, *me* – look unforgivably foolish, and for that you have lost your command.' He let his gaze fall to the smoulder-ing logs, his voice becoming distant. 'But there will soon be battle.'

Hogg leaned in a touch. 'You are certain, sir?'

Collings did not look at him. 'Without doubt. The barbaric Cornish will not stand blithely by as we burn Truro and stroll to Land's End.' His head lifted then, but the eyes fixed on Wild. 'And when there is a fight, Colonel, you become undeniably useful. I, on the other hand, despise such base pursuits. My war is of a more,' he tapped lightly at his temple, 'cerebral nature. You are to be my personal aide, Colonel Wild. My guard.'

'Is there nothing I can say?' the colonel said, voice pitched higher than usual. He spread his big palms. 'Do?'

'Pray Stryker is with Hopton,' Collings replied bluntly. 'When the king's men are broken, I will release you as I would release a hound. And you will hunt him down. I am greatly displeased with you, Colonel, but things may go better should that bastard perish on the field.' His attention turned abruptly to the men across from him. 'You will remain with the army, Master Hogg.'

Hogg was aware of his mouth falling open, but felt unable to prevent it. 'But, sir—'

'Enough!' The major-general cut him off with a wave of his hand and a look of pure iron. 'You have failed me too, Witch-finder. I pay you well for your dubious service, and I expect a return on my investment. Instead you run before Stryker like a scolded infant.' He rose to his feet, stooping briefly to rearrange the bucket-shaped leather folds at the tops of his boots. 'You will remain with the army, Master Hogg, for we shall require your powers of coercion when the enemy is defeated. *Kernow*,' he said the word as if his mouth had filled with poison, 'will be in dire need of subjugation.'

Collings turned and stalked into the night, leaving the three forlorn men to stare at the flames in silence. Osmyn Hogg's heart battered against his ribcage. Battle. He had seen it before. Indeed, he had witnessed indescribable massacres in the Low Countries, but there, as first a priest and later a witch-hunter, he had not been unfortunate enough to become embroiled in the blood and death. Now, all for the hatred of a single man, he was utterly entangled within the web of this brutal war. He shut his eyes and began to pray softly.

'We will kill him,' a deep, hard voice broke across his entreaty.

Hogg's eyes sprung open. 'Colonel?'

'Stryker. This is all Stryker.' Wild placed another plug of dark sotweed on his tongue and began to chew. 'He is a fighter, Master Hogg.'

'Your point?'

Wild sent a jet of brown liquid between his front teeth to bubble on a brightly glowing log. 'He will be with Hopton. And Hopton will come to us.' He jabbed a finger against his own sternum. 'And I will be watching. Watching and waiting. You and your goddamned diego—'

''Ey!' Ventura lurched forward, making to stand, but froze when he saw the promise of violence in Wild's eyes and the glint of honed steel in his fist.

Wild looked back at Hogg. 'You and your goddamned diego,' he repeated with the merest hint of amusement, 'wish Stryker dead too. So you will stay with me. And we three will search the faces of the men we fight and kill and capture, until we see a man with one grey eye. And then,' he turned the knife in his hand, the firelight dancing along its keen length, 'we will dig out that eye and cut off his stones and tear out his tongue.'

'And stretch his neck,' José Ventura added.

Osmyn Hogg's heart still kept a rapid pace. But this time it was not through trepidation but excitement. His old wound ached, but, strangely, he did not mind.

CHAPTER 18

The young officer reined in beside the two mounted men as they watched the town come alive with scurrying soldiers. He bent briefly, patting the snorting brindle with his good hand before straightening to adjust the leather strap that held his withered right arm in a permanent angled suspension. Jerking his head sharply from side to side so that his neck gave a couple of satisfying cracks, the officer blinked sore eyes and gave a short bow. 'Sir.'

Both of the waiting men returned the newcomer's gesture, though only one spoke. 'Mister Burton. You are rested, I trust?'

Lieutenant Andrew Burton studied the speaker, who seemed so small atop the skittish black charger. Sir Ralph Hopton, commander of King Charles's army in the southwest, was soberly dressed, indicating a man who, though loyal to his sovereign, held beliefs nearer to the Puritan persuasion than most in the King's Army. His face was serious, an effect exacerbated by deep lines. Burton knew him to be in his mid forties, but the stresses of the rout at Sourton Down made him appear a deal older. 'Aye, sir, well enough.'

377

Burton glanced across at the road where a thick forest of pike staves was steadily growing as men mustered in a cloud of dust, hurriedly finding their companies and files. There were perhaps four hundred already drawn up, with scores more approaching from the various lanes that criss-crossed the town like the threads of a vast cobweb. Sergeants and corporals stood along the road's edges, berating, cursing, and manhandling their charges into some semblance of order, the hawkish gaze of their officers an ever-present incentive. 'I see plans move on apace,' Burton said, genuinely impressed by the speed with which Hopton had mustered an army hitherto so widely spread around Launceston and beyond.

Hopton pecked a staccato nod. 'They do, they do. And necessarily so. I was just telling Colonel Trevanion of the dread word we have received.'

'Dread indeed, sir,' Burton replied, 'and I pray the news was not too late in the telling.'

The general gestured the intimated apology away. 'It is told, and that is what matters.'

'What I do not understand, sir,' Burton ventured, 'is why Stamford would choose Stratton. Is it not Sir Bevil Grenville's territory?'

'The area at large, aye,' Hopton answered, 'but not the town.'

'Stratton itself is one of the few rebel garrison positions along the frontier,' the man Hopton had named as Colonel Trevanion said abruptly. He craned forward to draw a wizened little apple from his saddlebag and bit into it, a pale bead of juice quickly tracing its way down his clean-shaven chin. He watched the various units take shape on the road as he chewed.

'It is also,' he continued when he had swallowed, 'an excellent crossing point for the Tamar. The river cuts a broad gash through the rest of the county. It is more easily defended by our lads. At Stratton, Stamford can simply walk round it.' He took another bite of the apple, before switching his attention to Hopton. 'We must engage him before he strolls into Cornwall.'

Hopton's face became grim. 'There will be much blood.'

Trevanion stretched his back as he picked his words. He was tall, with long brown hair and hazel eyes that twinkled with intelligence. 'I know you would favour some kind of blockade, General. Keep them stuck fast at Stratton, force them to venture south again where we might use the Tamar to our advantage.'

Hopton's fleshy head shook. 'I accept such a thing would fail, but a direct engagement carries grave risk. I understand Stamford's strength to be comfortably superior to my own.'

Trevanion tossed the apple core over his shoulder. 'Hit the bugger quickly, sir. Hit him hard. Push him on to the coast.'

Hopton turned back to the massing troops. 'It will be a rare fight. We are grievous outnumbered.'

Trevanion grinned at that. 'But you have the Cornish, sir.'

A trace of a smile twitched at Hopton's own lips. 'Aye, John, I have the Cornish.'

'Besides,' Trevanion said briskly, 'how, might I ask, do we know they attack? Is it certain? We have had no news for days.'

Hopton's wide brow shot up. 'Apologies, Colonel, I am

remiss.' He indicated Burton. 'I present to you Lieutenant Andrew Burton. The source of my new-found knowledge.'

Trevanion leant across, saddle creaking beneath his shifting rump, and stretched out a gloved hand. 'Well met, Lieutenant. I am Colonel John Trevanion.'

Burton shook the colonel's hand. He judged Trevanion to be no more than thirty, though his voice was strong and his bearing confident. 'I know who you are, sir, of course.' He glanced at the burgeoning ranks of pikemen and musketeers. 'These are yours, are they not?'

'The whole raggedy lot,' Trevanion said happily. 'Seven hundred at last count, and I'm proud of each. And with whom do you serve, Mister Burton?'

'I'm with Mowbray's regiment, sir.'

Trevanion's forehead wrinkled. 'Mowbray? Ain't he out watching the Okehampton road?'

Burton nodded. 'Aye, sir, he is. That is to say, lately my company have been on,' he paused for a heartbeat, '*detached* duties. I am come direct from Captain Stryker at Beaworthy.'

The youthful colonel's lips drew back to expose neat white teeth. 'Stryker?'

'You know him, sir?' Burton could not hide his surprise.

'*Of* him, Lieutenant. Prince Maurice speaks very highly of Stryker.'

That made sense, thought Burton as he nodded. 'The captain has served the Prince's brother many times.'

'Well if Rupert of the Rhine has cause to trust him,' Trevanion declared, 'then he must be a rare character.'

And, in the most unlikely of places, Burton was forced to think upon his captain. He had wanted to kill Stryker in that cave. Cecily Cade had turned Burton down, only to engage in a clandestine tryst with the captain. It must have been going on for days. They must have been mocking Burton's lovelorn advances the entire time. Yes, he had hated Stryker for that. But now, after daylight and distance had provided some small perspective, he was beginning to wonder if things had really been entirely as they seemed.

'Aye, sir,' he said eventually. 'He is a hero.' Perhaps it was worth discussing matters with Stryker. After everything they had been through together, the captain deserved that.

'When did you discover Stamford's purpose, Lieutenant?' Colonel Trevanion was asking.

Burton blinked to clear his thoughts. 'Two days since, sir. My horse stumbled, broke its leg. It took time to find a new one.'

Hopton snorted. 'And time to reach me, no doubt.'

Burton offered a rueful smile. It had indeed been difficult securing an audience with Sir Ralph without knowledge of the army's new field word. 'Your guards are scrupulous, General, aye.'

Hopton shrugged. 'What matters is that I know. I know Stamford has launched his offensive, and I know where he will strike. We are to advance northward at sunrise with as many men as we might gather hereabouts.'

'You have summoned Slanning?' Trevanion asked. He glanced at Burton. 'He has a thousand good men at Saltash.'

'Naturally,' Hopton nodded. 'And Lord Mohun from Liskeard. They will be with us by the morrow. We leave as soon as our forces are joined. With God's breath in our sails we shall reach Stratton in no more than two days.'

'Sir Bevil is already there?' enquired Trevanion.

Hopton twisted his little greying beard between a thumb and forefinger. 'He has twelve hundred troops in the vicinity, certainly. I have sent a rider to inform him of the enemy's approach and to order him not to engage. He must await my arrival.'

Trevanion sucked air into his chest, easing it out through clenched teeth. 'To Stratton then, sirs.'

'To Stratton,' Hopton agreed. 'Where we will destroy the rebellion in the south-west.'

NEAR MARHAMCHURCH, CORNWALL, 13 MAY 1643

The twin companies of Captains Innocent Stryker and Lancelot Forrester bivouacked in mist-fringed fields to the north of Marhamchurch. The village lay astride the road from Launceston, and it was along that road, Stryker hoped, that the army of King Charles would soon appear. To the north lay Stratton. They had visited the place that might soon become a battlefield, only for their scouts to tell of a populace roused for the cause of Parliament and of an approaching wagon train of provisions. That train might have been a tempting target for the weary redcoats, a chance to fill snapsacks and bellies, but the large escort of firelocks quickly put paid to the idea.

'At least we know Richardson's man spoke true,' Forrester said when he found Stryker squatting on a crumbling log and inspecting the stitching of one of his boot soles.

Stryker looked up. 'The firelocks?'

Forrester nodded, rosy cheeks quivering. 'Why send them unless there's more to guard than victuals?'

That was true enough, thought Stryker. Firelocks were employed to guard wagon trains when an errant spark could spell carnage. Their presence almost certainly meant that the convoy carried black powder as well as food. And that meant that Stratton was indeed the place where Stamford's forces were headed. But what could Stryker do, except wait this side of the little town and hope Burton had reached Hopton with the news? Now, as the morning mist was cleared by salty coastal gusts, his men rested and his pickets watched the north and east, their eyes trained on the horizon from which the Roundheads would surely emerge.

Forrester removed his hat, fanned his face with it, and went to sit beside Stryker, clay pipe appearing in his free hand as if conjured from thin air. 'Will Andrew come round, do you think?'

Stryker abandoned the scrutiny of his boot and jammed it back on to his foot. 'I don't know, Forry.'

There was a short but awkward silence as Stryker jerked the tall boot tight over his calf, while Forrester peered around at the small groups of men who squatted at fires, diced, or drank smoke. 'She's a singular beauty,' the latter said eventually.

Stryker looked across sharply. 'And?'

Forrester shrugged. 'And any man with red blood and an underused pizzle—'

'Nothing happened, for Christ's sake!'

Forrester lifted his hat as if to shield himself from his friend's wrath. 'I'm sorry, Stryker.'

Stryker relented as his fellow officer pretended to cower. He shook his head, half in exasperation, half in bewilderment. 'She thought to seduce me.'

'In order to convince you to let her leave the tor.'

Forrester returned his hat to its perch of thin blond hair and clamped the pipe stem between his teeth. 'But you held firm, and Burton let his jealousy get the better of him. You have done nothing to give concern.'

Stryker thought back to that night, to the dark cave and the pale-skinned woman. He wondered whether Burton had truly been mistaken. 'I almost took up the offer, Forry. Despite Andrew's interest in her.'

Forrester was lighting his pipe, pungent grey gusts swirling about his face as he sucked the tobacco into life. 'Then why did you turn her down?' He took the pipe from between his teeth, blew out the remnants of smoke from his lungs, and stared hard at Stryker. 'Not sure I'd have been as strong-willed.'

Stryker offered a simple shrug. 'Lisette.'

'*Ha*!' Forrester snorted, lurching back with the laughter so that he almost fell from the log. 'And yet *she*—'

'Have a care, Captain.'

The mirth left Forrester's moon-round face almost immediately as he caught sight of Stryker's hard, silver-streaked eye. 'Well, you know what I would say.'

'That she betrays me at every turn?' Stryker retorted bitterly. 'That she gallops off to God knows where at the click of the Queen's fingers? Does God knows what, with God knows whom?'

Forrester took another long breath from his pipe, letting the fingers of smoke drift lazily between his lips to envelope his head like a waterfall in reverse. 'That's about the size of it, aye.'

The quick anger had left Stryker now, for he knew his old friend was right. 'And yet I am faithful. Do you think me weak? An unmarried cuckold?'

Forrester stared across at Stryker for a long while, teeth clamped on the clay stem, gaze steady. Eventually the merest trace of a smile flickered at the corners of his mouth and he slapped Stryker's shoulder. 'Aye!'

Stryker began to laugh, but immediately something caught his attention. A man, tall and rangy, ran briskly towards them, the four men Stryker had set as pickets scuttling in his languorous wake.

'What is it?' Stryker called, recognizing Sergeant Skellen.

'We got company, sir!' Skellen bellowed through cupped hands, before turning back to the south.

Stryker looked beyond Skellen and the pickets to see a broad line of shapes moving within the veil of mist. At first the shapes were hazy, intangible, and a part of him hoped it was nothing more than a herd of deer, but a man's voice called sharply from within the white cloak, followed by the startling beat of drums. Stryker stared as the shapes resolved. They were men, hundreds of men, and they carried pikes and muskets, halberds, scythes, pitchforks, swords, poleaxes, and partizans. The first ranks darkened as they burst beyond the pale wisps, and Stryker searched them for signs of a consistent coat colour or field sign. Nothing.

Forrester was immediately beside him. 'See an ensign?'

Stryker shook his head for answer. 'Get your men ready, Forry. If it is Stamford, we must be ready to run.'

'God's fingertips,' Forrester muttered, fingering the sword-hilt at his waist, 'let's bloody well pray not.'

But then the first of the great standards appeared, looming from the mist like the prow of a Viking ship of old. It was a large flag of dark blue, hanging limp in the still air from a stout wooden staff, and, though it carried no device, his jangling nerves immediately began to settle.

'There are no blue ensigns in the Devon foot,' Lancelot Forrester was saying at Stryker's flank. 'Who could it be?'

Stryker shot his friend a rare smile. 'Sir Bevil Grenville.'

LAUNCELLS, CORNWALL, 13 MAY 1643

The grey edifice of St Swithin's Church dominated the village, casting its elongated shadow over most of the small, timber-framed hovels that clustered beneath mouldering thatches.

'Half granite, half soapstone.'

Terrence Richardson, intelligencer and double agent, frowned at his commander's words. 'Sir?'

Major-General James Chudleigh was standing at the big church's main entrance, head tilted back so that he could stare up at the soaring stone tower rising above the efficient Norman arch. Buff-sleeved arms folded across his chest, Chudleigh did not look round. 'St Swithin's. I have a particular interest in architecture. Of course, the proper term is polyphant, but soapstone persists.'

Richardson's shoulders bunched. 'If you say so, General.'

'I wonder what they would make of its current use,' Chudleigh said, almost regretfully, as his chin jerked down. He peered through the open doorway, listening to the whickering of horses from within the long nave.

'I do not suppose they'd be happy, sir,' Richardson said.

'No,' Chudleigh muttered, before finally looking round at the spy with a rueful smile. 'And he must needs go that the devil drives.'

'Quite,' Richardson replied, considering how apt Shakespeare's words were for his own situation. He had gone to such pains to hide his duplicity; lied, cheated, and murdered to keep himself concealed. And yet events had conspired against him. He had ambushed Forrester and Payne, and that had been beautifully planned and timed, yet the force of redcoats he had encountered was far greater than expected, and his plan to kill every last man had been quickly aborted. He had revealed himself to the enemy, and now he could never return to Hopton's side. 'Needs must.'

But the young general was no longer listening. His brown eyes had drifted across the intelligencer's shoulder to take in a new sight. His right cheek flickered slightly. 'You have brought her. Good.'

Richardson turned to face the woman who had accompanied him from her heavily guarded quarters in the village. She was clothed in a clean, straight dress of pale blue, her raven-black hair tightly imprisoned by a pristine white coif. He waved a hand to indicate that she should approach. She obeyed, shuffling closer.

'Do you know who is entombed here?' Major-General Chudleigh asked suddenly, eyes fixed on the woman. 'I dare say you do not. Sir John Chamond. A great man of Cornwall, by all accounts. High Sheriff of the county, Custos Rotulorum.'

'Keeper of the Rolls,' the woman said, eliciting a broad smile from the general.

'Very good, Miss Cade. But what else?'

Terrence Richardson moved aside as his superior paced towards their captive. 'Member of Parliament,' he said, addressing Chudleigh's back.

Chudleigh did not turn, his gaze instead fixed firmly

upon the woman. 'Member of Parliament. *Parliament*, Miss Cade. That is the crucial institution. The one to which a man – or woman – must look for guidance. Even a man like Sir John Chamond. A good man of Kernow.' Chudleigh had moved to within an arm's length of his prisoner, and he leant in further, voice low. 'Do your duty for the Parliament, Miss Cade.' He straightened suddenly. 'Well? I am waiting, girl.'

For answer, Cecily Cade's upper lip lifted at the corner in a derisive sneer. 'Girl? You are hardly my elder, sir.'

James Chudleigh's jaw stiffened. 'But I am most certainly your better.' He glanced back at Richardson. 'She remains stubborn?'

Richardson nodded, declining to detail the scorn with which Cecily Cade had rebuffed the interrogations of the days since her capture. 'She has told me nothing of worth.'

Cecily glared at him. 'I cannot tell you what I do not know, sir.'

'Ah,' Major-General Chudleigh interjected, 'but that is where things become somewhat difficult.' He began to pace around her in a tight circle, shoulders brushing hers as he moved. When he spoke, his voice was low, measured, as though he spoke to a child. 'You will have heard of a great victory for the Parliament at Sourton Down. One of our prizes at that hallowed fight was the portmanteau of General Hopton himself. It spoke of a great many important matters. One of which, it transpired, was the imminent arrival of a man who knew the whereabouts of a great deal of gold. That man, we later discovered, had been, once upon a time, in the service of the Spanish Empire, as an interpreter. It is said he amassed vast wealth from his dealings with King Philip.'

Cecily kept her head and shoulders straight, not deigning to follow the general as he paced. 'What of it, sir?'

Chudleigh halted beside her. 'That man,' he spoke directly into her left ear, 'was Sir Alfred Cade, your father.'

She did not flinch. 'I know nothing of this wealth, General. It is make-believe. A peasant's myth, conjured by poor men through green eyes.'

Chudleigh began to walk again. 'Except Mister Richardson, here, intercepted a rider from the men you were with on Dartmoor. And that rider said, unequivocally, that you had been told the whereabouts of this treasure before your father breathed his last.'

'It is true,' Richardson spoke now. 'Come now, Miss Cade, we have been through this time and again. We know you are privy to the location of the gold. Cease this game.'

'Speak up, Miss Cade,' Chudleigh continued smoothly. 'Surely after the coin I have spent—'

That seemed to touch a nerve, for Cecily rounded angrily on the Parliamentarian commander. 'You think a new coif and a fancy dress will buy a betrayal, sir?'

'Betrayal?' Chudleigh replied icily. 'Whom would you betray, since you no longer have any kin?'

Cecily Cade's green and hazel eyes narrowed to slits, her breaths thickening. 'A pox on you, sir.'

Richardson stepped closer now. 'Miss Cade,' he said gently, 'you must speak with us.' He had attempted to lever the information from her enough times to know that personal insults would only serve to fasten her mouth shut. 'Please, I ask you. Tell us the location of the gold. It is for your benefit.'

Chudleigh stepped abruptly between them, cutting across the intelligencer's words. 'I grow tired of this obstinacy, girl.' He drew close to her, pausing to tug the gloves from his hands, and propping them under an armpit. Silence followed as he casually cracked each of his knuckles in turn. 'I should not wish to make things— physical,' he said eventually, slipping the gloves back on. 'But I will if I am compelled, make no mistake.'

Richardson watched the pair eye one another. 'Please, Miss Cade,' he said quietly.

She stared ahead, focussing on some distant point, lips pressed together in a thin line. Chudleigh shook his head. 'Such folly.' He stooped briefly to pull up the tops of his boots, stretching the leather where it had bunched at his ankles. 'I assure you, Miss Cade,' he said when he had straightened, 'Lord Stamford will not be as forgiving as I.'

Cecily's eyes left their far-away focus then, flickering to meet the general's. 'A pox on him too.'

'Where is Lord Stamford, sir?' Richardson asked when Chudleigh turned his back on the prisoner in exasperation, cheek shivering manically.

'Away to the east,' he snapped irritably. 'The gout ails him terribly. But he will arrive in time to deal with Hopton,' he added, as much for Cecily's benefit as Richardson's. 'Do not doubt it.'

'Should I take her to him?' the intelligencer asked.

Chudleigh considered the question for a moment, gnawing at the inside of his mouth. 'No. I would not want our precious friend on the roads, crammed with soldiers as they are.' He stared at Cecily, eyeing her rigid stance coldly. 'No, Miss Cade, you will stay with me, where you can disclose your secrets in your own time. Perhaps you will be fortunate enough to witness the final destruction of Cavalier influence in the south-west. Then, of course, you will see that there is little point in this stubbornness.'

'And if I do not?'

He smiled, the gesture unpleasant. 'Then you *will* meet some of our soldiers. They will wish to celebrate our imminent victory, naturally. And they have been starved of female company for a very long time. Do we understand one another?'

NEAR MARHAMCHURCH, CORNWALL, 13 MAY 1643

Sir Bevil Grenville's men might have marched behind a blue standard, but their coats reflected no uniform colour whatsoever. They were a rough-looking force, clad in a spectrum of shades as diverse as their weaponry, men who had enlisted to fight in whatever clothes they possessed.

'The mighty men of Kernow,' Anthony Payne's rib-shaking tone jarred across Stryker's thoughts as he watched the massed ranks advance. 'They fight for their colonel, their county and their king.' His wide mouth split in a wolfish grin. 'In that order.'

Stryker twisted back to catch Payne's dark eyes. 'They look like a rabble.'

To his surprise, Payne's beam widened. 'The most formidable rabble in the land, Captain. Brutal, fearless, and ferocious.'

Looking at the dour expressions, the lean, hard physiques and the array of agrarian tools turned so convincingly to macabre employment, Stryker did not doubt it. He strode out to meet the larger force as the two groups converged in the misty field. As ever, the footfalls of his most trusted men sounded a short distance behind; Forrester, Skellen, Heel, and Barkworth. He guessed Payne would be there too. Further back, he imagined, was his own small force, waiting straight-backed and solemn, a wall of stoic redcoats in the face of more than a thousand grim Cornishmen.

'You are with General Hopton, Sir Bevil?' he asked of the only mounted man present as soon as formal introductions had been made.

Sir Bevil Grenville, resplendent in shimmering blue-green doublet, slid nimbly down from his big gelding and nonchalantly rolled his broad shoulders as he spoke. 'Alas, no. But he travels hither.'

Stryker glanced back at Forrester. 'Burton made it through.'

'I haven't the faintest notion of what you're about, sir,' Grenville said briskly as Forrester's head bobbed, 'but Hopton is on his way.'

'All is well, then,' a deep, guttural voice emanated suddenly from behind Stryker, causing Grenville's twinkling gaze to lift as though he searched for clouds beyond the pallid haze.

'Anthony,' the knight said with genuine warmth.

Anthony Payne took a gigantic pace forward, bowing low, though his head remained above that of Stryker. 'Sir Bevil. It is a grand thing to see you well.'

Grenville waved his manservant's pleasantries away. 'And you, sir, though I'd wager naught could see you harmed.' His eyes dropped to the third man in the group. 'And Captain Forrester. Well met.'

Forrester brandished an urbane grin. 'Well met, Sir Bevil.'

A shadow ghosted across Grenville's cheerful face suddenly, and he glanced left and right. 'Let us speak in private.'

'Captain Stryker was made aware of our mission, sir,' Payne's stentorian voice grumbled back. He winced as Grenville set his jaw. 'By absolute necessity.'

Grenville blew air out through his nostrils. 'So be it.' His voice fell to a coarse whisper. 'What have you to report?'

Forrester and Payne exchanged a sideways glance, the former clearing his throat. 'We have failed, sir.'

Grenville did not speak, but his eyes flickered up to stare at his manservant.

Payne winced and nodded slowly. 'It grieves my very heart to say it, but it is true. Sir Alfred is dead. Killed by brigands.'

Sir Bevil Grenville removed his hat, tossing it behind to be caught by the aide who held his horse's reins. His hair, lustrous and bronze despite the gloomy day, escaped at all angles as soon as it was released, putting Stryker in mind of a lion's mane, and he ruffled it vigorously with a gloved hand so that the curls cascaded across his shoulders, falling band collar, and silver gorget. 'Jesu,' he said heavily, 'then his knowledge is lost forever.'

'Would that were true, Colonel,' Anthony Payne growled. 'He had a daughter.'

A moment's silence followed as Grenville absorbed the revelation. 'And she has the location?' he asked slowly.

'Aye.'

'Then—'

Payne grimaced, mouth working tonelessly like a landed fish.

'Then,' Lancelot Forrester cut in, seeing Payne's discomfort, 'the rebellion will soon be a deal richer.'

The knight looked from the tubby officer to Payne, and back to Forrester. 'They have this woman?'

Forrester dipped his head, like Payne unable to hold the great man's searching gaze. 'We were betrayed, Colonel. A man named Richardson, Terrence Richardson, has foiled us with his treachery.'

Grenville's handsome face tightened. 'Richardson?' He scratched at his chin briefly, lost in thought. A memory evidently hit him, for his eyes seemed to bulge from their sockets. 'But I know that fellow. He is one of Sir Ralph's most trusted men.'

'Then he has turned his coat, Sir Bevil,' Stryker interjected levelly. 'He ambushed us with a troop of horse. A Roundhead troop. We fought him off, naturally, but not before he had taken the girl.'

Grenville's hand fell to his sword-hilt, and he gripped the handle as if to steady himself. 'And Cade's daughter has the information we seek?' he pressed, clear voice belying the strain Stryker could see in his eyes. 'You're certain of this?'

Stryker glanced at Forrester and Payne, but the pair could not bring themselves to meet the colonel's stare. 'Aye, sir,' he replied. 'We understand Richardson has taken her direct to Lord Stamford.'

Sir Bevil Grenville spun away, startling everyone present. He strode rapidly back to his horse, taking the reins and his wide, feathered hat from the blank-faced aide, and hauled himself back up into the saddle.

'Colonel?' Stryker called after him.

Grenville's apple-eyed gelding whinnied at the sudden

flurry of activity, and turned a tight circle, blasting steamy clouds from flared nostrils. Sir Bevil Grenville laughed, patted the beast's neck, and steadied it with a deft twitch of the reins. It immediately became calm. He stared down at Stryker and his men. 'If the rebels have Sir Alfred Cade's daughter, gentlemen, then by Christ we must get her back!'

CHAPTER 19

It was Sunday, and the common land just outside the little East Cornwall village had been transformed into a green cathedral. Blocks of men, arranged in regimental denomination, knelt on the dewy grass as their preachers bellowed thunderous sermons to the drifting clouds like so many angry magpies.

The Royalist army had grown since leaving its Launceston base. Sir Ralph Hopton's summons had had the required effect, and as the force made its gradual progress north and east its ranks had been swollen by the arrival of those units necessarily spread along the border with Devon. Five hundred roaming horse and dragoons under Lord Digby had cantered to Hopton's aid, while Lord Mohun's Regiment of Foot, nine hundred strong, had joined them from Liskeard, and Sir Nicholas Slanning had brought up his thousand men from Saltash. The numbers remained paltry in comparison with those the Earl of Stamford could bring to bear, but at least the king's western army was beginning to look more formidable.

Lieutenant Andrew Burton knelt towards the front ranks of Trevanion's, his adopted regiment. His head was bowed, ready to bob in dutiful unison with the rest when the moment called, but his eyes were wide open. He was not thinking of the Scriptures, or of the ranter's hoarse-voiced pleas for God to protect His righteous warriors in the bloody days to come. Burton's mind was a jumble of images and emotions, certainly, but ones that would sooner enrage the big, silver-haired preacher than delight him. The broad-shouldered cleric, black-smocked and clutching a small Bible in white-knuckled fingers, harangued Colonel Trevanion's men with a spittle-dowsed passion, and Burton was relieved his own thoughts would remain private, because at the very fore-front of them was an image of a woman. A raven-haired beauty of pale skin and round eyes that shimmered green and hazel. Cecily Cade.

From the moment he had set eyes on her amid the bullet-riddled remains of her father's coach, he had yearned for her. The smell of her hair when she wafted past had been intoxicating; the sound of her voice; the smooth lines of her body, hidden so tantalizingly beneath that delicate yellow dress. He had been in love, he supposed, from the very beginning. Or in lust, he chided himself ruefully. And now that he was away from her, away from Stryker, he was beginning to wonder if that lust had made a fool of him.

His stomach lurched suddenly, rumbled audibly enough for the man next to him to jab at his ribs with a sharp elbow. He hissed an apology, wondering what the man expected after they had dined the previous night on a single, weevil-ravaged biscuit each. How Sir Ralph expected his men to march, let alone fight, on such pathetic rations, he did not know. He hoped Stamford's army was equally as ill provisioned.

Stryker would never have let his men go this hungry before a brabble.

Burton sat back on his haunches, shocked by his own mellowing. He was still angry, would still happily crunch a fist into the captain's narrow chin, but the boiling, murderous fury had cooled. Perhaps he had misinterpreted the events of that fateful night. Stryker had protested his innocence, but he had taken Stryker's refusal to put him on a charge for such rank insubordination as a sign of guilt. But now, in the cold light of morning, he could not help but rethink things.

'Bow your head, man, lest you be struck down by His wrath!'

The cleric, wielding his Bible as though it were a weapon, had noticed the absent look on Burton's face among the rows of solemn godly folk. He hurriedly dropped his gaze, reacquainting himself with the bead-glistening grass, and found, for the first time in days, a sense of peace. And regret.

With prayers done, the Royalist army marched on towards Stratton.

The terrain was mostly flat, with long tufts of grass in abundance and the odd wizened tree casting macabre shapes at the sky. It allowed for a reasonable pace, with the horse and dragoons out in front and the blocks of pike and musket stretched out like a vast eel, the small wagon train placed at the centre.

Burton, afforded due honour for bringing the news of Stamford's raid to Hopton, rode at the head of the progress with the general and his illustrious staff. They were Cavaliers all, well dressed, brash, and confident. Despite having little practical military experience between them, they had already built a reputation as a group of fearless young commanders.

'Sir Ralph tells us you were at Stafford in the winter,' commented one of the men at Burton's side. The lieutenant glanced across to see Sir Nicholas Slanning. He had long, wavy hair that seemed like lengths of coke against his bright yellow doublet, and a face that was unshaven and remarkably fresh for a man known for being an uncompromising fighter. Slanning was in his early thirties, but had already served in the Scots War, and had built a solid reputation as one of Cornwall's leading military lights.

Burton caught the interest in the colonel's owl-like brown eyes. 'That I was, sir. The battle was fought on a sloping heath between the villages of Salt and Hopton.'

General Sir Ralph Hopton rode at the head of the group, and he twisted back to brandish a wry smile. 'Hopton Fight. I always wanted a battle named for me, and I am honoured with one at which I was not present!'

The group broke into warm laughter, surprising Burton with their easy camaraderie.

'It was a hard scrap,' Slanning spoke again, 'or so the pamphlets have it.'

Burton nodded. 'Aye, Colonel, that it was. Gell's foot held a wide ridge——'

'That base scoundrel,' Hopton muttered at the mention of the name.

'And Northampton's horse,' Burton continued, 'charged straight at 'em.'

'God rest him,' Hopton intoned sombrely. 'Spencer Compton was a brave man.'

'One of the bravest, sir.'

Colonel Trevanion, loping easily on his big destrier, cleared his throat. 'Did he really take many rebels to the grave with him?'

Burton let his mind drift back across that bloody expanse, to the forest of pikes crammed on the heath's God-forsaken ridge and the fetlock-snapping coney holes that had unhorsed so many of the king's finest cavalrymen. One of those had been Spencer Compton, Earl of Northampton, and that man had refused quarter and been slaughtered for his stubborn bravery. Another man had been with Northampton that day, Burton knew. Cleaved his own blood-soaked passage through the armour and flesh in a forlorn bid to rescue the lord, but never found fame in the printing presses. Captain Stryker had come so close to saving Northampton's life, and nearly perished in the attempt. The ban-dog of the aristocracy, Captain Forrester often called Stryker. That was too true, thought Burton, and he stifled a smile.

'In the end he was swamped,' the lieutenant said. 'But he fought like a lion.'

'You fought with the horse that day, Lieutenant?' Slanning enquired with surprise.

'A strange twist of fate for an infantryman, sir, I grant you.' He shrugged. 'It is a complex tale.'

'Never fear, sir,' Trevanion announced brightly. 'We have ample time for the telling!'

'What the devil?'

It was Hopton who had spoken, and the sheer tone of his voice was cause enough for alarm. Burton and the assembled colonels stared after the general, mouths gaping, as he pointed frantically up at a low ridge to the west.

'There! See?' Hopton spluttered, standing in his stirrups as he fished for something in his saddlebag. In moments his hand came away with a battered little spyglass, and he trained it on the place that had so ensnared his attention. 'Horsemen on the right flank!'

Already many of the non-commissioned officers stalking along the army's right side had spotted the threat and were instinctively arranging evasive action. The column juddered to an abrupt halt amid a storm of snarled instructions.

'Get Digby back here!' Hopton called to his nearest aide. The five hundred mounted Royalists were some distance up ahead, obscured by a dense stand of trees, and it was not certain they would have noticed the men on the ridge. The aide kicked his horse into thrashing life, racing away down the road with his dire news.

'Whose are they?' the general snapped, tossing the spyglass to Slanning.

The huge, owlish eyes pressed against the brass rings for a second as Sir Nicholas slowly replied. 'I believe that is Chudleigh, sir.'

'Which?'

Slanning lowered the glass. 'The elder, sir, to judge by the cornet.'

Hopton pursed thin lips and ground his teeth. 'Meaning we face only the horse, for young James commands the foot on Lord Stamford's behalf.'

'We will hold,' Slanning said confidently.

'Have to pay them their dues, I suppose,' Colonel Trevanion said, seemingly as unflustered as Slanning, though all about him the pikemen shuffled into position. 'They risk a great deal by sending their horse against us, but it is a bold move.'

'There is no deliberation here, John,' Slanning muttered derisively. 'They were travelling south, I'd wager, and blundered into us. Sir George is compelled to give battle, though I guarantee he'd rather not. When he sees this will be no Sourton he will disengage.'

'Then what in Jesus' name are they doing here?' General Hopton replied absently, but no reply came. The enemy were coming.

Lieutenant Burton was staring at the advancing cavalry with a mix of trepidation and awe. It was a large force, comfortably more than a thousand, and they swept down from the high ridge in a whooping, silver-crested wave designed to smash into the Royalist right flank. But they had attacked early, giving credence to Slanning's guess that they had been as surprised to find the King's Army as Hopton had been to see them. There was still a good half-mile to cover, giving the Royalist officers, sergeants, and corporals ample time to prepare a defence with shrill orders and bawled threats, and the men on the right flank turned smartly to face the ridge, blocks of pikemen stepping to the fore, musketeers arranged, three ranks deep, in between.

Burton watched in stunned silence as the Roundhead wave coursed across the damp turf with a growing roar. He instinctively adjusted his arm strap, as he always did before battle, though he knew his position with General Hopton would probably negate the need to fight. Sure enough, a group of heavy-set men, pikes facing outwards in a protective ring, moved into position around the general and his young commanders, ushering them towards the safer left flank.

The first horsemen were soon in range, and the rapidly

barked orders to *fire by introduction* were spread along the threatened flank. The foremost rank of musketeers snapped back their triggers, tongues of flame lashing out in front. Immediately the rank behind moved between that forward rank and fired, followed in quick succession by the third, thereby offering an almost continuous fusillade. A great storm of smoke and flame pulsated across the Royalist force, belching violence towards the encroaching peril.

The range was still great, and only two Parliamentarians were knocked from their saddles in that early barrage, but the Cornish cheered their defiance like a horde of Celts facing the might of Rome, and they snarled and spat and cursed at the advancing enemy.

The first rank fired again. A few more of Sir George Chudleigh's cavalrymen went down this time, and the Royalist jeers grew like a Penzance squall, but time was against them and they stepped rearward as pike blocks shuffled to the fore, great shafts of ash angled upwards, braced against each man's instep, presenting a glinting barrier of razor points for the white-eyed storm to drench.

The wave broke with a clash of steel that rippled all the way along the human storm-break. The noise of man and horse, musket butt, pike, halberd, and sword mingling in deafening crescendo, echoing like a thunderclap all the way back up the ridge.

But the momentum had gone from the charge. The musket volleys had slowed the Roundhead attack, and the pikes, thrust into the faces of Chudleigh's horses, had made the frightened beasts shy away from the fight. They wheeled back almost as one, understanding that their beating broadswords would not cut enough holes in the Cavalier defence to lever a breach.

Burton was leaning across his own mount, whispering softly into the pricked ear to sooth the animal's frayed nerves. His eyes, though, were still fixed over the heads of the Cornish infantry to the chaotic front line where the last of Chudleigh's attackers were extricating themselves from personal duels, desperate to be free lest they become isolated and abandoned. Somewhere to his left a trumpet screeched, all eyes shifting to meet the new sound. Burton peered too, searching the dark tree line for the origin of the startling note. There, bursting out on to the road like so many avenging angels, were more horsemen. This time, though, the Royalist column did not have to brace itself for action.

'It's Digby,' Sir Nicholas Slanning announced from somewhere behind Burton. 'About bloody time, eh?'

Another cheer went up from the grizzled foot, but its tone was rueful rather than joyous. Slanning grinned. 'The horse can chase Chudleigh into the hills, but our lads know who won this day.'

Sure enough, the Roundhead force, so irresistibly large, was already making for the safety of the ridge, desultory pot-shots sent whistling in their wake by optimistic musketeers. And there, on the top of that gentle slope, they regrouped. But this time there was no malice in their movements, no drawn blades or screamed challenges. There would be no repeat of the attack, it seemed. No relentless charges like those Burton had witnessed at Hopton Fight. The enemy were leaving.

All around Burton staff officers nodded congratulations to one another, though their eyes remained warily trained on the horizon. It was a hollow kind of victory. They had survived with only minor casualties, and yet the direction in which the Parliamentarian party were headed seemed to be cause for concern. They were not waiting around to watch Hopton's army, nor racing north to the main rebel hub at Stratton, but filing quietly away to the south, funnelling on to the road that would lead them deeper into Cornwall.

The Royalist column took pause for around two hours after the skirmish below the ridge. They had come through it relatively unscathed, but burials had to be organized and land had to be more thoroughly scouted.

'What the devil were they about?' a pink-jowled Hopton snapped when relative calm had returned. 'What was Chudleigh doing here, damn his hide? And where did they vanish to?'

For answer, a barrel-chested horseman in full harque-busier armour cantered up to the group. He lifted his hinged visor, revealing pock-rutted cheeks, bulbous eyes, and a syphilitic nose. 'Captain Newbury, sir. Compliments o' Sir John Digby, an' I'm to tell you we took a couple o' the scrofulous villains, if you'll pardon m' language.'

'Well?' Hopton replied impatiently.

'Their treasonous tongues flapped readily enough, General.' Newbury rubbed a gloved forearm across his disease-ravaged face, mopping up the beading sweat that clung to his bushy brows. 'They weren't here for us, sir. They discovered us by accident and gave steel, but we were not his target.'

'Oh?'

'What did I tell you?' Sir Nicholas Slanning whispered as he caught Burton's eye.

'Sir George Chudleigh,' Newbury went on, 'is charged with the blockin' o' Bodmin.'

405

Hopton frowned. 'Blocking?' He shot a wary glance at Slanning and Trevanion. 'They know about the militia?'

The cavalryman nodded, sweat running from his chin to speckle his breastplate and the waxy hem of his coat. 'They do, sir. Chudleigh is tasked with preventing the posse's muster.'

Slanning spat a clump of powder-spotted phlegm on to the hoof-spoiled grass. 'And with that many troopers I'd wager he'll succeed. He must have had fifteen hundred men.'

'If Chudleigh rides to prevent the raising of Bodmin, then Stamford's thought remains bent on Stratton,' Hopton mused. 'And without the Bodmin posse, we must be about our business with half the men he has.'

Burton coughed nervously. 'General? Is there no time to gather more troops?'

Hopton's round head shook. 'We will rendezvous with Grenville imminently, which will bring us to full strength.' He grimaced. 'Barely three thousand.'

'Against Stamford's near six,' Slanning added grimly. 'With a thousand and a half horse roaming Cornwall.'

'And that,' continued Hopton, 'is why we must break him soon, before his horse return. We know Sir George Chudleigh will be a goodly while at Bodmin, so there is time.'

Andrew Burton could feel the colour drain from his face, but was powerless to prevent it. These brave, reckless men were marching to war against insurmountable odds, and he was marching with them.

To his surprise a fist thudded sharply into his left shoulder, and he looked across to where Sir Nicholas Slanning perched atop his muscular charger. The colonel's lips pared back in a wolfish grin. 'Do not fear, Lieutenant. Without his cavalry Stamford will be forced into a straight fight between armies of foot.' He swept an arm out in front to indicate the solid lines of rough-hewn infantry. 'And for such a task, sir, there are none better than the Cornish.'

In that moment Lieutenant Andrew Burton believed him. Believed the power in Slanning's voice and the devilry in his glistening eyes. Despite himself, he felt a surge of hope. 'Aye, sir. We'll send him packing.'

'Back to Devon, Lieutenant! That's the spirit!' Slanning beamed. 'So long as he does not find a bloody hill to climb, eh?'

NEAR STRATTON, CORNWALL, 14 MAY 1643

The hill was ideal.

Looming over the village from the north, it was steeply sloped and flat-topped, protected to the south by a patchwork of hedged fields and to the east by a wooded escarpment that was far too sheer to scale. Furthermore, the River Strat gushed at its foot, and an ancient earthwork provided stout defence at the summit.

Yes indeed, thought James Chudleigh as he gazed down at the cluster of pale dots that was Stratton, the hill was perfect. As commander of Parliament's army – at least until Lord Stamford arrived – the task of scouting the land had fallen to him. And he had been guided by God to this spot. Ordinarily it would be madness to camp on the top of such a high place, but his army was well supplied with ammunition and provisions, and he could stay there for as long as was necessary. Thus, he had decided to march up to the flat crest with his five thousand men, and challenge the Cornish Royalists to knock him off. Soon the malignant horde would come to this hill, flounder on its steep slopes, and be overwhelmed by Chudleigh's much larger force. The coup de grâce, of course, would be the triumphal return of his father's cavalry from Bodmin. They would smash into the Royalist rearguard, sweeping them from the field, and from England, in one decisive victory. All he need do was hold the position and wait.

'You see the trees lines?' Chudleigh said, thrusting an arm to the west to indicate the network of hedges and sunken lanes that webbed the lower third of that steep face.

The woman standing beside him shrugged. 'I see them.'

'That is where the king's men will flounder.'

The woman gave a contemptuous snort. 'You pray.'

'I do not need prayer, Miss Cade,' Chudleigh said, not deigning to look at the infuriating bitch. 'If they choose not to fight then I will await my father, who comes with near two thousand horse. When he arrives I will march down there to meet him and together we will smash Hopton's pitiful army between us.'

'It is the Cornish,' Cecily Cade retorted waspishly. 'They will fight.'

Chudleigh shrugged. 'Then I will have men – *hundreds* of men – in those lanes and hedges, and they'll cut the malignants to shreds before they so much as spy the summit. A few will doubtless make it on to the open terrain.' He glanced at the big artillery pieces being dragged into place a little way down the hill where the lanes petered out, leaving open pasture all the way to the summit. There were thirteen such guns, and, further back, a huge mortar, squatting like a black mastiff against the green grassland. 'And those will be shredded in seconds.'

'You are confident, General.'

'With good reason, Miss Cade. With good reason.'

Cecily Cade stared up at the young Parliamentarian. 'Why did you feel the need to show me all this?'

Now Chudleigh met her gaze, his face serious, his right cheek twitching slightly. 'Because you must see your folly. Witness the end of the war in the south-west. Understand that to join the rebellion is to join God's own cause. We are on the cusp of change, Miss Cade. England will soon be made anew.' He grasped her shoulder suddenly, making her shudder. 'Tell me the location of the gold and the new nation will be yours for the taking. You will be a heroine of the rebellion.'

Cecily Cade looked the major-general straight in the eyes. 'I would sooner be dead than betray my king.'

He sighed in resignation. 'You will certainly pray for death before too long.'

She looked up at him with utter scorn. 'You will hand me to your vile men? I am not afraid, sir.'

Major-General James Chudleigh shook his head sadly and began to walk away, leaving his prisoner to the guards who now converged around her. He looked back briefly. 'I shan't give you to the men, Miss Cade. I am not a monster. No, you will be questioned by another.'

'Who?' she called after him.

'You are not afraid?' He shook his head. 'You should be.'

An hour later, in the shadow of the hill that had become a rebel fortress, three men strode purposefully through fields left untended and abandoned by terrified farm workers. Their boots trampled green crops, sank in soft soil, and slipped when planted in the slick droppings left by the horses and oxen used to haul Chudleigh's big guns into position.

'Curse this *mierda*!' one of the men, lagging behind the others, hissed in heavily accented English as he shook his leg to free the toe end of a particularly sticky piece of faeces. He was a short man, dark of skin and hugely fat, his black cloak, designed to be voluminous, stretched tight about a morbidly fleshy frame.

The taller of the fat man's companions, keeping up a brisk lick despite leaning heavily into a knotted walking cane, turned back brusquely. 'Keep up, José!'

José Ventura, Spaniard, Protestant convert and faithful servant to witch-finder Osmyn Hogg, muttered something unintelligible in his native tongue and launched into a jowl-shaking scuttle to regain the pace. 'Where we go?' he added breathlessly.

The third man, a pale creature with beady black eyes and skin so taut it was almost translucent, did not look round. 'Into the village. Well, the outskirts, to be precise.'

Osmyn Hogg, limping beside the pale man, glanced down at him, instinctively suspicious of the Parliamentarian power broker. 'Oh?'

'I have something to show you,' Major-General Erasmus Collings answered nonchalantly.

That did not fill Hogg with confidence. He made his daily bread by hunting out and purging evil-doers from God's realm. Sometimes it meant that difficult decisions were made; blood spilled, children frightened, and folk killed. But whatever he and Ventura did, they did it in the name of God, with His blessing. Yet Hogg had returned from the New World to find an England full to bursting with men like Collings. Those who would inflict pain and suffering, would lie and cheat and steal and betray for their own advancement. For earthly rewards. He mistrusted such men.

'Why we leave Colonel Wild?' Ventura asked suddenly.

Again, Hogg noticed that Collings did not lower himself to address the Spaniard directly. He offered a cursory reply as he studied the ground, careful to avoid the dung. 'Because this is none of his concern. He will spend the rest of the day sulking, no doubt.'

'He feels,' Hogg answered quickly, as much to curtail Ventura's abrupt line of questioning before it was perceived disrespectful as anything else, 'he should not have to suffer such indignity.'

'He is a failure in the Parliament's army, Master Hogg,' Collings answered as though he spoke to a halfwit, 'and he will suffer whatever indignity I perceive fitting. His troop are good. One of the best we have, in fact, and he will get them back. But he should be put in his place.' He looked at Hogg then. 'And when better than during a battle at which his harquebusiers would have been utterly impotent?'

'They would?'

'Of course, sir. Hopton will have pike blocks, so we will crush them with pike blocks. Besides, we have near six thousand men on top of that small crest. Where would we put horsemen as well? No, they are better employed down at Bodmin with Chudleigh the Elder.'

That seemed reasonable enough to Hogg. Still, he thought, Wild's rage smouldered bright and hot. They had spent much time in his presence since arriving at Stratton, both for their own protection and because, when battle came, Hogg felt that would give him the best chance of finding – and killing – a certain Royalist officer. 'He is angry.'

Collings's deep-set eyes, like twin sepulchres in his lily-coloured face, narrowed with malice. 'He is pathetic.'

Hogg thought about that. About the scornful treatment Wild had received since their ignominious return from the defeat on Dartmoor. It seemed to him as though Collings had gone out of his way to puncture the colonel's hitherto inflated sense of pride. 'You would have him hate you?'

Collings halted, purple lips twitching at the corners. 'I understand the workings of his simple mind, Master Hogg. He will blame Stryker for this. For the defeat, quite rightly, but also for the humiliation he has since suffered. Even now he will be plotting his revenge.'

Hogg nodded in sudden understanding. 'And strive all the harder for the villain's downfall.' Collings was deliberately goading Wild into a frenzy of hatred and bloodlust. When the time came, the general would release him knowing that Wild's only thought would be murder. When he looked into Collings's face, Hogg saw that the general regarded him with renewed interest. 'Sir?'

'You yearn for Stryker's demise as well,' Collings said. It was not a question.

Hogg breathed in through his long nose, held the breath for a heartbeat, and released it slowly. 'He and I have a shared history.'

'A history that has set you against one another?'

'Aye, General.'

Collings began to walk again, ragged corn stems

412

rustling against his shins. 'Stratton is ours,' he said as the first of the village's low buildings came into view. 'Yet the king's champion, Sir Bevil Grenville, has a home here. Ironic, is it not?' When Hogg did not answer, too engrossed in his own thoughts to think of the paradoxes of this conflict, Collings spoke again. 'That is why you would remain at Wild's side, yes?'

The question jolted Hogg. 'Sir?'

'Your personal antipathy towards Stryker. I ordered you to remain with the army, but not necessarily with Wild. You choose to stay close in the hope that he is able to hunt the man down.' He bobbed his head as they drew nearer to Stratton's outermost buildings. Small timber-framed structures with filthy ancient thatches. 'Reasonable. I'd have done the same. And yet you have another duty to perform before you seek any vengeance.'

'Oh?' Hogg enquired warily.

They had reached one of the shabby buildings. Its beams were rotten and worm-ridden, and, even from several feet away, Hogg could smell the ripe odour of damp and mould. Collings rapped knuckles briskly on the low door. It creaked open, the face of a soldier appearing from the far side. Collings looked up at Hogg. 'Speak with a prisoner for me.'

Hogg stayed still. 'I am a witch-catcher, sir, not a soldier. I cannot employ my more—*rough-handed*—techniques for a secular task.'

'Upon the orders of General Chudleigh,' Collings retorted calmly.

Hogg frowned and moved his stick from one hand to the other as his palm began to ache. 'Is Lord Stamford not in charge here?'

413

Collings's grunt dripped contempt. 'When he arrives, yes, but he has yet to show his face.' He smiled unpleasantly. 'Perhaps the gout has spread to his horse.'

Collings led Hogg and Ventura into the room. He stepped to one side, allowing them to peer unhindered at the ghostly figure at the room's far end.

Hogg blinked rapidly as his eyes acclimatized to the poor light, though it was Ventura who recognized the figure first. 'She was one on the tor,' he hissed in his master's ear.

And then Hogg found he could place her too. It was surreal to find her here, of all places, but here she was. 'The witch.'

'Well now she is our prisoner,' Erasmus Collings said from his place beside the door.

Hogg stared back at him. 'She was with Stryker.'

That seemed to elicit a flash of interest from Collings's magpie gaze. 'She was with a large group of enemy foot when captured.'

'And Stryker?'

'I was not told. Our man mentioned a much larger force than he was expecting.'

Hogg nodded. 'Wild's troop were bested because Stryker received reinforcements. They appeared right out of the wood as though spawned by the very trees.'

To his surprise, Collings shrugged. 'No matter. Miss Cade is of greater import. It appears she knows the location of a goodly store of treasure. Chudleigh would have her share that location with us.'

The woman's eyes were wide, unblinking, but her headshake was firm. 'I'll not speak a word.'

'Do you recognize me, girl?' Osmyn Hogg asked. He

stepped closer so that she could see his face more clearly. 'Or Señor Ventura, perhaps?'

There was a long silence before the light of understanding seemed to flood across the woman's face. Her eyes darted manically between Hogg, his walking cane, and his assistant. 'Murderers!'

'Witch-hunters, my dear,' Hogg replied smoothly. 'And you are one such imp-suckler according to the man, Otilwell Broom.'

Cecily Cade's hands shook now. Her face was ashen grey and her bottom lip quivered violently. 'You killed him in cold blood.'

Hogg calmly fished within the folds of his black doublet, drawing out a square of paper, which he carefully unfolded. 'I killed him in God's righteousness.'

Collings took the paper and scanned through its inky scrawl. 'Broom named her as Satan's whore?'

Hogg gave the hint of a nod. 'To you this woman is but a prisoner. To me, she is a witch.' He stabbed at the paper with an outstretched finger. 'You hold my proof.'

Collings stared at the paper a while longer. When he looked up, his eyes glittered like black diamonds in the murky room. Cecily staggered back against the far wall, a high-pitched mewing sound escaping her throat, but all he did was smile.

'Then treat her as such.'

CHAPTER 20

Stryker paced briskly through the dark, the imposing structure's solid black mass blocking out the stars behind.

It was two hours before midnight, but Ebbingford Manor seemed abuzz with activity. Bude itself was a little community nestled against the north Cornwall coast, around a mile to the west of Stratton, and the logical staging post for Hopton's move against the Earl of Stamford. But within the unassuming village, full of plain thatched houses and drab fishermens' hovels, one home stood out above the rest. It was a grand house of hoary granite and intricately carved archways, of low outbuildings, expansive courtyards, and imposing, high-beamed roof. The largest and best-appointed building in the area, its owners had fled when rumours of war had been whispered some days back. Thus, Sir Ralph Hopton, General of His Majesty's Army in Cornwall, had chosen Ebbingford Manor as his headquarters.

Stryker made his way briskly across the courtyard, flames lighting the way, dancing at the ends of torches that sprouted from the exterior walls. He made straight for the main entrance, the open doorway flanked by a pair of thick-set sentries, each sporting a gleaming halberd and stony grimace. They waved Stryker through at the mention of his name, and he strode across the wooden floors of the reception hall and into a narrow corridor, the tapping of his companion's boot heels mingling with his own.

'This will not go well for us.'

Stryker glanced back to look at the tubby fellow scuttling at his heels. Like Stryker, the man was dishevelled and tired, the lines framing his perpetually red cheeks ingrained with grime. He wore a stained brown doublet beneath a well-worn buff-coat, waxy breeches appearing above the creased leather of tall boots, and a hat on his head that had seen far better days. Stryker offered a wan smile. 'Come, Forry, we were betrayed.'

'Betrayal or no,' Lancelot Forrester bit back anxiously, 'Payne and I were charged with bringing Sir Alfred Cade safely to Hopton. Not only did we fail in that, but we lost the old man's bloody daughter too. And do not think you'll escape with a clean nose either, Stryker, for you held the proverbial reins when Richardson galloped off with her.'

They made their way between a couple more surly, if respectful, guards and reached a heavy door of reddish wood and black rivets. Stryker knocked sharply, waited as the door creaked open, stole a last look back at Forrester's nervous face, and stepped beneath the lintel.

The room glowed dull orange as flames from a big hearth and a dozen fat beeswax candles fought to break through the fug of several billowing pipes. Stryker's single eye immediately began to water, stung by the sheer amount of pungent smoke roiling about the men, the furniture, and the stout beams above. He blinked as fast as he could, eager to appear focussed in the presence of such company.

As the blurred shapes became distinct lines, he noticed that the room, for all its modest size, was fairly crowded. A couple of faces he recognized immediately, most he did not, but all, he knew for sure, were men of renown. Their bearing was confident, their clothing of obvious quality, and their faces expressed an innate sense of their own abilities. He snatched his hat clean away, bowing before the men he knew to be the driving force behind the king's western war machine. The young, brash, courageous Cavaliers of Cornwall.

One of the assembled men, the only one sitting, looked up from the far side of a sturdy desk of broad surface and short legs. 'Captain Forrester,' he said brightly. 'It is good to see you again. And the famous Captain Stryker. I should thank you for bringing me the extra powder and guns, sir. It is more welcome than you know.'

'Sir,' Stryker murmured, dipping his head in acknowledgement, though his insides burned with the knowledge that the gift might have been so much greater.

'And how fares Sir Edmund?'

Stryker returned his gaze to the seated man, the man he knew to be Sir Ralph Hopton. He kept his expression impassive, but found himself wishing he had spent more time cleaning himself up. 'In truth, sir, I have not seen our colonel these past three weeks. My company has spent much time out towards Bovey Tracy. But I understand the regiment is strong.'

Hopton's round, fleshy face twitched in a tight smile. 'A shame they could not join us for our current expedition, but I required solid men to protect the rest of the county.'

'I understand, sir. I only hope Captain Forrester and I will represent Sir Edmund as well as he might expect.'

Hopton nodded. 'I am sure you will. And I would thank you both for sending your young lieutenant to warn me of the enemy's plans.' The general jolted upright suddenly, peering through the fragrant smog at the other men assembled. 'My apologies, Captain. Introductions must be made. You will know the names, naturally, but perhaps you have never been fortunate enough to have met my young Cornish scrappers?'

Stryker let his gaze move around the room. Two of the pipe-puffing men stood behind Hopton like foppish sentinels, another pair leaned nonchalantly beside a window, and others had been standing at the corners of the general's big table, evidently studying the huge campaign map spread out across its surface. 'I fear not, sir.'

'Then let us redress the situation.' Hopton nodded towards a point on the wall at Stryker's back. He and Forrester turned to see a pair of faces they knew well. 'Sir Bevil you know, of course, and his man, Anthony Payne.'

The captains bowed low, each with a smile of greeting for the huge Payne, a man they had come to revere.

'And I would introduce you to Sir Thomas Basset, my Major-General of Foot,' Hopton said, eliciting a short bow from one of the men beside the window. 'And here we have Colonel Sir John Berkeley, Lord Mohun, and Colonel John Trevanion.'

Stryker nodded to each one in turn, praying that he would remember which smoke-shrouded face belonged to which great man. 'Well met, sirs.'

'Colonels Sir Nicholas Slanning, William Godolphin,' Hopton continued, finally pointing a slender forefinger at one of the men who had been craning over the map, 'and the man charged with leading our mounted troops, Sir John Digby.'

Stryker bowed low again. He found the presence of such powerful men extremely discomforting. What exactly did the Cornish commanders make of him? Their respective regiments were famed for coarse manners, after all, and each company and tertio raised in defence of the ancient county boasted rank upon rank of rough-hewn, scrap-toughened men, the like and frequency of which were found nowhere else. But tonight they beheld a man of slim, sinewy stature, with a head of long, raven-black hair tied at the nape of the neck. A man of narrow, angular face, one half of which was mutilated fit for nightmare, the other dominated by a bright, quicksilver eye that would not have been out of place on a wolf. He felt their collective gaze falling upon him, and fought to keep his well-practised stare, unflinching and iron-cold, on a point on the oak-panelled wall behind Hopton.

The first Stryker had seen of Sir Ralph Hopton's army was the smudge of slate-grey on the southern horizon. Sir Bevil Grenville's regiment, twelve hundred of Cornwall's most grizzled fighters, had remained in the environs of Marhamchurch until, as dusk spread its stealth over the land the evening before, a scout from General Hopton had arrived to say that the larger Royalist force was drawing closer. Hopton had been waylaid, the scout informed them, by a skirmish with rebel cavalry, and had been forced to bivouac at a place called Week St Mary before pushing on towards Grenville's position. The delay had been irritating for all concerned, for it meant that the Devon Roundheads would have an extra day to prepare for whatever engagement lay ahead, but at least, finally, the king's men had rendezvoused, combined, and marched into Bude.

They had not had things all their own way, of course. The River Neet bisected the land between Royalist Bude and Parliamentarian Stratton, and Roundhead pickets had been placed at the various crossing points to snipe at any vanguard sent across by Hopton. Sir Ralph, though, was in no mood to dally any longer, and sent a solid party of musketeers to clear one such crossing. This they did by cover of dusk, pushing the enemy pickets, and those stationed elsewhere along the river, back to the main rebel position.

After securing the river crossing, Hopton had ordered the bulk of his force across the Neet and eastwards beyond the town. They had reached a patch of high, sandy common ground overlooking the sea. It was the land separating Bude from Stratton, and there, amongst the coarse tufts of wind-harried grass and barren dunes, the men made camp. Or at least, Stryker mused, a camp of sorts. In truth there would be no tents, no drinking, and no fires. No dice would be thrown and no women would make their way up from the countryside to earn some coin. Sir Ralph, acutely aware of the enemy's remarkably strong position, was mindful of a night attack by the waiting rebels, and had ordered the Royalist troops to stand at arms during the starry night. Stryker and Forrester had been organizing their men in the chill coastal breeze when the summons came from Ebbingford Manor.

'Have no fear, gentlemen,' Hopton was saying now, 'Sir Bevil has explained Richardson's treachery. You are not responsible for losing Miss Cade.'

Losing Miss Cade. The three words alone sent a pang

up and down Stryker's spine, finishing in a knot within his guts. 'I wish I could make amends, sir,' was all he could think to say. Behind him, Forrester echoed the feeble sentiment.

Hopton straightened. 'But I would have you bring her back.'

Stryker glanced across at Forrester.

'I cannot exaggerate the importance of the Cade fortune, Captain,' Hopton went on when Stryker had evidently paused too long. 'It must be retrieved at all costs.'

Forrester cleared his throat. 'But Sir Alfred's daughter will be with Stamford, sir. She may even have shared her knowledge by now.'

'My intelligencers do not believe the earl has yet arrived on the field.' The general shrugged. 'It may delay their dealings with her. I'd guess she is confined somewhere in Stratton itself.' Though Stryker still examined the wall beyond Hopton, he could feel the general's gaze rake across his face. 'Choose a man, Stryker. Send him into the village tonight. Discover her whereabouts.'

That surprised Stryker, and he risked a glance directly at Hopton. 'I will go.'

'No, sir, you will not. There will soon be a fight, and you must be here to lead your men. I'd send Mister Payne, for he would see this mission through to its conclusion. But he is a tad conspicuous for the task. With the utmost respect, Mister Payne.'

Stryker could not see the giant's response, but Hopton's quick grin told him no offence had been taken. 'I will pick one of my best, sir,' he said when Hopton's gaze returned.

'Will we join battle on the morrow, General?' Forrester asked abruptly.

For answer, Hopton waved him and the rest of the men closer, and they converged around the huge map. Stryker stared down at it. At first he had no idea what he was studying, for it seemed like no map of England he had ever seen, but then he noticed the looping ink scrawls that labelled Bude and Stratton, saw the jagged line representing the coast, and the tapering V shape that sat in the very centre like a fat spider in its web.

Hopton stabbed the spider with his thumb. 'The enemy are camped on the summit of this damned hill. It is steep, it is difficult to approach, and it is crammed with five, perhaps nearer six, thousand souls. We are also aware of several fieldpieces. A dozen or thereabouts.' He looked up sharply. 'And yet we have one advantage, gentlemen.'

'They have no horse,' Sir Bevil Grenville replied.

'And ours,' Sir John Digby cut in swiftly, 'cannot assault such a sheer position.'

'True enough,' Grenville agreed patiently, evidently sensing the cavalry commander's tension. 'But our foot will carry the day against theirs.'

'With half as many men?' Digby persisted.

Grenville stepped further into the room, leaving Payne silent and watchful beside the doorway like the Colossus of Rhodes. He made his way to the table and its detailed map, the others looking to him with interest. 'Difficult odds, Sir John, I readily accept. But Sir George Chudleigh has a flying column of horse here,' he thrust a gloved finger on to the map and snaked it south-westwards from the north Cornish coast to rest upon one of the handwritten labels scrawled at a place in the centre of the county, 'at Bodmin. Either we engage the Stratton multitude now, or wait until they have twelve hundred harquebusiers at our backs.' His other hand hovered over Stratton and, with deliberate slowness, he slid it across the page to collide with the one at Bodmin. 'Between the two, we'd be crushed like a rotten apple in an eagle's claw.'

Digby took a long, lingering drag on his pipe, the embers in the blackened bowl roaring to life, and blasted the smoke out in a long jet from wide nostrils. Stryker sensed the cavalryman wanted to argue, but knew it would be futile.

'So you see,' General Hopton said, drawing attention back to him, 'it is a hard fight now or an impossible one later.' He paused to let the words sink in, reaching to his right to pick up a small glass. As he lifted it to his lips, Stryker noticed the dark liquid glow crimson as it caught the candle glow, and found himself wondering how Sir Ralph had managed to find a supply of wine when the rest of the army were forced to make do with sour beer and gritty biscuits.

Hopton swallowed, the glass clinking as he set it down. 'We must take the fight to Stamford and the Chudleighs, gentlemen.' He looked down at the map once more, this time concentrating on the hill itself. 'We shall divide our force into four equal columns and advance upon the west face.'

'Is the north not the shallowest option, sir?' Trevanion ventured, frowning at the map's contours.

Hopton nodded. 'But the scouts say it is too heavily defended for us to work around that flank. So it is the west face we scale.' He pointed to the southernmost tip of the V-shaped hill. 'Lord Mohun and I will attack here, with six hundred men.'

'And I, sir?' Grenville asked eagerly, keen to take an active part.

'You, Sir Bevil, will lead the second division, another six hundred, to my left, supported by Berkeley.'

Grenville and Sir John Berkeley leaned over the map, studying their point of advance. The latter planted a hand on a thin, jagged line leading half way towards the hill's summit. 'A lane?'

'Aye,' Hopton confirmed. 'Sunken and wooded. We must traverse those channels to reach the upper part of the slope. But have a care, sirs, for they will surely place men in the trees to stop us.' He glanced at Slanning and Trevanion in turn. 'Your regiments will form our third division, gentlemen. You will advance upon Sir Bevil's left flank. Whilst Sir Thomas—'

Basset, Hopton's Major-General of Foot, raised bushy brows. 'Sir Ralph?'

'You will lead the fourth division with Godolphin's men, here,' he pointed to the most northerly part of the hill's western slope, 'protecting the third column's left flank.'

'And who will protect our left flank?' Basset asked wryly.

Stryker held his breath, bracing himself for a tirade at what seemed a grossly impertinent comment, but Hopton merely jutted his bearded chin towards Digby. 'Sir John will take the horse and dragoons out to the west. Thus, they will guard your flank while watching for the rebel horse's return.'

Basset bowed. Digby's nod was cagey. 'Sir George Chudleigh commands near three times my number.'

Hopton simply sat back, folded his arms. 'Then pray we carry the day before he fills the horizon.'

* * *

'I should see to my lads,' Forrester said when he and Stryker had been dismissed.

They reached the manor's main doorway and shook hands beneath the lintel, candles in the nearest corridor guttering frantically in the draught whipping in from the now empty courtyard beyond. 'I'll be across presently,' Stryker replied, thinking his own men, camped with Forrester's up on the dune-blemished wasteland, would need their commanding officer present to compel them to stay awake. 'It'll be a long night.'

'That it will.'

'The morrow, then.'

'The morrow.'

Stryker watched his friend vanish into the shadows, and said in a loud voice, 'You two hide like a pair of striplings.'

As if conjured from the night itself, two men suddenly emerged from the courtyard's shadowy recesses. One was tall, with long, sinewy limbs, a near bald head and small eyes that were sunk deep in cavernous sockets. His companion, by contrast, reached barely beyond the first man's waist. He might have been a child, had his grey uniform and jangling weaponry not given martial credentials away.

'We weren't hidin', sir,' the taller man protested. 'Just waitin's all.'

'And what did you want, Sergeant Skellen?'

The short man coughed, drawing the others' eyes down to his. 'We fightin' then, sir?'

Stryker nodded. 'Dawn, Mister Barkworth. General Hopton would have us attack the hill directly in four divisions. We're with Sir Bevil's party.'

'What of Miss Cade, sir?' Barkworth croaked.

'Plans are afoot to locate her.'

Skellen gave his typical sardonic snort. 'So once we knows where she is, we just need to survive the bloody battle and go rescue her.'

Barkworth winked at the sergeant. 'Simple, eh?'

'The men are ready?' Stryker asked impatiently.

Skellen's small head shook. 'Not 'specially, sir. They're exhausted. The army's got barely enough powder to go round—'

'And we dine on a single shitty old biscuit a man,' the little Scotsman added bitterly.

Stryker sighed. 'Nothing changes. Get up to the camp, lads. Keep the men alert.'

'Sir,' both men grunted, turning away to begin the trudge back up to the sandy common where two and a half thousand musketeers and pikemen waited to march upon an enemy army more than twice their size.

Stryker lingered in the courtyard a moment longer. He had no more business in Bude, but did not wish to discuss the forthcoming battle any further. The walk back to camp would be more peaceable alone.

He heard a crunch of feet on gravel somewhere at his back. Swinging round in alarm, his sword rasped free of its scabbard and wavered out front, a viper ready to bite.

'It is I, sir,' a tentative voice rang in the shadows.

Stryker could still see nothing, but he knew the voice as he knew his own. 'Andrew?'

Lieutenant Andrew Burton stepped into the dancing torchlight. The reddish glow cast dark shapes and lines across his narrow face, ageing the young man by a decade. 'I heard you were in town.'

Stryker was thrown by the lieutenant's calm demeanour. 'Captain Forrester and I stumbled across Grenville's regiment after you left.' He hesitated. 'I am glad to see you made it through.'

Burton shrugged. 'Hopton would not otherwise know of Stamford's advance, sir.'

'I meant I was pleased to see you reached the general safely, Andrew.'

Burton smiled tightly. 'Thank you, sir. A shame Sir Edmund is back in Launceston, though. They shall miss all the fun.' For a second he stood stock still, evidently weighing up his next words, and Stryker half expected an attack, but then he stepped forward, words tumbling from his mouth, 'I—I am sorry, sir. Truly. I do not know what came over me. I was bewitched by her.'

Stryker held up his palms to calm the lieutenant. 'You sound like Osmyn Hogg.'

Even in the flame's tremulous light, Stryker could see his protégé colour. 'A poor choice of words, sir.'

'I understand, Andrew. We have all been burned for the love of a woman.'

Burton swallowed hard. 'The lust.'

Stryker offered a wry smile. 'Aye, the lust. But you must hear me when I say that not a thing happened. Cecily Cade was never interested in either of us, Lieutenant. She picked me to seduce for sheer expediency, thinking I would let her escape the tor.'

Burton nodded, and, for the first time, Stryker could see that the shroud of jealously had been removed from his eyes. 'Because of what her father told her.'

'Aye.'

With that, Burton's good hand dropped to his

428

sword-hilt. Stryker's blade was still naked, and he flicked his wrist upwards in preparation for the coming attack.

'No, sir!' Burton blurted when he saw his captain's reaction. 'Wait!'

Stryker stayed his sword and took a small step back, making sure he was out of range. To his surprise, the lieutenant proceeded to ease his blade free of its long scabbard, but instead of pointing it at Stryker, he reversed the steel, holding the tip in his hand and offering the hilt to the captain.

'I am in your custody, sir.'

Stryker was taken aback. 'Custody?'

Burton was crestfallen, his voice sombre. 'For my ill words to you, sir. You are within your rights to try me for my foul conduct.'

'Indeed I am,' Stryker replied casually, before offering a half-smile. 'But you are a fine soldier, Lieutenant Burton, and I would rather you were commanding my redcoats than rotting in some cell. Are we in agreement?'

Burton returned the smile. 'We are, sir. Thank you.'

'Now put your blade away, man. We must to camp.'

Burton did as he was told, suddenly embarrassed at his solemn display of fealty. 'Aye, sir, aye. We must keep the men vigilant.'

'Not only that. Hopton would have me send a man into Stratton to find Miss Cade. I must select the fellow while there is still enough darkness for him to go about the task.' He made to leave, but Burton immediately stepped into his path. Stryker caught the look on the younger man's face, and shook his head firmly. 'Not you.'

'But I am eager to make amends, sir.'

'Not you.'

'I am the best man for the task, sir,' Burton protested, refusing to move out of Stryker's way. 'You know it.'

In truth, Stryker knew Burton spoke sense. He had conducted many such clandestine missions for the company, and, despite the obvious disadvantage of having only one useful arm, the young officer had worked hard to compensate, with blade and in the saddle. But the recent estrangement had made Stryker realize that Burton was more than a protégé to him. He was like a son. A son he had already lost once. He was not inclined to risk him again so soon. He thrust his own sword home and placed a firm hand on Burton's shoulder.

'Not this time, Andrew. Back to the company with you.'

Lieutenant Burton's eyes searched Stryker's face for a second longer, but eventually they flickered down to look at the gravel. He stepped out of Stryker's path. 'As you wish, sir.'

STRATTON, CORNWALL, 16 MAY 1643

Cecily Cade was a shadow of her former self.

By the pitiful light of a single brazier, she had been subjected to one of witch-finder Osmyn Hogg's most efficient tools of interrogation, and, he prayed inwardly, soon she would surely snap.

'You have enjoyed your stroll so far, Miss Cade?' Hogg said with a smug sneer.

Cecily was standing at the centre of the room, propped against the bulk of a sweaty José Ventura. She lifted her head slowly, revealing a face that had changed from its natural paleness to a sickly ashen pallor, with eyes that appeared dark and hollow. 'Father and I always enjoyed a brisk constitutional. It does so keep the ill humours at bay.'

Hogg laughed at her defiance, hoping she would not sense his frustration. He and Ventura had walked her for the best part of five hours now, ever since Collings had authorized him to treat her as he would any other named witch. It was a bloodless technique, of course, and often seemed to be rather timid to the outsider, but he had had many successes with it. Deprivation of sleep was a power-ful tool, and when combined with constant walking – with no pause for rest, food, or drink – it could be more effect-ive than even the sharpest pricker.

And yet Cecily Cade was a stubborn cow, determined to take her punishment with solemn bravery and a tightly shut mouth.

He shook his head as if exasperated by an errant child. 'Are you ready to speak with us properly, Miss Cade?'

She forced a smile. 'We are speaking now, are we not?'

He shrugged. 'Have it your way, girl.' He glanced at Ventura. 'Walk her another hour, señor.'

Cecily Cade watched the witch-finder stalk furiously away but felt no solace in her small victory. She was exhausted, uttterly empty in body and mind. She prayed her torturers would not read that terrible truth in her eyes, but feared it too obvious to mask.

And yet mask it she must. Bite down her woes, bury them deep within her chest and refuse to show them the light of day. They could walk her all night. Prick the very skin from her back as they had done poor Otilwell Broom, but her knowledge would not be spoken aloud.

'Come, señora,' the corpulent Spaniard was saying, the

acrid stink of his clammy flesh ripe and nauseating in her nostrils.

'I am surprised your heart has not given way before now,' she hissed as caustically as her weak body would allow.

Ventura licked his lips so that they glistened. He winced as he broke wind, reaching behind to pick his breeches from his huge backside. 'I have done this many times, señora. And I will soon rest, while Master Hogg takes my place. You, however, will walk all night.'

He lurched forward, dragging Cecily at first before she gradually found her feet. They were sore. Her knees hurt too, and her hips pounded with a dull ache that seemed to creep around just below the skin like some kind of insidious parasite.

But she would walk, nonetheless. She had to suffer this torment, just as she had had to attempt the seduction of Stryker. It was her duty. Besides, she thought as they made the first of many more turns at the end of the chamber, what she knew had to be protected at any price.

Any sacrifice.

THE COMMON NEAR BUDE, CORNWALL, 16 MAY 1643

It was five hours into a new, mist-clogged day when Stryker took his turn to patrol the area of the encampment populated by the redcoats of Sir Edmund Mowbray's Regiment of Foot. He screwed up his bleary eye, yawned, and rose to his feet, buckling on his scabbard without thought. He had allowed his men to sleep, but in shifts of no more than an hour at a time, so that they would be ready to move if the rebel army decided to march down from their hill. If that strict policy was to be observed by his fighters, he had decided, then it would be observed by their leaders too. Thus he had taken his turns, stared into the blackness, listened to the owls and the gulls, and now, as the morn chipped away at the eastern horizon, felt dog-tired as a result.

He strode carefully over the legs of snoring men, past a pair of hounds growling at one another over a dead crow, and lifted his hat to a grim-looking sergeant-major wearing a broad red sash, billowing pipe stem propped in the hole left by a long-rotten front tooth. The camp was quiet as men considered the day to come, gazed out across the dark grey sea or eastwards to Stratton and its deadly hill.

He reached the deep, bramble-thick hedge that divided this part of the common from the next, and began to walk beside it. To his surprise, Stryker soon strode past a man he recognized, seated on the messy turf of compacted sand and grass. He was of middle age, with short hair that had once been dark but was now speckled liberally with shards of silver. He was carefully cleaning his musket's serpent with a small piece of rag. 'Abbott?'

The man, one of his musketeers, clambered smartly to his feet, leaning lightly on the tall gun, its wooden stock propped against the ground. 'Sir?'

'What the bloody hell are you about, man?'

Abbott looked nonplussed. 'Don't follow, sir.'

Stryker could not believe his ears. This was the man chosen, only hours ago, to travel beyond the enemy's lines and search for Cecily Cade. It was all he could do not to crack the man's jaw with his fist there and then. 'Should you not be in Stratton?'

The redcoat displayed his evident consternation with a frown of deep lines that travelled all the way up to his receding widow's peak. 'L'tenant Burton told me to stay put, sir.'

Stryker's heart almost stopped. He gritted his teeth, feeling his gums ache. 'Why, Musketeer Abbott?'

Abbott's gaze, hitherto fixed on some faraway point, suddenly focussed on his captain's single grey eye. ''Cause he was goin' down there 'iself, sir. Far as I could gather. Didn't you know?'

Stryker's mind began to reel, but, just as he had got to grips with his lieutenant's rash insubordination, a solitary cry rippled out across the sandy encampment. Something about the sound jarred, because the shout, far from being the usual dawn chorus to rouse half-drunk or march-weary troops, did not ring true. It was louder and more shrill than those he had become inured to. Someone further along the dense hedge was desperately raising an alarm.

Stryker squinted to a point at the hedgerow where a man in morion helmet, breastplate, and jangling tassets was pointing frantically at the thick bushes. Some of his comrades were staring too, following his outstretched arm, and Stryker noticed that they, in turn, were beginning to echo the cry.

'Jesu,' a man muttered, appearing at Stryker's blind left flank. 'What's the din?'

Stryker did not bother to look at the speaker. 'Something's happening down there, Will.'

Sergeant William Skellen belched, casually tapped a fist against his sternum, and spat a globule of mucus on to the sandy earth. 'Can't be the Crop'eads. We'd have seen 'em before now.'

But Stryker wasn't so sure. An ink-black night had given way to murky daybreak, and he imagined a determined and disciplined force creeping down from Stratton Hill without word or lighted match. Could they have reached this far west without being spotted? He could see nothing definitive at the place where the rapidly frenzied pikemen were gesticulating, so allowed his gaze to rake its way along the hedgerow, resting finally on the portion of tangled branches that ran adjacent to his own company's section.

'Oh no,' he whispered, catching a flash of what looked to be steel through a tiny gap in the foliage.

'Sir?' Skellen prompted cautiously. 'What d'you see?'

Stryker stared at the hedge for what seemed a long time, but could only have been seconds, searching for movement not thirty paces away.

There they were again. Shapes shifting quietly on the far side of the green barricade. He wondered if they were animals at first. Horse or deer or cattle. Perhaps the metallic glint had been a bridle or bit. But then the distinct glow of smouldering match penetrated the tangled branches and his guts began to churn. The shapes were men. Two, a dozen, then a score. Perhaps as many as fifty; snaking along the far side of the natural barrier as though they were part of the mist, their very bodies made from the white miasma. Another shout went up from the Royalist side, someone at the other end of the hedge had seen them too. More shouts. More alarm. But now there were more specks of burning match appearing through the hedge like a sudden swarm of flaming wasps. And then the firing began.

It was a single, hopeful shot that punched through

the hedge, whistling harmlessly across the encampment. But then it was joined by a brace more, then half a dozen, then too many to count, crackling in a sporadic volley along the enemy's side of the deep obstacle, turning leaves and branches to flying mulch, vomiting a new, dirty smoke cloud to overwhelm the mist.

Stryker, like many officers all the way down the Royalist line, began barking frantic orders at his men. There was no cover on the common, save a few sandy dunes, and he quickly understood that his options were limited. Fight or run.

But they could not give up the ground so easily, for if the Parliamentarians held the flat terrain between Bude and Stratton, Hopton's proposed attack would be over before it began, so he stepped forward, knowing that a lump of lead could burst through the hedge at any moment and hammer the life from him, and began snarling at his men to return fire. A line of wide-eyed musketeers in the red coats of Sir Edmund Mowbray shuffled up on his command, and he berated them for their sluggishness as he set about preparing his own weapon.

Loading the cumbersome long-arm with powder, ball, and wadding may have been a slow process, but it was mercifully uncomplicated. Some drill manuals Stryker had seen would teach up to four-dozen postures, and these would often be taught ad nauseam to raw recruits, but they were designed to show the mechanical prowess of a company. In reality, when a man stood in line with his comrades and was ordered to spit very hell at the enemy, any musketeer worth his salt would know how to prepare and fire his weapon without the need for postures or drill sergeants. He would know – as a matter of pride and of instinct – how to load and prime his piece, to blow on his match till it glowed red, to pick a target and pull the trigger. Anything more complex was unnecessary, and would likely see a man finish the day in a cold pit, dusted with lime. Sure enough, the musketeers arranged to his right and left began offering regular fire. They slammed bullets straight into the hedge, never knowing if the shots found flesh, but always aware of the enemy scuttling this way and that behind the clawing curtain.

It was a strange fight. Muskets were not accurate at the best of times, but here the redcoats could not even take aim. There was nothing for it but to level the barrel at the hedge, ease back the trigger, and hope a Parliament man was unlucky enough to be standing in the ball's path. The odd disembodied scream told them a toll was being taken. But men fell on the Royalist side too.

Stryker shouldered his musket, trained his eye along the length of the barrel. Blood rushed in his ears, and he felt a thick pulse appear somewhere below the broad mess of scar tissue that cast mottled shapes over the left half of his face.

There it was. Movement. Fleeting but certain on the far side. He let the shot fly, never to know if it had found its elusive mark.

Scores were involved now. Perhaps even hundreds. The musketeers of Devon and Cornwall pouring fire through the hedgerows in a skirmish of pure attrition. The air, so fresh just moments earlier, now stank of sulphur as more and more powder charges ignited to throw lead forth with tongues of flame. It might have been impossible to pick out a definite target through the accidental breastwork, but men died nonetheless, plucked back by shot as it shredded the dense foliage in a shower of greens and browns.

Stryker reloaded his musket, wincing as the air felt suddenly hot beside his cheek. There was no protection here, only the hope that a ball would strike the man next to you, and Stryker tried not to flinch as more bullets spat low and high. Two hit the grass barely more than three paces away, another went clean between his legs and a fourth clanged on the billhook of a halberd wielded by a man some distance to the rear. The pole-arm skittered from the fellow's grip, bounced as it hit the ground, and he scurried to retrieve it, only to take a musket-ball in the rump. He screamed. No one listened.

Stryker fired his weapon, blinking quickly as his eye was spattered with grit. When his vision cleared, he saw that the huge Royalist line was falling back on the command of bawling officers. He followed suit, drawing his redcoats back so that the range was not deadly, and called for his pikemen to form up into solid blocks. They would charge the hedgerows, slash gaps through which the hard men of Cornwall would stream, and force the rebels back to their looming hill. And then they would follow, surging up the western face in their great columns, cutting the Devon army to bloody pieces and throwing the survivors into the sea.

The Battle of Stratton had begun.

CHAPTER 21

On the flat summit of the formidable Parliamentarian position, Major-General James Chudleigh, de facto commander of the day's rebel forces, listened to the distant sounds of musketry from atop his skewbald gelding. It was a surreal experience, to be positioned on the huge vantage point, surrounded by thousands of fresh troops, and clothed in full battle regalia. For the crackling exchange of fire was shrouded by mist and trees, and only a dark pall of gun smoke could be seen to pinpoint the bitter skirmish. It was like being within the battle and yet outside of it. Part of him yearned to be down below, on the unseen common, bloodying his blade as a leader should. He said as much to an aide reining in at his right hand.

'There'll be plenty opportunity for that, I fear, General,' the aide replied dourly. 'The enemy advances o'er the scrubland to the west.'

Chudleigh stared at the drifting smoke. 'We have men out there, do we not?'

'Aye, sir, that we do,' the aide agreed, 'but not enough to hold them. Our musketeers have fought well, but the malignants deployed pikes to cut through the hedges and simply overwhelm us. The musketeers fall back even now.'

'Then Hopton comes.'

'He does, sir.'

'It is a brave thing.'

'A stupid thing, sir.'

Chudleigh hoped so. Prayed so. His position was certainly formidable, demanding that the Royalists fight uphill, carrying pike and musket along the steep, wooded lanes to face the waiting Roundhead ranks on the summit. But the Cornish were a strange breed: one step away from savagery, and ever relishing a fight. He removed his helmet, propping it on his lap, and glanced at the aide. 'How does Hopton proceed, Cripps?'

Cripps pursed his lips as he totted numbers in his head. 'Four divisions of foot, sir, each p'raps six hundred strong. A mix of pike and shot. Each appears to have a brace of brass cannon.' He wrinkled a nose that was crooked from an adolescent break. 'Nothing to concern us.'

'Horse?'

'Seems they'll loiter in the rear. They're useless against this hill, so one can only presume Hopton has 'em watching for Sir George.'

Chudleigh nodded gravely. 'Pray God my father returns swiftly.' He twisted, saddle creaking, and scanned the land to the south and east. 'And where is the earl, by Jesu's wounds?'

Cripps visibly winced. 'I know not, sir.'

'My apologies,' Chudleigh muttered gruffly when he read the discomfort on his aide's face. 'You are of the Puritan thought, are you not? Then I will curtail my oaths.'

Just then a rider Chudleigh recognized as one of Stamford's servants spurred on to the summit from the direction of Stratton, slashing at men with his whip if they stepped into his path. The major-general wheeled his mount round to greet the newcomer. 'My lord Stamford arrives?'

The servant hauled his grey steed to a snorting halt, doffing his cap. 'He will be here soon, sir. He is indisposed.'

Chudleigh thumped a fist against the crown of his helmet, making his own mount whinny in complaint. 'Indisposed? Christ, but he has an escort of seven-score seasoned harquebusiers. I would have them on the field.'

The horseman grimaced. 'It is the gout, sir.'

Chudleigh spat. 'A pox on that, sir.' He patted his right thigh. 'We all have gout.'

'But he says to inform you, sir, that he will be on the field in a matter of hours.'

'Hours?' Chudleigh exclaimed incredulously. He cupped a hand to his ear, turning the skewbald back to face the west. 'Do you hear that, you blithering dolt? Musket fire out on the common. The enemy advances now. Not tomorrow, not even this afternoon. Now.'

'Sir, I—'

'Be gone with you,' Chudleigh ordered with a derisive wave, 'back to your gouty master. Go on! Get out of my sight, sir! Lest I hand you a musket and send you down there!'

Lord Stamford's servant followed Chudleigh's outstretched finger to gaze upon the mist-smothered common where small bursts of light flared a fraction of a second at a time within the miasma. For a while he simply stared, unable to tear his gaze away from the strange scene, knowing a battle raged beneath the white blanket. But then he looked back at

Chudleigh, nodded briskly, wrenched hard on his mount's bridle, and kicked for the south-east.

Chudleigh shook his head scornfully. 'There is nothing for it. I will assume command.' He bent to snatch a small flask from his saddlebag, twisted open the cap and tilted back his head to take a lingering draught. The wine, good-quality claret he had taken from Okehampton, brought instant warmth to his throat, reinvigorating him like a mythical elixir. 'Now, let us prepare to receive these Pope-turds, eh?'

Cripps grinned. 'Sir.'

'Fetch Northcote. I want a goodly number of his best muskets down on the low ground. Tell him to harry the enemy where they are forced to funnel into the lanes. It will be the easiest of pickings.'

Cripps offered a crisp bow. 'If it please you, Major-General.'

'And carry a message to the rest of the staff. Tell them I want two lines across the summit, like so.' He swept an arm from left to right, indicating a front of approximately nine hundred yards. 'Best troops in the first; Northcote's boys, and Merrick's greycoats. Trained Bands to form the second line. Wouldn't want them facing the bloody Cornish unnecessarily.'

Lord, he thought, but he did not wish those craven bastards to face the mad Cornish at all. Northcote's twelve-hundred-strong Devon regiment were as tough as they came, and Merrick's greys were a useful and seasoned force. But the Trained Bands were reliable only as a reserve. He prayed they would not be needed this day.

'Should I bring the men back from the north, sir?'

Chudleigh nodded. The gentlest slope was that to the

north of the hill, and he had been concerned that the enemy would somehow work their way on to that front. 'That horse has bolted. They're committed now. We look west.'

'The ordnance, sir?' Cripps was saying. 'Should they remain in position?'

Chudleigh peered down at the open grassland that swathed the upper half of the hill. At the lower part of the incline, immediately above the wooded lanes, his thirteen fieldpieces had already been positioned at regular intervals. He nodded. 'Aye, we will leave the cannon in place. If the buggers are hardy enough to push beyond the lanes, we'll make them a gift of iron.' His cheek began to twitch.

'No word, sir?' Sergeant William Skellen asked of his captain as the red-coated company filed across the last of the common's rough ground and into the first stand of trees. There were more copses along the track that took them east, becoming thicker and more frequent until, in about a hundred paces, they finally came together in a small forest. Beyond that forest, climbing towards the sliding clouds, stood Stratton Hill.

'None,' Stryker replied as he kept a rapid pace for his men to follow.

Skellen sniffed at his side. 'Ballocks.'

Stryker looked up at the lanky sergeant. 'My sentiment exactly. Mister Burton left hours ago.'

'Think he's been taken?'

Stryker shrugged. 'It's daylight now. If he's still in Stratton, he'll be in a deal of danger.' He slapped the butt of his musket. 'Foolish boy.'

'Maybe he came back,' Skellen said hopefully, 'but lost us in the fight at the common.'

'Or maybe he's in a rebel cell,' Stryker answered sourly. 'Nothing we can do now, Sergeant. We're at the muster point.'

The four Royalist infantry divisions gathered at the south and west of the hill. They could not see the summit, for the view was clogged with the leafy boughs of huge oaks and gnarled beech, but their commanders announced that they had reached the foot of the escarpment and that the rest would be akin to a morning stroll. The reality, of course, was not so simple, for rebel musketeers, repelled from the sandy common by sheer weight of numbers, had secreted themselves within the trees, moving in squads, firing from behind broad, shielding trunks. Even General Hopton's most fresh-faced novice would know that this was to be a hard fight.

Captain Innocent Stryker marched at the head of his company of redcoats and they, in turn, were positioned a short way behind the vanguard of the large column of pikemen and musketeers led by Sir Bevil Grenville. To their right, down towards the southern tip of the hill, Hopton himself led another column, while to their left two more began their own grim march, commanded respectively by Sir Nicholas Slanning and Sir Thomas Basset.

'Shoot that fucker!' a sallow-faced sergeant bawled somewhere ahead of Stryker. He saw a musket-wielding teenager step out of rank, prop his long-arm on a rest that he drove into the soft earth, and pick out the enemy marksman that had drawn the sergeant's attention. The range was about forty paces, and the shot probably missed, but the Roundhead vanished into the tree line all the same.

And then the drums began. They beat a rapid rhythm

that ordered the advance, a deep thrum reverberating around the lanes of the lower part of the slope, telling the waiting rebels that the king's men were on the march. The sound shook Stryker's bones like a perpetual cannon blast, rolling its way up from his toes to his skull, making his chest shiver and his spine tingle and his pulse quicken. His guts churned, his eye focussed, and his hearing sharpened. He felt terrified in that moment. But, by God, he felt alive.

Sir Bevil Grenville stepped out in front. He wore a silver-laced buff-coat, tall, black boots, and a wide-brimmed hat from which sprouted a huge feather of deepest green. He drew his big sword with a gloved hand and held it aloft for all to see, tracing tight circles with the fine tip. His gigantic manservant, Anthony Payne, was there too, ever at his side, the colonel's own personal titan. The Cornish cheered them. They bellowed jeers at Parliament, at Puritanism, at the Earl of Stamford and at the men of Devon. They blew gently on smouldering matches, tightened spare lengths of cord that were wound around wrists and waists, and shook hands with their mates for perhaps a final time.

And then the column rumbled forwards, contracting to squeeze into the ancient lane made dark by overlapping branches, the incline immediately growing steep. Pikes were deployed in narrow, deep columns in the sunken thoroughfare, blades scraping and snagging the light-stealing canopy, with teams of musketeers moving more rapidly along the flanks to provide protection. Stryker left the column at this point, taking a score of his redcoats with him to claw their way up the left-hand bank. They kept pace with their pikes down on the lane, ready to do battle with any who would threaten them. Still the drums hammered out their dread beat.

Stryker gazed through the forest of pike staves, the blades of the shortest poles now level with his eye line, and saw that the opposite bank was full of men too. More musketeers scrambled like herds of mountain goats over slippery earth, tangled tree roots, and fallen branches, ever vigilant for enemies hidden up ahead. It was a mild morning, but the wind, funnelled down this unnaturally busy lane from up on the bare crest, whipped in spiteful gusts, slashing along the sunken corridors to sting eyes and dry lips, shaking the full branches and drowning out the column's footfalls for just a moment.

Stryker walked on, leaning into the bank to keep his footing, reassured by the sight of a giant at the column's head and the drums' relentless percussion. For a minute or two there was no shooting as men on both sides paused to reload, and they made reasonable progress, though still he intermittently breathed life back into the tip of his match, keeping the saltpetre-impregnated cord hot for when it would be required.

Shadows moved at the far end of the lane. They looked like men but moved like wraiths, drifting in and out of the half-light, grey and nebulous. Stryker bit down his anxiety, telling himself the shapes were the shadows of wind-whipped branches. But then a small flicker of light danced before one of the figures, a hovering pinprick of furious orange against the drab morn. Before Stryker could call the warning, the light flicked suddenly downwards in a tight arc, racing to what he knew would be a pan full of black powder, and a bright flash spat into the gloom.

A corporal, down on the lane, came to a sudden halt,

throwing the step of the ranks behind. He made a strange squeaking sound and swayed for a heartbeat before his left leg crumpled from under him, seemingly no longer within his control. He staggered back, crashing into the pikemen to the rear, blood showing on the white fringe of his collar. Then the other leg went too, limp and hanging, so that he collapsed in a heap like a puppet whose strings had been cut. He squeaked again, but the sound quickly deepened into a gurgle, crimson bubbles exploding past his lips as he tried to mouth final words.

The lane erupted in noise. Eight or nine men from both banks gave fire in reply, even as the column juddered into life again, men stepping inexorably over their fallen comrade, but it was impossible to see if any of the vengeful shots had flown true. And from the top of the lane came more fire, more leaden death, as the Roundheads gave rapid reply. Bullets fell around them like rain, punching the air at their ears and splintering trees. These were not wraiths, but flesh and bone. Men who were waiting to pour their malice into the Royalist column as it climbed a lonely hill where the soil would soon be red.

There was another abrupt squall of musketry, spraying the trees in a cacophony of splintering bark. Stryker half shut his eyelid as he searched for the assailants amid the trees, eventually spying splashes of tawny where enemy scarves could be glimpsed behind fat tree trunks some fifty paces along his side of the lane. He took a knee, shouldered his musket, and looked for a man to kill.

Colonel Gabriel Wild, armour slick with newly applied oil, whispered soothing words in his horse's pricked ear.

The beast shook its head, complaining at the unforgiving metal bit that pulled at its black lips, but let out a calm whicker all the same. Wild patted its muscular neck, feeling happier than he had for a long time. Since a time before, he noted ruefully, he had been sent to fetch an ammunition cache in the rugged Dartmoor hills. Now, at least, he was on horseback, swathed in buff leather, gleaming Milanese plate, and a helmet with long lobster-tail neck guard, three-barred visor, and a huge feather plucked from the body of a Great Cormorant. He might not have his beloved troop at his back, but he was ready for battle, nonetheless, and the feeling was good.

Wild peered down the western slope of the hill from his position on the flat crest. Before him, still in the throws of mustering, were the packed ranks of Parliamentarian infantry. Ordinarily, of course, he would only pour scorn on such men. Pike, gun, pole-arm hefting plodders, one rung further up life's social ladder than gong farmers and jakes diggers. But today, he inwardly admitted, they looked impressive. Two sprawling lines stretching right across the slope, divided into intermittent blocks of pike and musket. They were a huge, immovable, fresh, well-fed force of killers, and he was glad to be positioned behind them.

'Small guns,' a grunt of a voice, heavily inflected with the accent of the Mediterranean, stabbed through Wild's thoughts.

He glanced sideways at the huge form of José Ventura, perched like a vast toad atop his struggling bay. 'We have thirteen cannon pointed at the mouths of the lanes, señor. They are small, aye, but effective against massed blocks. They cannot miss.'

'I not un'erstand why these kingmen here,' Ventura muttered. 'They cannot win. We have too many.'

'Well observed,' Wild replied sardonically. He glanced across at the man mounted on a piebald gelding to the other side of the Spaniard. 'Congratulations, Master Hogg. Your creature can count.'

Witch-finder Osmyn Hogg sneered at the barb, his long, hooked nose wrinkling as he addressed his assistant. 'The king's men are Cornish, señor,' he said as though that were explanation enough.

'But they will lose all the same,' Wild added, relishing the hours to come. 'And I will ride into the melee and hone my sword on their Rome-suckled skulls.' He shivered involuntarily, the promise of blood-drenched glory making his skin tingle deliciously. After the ignominy and shame of his defeat to the one-eyed fiend, he had yearned for an opportunity like this.

'Not yet you won't,' a fourth voice clamoured for Wild's attention.

The harquebusier lifted his visor and twisted to his left. 'Major-General Collings.'

Collings ignored Wild's brusque tone. 'Fetch Miss Cade.'

Wild blanched. 'Sir?'

The major-general wore an impressively expensive set of armour. His helmet, back and breast plates, short tassets and elbow gauntlet were all blackened and studded with gilt rivets. Beneath those pieces his skeletal frame was covered by a bright yellow buff-coat, with loops of metallic lace adorning the sleeves. The falling band collar was obscured by a knotted neckcloth, giving extra protection for his throat.

Collings took off his helmet, revealing the pallid skin of his small, bald head. His eyes were as black and lifeless as his breastplate. 'Go down to the village and bring her up here, Colonel. Major-General Chudleigh would have her see this for herself.'

Wild swallowed hard, forcing a stinging retort back into oblivion. 'As you wish, sir,' he said tightly.

'It is as *he* wishes,' Collings corrected, thrusting his chin in the direction of another group of mounted men some hundred yards further along the summit. 'Chudleigh does not believe Master Hogg's methods are bringing results.'

It was Hogg's turn to bridle, and he kicked his horse beyond Ventura's bulk to see the major-general. 'It is not as simple as all that. People – soldiers especially – are not fond of men who torture women. Particularly young, pretty women. We have walked her, sir. Walked her all night. It is a crueller technique than it sounds, General, I can assure you. The exhaustion alone often breaks a soul.' He cleared his throat awkwardly. 'But I confess she remains tight-lipped as ever.'

Collings licked narrow, purple lips. 'Then move things on as soon as this damned battle is done with.'

'You cut that man on the moor,' Wild offered.

'Pricked, Colonel, aye. But—'

Collings hauled his own horse round now, facing Hogg. 'No buts,' he snapped. 'Did it work?'

Hogg rubbed his big nose. 'Aye, sir, he confessed to witchcraft.'

'Then do the same to Miss Cade,' Collings ordered flatly. 'I want the location of that gold, Master Hogg, or you will be held responsible.' The beady gaze darted to

Colonel Wild like a magpie sighting silver. 'Bring the bitch to the hill. Let her see the destruction of her precious malignants and then, if she maintains her bovine obstinacy, our friends here will prick the words out of her.'

The battle smouldered like the thousands of match-cords carried along the western face of the hill. Grenville's division pushed on, desperate to break free of the deep lanes that forced them into narrow lines, nullifying their pikes to utter impotency, but there were so many Roundhead shooters in the trees, picking at them, plucking men out of line, forcing them to stall.

The morning progressed rapidly. Ten o'clock passed, then eleven, and as the sun glimmered in warped chinks through the canopy immediately over their heads, the king's men knew that noon approached. But still they had not broken free. Still they could see nothing of the upper half of the hill, the open land where the bulk of Parliament's vast horde awaited them.

The pikemen in the lane moved painfully slowly, kept to shuffled advances of a few feet at a time, all the while battered by the enemy gunmen. Their own musketeers still flanked them, skirmished along the high banks, fought tooth and nail to keep the enemy shooters at bay, but there were simply not enough of them to free the column up.

Stryker's eye was full of powder grit, his face singed, his fingers black. But he fired and reloaded and fired again. A fresh volley of musketry crackled madly somewhere to his right. His gaze drifted there, expecting to see some new line of foes, but he looked only upon a thick mass of branches and leaves. The fight – this same contest between determined pikemen and sniping musketeers – was playing out in the next lane along, and the next, he presumed, and the one beyond that. All four Royalist divisions would be marching through this same torment.

He tripped suddenly, cursing as he pitched forward, looking back to see what branch had snagged him. But there, flat on his back, was a grey-coated man with a thick, black beard and wide orange sash. He had been wounded, a messy bullet hole glistened at his groin like a huge ruby, but he still had strength enough to lift a pistol. The shot cracked out, pitched high, deafening at this close range, and Stryker fell back on his haunches, fully expecting the world to turn black. But the thud on a tree behind told him he had survived, and he scrambled rapidly to his feet. The prostrate Roundhead clutched a tuck in his other hand, and he made to hurl it at Stryker, but the captain reached him first, burying his leather-bound toes deep into the bearded man's wound in a savage kick. The Parliamentarian screamed, pure and penetrating, and Stryker kicked him again, this time in the face. He slumped back, head bouncing on the bed of fallen leaves.

'*On! On! On!*' an officer bellowed down on the lane, willing his pikemen onwards like a herd of terrified cattle. But they were still painfully slow. The foremost men flinched as sporadic shots flashed forth from deeper into the lane. They knew their comrades on the banks were fighting well for them, for the reports of Royalist muskets rattled just as loudly as those of the rebels, but a man gripping a sixteen-foot-long pole could not protect himself from a flying lump of lead, and their instinct was to turn tail and run. The sergeants threatened them. They snarled and cajoled and prodded with their halberds, and the

452

frightened pikemen did not turn. But, with each passing moment, with every man thrown to the mud by an unseen gunman, the advance was gradually beginning to stall.

Colonel Gabriel Wild spurred his horse into Stratton, its hooves clattering over a patch where the road was cobbled. He knew where Hogg and Collings had kept the pasty-faced wench, and turned his snorting beast into the alley that would lead him to the secluded building at Stratton's periphery.

The alleyway was clogged with mud, cloying reddish filth churned to slop by soldiers, horses, cartwheels, and villagers. Wild's mount sank to its fetlocks, but he raked his spurs all the way along its heaving flanks, making it clear that no argument was to be tolerated. But the going was slow all the same, the unhappy animal whinnying its protest as it picked a tentative route between the timber-framed homes and businesses that leaned over the alley.

'What happens, m'lud?'

Startled, Wild peered down through his vertical face bars to see a haggard old woman stagger out from one of the low doorways. 'Christ, you venomous bloody harridan,' he rasped, turning his face away from the woman, 'I can smell your damned stench from here.'

The crone lurched at him, grasping the horse's bridle in a clawlike hand. 'But what 'appens, sir? Up on the hill? My poor boy, James!' With her free hand she pointed down the alley in the direction from which Wild had come. 'He fights!'

'Get your vile skin away from me, bitch!' Wild snarled, jerking his boot from its stirrup and smashing it upwards into the villager's wrist.

She yelped in pain, rocked sideways, and landed heavily on her rump in the mud. Long strands of coarse, greying hair tumbled from beneath her coif to fall across her face and the material of her sleeve quickly began to turn a bright red hue as though a huge rose blossomed there. She stared down at the forearm. 'But my boy, James, m'lud,' she moaned, beginning to sob, 'he did not wish to fight. He bain't the fightin' kind, see? They forced 'im.'

'Pox on your gibbering tongue, palliard's whore,' Wild hissed, clambering down to the sticky morass. Holding his breath, he thrust hands under the woman's armpits and dragged her from his path, dropping her by the side of the alley, her spine-ridged back flush against one of the dirty walls.

As he straightened up he noticed a small group of soldiers up at the far end of the alley. There were five of them, all but one dressed in civilian clothes, though straight tucks clattered at their sides and he could see withered oak sprigs in their hatbands.

Wild tethered his horse using the iron ring of an open doorway, and paced towards the men. 'Northcote's?'

The group paused, the nearest man squinting down the alley at him. After a moment's reckoning, the fellow – a flat-faced, stubble-jawed man with one twitching eyelid and teeth protruding out over his bottom lip – doffed his hat, the rest following suit. Wild's expensive armour, the ostentatious helmet feather, and his sheer build and bearing clearly shouted his credentials. 'What can we do for you, sir?'

But Wild kept his steady, purposeful pace, closing the distance between him and Northcote's men, because they could do nothing for him. It was not the four sprig-donning soldiers that he wished to see, but the fifth man, face hitherto concealed by the rest. 'Who is that man?'

The buck-toothed soldier stared back with a slack-jawed expression. 'Sir?'

Wild drew his sword, levelling it at the centre of the group. 'That man, damn your beef-witted impudence!' There it was again. The glimpse of a narrow leather sling. His heart raced. 'What is his name?'

The spokesman for Northcote's men took a faltering step backwards as the big armour-clad horseman strode ever closer. 'I—I know not, sir,' he stuttered, evidently too frightened of the poised blade to give a proper answer.

Wild was only a matter of five strides from the group now, and one of the other soldiers shoved his way past his dumbstruck comrade. He glanced back at the object of Wild's attention. 'He was taken an hour after midnight, sir.' He shrugged apologetically, moving out of the way so that Wild could finally get a good look at the prisoner. 'He was sneakin' around the village, that's all I know. They've roughed 'im up a tad, so we're to take 'im to one o' these rooms under guard.'

Wild stared at the beaten man. At the swollen eye sockets, the dishevelled hair, the split, weeping, puffed-up lips, and the newly twisted nose. He would not have recognized the fellow if it had been anyone else, for the man's injuries were so remarkably disfiguring. But this man was different. His right arm, withered and immobile, was pinned against his torso by a leather strap.

Colonel Gabriel Wild sheathed his sword slowly, and grinned.

*

455

Down in the sunken lanes the fighting went on.

Stryker's redcoats were there, his musketeers ahead and on the flanks, locked in bitter skirmish with their rebel counterparts, while his pikemen waited within the large column, creeping along the tree-hung lane an inch at a time. But creep they did. The Parliamentarian musketeers had been sent down from the hill to knock them back; to batter them and bruise them and send them back to Bude. And for a time it had looked as though that might happen, but, though they had winced and paused, seen men wail and witnessed friends die, the column had gained ground.

Stryker loaded his musket behind a broad oak trunk, stepping out into the open when he had tested that his match would shift true to touch the powder in his pan. He flicked the pan cover back, exposing the charge.

'Sir!' Simeon Barkworth's noose-wrung voice sounded away to Stryker's right.

He looked over, seeing the little Scot, face grim and blackened. Barkworth pointed frantically past him, indicating something on Stryker's blind left, and he swiftly turned his head to see a flash of tawny smear the air between two thick bushes. He twisted his shoulders, swinging the long-arm across his front, eye still trained along the black barrel. The target was there. A musketeer with a dishevelled scarf around his waist, and that man pulled his trigger first. The ball missed, chipping bark from the oak beside Stryker. He fired his own shot in reply, but missed as well, and the rebel scampered back into the wooded gloom to reload.

'Ne'er mind,' Barkworth called, when he heard Stryker's toxic curse. 'Least he can't shoot either!'

Sir Bevil Grenville's column marched on, edging ever

closer to the upper part of the slope where the terrain was an open expanse, friendly to their ferocious pikemen. But all around them the muskets of Parliament were loaded and loosed, loaded and loosed, gnawing away at the resolve of the approaching Cornish. And so the afternoon wore on.

Witch-finder Osmyn Hogg was a true believer. He believed in God's power, and in Satan's grip on the weak of mind, and in the notion that prayer – constant, heartfelt prayer – would see a man's deepest desires come to pass. And as he looked to the south-east corner of the hill's broad summit his belief increased a hundredfold. 'I recognize that man,' he said to Colonel Wild as the harquebusier walked his mount over the long grass to greet the group.

Wild, resplendent and proud atop the muscular destrier, signalled to two young boys brought up from the village to support Chudleigh's huge force in return for a few coins and the promise of safety. They scampered over to the horseman and helped lift his unwilling passenger from where she lay in front of him, face down across the horse's ample back. He stared dispassionately at her, unmoved by the ordeal that had turned her from raven-haired beauty to the dishevelled, gaunt, stooping figure she had become. He remembered her from the tor; how she had bolted down from the granite-strewn heights to scream at the men who had killed the prisoner, Otilwell Broom. That pith she displayed, the vigour and the venom, it was all gone now. Drained clear away by whatever torments Hogg and his oily servant had dreamt up.

When Cecily Cade had been dragged over to stand beside Hogg, Wild lifted his visor, lips peeled back in a white-toothed grin. 'I expect you do, Master Hogg.' He removed his helmet and twisted back to stare at the man tethered at the end of a short rope affixed to his saddle. Only the man's left wrist was bound, for his other arm was clearly useless, hanging inert and emaciated by a leather strap that kept it braced to his chest. Lifting a gauntleted hand to ruffle the silver badger stripe bisecting his otherwise dark hair, Wild added, 'He is one of Stryker's lackeys. His lieutenant, no less.'

The witch-catcher's eyes bulged from his face as Hogg looked beyond Wild to the tethered man.

Hogg kicked his mount forward a touch, glancing from the prisoner to Wild and back again. 'He is here?'

Wild nodded energetically. 'Oh yes.' He gazed down at the wooded area that stifled the lower half of the hill. Musketry, screams, and smoke still wafted up from that place of unseen horror. 'Down there, to be exact.'

'What is the meaning of this, Colonel?'

Wild looked to his right, to where the new voice had sprung forth. 'Major-General Collings.' He reached back, grasping the grimy rope, and gave it a swift tug. The man fastened to the far end came stumbling forwards, almost colliding with the horse's rump. 'A spy, sir. Found in Stratton during the night. Caught red-handed.' He allowed himself a malicious smirk, jerking the rope. 'One-handed.'

Erasmus Collings raked Wild's captive with his dead eyes. 'You know the orders, Colonel. All spies and Irish are to be hanged.'

Wild nodded. 'And this one will be, I promise you.' He leaned down, saddle groaning at the action. In a low, conspiratorial voice, he said, 'He is Stryker's lieutenant, sir.'

The black beads twinkled in Collings's lamb-white skull. 'Stryker?'

'Stryker,' Wild echoed. He thought about the familiarity of speech he had witnessed between the villainous captain and his men back at Bovey Tracy. 'And he holds an—*affection*—for his men, if memory serves. They are friends.' He almost hissed the last word. 'I would have this wretch watch the battle.'

Collings's thin, bluish lips twitched in amusement. 'You are a vindictive man, sir.'

Wild sniffed, cleared his throat, and deposited the resulting yellow globule at the prisoner's feet. 'Stryker humiliated me, sir. I would rather take my vengeance against the captain himself, but I must make do with his lieutenant. Until I meet that scarred demon again, leastwise.'

Collings seemed satisfied enough. 'Very well.' He let his gaze drift to the girl. 'Have you chosen to speak to us?' Silence greeted the question. 'No matter, Miss Cade. Your stoical hush has only harmed you, for your reward is a position of honour on this hill. From here you may witness the very death of the cause you so admirably strive to protect.'

Lieutenant Andrew Burton forced one of his eyes open. It was sticky, near glued shut by swelling tissue and congealed blood, but eventually the puffy lids parted, stinging intensely as the tangled mess of lashes and gore finally peeled free, and he lifted his face a touch. The breeze kicked up then, making the small, knuckle-carved lacerations in his lips and cheeks smart like a thousand paper cuts, while even the tiniest breaths stung at his nostrils and chest. What he saw was a forest. It appeared beautiful at first, crowned by a drifting halo of cloud that seemed to glow yellow in the sun. But then his ears, still ringing from the kicks and punches of the night, caught a muffled crackle, like damp logs in a blaze. And he knew. The sounds were the music of battle, the clouds were the stinking, acrid fumes of burnt black powder, and the forest was where his friends were, even now, fighting and dying.

He stole a glance at Cecily. At least he had found her, he thought. She did not look at him, but stared off into the middle distance as if deeply enmeshed in a dream. A white-faced man with no hair, mottled blue and purple lips, and the smallest, blackest eyes he had ever seen was speaking to her now. Burton did not listen to the words. Nor, it seemed, did she.

'I want you to see this, Lieutenant,' a new, stark voice now entered his mind, searing out above the perpetual chimes. The speaker was the man who had, until now, been saddled, dragging him along like a fisherman with a hooked trout. Now, though, he was right there beside him. 'Your Pope-fucking friends have less than half our number. They cannot hope for victory. I want you to watch their deaths from up here. With me.'

Burton knew that voice. He had recognized it down in the village, but, in the midst of capture, and torture, near blindness, and the terror of knowing that he would surely be executed as a spy, he had not been able to place it. The bastard had been wearing the dress of a harquebusier, and that was rare, for the rebels had very few cavalrymen in Stratton, but still the name had eluded him, even as he was hauled up the steep hill at the end of a wrist-burning rope. But something in this new, whispered threat had jolted his memory, and his mind flew back to a forest west of Bovey Tracey and a wagon full of munitions.

'Colonel Wild.'

Someone patted him on the shoulder. 'Very good, young man.'

Burton tried to turn his head to see his enemy, but his neck convulsed, compelling him to remain focussed on the foot of the slope. He affected a bitter laugh that seared his broken ribs. 'Where's your troop?'

Wild hit him. It was not a heavy blow, more a shortened jab into the flesh of his shoulder, but Burton, weak, wounded, and flat-footed, went sprawling to the long turf. He sensed the big Parliamentarian standing over him.

'Never speak of my men, Lieutenant.'

Burton coughed up a glutinous gobbet of blood and tried to spit. His enfeebled lungs meant that it simply slid down his chin, mingling with the grass where he lay. He craned his head to look up at the fearsome silhouette. 'Stryker is down there, Colonel. He's coming for you.'

Wild laughed, a hearty, savage laugh. 'No, sir. I am coming for him.' He knelt suddenly, leaning close to Burton's prone form, speaking directly into his ear. 'If he survives the battle, I will find him, and I will make good my promise. And once I have his stones in my fist, I will hand him to the witch-hunters, and they will dangle him from a high branch for the demon he is.' A strong thumb came down at Burton, pressing into his chin, grinding a pathway into his cracked jawbone.

Burton screamed.

Wild chuckled again. 'You will follow, Lieutenant. As will the rest of your company. You will swing, and you will dance, for the drop will be short, I assure you. *Nothing* will break, save your spirit. And you will all know that you died the day you crossed Gabriel Wild.'

Captain Innocent Stryker was only a company commander, and his men were only attached to Grenville's division by an accident of fate, but that did not mean he would fail to seek an explanation.

The battle had smouldered throughout the afternoon, reaching three o'clock without even the foremost rank of the column's pikemen reaching the last of the light-blocking oaks. But the Royalist advance had continued a few paces at a time, at least in the only lane Stryker could see, and it had seemed foolhardy in the extreme to halt such hard-won progress when there was still daylight.

But halt they had. Grenville, still out in front, blade at the ready, and in full view of enemy marksmen, had been accosted by a rider who had spurred along the narrow lane from the rear of the column, clipping the thighs and shoulders of the tightly packed pikemen as he went and spawning a chorus of jeers and oaths as his chestnut mount flung thick clods of earth in its wake.

Now, with the rider kicking hard towards the rear of the division, the column had been ordered to stop, a screen of musketeers deployed beyond the front rank to protect them from marksmen.

Stryker, watching the hasty conference from up on the wooded bank, was shocked that Grenville would surrender what little momentum his division had built up, and he leapt from the loose-earthed edge, sliding headlong down the short escarpment. Sword sheathed and musket gripped across his sternum in both hands, he stepped along the column's left flank, passed stoic pikemen and sooty musketeers, until he reached the Cornish talisman.

'Sir?'

Sir Bevil Grenville was in hurried discussion with the huge form of Anthony Payne, gesticulating with his naked blade while bullets whistled around them. For his part, Payne seemed more agitated than Stryker had seen him before, the halberd he gripped – like kindling in his paw – twitching with each word he spoke.

They broke off when the colonel saw Stryker, and he turned to stare at him with red-rimmed eyes. 'You want to know why we stop, yes?'

Stryker nodded wordlessly.

'Well you're in luck, for I was just explaining the same to Mister Payne.' He waited for Stryker and Payne to share a nod. 'The messenger came direct from Sir Ralph, whose division fights parallel to ours to the south.' He cleared his throat awkwardly. 'It appears we are down to our last four.'

'Last four, sir?' Stryker repeated, utterly nonplussed. 'Last four what?'

'Barrels,' Anthony Payne rumbled cheerlessly.

'Powder,' Grenville added. 'We have four barrels of powder left.'

Stryker jammed his musket butt into the soft earth and leaned against the long weapon while he rubbed sweat and powder from his eye. His mind raced as he silently totted figures. 'Should be enough if we make good headway, sir.'

Sir Bevil Grenville shook his head, teeth gritted. When he spoke again, his voice was barely more than a whisper. 'Our army has four barrels of powder left, Captain. Our *entire* army.'

463

Stryker felt his jaw sag, powerless to stop it. 'We'll—' he stammered, reeling from the news, 'we'll be through that in no time, sir. Jesu, it's taken us all day and we aren't even beyond the tree line.'

'And that, Captain Stryker,' Grenville replied gravely, 'is why we are to make one last push. A final advance. In silence.'

It began with cannon fire.

The brace of small fieldpieces, so far left cold at the rear of Sir Bevil Grenville's beleaguered division, were dragged forth by teams of grunting musketeers and gunners. Positioned at the very head of the column, like the fangs of a vast snake, their small muzzles were aligned directly along the lane. The gunners primed them, shoved the three-quarter pound iron spheres down the barrels, and awaited the order. And the quaint, rural track, sunken over the centuries and enclosed by mighty trees, exploded in flame.

As they had dared hope, the sudden artillery fire, small though it was, seemed to quieten the rebel musketeers ahead. Those men shrank back behind their lead-pocked trunks or retired to the open ground further up the slope, and that was all the respite the Royalists needed.

'*Forward*!' the call screeched from the front, echoing instantly down to the men at the very rear, and Sir Bevil Grenville's column juddered into life. Drums repeated the order, hammered it home for the first yards before shifting into a sprightly pace-setting rhythm. For the silent advance was not to be wordless or drumless. It was to pass without a shot being fired.

Stryker was near the front, alongside Grenville and

464

Payne, and he heard the same sounds roar throughout the wooded slopes as each of Sir Ralph Hopton's four divisions followed suit. A single volley from the ordnance, then a quick step towards the enemy. He patted his long-arm, held diagonally across his chest, muzzle pointed at the canopy. It was loaded and ready, his match glowing hot, and he blew gently upon that reddened tip to keep it bright, but he was not to shoot. Sir John Berkeley, commanding the musketeers flanking Grenville's body of pikes, had reiterated Hopton's decree. No man was to fire his weapon until the order was given. No explanation had been forthcoming, for the hasty orders from Hopton had included a warning not to reveal the dire situation with powder supply, lest they damage morale, but the troops marched up the rapidly increasing incline regardless. Anthony Payne had told Stryker of the Cornish loyalty to their commanders above all else, and here the claim was borne out before him. The Cornish had been told to march into the face of a vast rebel army without the use of their muskets, and not a murmur of dissent had been heard. Truly, he realized, they would march into hell itself if their Cornish lords – Grenville or Slanning or Trevanion or Godolphin – asked it of them.

'God speed you, Stryker.'

Stryker turned to see Lancelot Forrester at his back. 'And you, Forry.'

Forrester's fleshy face was more rose-tinted than usual, his jowls glistening, his sandy fringe clumped and darkened by sweat where it poked out from beneath his hat. He rolled his eyes. 'It's madness, of course. We'll all bloody snuff it.'

And in that moment Stryker laughed. It was that or cry,

and he'd be damned before he died with tears on his cheeks.

The first shots came at them from the enemy marksmen, emboldened now that they knew no more cannon fire would rent the afternoon. But the king's men had gathered such a pace behind their dashing Cavalier and his goliath-sized manservant that they could no longer turn back even if they had a mind to, for they would be crushed by the men behind.

Nothing could stop the advance now, thought Stryker. This was it. The last-ditch attempt to break through to the upper slope of Stratton Hill. Hopton's final throw of the dice. Dusk would not be long in coming, and that alone would hinder his advance, but more certain was his imminent exhaustion of black powder, and that would not only trigger stalemate but also a crushing defeat. Stryker felt his skin prickle, felt his senses sharpen as they did when faced with the very real chance of death, and revelled in his newly racing heart. He did not know if this thrust would prove successful. Indeed, they were still vastly outnumbered, even if they made it out of the ensnaring lanes, and Cornwall would almost certainly fall to the Earl of Stamford. But here they were, advancing all the same.

And then the day brightened. Gradually at first, but inexorably, as more and more shafts of light stabbed through the branches above. Stryker glanced up, realizing that the canopy was becoming thinner, and, just as he absorbed the implication, Sir Bevil Grenville turned back with a broad, wild-eyed grin.

'We've made it, my boys!' he screamed over their heads. 'They thought to stop us! But who may stop the men of Kernow?'

A vast, rippling cheer drowned out the sporadic cracks of rebel musketry, and the pace quickened again, so that they were nearly at a full run. And then they were out in the open, standing on a wide, rolling expanse of tall grass, without a tree in sight. They fanned out, sergeants and corporals braying for order as the eager pikemen shifted and bustled their way out of line and into their more familiar blocks.

Units of musketeers formed at the flanks of each bristling square, and Stryker and Forrester found the one containing their redcoats. They ran to join them, blowing again on their matches for when the time was right, and offering words of encouragement to any man who caught their eye.

But most did not. Indeed, most did not look at their comrades or their officers or their weapons at all. They simply stared up at the hill before them. And at a flat crest stained black by men. Thousands upon thousands of men.

CHAPTER 22

Major-General James Chudleigh had not expected to lead Parliament's army, for his position had only come about as a result of Lord Stamford's slothful advance through Devon, but he thanked God for such fortune. He was hardly a novice, of course, having fought in the Irish wars and recently engineering the victorious rout at Sourton Down, but this battle, of all battles that might have fallen into his lap, was an indisputable godsend. Because he simply could not lose.

Chudleigh spurred clear of his staff officers to take up position on the left flank of his first line of infantry. He stared down at the smoke-wreathed forest choking the hill's foot, and at the Cornish soldiers who spread out across the grass before it, shifting with admirable proficiency into recognizable lines of battle. There were not many; less, in fact, than he had expected, and he quickly realized that only the colours of Sir Bevil Grenville and Sir John Berkeley had so far emerged.

Chudleigh watched as a horseman galloped up the face of the hill towards him. He was in civilian dress, though the orange ribbon tied at his wrist spoke clearly of his allegiance, and he urged the heaving animal mercilessly

468

on until it began to drift sideways as the incline proved too much. He slewed the froth-muzzled beast to a halt, slid off the saddle, and threw his reins to an infantryman, deciding to climb the last few paces himself. 'They have broken out of the lanes, sir,' he rasped breathlessly, bending to brace hands on his leather-bound knees.

'I can see that,' Chudleigh muttered irritably.

The messenger lifted his head. 'But that is not all, sir. They refuse to give fire.'

'I heard artillery.'

'Aye, sir. They fight in four columns, each with a brace of robinets, or the like. They fired those, then launched into a near run.'

Chudleigh frowned. His pulse quickened, though he was not sure why. The cheek began its dance once again, forcing him to clamp a hand hard across the right side of his face. 'Without shooting?' When the rider offered a rapid nod, he asked, 'Then how did they manage to reach this far?'

'Speed, sir. And they have the greater numbers in the wood. Our musketeers were forced to fall back. They give fire even now, sir, but it will not be long before the rest of the malignants reach the open ground.' His face screwed into a look of embarrassment. 'To tell it true, sir, I fear the men are unsettled. The enemy advance without returning fire. It is unnatural.'

Chudleigh drew a deep breath that made him feel light-headed, and sucked at his upper lip in thought. Hopton's strange tactic had thrown him, he inwardly admitted, though it was surely irrelevant. He glanced at the messenger with new-found resolve. 'Get back down there. Tell the gunners to wait until Hopton's full force is mustered in the open, then flay the king's men till there's not a soul left standing.'

The messenger bowed, puffed out his cheeks in readiness for the next lung-bursting errand, and went to his horse.

Out the corner of his left eye James Chudleigh caught sight of a group of figures a little way along the ridge. Most were mounted, studying the scene around the forest, just as he was, but a couple were on foot. That in itself was not strange, except that one of them seemed to be tied by a short rope to a harquebusier's saddle and the other was a woman. He went to investigate, pausing only to sear one last image of the lower slope on to his mind.

Yes, he thought, he could not lose.

Sir Bevil Grenville's division was formed up on the open ground.

The Cavalier knight stood at the head of his pikes with Payne at his side, careful to be a conspicuous spearhead for the men to follow. To their right the column's skirmishing musketeers, still forbidden to fire, formed into a single body led by Sir John Berkeley.

Grenville turned to face his troops, blade held high. The bristling forest of ash and steel erupted in a low, spine-chilling cheer. They swayed as one, shimmering like a vast shoal of fish, and jolted forward, the massed pike block finally unleashed on ground to which they were suited. The pikemen had seethed down in the lanes, rendered ineffective by the terrain and by an enemy who stayed well away from the killing tips, but out here, on open ground and gathered en masse, they were lethal. They lumbered up the steep slope, spurred on by the relentless thrum of drums, protracted lines of musketeers keeping pace at the flanks. Sergeants bawled oaths of threat and encouragement, waving partizans, pole-axes, and halberds high, ensuring their charges understood that to fight was safer than to desert.

Captain Stryker, with the musketeers at the side of Grenville's huge human hedgehog, felt every muscle and sinew in his scarred body tense. He marched to battle yet was forbidden to fire. The immediate threat from the Roundhead musketeers had diminished now, thankfully, for they seemed to have pulled back to join the main body of men standing on the high summit, but it remained a terrifying prospect to stroll into the face of the enemy without first softening their spirits with flying lead.

'Always knew I'd die with a gun in me 'and,' a voice droned from Stryker's blind side. 'Just didn't realize I wouldn't be allowed to use the fuckin' thing.'

Stryker smiled, more due to the knowledge that William Skellen was with him than to the tall sergeant's sardonic commentary. A constricted sound emerged from beyond Skellen, as though someone stifled a sneeze, and Stryker looked across to see Simeon Barkworth chuckling.

He opened his mouth to speak, but never heard the words. They were obliterated by a bone-fracturing explosion a hundred and fifty paces up the slope. The first of Parliament's cannons had fired.

The whole of Grenville's division seemed to stagger back a step, shrinking and wincing as if each man believed he could keep his head if he could retract it far enough into bunched shoulders. In the sudden, muffled aftermath, Stryker peered around, searching for casualties. He heard the screams before he saw the wounded, somewhere away to his right, and it was then that he saw another full division of men, frantically forming up on the grassy slope. Hopton's column, attacking from the south, on Grenville's right flank, had made it to the upper section of the hill, only to be summarily smashed by rebel artillery.

Stryker shook his head clear, the silence quickly replaced by a high-pitched ringing, only to hear Grenville's voice bellowing at the head of his men. It did not matter that he was still unable to discern the order, for he was immediately swept up in the motion as the Royalist division rumbled into life again.

'By God's blessed kneecaps,' he heard Forrester intone nearby. 'We're marching into the bloody ordnance.'

Sure enough, the rest of the iron tubes, arranged like a line of black toads, squat and ugly on the steep slope, belched into life. Some were double-charged, and they roared their anger with tongues of bright flame and billowing smoke that filled the air with the stench of rotten eggs. They hurled their iron lumps down the face of the hill to tear a swathe of gore through the flinching Cornishmen.

To Stryker's left marched the divisions commanded by Slanning and Basset, and they seemed to be taking the brunt of the volleys' ire. He saw three shots race down the slope, one flying overhead, but the others sailing true, plucking men out of line like a child tossing aside his toys.

'Can we shoot yet, sir?' the tremulous voice of one of Stryker's musketeers reached him from the redcoats at his back.

He twisted back angrily. 'No you damn well can't, Godwin! Not till I say. Sergeant Skellen?'

'Aye, sir,' Skellen replied smartly.

'Any man shoots, stick your halberd up his arse.'

'Sir.'

Three of the cannon were aligned directly with Grenville's block of pikes, and they each spewed forth smoke as their charges ignited. The men braced themselves for impact, step faltering in that horrific moment of expectancy. And what a short moment it was, thought Stryker, remembering the high, looping cannonades that had marked his last battle, Hopton Fight. There, the slope had been gentler, and the distance far greater, so the balls had been sent in high arcs to plummet on to their targets. Here the range was tiny and the guns were aimed directly down the steep descent, so that they scythed the air only feet above the tall grass.

One of the balls fell short, skipping up off the turf like a flat stone skimming a lake, and took a musketeer's leg clean away in a fine red mist. The others hit home, flattening files of pike, pulverizing the men it hit and causing the survivors to scream their terrors to the hills. Sergeants moved immediately in, snarling their practised threats so that the tight formations did not bend or break. Men wiped away blood and bone and brain from their ashen faces with trembling hands. The regimental preachers strode across the rear ranks, bellowing prayers and encouragement at men who heard only their own hearts beating.

Up ahead, perhaps eighty paces now, the gunners pushed more spherical iron balls into their barrels, stepping away for their crews to set to work.

'We'll never reach them!' a near sobbing man shrieked in querulous panic.

473

'Yes we will, you chicken-hearted bastard!' another snarled at him, clipping his ear with a swift slap.

Stryker looked back up at the big guns. The snarling man was right, they would close the distance eventually, but at what cost?

The ordnance lit up once again, each one firing from left to right so that the slope erupted in a great wave, the fieldpieces careening backwards on their split-trail carriages.

The air pulsed. More men died, another corridor was ripped open in Grenville's dense block of pike. Stryker stepped over a man, wailing, inconsolable, begging for his mother. His fingers, stained deepest red, groped at the ragged stump that was once his leg, the limb obliterated below the knee by a bouncing round shot.

'Jesu,' Stryker whispered.

'Bad business, sir!' Skellen shouted above the screams.

Stryker looked at him, realizing the sergeant thought his blasphemy was for what he had seen. In fact, it was for what he was about to do. 'Are you with me, Will?'

Skellen affected an amber grin. 'Always, sir.'

Up at the high Parliamentarian position, Major-General James Chudleigh had reined in alongside his fellow major-general, Erasmus Collings, as the ferocious artillery burst to life. They exchanged pleasantries as briefly as possible. Chudleigh disliked the Earl of Stamford's spymaster and knew the feeling was mutual. He shifted his gaze to the pair of prisoners.

'They seem rather distracted.'

Collings raised a hairless brow. 'One is a spy, and has been soundly beaten, sir. The girl has been walked.'

Chudleigh looked up from the dishevelled captives. 'Walked?'

Collings's face was expressionless as his hard little eyes met those of the rebel commander. 'A method to extract confessions from those suspected of witchcraft.'

James Chudleigh did not consider himself a bad man. Stubborn, yes, fractious on occasion, but not wicked. And yet in his frustration with Cecily Cade he had handed her over to Collings in the hope that his threats, perhaps even his evil, coal-pebble eyes, would frighten her into giving up her secrets. He had not, it seemed, fully considered the implications of such a decision.

'Christ on His cross, Erasmus, I asked you to interrogate her. If it comes out that we tortured a woman as we would torture a damned warlock—'

For answer, Collings beckoned one of his companions over with a wave. He was a dark-clothed man of average height, with straight, shoulder-length auburn hair, a brown beard flecked with silver, a huge, hooked nose and teeth that were so large they might have better suited the horse on which he perched.

'Osmyn Hogg,' he said smoothly. 'God's chief witchfinder, sir.'

Chudleigh offered a brusque nod. 'Well?'

Hogg waited as a new barrage of cannon fire reached its world-shaking climax, clearing his throat as the thirteen explosions began to ebb. 'She is your prisoner, Major-General, of course. But she is also charged with making a vile compact with Satan.'

'So you see,' Collings interrupted swiftly, 'I am at liberty to employ the most expedient methods in this case.'

'And did she talk?'

475

Collings threw Hogg a venomous glance before shaking his head. 'No, sir. Not yet.'

Chudleigh gazed down at the girl. She looked gaunt and weak, but news of her continuing obstinacy eroded what little compassion he had been prey to. 'Are you ready to watch your precious king's men die, Miss Cade?'

Just then a loud murmur swept along the deep lines of infantrymen ranged to the group's right. It was as if each of the five thousand men had drawn a simultaneous breath, easing it out upon a few whispered words. Chudleigh looked across, seeing that something had indeed set them to feverish gossip, and he was about to berate their officers for allowing such behaviour in the ranks, when he noticed one of the sergeants gesticulating frantically at something down on the slope with his halberd.

Chudleigh wrenched his horse's head so that it turned to face Stratton Hill's western slope. His gaze raked across the grass, over some of his more advanced musketeers, and to the line of smoking fieldpieces. Men scuttled around them, hurried to and fro like ants about a nest, and he expected them to belch forth at any moment. Except they did not belch. Indeed, they did nothing at all. Now they were silent.

'Dear God,' he whispered.

Stryker and Skellen had burst from Grenville's increasingly ragged division and sprinted towards the line of artillery pieces that had punished them so severely.

At first Stryker had not known what exactly he was going to do, but one thing was certain, the guns needed to be taken out of the fight. He had thrown his musket to the

476

nearest man, for speed was crucial, and bolted free of Berkeley's silent detachment, bounding up the hill as fast as his aching legs would allow. Even as he ran, he considered the foolishness of the idea, wondering what exactly two men could do against thirteen cannon and their crew, but then more thumping steps could be heard behind and he risked a brief glance over his shoulder to see twoscore redcoats careening in his wake. They were not just his men either, but Forrester's as well, his old Brother of the Blade leading the way.

And then they were at the guns, swords drawn, banshee cries shrill and demonic, and the gunners were already on the back foot, stunned and terrified by the sudden ferocious charge, as though they faced frantic-eyed berserkers from days of old. They panicked, began to run. Stryker hacked a man down with his big, basket-hilted blade, the expensive Toledo steel, commissioned for him by Queen Henrietta Maria herself, flashing through the man's face as though he were made of silk.

He ran to the nearest cannon, kicked another gunner away in case he was attempting to fire the iron beast one last time, and immediately had to crouch behind the barrel as a musket-ball pinged off one of the big wheels. But the ball landed at his feet, barely dented, and he realized the shot must have come from a great distance, for it had been almost powerless when it reached him. He rose to his feet, stared into a dense patch of smoke until the breeze shifted it, and there, midway between the ordnance line and the bustling crest, he spotted the closest team of rebel musketeers.

'They're too far away!' he shouted to anyone who would listen. 'Keep going, lads! Send the bastards back!'

The men responded, hacking and bludgeoning their way through the bravest – or slowest – of the gun crews, suddenly confident that the enemy marksmen were too far out of range to pose any real threat.

Skellen was nearby. Stryker could not see him at first, for the area around the cannons was thick with powder smoke, but he heard the sergeant's roar, a battle-cry born in the gutters and taverns of Gosport and honed on the bleeding lands of Saxony. Barkworth was there too, screaming unintelligible Gaelic curses at men who must have thought a true demon puckrel had come to claim their souls for the underworld.

'Spread out!' Forrester's tone, strained with battle but still distinct in its educated cadence, reached him through the stinking fog. 'Take the rest of the guns, damn you! Take them all!'

Stryker repeated the call, realizing they needed all thirteen pieces decommissioned before Hopton's divisions could gather pace, but he quickly saw that the last vestiges of the enemy crews were gone, high-tailing it up towards the safety of the summit. He stopped, heaving in a few massive breaths to steady his heart and mind. The guns were captured, just seconds after they had fired their last, and he jabbed his bloody sword at the air, a banner to which the tattered Royalist columns could flock. And there, no more than fifty paces away, he saw the huge ensign of Sir Bevil Grenville surge through the acrid mist like the prow of a warship.

The king's men were coming.

James Chudleigh slapped a hand against his right cheek to suppress the tick. Somehow it would not relent, the skin flickering madly beneath his eye.

'They have captured the ordnance, sir,' an aide murmured at his side. 'Without a shot fired.'

Chudleigh rounded on the unfortunate man. 'God's precious blood, man, I can see that!'

The cheek twitched ever more violently.

'No matter,' Major-General Collings, still beside Chudleigh on his smaller mount, intoned nonchalantly. 'They must now march uphill into a force more than twice their size. It is lunacy, and they will lose.'

But Chudleigh was staring down at the advancing Royalists, his heart beginning to rattle inside his chest. He ignored the tick, leaving it to shiver wildly, and hurriedly drew an ornate spyglass from his saddlebag. He trained it on the lower slopes, taking in the overrun cannon and the bodies of pike and musket that were now this side of those impotent emplacements. And then he shifted the glass further back, towards the tree line, and took in the men and colours that still spewed from the hidden lanes. 'Hopton is down there.'

'General?' Collings prompted warily.

Chudleigh lowered the glass, glanced across at the skeletal face with its jackdaw eyes. 'Only Grenville's men have advanced beyond our guns. The rest of their pitiful little army still muster against the trees.' He thrust the glass back into the saddlebag and slammed a fist into his opposite palm. 'He has overreached himself, gentlemen, and we can destroy him while his friends dither.'

The tongue-lashed aide found his voice again, clearing his throat awkwardly. 'Sir, we will let them come to us, yes? Dash themselves on our steady ranks. They do not have the numbers to trouble our position, and soon your father will return with our horse.'

But the young major-general was not listening. Instead his gaze was fixed firmly upon the most advanced of the Royalist ensigns, a gigantic blue standard cutting its way through the drifting smoke. 'That is Grenville. The popinjay leads his cankerous whoresons ahead of the rest. Thinks he can cow our men by holding his fire.'

'He's probably run out of powder,' Collings interjected levelly.

Chudleigh shook his head. 'It is a knavish trick!' The twitch had gone, and Chudleigh inwardly thanked God for the sign. 'Believes he can best me on his own, does he? By God I will show him.'

Chudleigh raked his spurs viciously along his mount's flanks so that the beast lurched into action, and he steered it right to the edge of the flat summit, cantering along the front of the first of his two vast lines of infantry. This first line was filled with the best men of Devon. His own pikes were here, and those of Sir John Northcote, and even Merrick's redoubtable greycoats. Perhaps three thousand in all, stretched into a line that covered the better part of nine hundred paces.

He looked for Northcote's banner and galloped directly towards it.

'My pikes, Sir John!'

Northcote, a dour fellow with tightly trimmed whiskers, clear blue eyes and close-cropped hair that did not show beneath his hat, offered an uneasy frown. 'Shall we not simply wait for them to struggle up the slope, sir?'

'No, sir, we shall not. I would take my pikes down to thrash Grenville while he is without support. Some of your men too, and a body of the greys.' He peered back down at the foremost Royalist division, gauging their

480

strength quickly. 'He has five or six hundred there, so I will take a thousand.'

'But, sir—' Northcote began to protest.

'But nothing, sir!'

Chudleigh wrenched his horse away, leaving the colonel no option but to obey, and stood high in his stirrups as his detachment took shape a little way down the slope. Of the thousand, the vast majority were pikemen, with a hundred or so musketeers in support, and they shuffled dutifully into place.

When they were ranged before him, he drew his sword, revelling in the rasp as it cleared the scabbard's throat, and pointed the keen tip down at the steadily marching foe. 'Let us flense these savages,' he bellowed so that the men in the packed ranks could hear, 'and toss their remains into the sea!'

'*Huzzah*!' came the cry, rippling through the bristling new body of men.

'Take heart! These are not your countrymen. They are dirty, Pope-loving Celts! Heathen men, no better than those the Lionheart crushed so many years ago. Now take up his legacy! Complete his journey! God will reward every man here!'

The men cheered again, but this time the cry was taken up throughout the entire rebel force, surging across the hill's summit like a rain-swollen tide. They stabbed their pike staves up at the clouds, thousands of points of light glimmering from thousands of blades.

Major-General James Chudleigh slid down from his horse, tossed the reins to a waiting officer, and strode out to lead his men to battle.

*

Stryker saw the Parliamentarians move off the crest, slowly at first, but picking up speed with every pace as they hit the hill's steep incline, and he knew the real killing was about to start. The skirmishing – so bitter and drawn out – had been no more than the day's opening exchange. Here, on this grassy slope between the dense forest and the flat crest, the land would become a charnel house.

He retrieved his musket and returned to Grenville's column as it began to fan out, pikes on the left, muskets to the right. Stryker looked back, hoping to see the rest of Hopton's army, and there, swarming up from the tree line like God's own host, came the remaining trio of Royalist columns. But they were too far back to influence the fight, at least for the moment, and Grenville's men were on their own.

'It's Chudleigh!' he heard someone call. 'That's his banner!'

Sure enough, a figure in fine, gleaming armour paced confidently at the very front of the Parliamentarian advance.

And then Stryker's attention switched to his own side, as another lone figure scampered out to stand before the Royalists, waving his sword in sweeping arcs above his head. A giant soon joined him, shielding his body from any in the closing rebel ranks that might try a lucky shot, and Stryker realized the smaller man was none other than Sir Bevil Grenville.

An eerie hush descended upon the Royalists then, as the Cornishmen, so grizzled and ferocious, gazed upon the man they revered above all others.

'It is a day for swords!' Grenville brayed. 'A day for fire, and for blood! A day for death! God is with us, my brave lads! Long live the King!'

The Cornish soldiers howled their support, screamed their obscenities, and surged up the hill with an ever-quickening pace. But their cries were quickly enveloped by those coming from higher up the slope, for the oncoming Roundhead force was nearly at full charge now, pikes beginning to lower from their shoulders, points level with the heads and chests of the king's fighters. The sound of Chudleigh's pikemen was deafening, overwhelming. There were just so many of them. Snarling and spitting and cursing and raging.

At once the cry went up from the Royalist side to charge their pikes, and down they came like a forest of felled trees, jerked from their breastplate rests to train upon the enemy.

Stryker watched, catching sight of his redcoats within the bristling mass. This was not the protective posture his men had employed to such good effect against Wild's slashing harquebusiers. They were no longer the barrier to keep horsemen at bay. No more a screen for the musketeers. This time they were the aggressors, the chargers, the killers. He silently wished them godspeed.

On the enemy flank the Roundhead musketeers slowed their run, formed up into a wide line, and fired a huge volley, flames swelling across their front. It should have been devastating, should have torn Grenville's densely packed pike block to fleshy ribbons, but the king's men moved too fast and most of the balls whistled into the rearmost ranks as they passed by. The front ranks were safe. They levelled their own spears to meet Chudleigh's, lowered their chins, braced their shoulders, tightened grips, and swept into the Parliamentarian *battaile*.

The pikes stabbed in, pressed irresistibly onwards by

the men at their butt ends, eleven or more feet further back. They crossed in the air, forming a tangled lattice-work of wooden shafts. And then they crunched home. The sound was horrific. The clang of metal overlaying the wet slap of punctured flesh, like a cleaver slammed into a butcher's block. Some of the pikes found immediate flesh, driven hard into faces and necks. Most missed, drilled between the shoulders of the men opposite, suddenly entwined with the myriad other staves that were now locked amongst the bodies of the men they had meant to kill.

And then the strange, low grunt of the push of pike rose up from the press. Stryker knew it well, had heard it so many times before. After the initial smashing, murderous collision, the opposing blocks would stall, for their pole-arms were entwined with those of the enemy and their sword hands were concerned only with maintaining a grip on the pikes. It was now a time for brute strength and courage. The first ranks, those fortunate enough to have been missed by the initial barrage of slicing steel tips, would lean forward, digging heels into the earth like so many mules, thrusting shoulders into the press, driving every ounce of strength they could muster along the length of ash. Many of the pikemen would have spent countless summers hauling on ropes, representing their respective hamlets in the tug-o'-war with neighbouring communities. The push of pike was a similar experience, only in reverse. Men groaned and cursed, they spat and they screamed and they gnashed teeth and heaved until their hands and arms and backs and thighs were fit to burst. And for a moment, one fabulous moment, it seemed as though Grenville's famed Cornishmen would achieve the unthinkable and break through the far larger rebel block. Chudleigh's Devonshire force rocked backwards, stunned by the ferocity of the Royalist press and aware that their musketeers had fired too soon. They took a step to the rear, then another, and it seemed as though they might cut and run, but the men behind leaned in, willing them on, shoving them roughly back down the slope.

Sheer momentum took over. The weight of the larger Roundhead *battaile*, combined with the fact that they were fighting downhill, seemed to turn the tide. It was slow to begin with, Grenville's hardy Cornish troops digging in, crouching low, grinding back up at them, but the powerful rebel drive staggered forth for the first time since pikes had crossed, and the entire Royalist body shunted backwards, unable to resist.

Stryker looked on in horror as Chudleigh's broad, deep *battaile* began to bow, its flanks curving round the smaller pike block, threatening to completely encircle it. But then he heard a new voice bellow out above the din of battle. It was sharp and strong, stentorian and confident. He looked to his right, only to see Sir John Berkeley step out of line. The man commanding Grenville's muskets, dressed superbly in a suit of yellow, with open-sleeved doublet and embroidered buff-coat, cupped a hand to the side of his bearded mouth and shouted again. Stryker heard him properly this time, and moved with the rest of the musketeers, the entire body wheeling round from the Royalist right to face the locked push.

'Give fire!' Berkeley roared, fist punching the air.

The Royalist musketeers had finally been freed to go to work. Stryker raised his own musket, blew on the match one last time, and eased back the trigger. He did not aim, for it was not necessary at this range. The huge, tightly packed body of rebel pikemen was there for the shooting. Had they waited a few seconds more, waited until Grenville's pikes finally capitulated, a savage melee ensuing, it would have been an unthinkable manoeuvre, for to distinguish between friend and foe would be impossible. Yet now, while Chudleigh's men were still braced at pike's length from the beleaguered Cavaliers, it was near impossible to miss.

All along Berkeley's flanking party muskets flashed in rhythmic volleys, one rank, then the next, and the next. The nearest files of Chudleigh's column convulsed, shrank instinctively away from the devastating bullets. And then Stryker saw Sir John draw his sword, and witnessed his lips give a command that was drowned completely by gunfire and screams, but knew what he asked all the same. He reversed his musket, hefting it by the barrel, heavy wooden stock presented like a club, and charged with the rest.

They smashed headlong into Chudleigh's already battered flank, forcing the confused Roundheads in on themselves. And, in turn, those Roundheads did not know whether to fight the pikemen at their front or the musketeers at the side, and so they did neither. Some of Chudleigh's musketeers raced around the press of bodies to resist the assault, but they were few compared with Berkeley's force, and they soon gave ground, unable to reload long-spent weapons.

The braying Cornish pikemen threw them back, hurled themselves into the splintering enemy like a herd of maddened bullocks, forcing the rebels to climb the slope as the king's men had climbed all day.

The first pikes were thrown down. Men in the front ranks, those facing Grenville's newly invigorated block, twisted and turned like rats caught by the tail, desperate to flee but unable to move for the press of bodies and the tightly knit staves. Some of the rebels at the back saw their fear, heard their cries, and began to peel away. The men in the centre could not see what was happening, but they sensed the new fear, saw their comrades' pikes fall like oaks in a gale, and began to jostle their own paths out of the hitherto solid formation.

The Parliamentarian pike block stalled, juddered backwards, cohesion draining away like rainwater through sand, and then collapsed. They turned, racing for the summit as though Satan himself snapped at their heels.

'We got 'im!' a man exclaimed. His voice was just one more noise in the cacophony of the fight, but it was somehow different to the others. A vein of surprise, shock even, raised it to a particular pitch that made men peer into the melee to see what exactly he meant. 'We got Chully 'iself!'

Stryker ran to where the push of pike had fractured into a hundred personal duels, desperate to see if the proclamation was true. He leapt clean over a grey-coated musketeer's twisted cadaver, rounded another man whose orange-sashed torso was spattered in fresh blood, and jammed his musket butt hard into the chin of a kneeling rebel who made to draw a thin dirk. In moments he was there, in the thick of a fight that had already dissipated, the Royalists crowing their victory up at the grim-faced onlookers gathered on the crest.

'He's mine!'

That voice again. Stryker looked left and right, scanning the bodies of the elated and the routed, until finally his eye fell upon a stocky man in pikeman's corselet, though it seemed his pole-arm had long been discarded. His face was heavy with stubble, his eyes slightly crossed, and his mouth almost entirely devoid of teeth. And that mouth grinned, broad and predatory, for beneath him, prostrate at the end of his blade but evidently unhurt, lay the man Stryker had first seen as the rebel force had rushed so irresistibly from the ridge.

Major-General James Chudleigh.

There was no such joy on the summit of Stratton Hill.

Henry Grey, First Earl of Stamford, had arrived late, and, for the briefest of moments as he scaled the slope from the less formidable north, he had feared that his absence would somehow prove costly. But then, he had reassured himself, young Chudleigh knew the terrain, had a superior army, and also all the logistical and tactical advantages afforded by this formidable position. Indeed, he even commanded more loyalty from the Devon troops than they ever displayed for Stamford.

And yet now, staring open-mouthed at the blood-blackened slope before him, the earl felt physically sick. Because Chudleigh had come dangerously close to throwing it all away.

But all, he knew, was not yet lost.

Stamford had brought one hundred and forty steady cavalrymen with him, and he left them at the hill's northern periphery, cantering alone through the undulating network of Iron Age earthworks and across the hill's crest, the two lines of foot stretching out to his right. Over at the southernmost fringe of the summit was a small party of horsemen flanked by a number of men holding the limp colours of various rebel units, and he decided it was there that he would find the army's senior men.

'What, in the name of the living God, has that boy done to my army?'

Almost every head in the mounted party turned to him, the ring of standard-bearers moving swiftly out of his way.

One of the group, a small-framed man encased in blackened, gilt-riveted armour, spurred out to greet him. 'My lord.'

Stamford stared at the armoured man, then down at the anarchic slope. 'You let him charge out on his own, Erasmus?' he asked coldly.

'He commands, my lord.'

Stamford looked up. 'Not any longer, Collings. I saw that disaster. James Chudleigh is gone, captured or worse, and his ill-advised counterattack has cost me a goodly part of my most seasoned troops.' He stared back down at the slope. There, without resistance from rebel pikes, and still too far away to be hindered by musketry, the four small Royalist hordes were steadily coming together. 'There will be no more stupidity this day, by Christ. No more. We still have the advantage of numbers.'

'Will you send in your horsemen, my lord?'

Stamford glanced back at the mounted men, but shook his head. 'They will not be required. Let the malignants clamber up to find us. We have four thousand men itching to greet them.'

The Royalist army converged to the right of the advance, naturally veering towards Sir Ralph Hopton's column.

All four divisions had marched straight up the steep

western face of the seemingly unassailable hill, not firing a single shot until they were almost at the summit, and now they had joined. One large, surging, ferocious force, new in confidence, bearing down – or, rather, up – on the heart of the rebel position.

'He's been hurt, sir,' Anthony Payne said as Stryker ran to him.

Stryker quickly apprised the man in fine green clothes who was able to walk only by Payne's bracing arm. 'How bad?'

'Bruising is all,' Sir Bevil Grenville replied angrily, but winced and swore at a new wave of pain. He had been in the thick of the push of pike, losing his step early on and being swiftly trampled by the boots of friend and foe alike. 'Damn it, Anthony, let me go!'

Payne shook his head firmly, hauling his master up when the colonel's legs began to wilt. 'You must rest, sir.'

'Mister Payne is right, Colonel,' Stryker added, acutely aware that morale would take a severe blow if the Cornish knew that their irascible talisman had been injured.

But Grenville managed to shrug himself free of the giant's bolstering embrace, and forced himself to straighten, breathing deeply through gritted teeth. 'Be off with your nannying hands, by Christ! My sword!'

Payne had retrieved Grenville's sword when the rebel block had ruptured, and he handed it to the colonel, hilt first.

Grenville grinned broadly, blood welling bright from a crack in his bottom lip. He raised the blade for his men to see. 'On!'

They marched on, a single army at last, divided into alternate bodies of pike and musket, drawing ever closer to the waiting rebel lines. Stryker and his men were there, his pikes intermingled with the metal-clad hedgehogs on either side, his musketeers clustered about Ensign Chase and the huge red banner with its two white diamonds. Stryker paced at the head of those musketeers, willing them forward, face grim, words brutal. They were still grouped within the larger force commanded by Grenville, and Stryker shouted for them to walk with heads high, to show their Cornish comrades that they were equally as fearsome. Skellen and Barkworth were with him still, the latter's eyes gleaming like a cat's in moonlight, alive with the battle-lust he so relished. Forrester was somewhere near too, leading his own musketeers, for he could hear the captain's distinctive voice in the crowd, and he felt suddenly sorry that his friend's own colour was not on the field. A man, he believed, should be allowed to die beneath his own standard.

Musket fire began to crackle loudly from above, two men fell in quick succession to Stryker's right, and he realized with a sudden bowel-loosening dread that they had advanced to within effective range.

'Hold fire!' Grenville called from the front. 'Hold, I say!'

Stryker, like the rest, held his shot. They had briefly used their powder to break Chudleigh's attack, but now the orders from Hopton were to save the precious powder for as long as possible. The whisper that hissed throughout the rank and file – not party to the dire situation with supply – had spoken of a devilish plan to frighten the enemy. To show the Devon folk that men of Cornwall needed no guns to win a fight. Stryker had been amused at the notion at first, but now, as they waded into ever more dense enemy fire, he wondered if such a tactic – albeit an accidental one – might actually work.

And then they were at the summit, the wide expanse where Stamford's army waited for them, and the drums crashed out a new rhythm. It was the order for the united force to wheel to the left. Hopton's column, having advanced to the south of the hill, were furthest right, and they took a wide berth, while the leftmost division, Basset's, would stay put, becoming the anchor for the broad line. Stryker, with Grenville's bloodied but exultant force, was in the centre.

Just as the Royalists completed their sweeping turn so that they faced due north, cutting off any retreat into Stratton, their right flank was quickly engaged by a desperate block of greycoats. Stryker watched as the men of Hopton's column endured a storm of musketry, before meeting the rebels at pike point, the long staves passing one another, overlapping like hundreds of interlinked fingers. He stared at that fight, so close to him and yet out of his influence, and he willed Hopton's companies on, as if some of his own determination might reinforce their bones.

'*Sir*!' William Skellen's loud voice ripped through his skull, forcing his attention back to the front, and he saw that the warning came just in time. More broad, dense blocks of grey-coated pikemen, flanked by units of musketeers, were bearing down on his own position.

'*Muskets*!' Sir Bevil Grenville screamed from his position at the front-right corner of the pike block. He was bruised and battered but still enthused by a remarkable energy, and in this terrifying, exciting, blood-bubbling moment, Stryker understood why the Cornish Royalists would fight so hard for this man. Because, he realized, Grenville would fight for them too.

'*Muskets!*' Sir John Berkeley, hidden in the black void that was Stryker's blind left side, echoed the order. It was repeated up and down the line by captains and lieutenants and sergeants alike, and, with the greycoats moving swiftly in, scores of musketeers moved to form a swathe of bodies in front of the pikes.

In came the greycoats, pace by thundering pace, their banners waved aloft at their backs, their faces twisted in pure hatred. Fifty yards. Thirty yards.

Twenty-five.

'*Fire!*'

Stryker picked the chest of an advancing pikeman and pulled his trigger. The serpent snapped down in its short, vicious arc, the match plunged into the firing pan, and the charge ignited. He jolted back as the heavy stock kicked at his shoulder like an angry stallion, and squinted into the gritty, stinking smoke cloud that immediately wreathed his head. He did not wait to see what became of the man he had marked for death, for he knew the advancing pikemen would not have been stopped by the volley, and he twisted away, moving quickly to form up with the rest of the scuttling musketeers as the opposing pike units collided.

The wrestling match had begun, just as it had on the slope, and, as before, the Royalists were outnumbered. This time, though, the two armies faced one another in a broad line that stretched right the way across the hill, so Berkeley could not send his musketeers to hit the rebel flank.

Mind pulsating with equal measures of fear and

excitement, Stryker threw down his musket and ducked beneath the tightly crossed pikes. It was as if he had entered a room newly erected on the pinnacle of this bloody hill, for the wooden shafts above him were so snugly packed, so interwoven, that they formed a ceiling. Neither side could advance, none would go back, and neither could so much as move, so entwined were they in each other's ash-poled mesh. Stryker stayed low, crouched beneath what seemed like a wattle fence formed miraculously four feet from the ground. There was no room to wield a musket, nor to draw a sword, so he unsheathed his dirk and crawled on hands and knees to the Roundhead front rank.

And he started to kill.

The first man, both hands gripping his outstretched pike, did not even see Stryker. He crumpled in a matter of seconds as the Royalist captain opened a gaping hole in his groin. Blood pumped thickly in a steaming spray, dowsing Stryker's arm, chest, and face. The man at his side saw him fall, looked down through the shifting lattice and called a warning. Stryker pushed up between two pikes, stabbed him in the throat, and dropped back out of sight.

But the cry had gone up now, spreading like wildfire, and soon the Roundheads had sent their own men into the bloody world where the knife was king and a man fought on his knees.

One of the rebels came at him quickly, scrambling across the grassy no-man's-land, a dirk in each hand. He reached Stryker, and slashed at the Royalist's face with one and then the other in rapid succession. Stryker swayed out of range for both swipes, but his own lunge missed,

494

clipping the Parliament man's earlobe but nothing more. The rebel came again, and this time he seemed to favour his left hand, jabbing the blade forth with three or four staccato thrusts. Stryker dodged them comfortably, only to see his assailant's right arm snap forward. The man had read Stryker well, guessing he would see an attack from that side late, and he threw himself backwards as the dirk slashed home, avoiding its deadly point by a hair's breadth. But then he was on his back, staring up at the tangled mesh of pikes that crossed above, and he heard the rebel scramble towards him.

'Two blades?' a voice Stryker knew suddenly rasped nearby. It was a constricted sound, more of a croak than a real voice, and inflected with the accent of Scotland. 'Now that's fightin' dirty.'

Stryker forced himself up, grinning as he laid his eye upon Simeon Barkworth. The dwarf could stand beneath the ceiling of pikes, so short was he, and that made him lethal against men on all fours.

Barkworth grinned, snatching one of the blades from Stryker's would-be killer, a man whose throat he had evidently slit. 'Still,' he said happily, holding up a dirk in each little fist, 'I've always believed fightin' dirty was the only way to do it.'

'Come 'ere, you fuckin' 'alf-man!' a spittle-laced snarl erupted from behind the Scot.

Barkworth spun on his heels and held up the dirks. 'Half-man, is it?' He lurched forward, agility unaffected in this gloomy place. His challenger responded, but he was on his knees, and that made him terribly cumbersome. In a flash he was dead, one of the dirks lodged in the roof of his gaping mouth.

Stryker quickly thanked Barkworth for saving his life. The blood-spattered dwarf offered a bow. 'Skellen would've helped, o'course,' he said, 'but the lanky streak o' English piss could'nae get under here wi'out puttin' his back out.'

Stryker grinned and went at the enemy pikemen again. He chopped away at the knee of one, hamstrung another, and sliced a yawning horizontal gash in the belly of a third. And as the men fell, their comrades stepping up to plug the gaps became ever more sluggish to take their places. And the Royalists at Stryker's back heaved and they roared and they began to gain ground.

Henry Grey drummed his fingers nervously against his thigh.

He had spurred back towards the safety of his seven-score horse, followed swiftly by Collings's group as the Royalist *battailes* reached the brow of the hill, and had watched proceedings from behind the two lines of foot. And now, as he watched with burgeoning horror, the first line was not annihilating Sir Ralph Hopton's little army, but shuddering, rocking back, giving ground.

Stamford wore plate on back and chest, a gorget at his throat, tassets over his thighs, and on his head sat a Dutch pot, a fixed peak helmet with sliding nasal bar. And suddenly he began to feel hot, as though his skin boiled beneath all the armour. He breathed deeply, snatched off the helmet, and fiddled with its chin strap.

An errant musket-ball flew past. There was nothing deadly about it, for its power had long since dissipated, but he went to put the pot back on. When he looked up, he saw the second – as yet untouched – line of infantry begin to quiver, as if readying to march. Yet they were not advancing. He looked on as their officers called for them to stand firm, their sergeants and corporals threatening them with bullets between the shoulder blades should they take a single step back. But the land before them was littered with the dead and wounded, the cannons were gone, the grass was black with blood. And step back they did.

'What in the name of—' Stamford whispered. He peered around, looking for an explanation and laying eyes on the staff officer encased in jet-black armour. 'Collings!'

Collings spurred to his side. 'My lord?'

Stamford pointed at the reserve line. 'What the devil are they doing?'

Collings lifted his hinged visor. His expression was blank as a corpse. 'They fear the Cornish, sir.'

'But Sourton—'

'Went some way to rectifying matters, but I rather think a march up a steep slope with fewer men and hardly firing a shot has somewhat reaffirmed the mystique.' He slammed the face bars back down, beady eyes glinting from within their steel cage. 'Besides, word of Chudleigh's capture has spread to them, my lord.'

'Then they must strive for his rescue,' Stamford blustered, feeling himself flush again.

Collings shook his head. 'I fear not, sir. The men in the second line are of the Trained Bands. Here under duress. Without their general, their hearts will fail them.'

Stamford's tassets clanged as he slammed a fist on to his thigh. 'But I am their general, by God!'

Collings turned his horse away. 'You were not here, my lord.'

CHAPTER 23

The sulphurous gun smoke had transformed the afternoon into premature dusk, but the ebullient Royalists rumbled on. They hammered and slashed and tore at the rebel front line, and that line, facing south now and weakened by the loss of their best troops in Chudleigh's abortive charge, was beginning to crumple under the strain of an enemy that smelled blood and sensed victory. It should not have been this way, for their sheer numerical supremacy should have carried the day, but morale was ebbing like a fractured dam, and in the whites of the Cornish eyes the men could see their own deaths.

The musket fire, such a storm throughout the day, was desultory now, flames licking forth from blackened muzzles as soon as men could charge them. But most entered the fray with their weapons upturned, taking the butt ends to break the bones of their enemies.

With each heartbeat that thudded in the chest of a king's man, his ragged opponents shunted backwards, edging towards the rear of the hill, aware that on three sides they were already hemmed in. And the enemy reserve, still formidable by sight, was not moving forward. They should have been surging up to fill the gaps between the tattered blocks of Northcote and Merrick, but instead they did nothing, simply stopped and stared to the rear like a vast flock of sheep. The Royalists guessed at their fear; Hopton and his colonels sensed it and urged the thin Royalist line forth, promising the unlikeliest of victories.

And the Parliamentarians began to run.

Eighty or so paces to the rear of the Parliamentarian force the great and the good of Devon's rebel army were taking their leave.

Major-General Erasmus Collings watched the Earl of Stamford's back bob up and down as his destrier carried him to the protection of his cavalrymen, and to the safety they would ultimately find. Stamford would run now, live to fight another day, and, Collings did not doubt, would blame this debacle on James Chudleigh.

'I am leaving,' he said to Wild, slamming down his black visor.

Wild, at Collings's left side and still dragging Stryker's battered lieutenant in his wake, opened his mouth to protest, but Collings raised a firm hand. 'Do not waste your breath, Gabriel. The battle is lost. Our best men are falling back, while our Trained Bands already look to the hills.' He cast his gaze across the rest of the group. 'Save yourselves or stay for martyrdom. I care not.'

'What of the girl?' Wild asked, glancing down at Cecily Cade.

Collings urged his horse over to where she stood. He stared down at the wan-faced bitch for a moment, then waved for a pair of aides to help him haul her into his saddle. She did not resist, so broken was she by the night's ministrations, and he gripped her waist tightly. 'Stamford forgets her in his flight.' He grinned suddenly, understanding that his own star would rise this day, regardless of the rebel cause at large. 'She will go to London, with me. Pym can weed out her damned secrets.'

'I had hoped to find vengeance,' Colonel Gabriel Wild said as he turned away from the gentle escarpment down which Collings had galloped. He stared, dumbstruck, at the line of battle that was now nearer sixty paces away. The Roundheads still fought, but they were giving ground with every passing second.

'Well, you will find nothing but death if you stay,' witchfinder Osmyn Hogg replied tersely.

'Aye,' José Ventura agreed, licking those fat lips.

'So you leave?' Wild asked. 'Abandon your search for Stryker?'

Hogg shrugged, already turning his horse away from the fight. 'It has taken a decade to find him. I have learned patience.'

'But if I gave you a chance for revenge,' Wild asked, 'would you take it? Even now?'

Hogg looked back at him, nonplussed. 'Aye. I should give much to see that evil-doer swing.'

Wild did not speak again. He simply smiled and stood in his stirrups, pointing at a bullet-riddled piece of cloth hanging from a pole that rose near the right of the Royalist ranks. It was a big thing, made of taffeta and dyed blood red. It had a Cross of St George in canton and two white diamonds in the field, occasionally flourished on a vagary of wind. And Gabriel Wild's heart was in his mouth, because he had seen that banner before. On a lonely tor in Dartmoor.

Captain Innocent Stryker had been in many fights. Seen more blood spilled than he cared to remember, witnessed more triumphs and defeats than was natural for a man to bear. But he had never been part of something as stunning as this.

The Roundhead army, apparently so invincible when the sandy common at Bude had erupted at daybreak, was being routed. The two armies faced one another in a long front that stretched west to east across the breadth of the summit, and to an onlooker it might still look as though the huge Parliamentarian line would simply swamp the shallower Royalist force, but the steep slopes at either flank meant that they could not encircle Hopton's army, and their tired bodies and shrinking morale saw that they were no longer willing to stand in the face of the rampant Cornish.

Stryker had taken a step back to load his musket, and, as he shoved his way back to the front line, he saw the first pikes topple, thrust down by men looking to flee.

'They're off, sir! They're bloody running!'

Stryker twisted his head to the left and saw that Skellen, who had somehow found himself a discarded halberd amongst the strewn weapons, was, as ever, by his side, instinctively shielding Stryker's blind flank. It was not just Grenville, he considered wryly, who had his own ferocious bodyguard.

'Keep at them!' Stryker snarled back. 'They're not all done yet!' That was all too true, he thought, as he hefted his musket. Plenty of units, the ones dressed in grey coats and those wearing oak sprigs in their hats, fought on, lips peeled back in macabre grimaces, turned to animals by terror and blood-rage. He fired, the rebel line immediately vanishing in his powder cloud.

Seemingly in response, a group of enemy musketeers some twenty paces away let fly with a spatter of fire that ploughed straight into Stryker's position. One of his redcoats, half a dozen places to his right, fell backwards suddenly, thumped from his feet in a fine spray of crimson that settled over the faces of the nearest men. Another toppled at the same time, hands pressed to his guts, wailing into the boot-pulped soil.

A single shot flashed from the direction of the enemy like a bright spark from an anvil, and Stryker heard its whine close to his face. By the high-pitched report, he guessed it had come from a pistol, and, sure enough, he quickly noticed an orange-sashed officer standing alone between the musket blocks, arm still raised.

'Get the bastard, Will!' Stryker called to his blind left side where he knew Skellen would still be standing. The tall sergeant, clutching his halberd in huge, thin-fingered hands, gave a single, guttural grunt and lurched out of the line. The officer saw him coming, called for help, but none of his men would leave the safety of the block. He tossed his smoking pistol aside, drew his broad-bladed sabre, and composed himself in a cultured riposte. Skellen knocked the weapon aside as though he were swatting a fly, the blade snapping from the force. He stepped in, feinted high, swept the pole-arm low, and opened the Parliamentarian's thigh. The wounded man stumbled back, dropped his broken sword to clutch the spouting wound, and Skellen brought the halberd back in a return sweep that cleaved away the rebel's lower jaw.

A huge cheer went up from the Royalists around Stryker. Skellen, drenched in his victim's blood, wading through drifting gun smoke, and screaming like a creature from Satan's infernos, held his halberd high and grinned at the rebel ranks. And they broke.

Stryker could not see clearly what was happening to the left and right of his position, but the blocks of pike and musket immediately facing his own men threw down their arms and turned tail. His men followed, keeping tightly together so as not to lose cohesion, and slashed at the routed Roundheads' backs. The bravest rebels rallied in small pockets of resistance, but they were quickly overwhelmed and died where they stood.

Stryker surged on, moving to Skellen's right again so that the sergeant could stand sentry in the spot where the world was all black to him. There was no time to reload his musket now, and he made to discard it and draw his sword, but a Roundhead musketeer was on him too quickly, and he was forced to duck below the heavy swipe of the burly man's wooden stock. He drove his own firearm up into the man's sternum, winding him, and reversed the cumbersome weapon, jabbing the stock at the man's nose, breaking it with ease. The rebel staggered back a pace as Stryker swung it in a wide arc, wrenching his own shoulder muscles in the process but connecting with the musketeer's temple. The man crumpled as though his entire skeleton had been sucked from his flesh.

The Royalists gushed onwards like water in a storm drain. Stryker slipped on a gelatinous patch of guts, pitched forwards and barrelled through a dazed pikeman's legs, smashing them from under the hapless greycoat like round shot through a wattle fence.

The musket was gone, tumbled away in the fall, and he hauled his sword free as he stood. A pair of bearded, wild-eyed rebels came at him now, and, perversely, he found himself wondering if they were brothers, even as one of them went down under Skellen's crushing halberd. The other, brandishing a frantic grin and a curved, scythe-like instrument that was probably adapted from an agricultural tool, lunged at Stryker, whipping the crescent blade left and right in heavy motions that might have been honed on Devon's crops. Stryker swayed out of range of the first flurry, ducked under the next few, and parried the last, the powerful blow reverberating all the way up his arm. Just as he thought he might be overpowered by the thickset brawler, the man's brown eyes widened in a look of utter surprise, and he slumped to his knees. Only when Stryker strode round him did he notice the bullet hole in the side of the man's skull.

He paused to catch his breath and stretch his jarred sword arm. Everywhere he looked fights raged, duels between Royalist and Parliamentarian, officer and commoner, pikeman and musketeer. The rebel blocks, so tight and dense at the start of the day, had disintegrated into groups. The bravest died, the rest ran. The Parliamentarian army, huge, fresh, and confident, had been routed by the redoubtable Cornish. They had been clawed from the formidable summit by a force less than half their size, smashed and scattered like white ash in the Stratton breeze.

And Stryker felt strangely elated. Here, amid the screams and the filthy smoke, the blood-drenched grass and the clatter of flying lead on pike staves, he was happy. This was what he knew. Where he felt most at home. Some men knew how to grow corn. Others – like his long dead father – could turn a sheep's grimy fleece into gleaming gold coins. But not Stryker. He knew how to fire a musket and wield a blade. He knew how to unhorse a cavalryman and deploy a pike block. He knew how to fight.

But the elation left him like wine from a punctured skin. Because, amid the mad, raging chaos of the battle, his single, gritty eye had caught sight of something – someone – he had not expected to see this day. It was the feather he saw first; tall, broad, black as a December night, quivering atop a gleaming helmet with the distinctive trio of face-guards worn by a harquebusier. Its owner was conspicuous, because on a hill crammed with infantrymen, he perched, proud and unflinching, on the back of a huge stallion. And that beast, snorting and mad-eyed, had a coat as black as the one beneath its rider's armour corselet.

Stryker stared at the cavalryman for what seemed like a lifetime, the clamour of battle blurring and muffling as he stared over men's heads and wavering pikes.

'Wild!' he bellowed. '*Wild*!'

The rider's eyes, pale blue like nuggets of fine glass, seemed to twitch at Stryker's call. He scanned the deep lines of men locked in bitter, private struggles until, in a moment that saw a slow smile form at the corners of his mouth, his cold gaze finally rested upon Stryker.

Stryker flicked his sword's tip, beckoning Wild to him, knowing the pair had unfinished business. He braced himself for the cavalryman's charge, to twirl away at the last moment or dive low to slice through the horse's thundering fetlocks.

To his surprise no attack came. He stared at Wild, surprised and baffled in equal measure as the colonel carefully turned his mount away. And then he saw it. The rope, knotted at the back of Wild's saddle. His eye traced its taut length until, in a single, gut-twisting moment, he saw the wretched man tied to its far end.

'O Jesu!'

In the north-east corner of the hill two men waited impatiently for Wild's return.

'We must leave,' Osmyn Hogg, witch-finder and reluctant Roundhead, hissed angrily when the colonel, prisoner in tow, steered his horse nonchalantly back from the southern part of the summit, where battle still raged. 'These craven fools are done. Finished!' He thrust out a finger, tracing it along the rear of the beleaguered remnants of the Parliamentarian army. 'Soon there will be none left, and we will be prisoners.'

Wild shot him a disparaging look. 'We have the horses, Master Hogg. Our escape will be swift when it comes.' His voice became low, acidic. 'Just wait a little longer, witch-catcher, and you will witness God's own miracle.'

'A miracle will be our survival,' José Ventura, Hogg's assistant, muttered.

Wild, the only soldier in the group, tore his horse round to face the corpulent Spaniard. 'Then get your greasy hide out of my sight.'

Ventura bridled, and Hogg had to raise a calming hand for peace. He nodded to his servant and cast his gaze back to Wild. 'He is right, Colonel. We should go. This is not our fight.'

Wild spat on the turf by his mount's wide hooves. 'A pox on you both! Go! Take yourselves down to Plymouth and catch the next ship to the New fuckin' World, for all I care. But you will miss the one thing you pray for most.'

Hogg was frightened. Petrified. He had thrown in his lot with the rebel army, only to find himself stuck on this God-forsaken hill while he watched Lord Stamford's mighty horde dash itself against Sir Ralph Hopton's rocks. He wanted to flee this vile place. And yet he had seen that ensign. Stryker's ensign, flown high above the men surging across the summit.

This was his chance. His one chance. It had been so long. He wanted to leave, but he knew he would stay.

Captain Innocent Stryker had worried for his protégé. When Burton had ridden into the darkness, he had fumed at the young officer's insubordination, but when the lieutenant had failed to return, that anger had turned to concern. In the heat and blood and commotion of battle, he had pushed such thoughts from his mind, daring to hope that his second-in-command was somewhere safe, perhaps watching the shocking Royalist victory from afar.

But now all that hope had gone. Andrew Burton was indeed watching the battle, but he was not at all safe.

'He goads you, sir!' Sergeant Skellen had warned as the pair stabbed and slashed and kicked and punched their way through the melee to reach the casually trotting Wild. 'Do not follow!'

Stryker knew it was a wise enough warning, for to break through to the land beyond the immediate fight was inviting trouble. That space at the rear of the remaining Roundhead line, towards the shallow escarpment that formed the northern slope of the hill, was still teeming with enemy soldiers, those waiting to see if the battle was truly lost or thinking to loot their own supply wagons.

Some, he imagined, simply waited to offer surrender and plead for quarter. To dash into that area, Skellen pointed out, was to risk overreaching themselves, becoming cut off from the rest of Hopton's still advancing force. Yet Stryker had seen Lieutenant Burton, tethered and led by Wild like an ox to slaughter, and he waved the sergeant's protests away.

The pair waded across the carpet of inert flesh, of discarded pikes, spent muskets, and dented metal that swathed the hill above Stratton. Men lay where they fell, dead-eyed and slack-jawed, macabre marionettes piled on the grass by some unseen puppet master. All around them, rebel soldiers ran away, taking their chances with the open land to the north or the sheer slope to the east. Some, formed in small but courageous groups, fought on. The majority were beginning to surrender.

One man stepped into Stryker's path having evidently decided to end the day in blood, jabbing at him with a partizan, the ornate blade at its head slicing towards his belly. Stryker blocked the blow with his sword before Skellen stepped out from the darkness of his left flank and cleaved the man's face clean in half.

Four pikemen, lethal poles still in hand, spied the pair as they strode on, and moved to intercept them. Skellen went to engage the grimacing men, and battered the first's pike aside with his halberd. He could not sever the killing tip because the pike's cheeks – strips of steel riveted to the staff below the head – held it intact, but he was already inside the weapon's killing range. The Roundhead released the pike as Skellen came at him, fumbling for his tuck, but the halberd's billhook had chopped through his ankle in the blink of an eye, and he was on the ground before he realized what had happened. His comrades, hitherto so brave with their snarls, dropped their own pikes and ran.

A fat sergeant with tawny sash at his portly midriff, blood-spattered sword in hand, made a surprise lunge from Stryker's right. The captain spun clear, parried the next blow, and kicked the sergeant in the guts, doubling him over. The fat Roundhead vomited, and Stryker opened the back of his skull with crimson steel.

Stryker pushed on, Skellen panting at his heels, and soon faced a braying musketeer. He made to check his advance, but slipped on a patch of blood, crunched on to a knee, and rolled haphazardly to his left. The move succeeded only in putting him at the feet of another enemy fighter, and he had to roll backwards this time to avoid the downward thrust of the man's tuck. The point drove deeply into the soil, becoming stuck for an instant, and Stryker lurched up, cannoning into the man's skinny waist with his whole weight. The pair crashed backwards in a chest-crushing tangle of limbs. Stryker found himself on top of the Parliament man, but his hands were pinned beneath the stricken Roundhead's shoulders, so he slammed his head down, breaking the man's long nose in a sickening explosion that sent a fine red spray up into Stryker's eye. He rolled away even as the man screamed, for he was entirely blinded, and frantically rubbed at his eye with a gloved palm. When his vision returned, the Roundhead was silent, Skellen standing over him, halberd buried deep in his chest.

And then they were clear, punching through the last of the Parliament's effective troops. Stryker realized that the reserve line, which he had spied during the throes of battle, had been routed and left the field.

'There he is!' Stryker pointed with his blade.

Sure enough, Wild's loping horse casually tore up the grass at the tree line at the hill's north-eastern edge, Lieutenant Andrew Burton in tow.

'Here!' Colonel Gabriel Wild called. 'Witch-finder!'

Osmyn Hogg caught the pistol cleanly and set about arming it. His fingers fumbled as they worked. 'We must do this quickly. They have overrun the entire army. Stamford is gone. Collings is away.'

Wild swore in exasperation. 'Do you wish to see Stryker die? Do you?'

'Aye.'

'Then hold your damned nerve. I will cut him down and chop off his stones. Once he has looked upon them, bleeding in my palm, I'll stick my blade in his heart and we will ride for Devon.'

'What if—'

'What if nothing,' Wild snarled. He jerked his head at the men who dashed in confused anarchic groups all about the hill, Royalists in pursuit. 'We have no insignia. No field signs that anyone here will recognize.' He patted his sword-hilt. 'They'll leave us for easier pickings.'

José Ventura picked his nose with his forefinger and inspected the produce. 'You promised we hang him.'

Wild turned on him. 'Do we have time for that, you swine-brained dolt? No, it must be over with quickly. You may go if you wish.' He stabbed a thumb at his metal chest. 'But I owe that bastard.'

'We will stay,' Osmyn Hogg intervened.

'And if I fail?' Wild asked warily.

Hogg patted the pistol. 'I know what to do.'

The colonel grinned suddenly. 'But I won't fail.'

Stryker and Skellen reached the group at the tree line. 'Wild!'

One of the horsemen turned at Stryker's call. The man, dressed in fine cavalry armour, slid immediately down from the saddle and strode across the grass, a half-smile on his lips.

'You humiliated me twice, Captain,' Colonel Gabriel Wild said, jauntily enough, but his blade appeared in his hand as he spoke.

Stryker shrugged disinterest. 'Perhaps you should think of becoming one of Stamford's clerks.'

Wild's amused demeanour slipped a touch as his face darkened. 'The powder wagon and then your trickery at the tor. I promised to kill you.'

Stryker let his eye drift beyond Wild to the three horses. One of those beasts, riderless now that Wild had come to challenge him, had a rope attached to its saddle. 'Just give him to me,' he said flatly, unwilling to look directly at Burton lest his friend's decrepit state put him off balance, 'and you can go free.'

Wild pursed his lips, dropped his visor into place and offered a sharp bow. 'Come and get him.'

'Want me to chop the fucker, sir?'

Stryker had forgotten his old comrade was there, and he glanced across at him. 'No, Will.'

Skellen sniffed. 'Thought not.'

The fight happened in the blink of an eye. Stryker barrelled into Wild with all the force he could muster, hammering his sword down at Wild's head in a great, bone-shattering strike. It slipped beyond the surprised rebel's guard, clipping his helmet, slicing down the left side and ricocheting off one of the rivets set into the cheek-guard. Wild darted out of range, sneered, brought his blade up sharply for the next action. He did not wait long, for Stryker lunged again, raining blow after blow at the Parliamentarian's head and torso. But Wild was quick, a classically trained fighter, and parried the strikes with little more than scorn, twisting away after half a dozen sure-handed blocks.

And then Wild went on to the attack, stepping in with sword high, tip angled down at Stryker's face, a serpent ready to bite. In a flash he made three quick downward thrusts that had Stryker skittering backwards, the great hill ringing with the song of swords. Stryker parried desperately, a ragged street fighter compared with Wild's cultured ripostes. But he had survived, defence still intact, and the pair stepped out of the killing zone, dragging rasped gulps of air into burning lungs.

Wild came back first, feinting at Stryker's right, then switching the blade to attack hard down his left side, eager to exploit so obvious a weakness. But Stryker was used to such a ploy, had long since learned to adjust the angle of his head when he fought so that he could perceive a deal more than his opponents imagined, and his sword, garnet winking in the pommel, was a match for the onslaught.

Wild stepped back again, and Stryker lurched at the Roundhead, suddenly aware of his enemy's own weak-ness. The cavalryman wore the full armoured corselet of his profession. His head, neck, chest, and back, even one of his arms, were encased in metal, and that would have set him in good stead on horseback, but here, on terra firma, fighting a man who had been fed on hand-to-hand combat since joining a company of mercenaries at the age of seventeen, he was dreadfully encumbered.

And Stryker felt a surge of confidence because he could already see Wild's reddening cheeks behind the visor. Stryker wore no steel, his only concession to protection being the buff-coat that would turn most blades, and it gave him far greater speed. He lunged again, one, two, three, four, five quick blows that forced Wild to retreat. Wild was alive to them, defended them with admirable skill, but Stryker could see that he was beginning to tire.

He drove again, aiming for speed above power, forcing the harquebusier to move quicker and quicker, combining lunges and cuts to keep Wild fighting for breath and for balance.

One of Wild's increasingly desperate lunges came too close, the blade slashing beside his neck, slicing the air with a gut-wrenching zing, but he knocked it down, the steel bouncing off his upper arm, its venom absorbed by the buff-coat. Stryker went forward again, remorseless, relentless, knowing his grey eye would be shining with the quicksilver of battle.

It was a musket-ball that changed things. Fired by a fleeing greycoat who had evidently spotted one of his comrades locked in mortal duel, he had paused in his escape, fired, and tossed the musket away, never waiting to see whether the ball flew true. Fortunately for Stryker, it hadn't. The bullet raced through the space between him and Wild, sailing beyond the assembled onlookers to tear a fresh, bright scar in the bark of one of the trees that cloaked the eastern escarpment. Stryker instinctively glanced to where it had impacted, but Wild did not, and the colonel lashed out with his broadsword in a blow that would have cleaved Stryker's head from his neck.

Stryker got his own sword up, but the parry was late, feeble, and the blade skittered from his grasp, leaving him to grope the air.

Wild grinned, and in that moment Stryker could see his own death. He saw the cavalryman's blade lift for the final execution, sucked in one last, chest-bursting breath, and bolted forward. Wild, gripping his blade in both hands, was powerless to resist as his intended victim took him squarely in the chest.

Stryker closed his eye as he barrelled in, feeling the cold breastplate against his cheek. The big Parliamentarian reeled backwards, dropping his sword, but he was a wily fighter, and he let Stryker come, gave ground willingly so that he would not lose his footing. When the pair slowed, both standing, locked together in a grotesque embrace, Wild slammed his head down, smashing the peak of his steel visor into Stryker's brow.

Stryker's world went red, then black, then white as he staggered back, a jet of vomit filling his mouth, harsh and acidic. He would not fall – could not allow it – but the pain flared through his head as if a mortar shell had landed on his skull. He put a hand up, felt the blood fountain from a ragged gash in his forehead, and wondered what had become of his hat.

And then Colonel Gabriel Wild was in his face, looming like a silhouette, laughing. Somehow he had retrieved his sword, and he held it out menacingly with one hand, removing his helmet with the other. He tossed the feathered pot clear, and shook out his long hair. Stryker gazed at him with blurred vision, at the silver stripe, broad and badger-like through the centre of Wild's brown locks.

'I'm going to slice off your ballocks, Captain Stryker,' Wild said in a low, silken voice. 'You have made me break too many promises of late, but this is one I intend to keep.'

And Stryker kicked him.

He kicked him once, right between the colonel's legs, a blow instilled with memories: of the tor, of the deaths and privations Stryker's company had been forced to endure, and of the gently swinging corpse of Otilwell Broom. It was a dirty move, he knew. One that would not have been employed by a gentleman. But Innocent Stryker was not a gentleman, and he cracked his boot home, pulping Wild's balls in a swift, violent second.

Wild howled, bent low, gripped his testicles, and Stryker stamped his boot heel into the side of the colonel's knee, grinding as hard as he could, feeling for the point where the joint began to buckle. It collapsed as he knew it would, bending inwards on itself with an audible crunch. The colonel brayed like a gelded bear and crumpled sideways, not knowing whether to paw at his smashed knee or his mangled groin. Stryker kicked him once more, this time in the chin, and the harque-busier commander, so proud and strong, collapsed in a heap on his back.

Stryker searched briefly for his sword, caught the twinkle of the garnet-set pommel, and went to retrieve it. When he strode back to Wild, the stricken cavalryman was just regaining some semblance of lucidity, peering up at Stryker with hate-filled eyes.

'I've beaten you again, Gabriel,' Stryker said, bending over him.

'Kill me,' Wild hissed through broken teeth. 'Kill me, you one-eyed bastard!'

Stryker shook his head. 'I think not. You're my prisoner.'

That seemed to enrage Wild further, and he made to stand. 'No. No! I would rather die!'

But Stryker's foot was on his plated chest, compelling him to lie back. 'Indeed,' he said quietly. He took a knee, whispering into Wild's ear. 'The dead don't remember, Colonel. And I want you to remember.'

'Captain Stryker!' The voice rang out like a church bell, clear and crisp, from somewhere near the trees.

Stryker cast Wild a last, withering look and stood. He wobbled there for a moment, the battle-frenzy draining from his legs, making him suddenly dizzy. Men rushed past them, Roundheads taking their chances with the steeply forested slope to the east and the gentler but more exposed route to the north, pursued by crowing Cornishmen, eager to kill and loot. The air was ripe with the stench of fresh blood. Gulls glided lazily overhead, bellies already made fat by their corpse feast.

The voice jolted him again. 'Stryker!'

This time he followed it, vision finally restored, and he saw the group of men who had been with Wild. One man was swarthy and disgustingly fat, his mount clearly struggling beneath him. The second, the one who had hailed him, had an unmistakably large nose, ridiculously prominent teeth that prevented him from completely closing his mouth, and appeared like a raven in black doublet, breeches, cloak, and boots. The sight of the third man made him feel physically sick. He was still tied to the rope behind Wild's riderless mount, face cast down, shoulders hunched. Stryker stared at him for a long time. He saw the welts at his lips and cheeks, saw the grotesquely swollen eyes that carried swirls of yellow, blue, and black, saw the smashed, crooked nose.

'Christ, Andrew,' was all he could think to say. He began to walk closer.

'Ah, ah, ah,' Osmyn Hogg muttered suddenly. He raised his hand, producing a pistol, flicking it between Stryker and Skellen. 'It is loaded.'

Both men froze, dropped their weapons. 'Andrew,' Stryker tried again.

The blackened, pulpy face rose to greet him as Burton peered out from eyes battered to slits. 'Captain,' he murmured, unable to properly speak.

Stryker tried to smile, to offer some kind of encouragement, but the expression became more of a grimace. 'I—I am sorry, Andrew. For everything—'

Burton seemed to offer a nod. 'Friends, sir.'

Stryker did smile then. 'Aye, lad, friends.'

'Enough,' Hogg interrupted. He smirked. 'All these years, Stryker. All these years I have waited to repay you. I limp still, terribly, did you know?'

'Yes.'

'And that kind of thing cannot go unpunished, now, can it?'

'I thought you wanted me hanged for a witch,' Stryker said, stalling for time.

'I did. Do!' He shook his head slowly. 'But sadly my hand has been forced. Or should I say *God's* hand?'

Stryker looked into Hogg's eyes and saw that the man meant what he said. He also read nervousness there, a vein of anxiety that might make a man's hand unsteady. Hogg

517

had just one shot. He would take his chances. 'You have me, sir. Revenge is yours.'

Osmyn Hogg chuckled. He glanced across at Ventura. 'Go, señor. Lead on.'

The Spaniard peered left and right, evidently gauging which route to take. Noticing the greater numbers of Royalists already beginning to gather on the northern slope, he kicked at his mount, steering it towards the lip of the forested eastern face.

Hogg straightened his arm, the pistol's black mouth gaping at Stryker, ready to spit its death. 'You would have me fire, Captain, because you feel I am a poor shot. Perhaps I would miss. And you would most likely be right. Besides, I cannot kill both you *and* your sergeant.' He smiled, a motion that barely registered beyond his lips. 'But revenge comes in many forms, wouldn't you agree?'

The shot seemed abnormally loud now that the battle was petering out.

Hogg's horse whinnied, turned a wide, skittering circle in its fright, and then it was gone, vanished with its triumphal rider down the tree-covered slope.

And Captain Innocent Stryker screamed.

He screamed because the witch-finder had not taken his chances with the range. Because he had swept his outstretched arm across his body and taken aim at the prisoner tied only a few feet away. Because the pistol flint had sparked bright. Because the small leaden ball, which might have been a lump of round-shot at such close proximity, had flown true. And because, in that terrible, deafening moment Lieutenant Andrew Burton had died.

*

The men of Sir Edmund Mowbray's Regiment of Foot, those that were not off scavenging for loot or intoxicated by bloodlust, gathered at the tree line.

There were around seventy of them, made up of the companies of Innocent Stryker and Lancelot Forrester, the regiment's second and fourth captains respectively. Forrester led them now, had maintained their cohesion when Stryker had broken from the line, and had kept the pikes tight and the muskets firing until, against all the odds, the rebel line had splintered. And then he had marched them in good order to the edge of a copse, where one of his men had spied their missing captain locked in a duel with a man many of the redcoats immediately recognized.

'Truss up that badger-skulled bugger,' Captain Lancelot Forrester ordered when his men first reached the prone form of Colonel Wild. 'He belongs to us now.'

Wild thrust palms into the earth and pushed himself up so that he was sitting. He gazed at Forrester, pale eyes blazing like fire on ice. 'I will kill you, sir.'

Forrester sheathed his bloody sword and folded his arms. 'Not hugely likely, is it?'

'*Sir!*'

Forrester looked up at the sharp hail, recognizing Simeon Barkworth. The Scot, every inch of his scarred face shimmering with blood, had found Forrester in the melee. He had fought bravely, ferociously, yellow eyes bright with each kill. Yet now Barkworth's eyes seemed dull, his shoulders strangely rounded. He was standing beside a tall man with bald head and hooded eyes, clutching a huge halberd.

Forrester beamed. 'Skellen! Glad you made it!'

It was then that he saw a man kneeling between the

pair, his back to the company. He wore a dark, nondescript doublet, but Forrester could see the long, raven-black hair tied in a ragged tail at the base of the neck, and he knew he had found his friend.

He strode past Wild, nodded happily at the blood-sheeted faces of Barkworth and Skellen, and tapped Stryker's back lightly with a toe. 'I've a bone to pick with you, old man. Why in Christ's name did you leave the line? That was fooli—'

Stryker turned to look at him then, and his narrow face, bloody though it was, was pale, his grey eye dull. And Forrester looked beyond him, saw that he cradled the head of a man in his hands, and only after several lingering moments did he recognize Lieutenant Burton. He straightened and took a step back. 'Oh Lord.'

Stryker was not listening.

He turned back to Lieutenant Burton's sagging body, finally released of its bonds by Skellen's deftly twitched halberd, and just stared. He stared at the eyes, open but unseeing, at the face made almost unrecognizable by pulping fists, and at the blood that glistened from the deep hole in his forehead. A pistol ball was small, but this one had been fired at horrifically close range. It had caught Burton to the right of his brow, just above the eye, and punched through skin and bone and brain, carving a tunnel that grew as it travelled, as the ball flattened with the impact, until it exploded through the back of the skull to nestle in the trees beyond.

Burton had died instantly, head punched back, rope snapped taut, legs turning to columns of water. Lieutenant Andrew Burton, who had come to war with a childlike view of the world, and had learned to fight like a warrior.

Stryker felt the thickness in his throat, felt his eye sting. Through the fog he caught the sound of Forrester's voice again, but this time it was a harsher tone, strained and querulous. Stryker forced himself to look away from Burton, and saw that his fellow captain had drawn his sword and was advancing upon Wild.

'No! Forry, no!'

Forrester spun on his heel, and Stryker saw that his friend's jaw quivered, his chest heaved, eyes glistened. 'What, Stryker? God, man, what?'

'It wasn't him.'

Forrester let his blade drop, struggling to understand. 'It wasn't him?'

Stryker shook his head, took his hand from behind Burton's head, wiped the blood from his fingers, and stood. 'It was Hogg.'

Forrester frowned. 'The witch-catcher?'

Stryker nodded mutely, still dazed by the fight and the murder.

Forrester stalked up to him. 'Well where, by the Virgin's blessed womb, did he go?'

'It will not go! *Culero*!'

Osmyn Hogg, thirty or so paces down the hill's eastern face, looked back up at his assistant. The pair had cantered straight over the brow of the hill, only to find that the slope, down which so many rebel troops had escaped, was far steeper than they had expected. It had been dreadfully difficult to negotiate the terrain, littered as it was with rocks and roots, brambles and vast beech trees, but Ventura, horse already struggling beneath him on the flat summit, was barely progressing at all.

'You're too fat, José! Get off and run!'

Ventura's sweaty jowls shook vigorously. 'I cannot manage slope.'

'Nor can your horse!'

Hogg stared up at the escarpment's highest point, checking for pursuers. A number of men wearing orange sashes and ribbons emerged from the trees, looking to flee from the crushing defeat, but they did not concern him. His only thought was of a black-clothed Cavalier with long hair and a hideously scarred face. By God, he thought, revenge had been sweeter than he could ever have foreseen. Now, of course, he needed to be away. 'By God, José, we must flee!'

And then he saw them. It was not the scarred man, mercifully, but at least a score of redcoats. They streamed out of the trees like a horde of demons, flowing down the near vertical slope in a great tide. He turned away. '*I must flee.*'

Ventura was staring, open-mouthed, at the thundering redcoats, and he turned back to see Hogg's horse begin to move. '*No!*' he screamed at Hogg's back. 'Señor, no! Do not leave me!'

The slopes of Stratton Hill claimed many victims. The routed rebels leapt down the escarpments with victorious Royalists at their heels. Some made it clear, some were captured, but many, too many, lost their footing in the panic and tumbled headlong into trees, breaking necks and backs. Twisted bodies blanketed the torrid land, escaping steel and lead only to fall victim to the terrain and their eagerness to be away.

But the redcoats of Sir Edmund Mowbray's Regiment

of Foot paid the Devon men no heed. They had won the day as much as the jubilant Cornish, had every right to chase down the fugitives or take well-earned respite or strip the hundreds of corpses that now offered up clothing, money, weapons, and trinkets to the victors. The redcoats had a new quarry now, however. They had all seen their lieutenant's broken corpse, had all felt the rage etched into the faces of their captains, and now they hunted.

William Skellen's tall stride took him to the front of the braying pack as they surged down through the trees like scarlet-pelted wolves. He leapt over the ruts and humps of the incline, the soil crumbling and sliding at his every footfall, acutely aware that one step out of place could see him in a shattered heap at the bottom of the hill. He saw the two horsemen, focussed on the nearest, and hurled himself forward.

Skellen caught José Ventura, pounced at him like a giant cat, careened into the Spaniard's blubbery side, and smashed him from the saddle.

The pair fell, tore at one another with bare hands, all the while rolling down the slope. Eventually they collided with the base of a soaring beech, and it was Skellen who bore the brunt of the impact, the unmoving trunk knocking the wind from him, his halberd long gone, bouncing and clanging its way into a dense patch of bracken.

Ventura was in no mood to fight, and he made to flee, scrabbling with fingernails at the shifting earth, but Skellen was up quickly, drawing breath into his squashed chest, desperately trying to keep up the chase. He scrambled on to all fours, sighted Ventura's wide body as the Spaniard negotiated the steep escarpment, and went to

523

run him down. In his haste he lost his footing again, and the earth burst from under him in a miniature landslide that carried him with it. He managed to stay upright at first, but the slide took him over an exposed tree root, his boot snagged, and the tall sergeant pitched violently. He rolled, bouncing off loose soil, clipping gnarled roots, crushing flowers, and praying that his head would not meet one of the jagged rocks.

In the whirling collage of browns and greens, of red coats, grey coats, lichen-crusted trunks, and boulders darkened by moss, Skellen could not tell which way was up, and he thrust out an arm, clawing at the ground, the air, anything, desperate to slow his descent. His fingers clipped something. He could not tell what, for the leather gloves removed that level of sensitivity, but he snapped shut his palm all the same.

He stopped. Suddenly, shockingly. A scream exploded from him as his arm stretched tight, snapped rigid, and his body jerked to a dead halt, tearing at the muscles in his shoulder. For a moment he lay there, white-hot tongues of fire licking down the side of his torso, but the pain soon ebbed, and he lifted his head to see the knurled bow of an exposed tree root in his fist.

'I'll pray every day,' Skellen murmured, glancing skyward. 'Least I'll try.'

He hauled himself up, clutching his wrenched arm close, sucking air through gritted teeth with even the tiniest movement. The damage was probably extensive, he thought, considering how bloody agonizing his upper arm was and, more worryingly, the fact that he couldn't feel his hand at all. But at least it wasn't all bad.

A call came from further up the slope: 'Is he dead?'

Skellen looked down at the contorted body of José Ventura. The Spaniard stared back at him, but his brown eyes, bulging from their sockets, had no light in them. One of his fleshy arms was bent in the wrong direction where the elbow joint had shattered, and, though his head faced the sergeant, the rest of his gross bulk seemed to be twisted in the opposite direction, a manoeuvre Skellen imagined only an owl could manage. Ventura had evidently fallen too, only his descent had ended in a snapped neck.

Osmyn Hogg thanked God. Not silently, not in sombre reverence, but in a howl that startled carrion birds from their cadaver banquet and echoed up and down the slopes. It was unbecoming of a man of his standing, but now, in this wonderful moment of skin-prickling relief, he did not care.

He had made it.

Hogg had been rewarded for his life of diligent servitude with the gift of the better horse. They had looked the same, his mount and Ventura's, but where the latter's would not negotiate the slope, Hogg's had proven its worth. It had bolted headlong down the escarpment. It had leapt branches where men tripped, had rounded blood-speckled bushes, powered past fleeing Roundheads and hacking Cavaliers, and taken the steep, loose, sliding, treacherous soil quite literally in its stride. And now he was at the lower portion of the slope, where the steepness petered out into a gentle curve as it approached the glistening river. For a moment his heart almost stopped as he realized that the waterway would need to be forded, but he could see that bodies had begun to pile up in places where men had been cut down or drowned, and between those dams of flesh the river had been reduced to a stream.

'Praise God!' he bellowed, wondering if the redcoats could hear, *hoping* they could. All those years of waiting for revenge. All those nights of sleeplessness he had endured, the terrible pain in his rump, put there by an arrogant boy's pistol. All those nights lying with that incessant ache, staring at the ceiling, imagining that boy's end. And now he had had his revenge. Not the revenge he had planned, but this was infinitely better. Stryker's face had been exactly as Wild had predicted – exquisitely twisted with anguish – and he would now live with the pain as Hogg had.

'Seek His will in all you do!' he cried as the horse splashed into the sun-dappled shallows, dyed murky and red. 'And He will show you which path to take!'

The sound of the shot pounded through the trees.

Hogg felt the horse shudder beneath him.

'No,' he whispered in disbelief. He kicked at the beast, thrashed at its neck with his hands. '*No!*'

It would not move. Would not respond at all. It let out a strange mewing sound, sidled to the left, slewed back, staggering like a drunkard. Hogg twisted in the saddle, peering into the trees to see if anyone pursued, but he could not see further than a few yards into the gloom. He turned back, kicked again, but the wheezing animal ignored him, blew a spray of bubbling foam from its flared nostrils, gave a final, juddering whinny, and slumped to its fore-knees. Hogg slid forward with a rasping cry, pitched clean out of the saddle, and tumbled across the beast's neck, scrabbling to grasp the coarse mane as he fell. He slammed into the stream, the splashing water ringing like laughter in his ears, breath punched out of him as he hit the slimy bed.

And then he was fighting, thrashing to free his hands

and knees from the sucking silt, wrenching his upper body up and out of the water lest he drown like all the others. Finally he was out, sitting, saved, praising God again as air filled his lungs. It reeked of sulphur, but he had never taken a more welcome breath.

He was facing the hill now, still on his haunches, the cold river reaching his belly. He stared into the woodland, at the tall beeches, at the broken bodies, at the dark slope that led up to a field drenched in blood. And in that second, that quiet, peaceful moment, he realized God had not shown him the right path to take. Because out from the shadows stepped a man. A man with a narrow face that was horribly scarred down its left side; whose hair was long and black as night, and whose clothes were stained in the blood of others.

Stryker let the smoking musket drop from his grasp and crossed the short distance to the river.

He stared down at the horse, its legs still twitching. 'Poor bastard. A bad shot.'

Osmyn Hogg peered up from the riverbed with eyes that were nearly all white. 'I am your prisoner, sir.'

Stryker drew his sword slowly, letting the delicious rasp of steel linger, revelling in the way it made Hogg's face convulse. 'Lieutenant Burton was your prisoner.'

Hogg swallowed hard, his neck pulsing in time with the muscles of his face. 'I—I—'

'You?'

'I accept quarter!' Hogg blurted, reaching out to Stryker with clawed hands, as a beggar would pull a rich man's cloak. Stryker thought he saw tears in the witch-finder's eyes, though it might have been river water.

He waded into the river, boots splashing in the stillness of this part made quiet by its morbid dam, holding his blade low, the tip nestling against Hogg's chest.

Hogg winced at the touch, flinched, but stayed put, too frightened to make any sudden moves. 'I accept quarter!' he shrieked again.

'No, witch-finder,' Stryker said calmly, voice low. 'None has been offered.'

That shook Hogg into life. His eyes hardened, face becoming rigid with hate. 'You are a devil, Stryker,' he spat. 'A wicked fiend who would shoot a man of God for a whore! That whore suckled imps. She deserved to die. And so do you.'

Captain Stryker thought of Beth Lipscombe then, the woman who might have died by Hogg's hand, and of Otilwell Broom and all the other innocents who had doubtless been tortured and killed by this man. Walked and swum and pricked and hanged. And he thought of Andrew Burton, his friend and protégé, who, even now, stared unseeing at the Cornish clouds. He shook his head. 'Not today.'

Stryker's arm moved with all the power those memories instilled, driving the blade upwards vertically from Hogg's chest, into his chin, and on through bone and skin and muscle and lips and teeth, stopping only when it hit his long nose.

Osmyn Hogg – priest, witch-finder, and Stryker's enemy – could not scream for his mouth was a glistening ruin, but a wet-sounding gurgle escaped from deep within his body. He rocked back, face cleaved near in two by a broadsword that had been a gift from a queen. The blade slid free, staying firmly in its wielder's grip, but Hogg kept falling until his torso, shoulders, and head broke through the water by turns.

Stryker stepped on him. He eased his heel into the softness of Hogg's throat, felt the witch-finder jerk back helplessly like an enormous speared fish. Bubbles erupted at the surface, red and manic like tiny volcanoes, but Stryker kept his boot there, hard and unyielding. He could see Hogg's wide eyes through the water, felt his body thrash, but the sword blow had smashed his senses, bled him to weakness, and the struggles were feeble. Stryker lingered, weight pressed inexorably down, watching for the bubbles to fade. And then they were gone, the stream flattening above Hogg's face, carrying his blood away to mix with the blood of all the other dead.

In that moment Stryker realized he had been holding his own breath, and he let it out in a great sigh that made him shudder. He paced back to the bank, allowing the body to float so that Hogg's enormous nose slipped above the surface like the mast of a wrecked ship.

'It's over.'

Stryker had been in a dream – a nightmare – since seeing the pistol ball dash Burton's skull to smithereens, and now, in the sudden calm of the forest, the voice of a friend returned him to crashing reality. He turned. 'Over, Will?'

Sergeant Skellen, clutching his right shoulder close, nodded. 'Aye, sir. You got 'im. You won.'

More nodding heads came into Stryker's dazed awareness. Faces he knew. Forrester was there, bloody and panting, Barkworth too, eyes shining in the gloom. Sergeant Heel had survived, holding a halberd that looked as though it had been dipped into a vat of crimson dye, and Ensign Chase still clutched the company's standard. They were all there.

Almost all.

'Won?' Stryker asked wearily. He turned back to the river, to the macabre dam and the cadaver floating at its surface. It was starting to rain.

EPILOGUE

The hill was empty, the armies gone.

The morning sunlight cast great, shifting shadows across the stained summit as clouds raced off the coast. Down in the villages, men still died. They would keep dying for weeks as wounds festered and blood became poisoned. At least in that, Stryker reckoned, young Burton had been lucky. Better to die outright than take a bullet that turned your flesh bad, stinking out some musty chamber while they waited for you to breathe your last. That was what he told himself, anyway.

The cart lurched suddenly as its driver whipped the lumbering nags into life. The men of Sir Edmund Mowbray's Regiment of Foot removed their headwear. So many hats, pots, monteros, and Monmouths snatched away out of deference for one of their own. They had lost many men in the great battle, and each had received a solemn burial. But this man, this body already white-skinned, purple-marbled, and stiff was an officer, and he garnered the utmost respect.

They had guarded him through the night, slept beside the trees on the summit, stared into the blackness like an army of grim-faced ghouls, shielding the lieutenant from the looters who crept across the hill, cloaked by the dark, stripping corpses and making new ones of those who still drew breath. And in the morning they had scared away the flesh-ripping ravens and found a cart, a pair of skinny dray horses, and a driver. A sombre preacher had bellowed at the dawn sky for Burton's soul, and then the lieutenant was away, trundling south to Stratton and a place in the grounds of St Andrew's Church. Stryker would write and tell Burton's soon-to-be heartbroken parents of his final resting place. He would be compelled to describe the young officer's death as well. He would lie.

'Stamford's in Bideford,' Captain Lancelot Forrester said as he fingered the hole in his hat, his eyes never leaving the cart, 'or so they say.'

Stryker, at Forrester's side, felt exhausted, utterly empty, but he managed a wry smile. 'Whispering of a great defeat for an army led by James Chudleigh, no doubt.'

Forrester shared the smile. 'Of course! But the King will be mighty happy. We took divers arms and supplies. Not to mention their thirteen wicked guns, a mortar, and more than threescore barrels of powder.'

Stryker looked at him. 'They had that much?'

'And we had four by the end. Would you countenance it?' Forrester shook his head at the improbability of it all. 'A damned miracle, that's what it was. A miracle.'

Stryker turned his gaze back to the cart. 'Butcher's bill?'

'No more than a hundred.'

'Theirs?'

Forrester pulled a dark grimace. 'Thrice that number, and we have seven hundred in our cells, with Chudleigh taken as well. Suffice to say, Cornwall is secure. They'll

532

make old Sir Ralph a bloody lord next, you mark my words.'

'He'd deserve it.'

Forrester lifted the hat, inspected the hole made by a musket-ball back in Peter Tavy. 'They all do. Grenville, Slanning, and the rest. Mad Cornish warriors, every man jack of 'em. They remind me of Rupert.'

Stryker nodded. 'You're right. Worried to fight with them, terrified of fighting against them.' He glanced at Forrester, seeing his friend still fiddling with the frayed hole. 'Did Mister Jays fight well?'

'Well enough, aye.' He paused as a drumbeat thrummed from the direction of Bude common. 'I'm pleased he took my offer of the king's commission. He'll make a good officer.'

'Lest he turn his coat again.'

'His coat is now red as that wound,' Forrester said firmly, eyes darting up to the deep, livid valley carved across Stryker's forehead by the peak of Wild's helmet. 'And if he is foolish enough to let it fade back to grey, he shall have me to deal with.' He replaced the hat, face becoming stern. 'I saw you speaking with Grenville after the battle.'

Stryker touched the throbbing cut at his head, feeling along the puffy skin and the raised, lumpy stitches. Grenville had come to him as he had been sewn back together by the light of a fire kindled by broken pike shafts. 'Sir Bevil has unfinished business.'

'You're going for her?'

'Colonel Wild is under lock and key, and he must sing for his supper,' Stryker replied, wincing as his fingertips brushed a particularly sensitive knot of skin. 'He claims

533

Cecily had told them nothing when last he saw her. She was taken to London by an intelligencer named Collings. I have been asked to go after her.'

'Asked?' Forrester echoed archly.

'Without leave to refuse, naturally.'

'Naturally.'

Stryker braced himself for the question he almost dreaded to ask. 'You'll come?'

Forrester rubbed his chin slowly, stared at the ground, at the trees, at the sky. Then he grinned. 'Thought you'd never ask. Will we be able to track down this Collings too?'

Stryker shrugged. 'Perhaps.'

'I imagine he would know where to locate a certain Terrence Richardson. Grenville may have unfinished business, but so, my dear friend, do I.'

'We'll get them, Forry,' Stryker said, and found that he believed his own conviction. 'We'll get them.'

Forrester whistled softly. 'But how in God's name will we discover the whereabouts of Miss Cade?'

'One of our agents is there already, so Sir Bevil claims, keeping watch upon Whitehall.'

Forrester frowned. 'Any idea who?'

'No.'

The cart had vanished from view, and the pair turned away, making for the place where they had left their snapsacks.

'Dangerous business,' Forrester said as he walked. 'We leave soon?'

Stryker stopped, nodded. 'In two days. I have one more matter to attend first.'

'Seek Wisdom, I—'

'You did what you had to, boy,' the old man interrupted. 'I can't blame you for that.'

Captain Stryker had returned to the tor with a deal of trepidation. He had left the place in a hurry. Such a hurry, indeed, that he had never been able to thank a certain Welsh hermit for all of his help. And, more importantly, apologize for destroying the tunnel that had been the former priest's secret protection for so long.

'It was the only way I could take down enough of Wild's troopers to make a difference.'

'I know, boy. I know.' He flipped back his head to stare directly upwards, pale eyes the same colour as the sky. 'The Lord Almighty knows too, don't you Lord?'

Seek Wisdom and Fear the Lord Gardner had not been the vision of anger Stryker had expected to find. The stoat-thin, filth-clogged recluse had rushed down from the granite parapet of the high tor upon glimpsing the small party of redcoats led by a man in black with a hideously disfigured face. And he had grinned his toothless grin and worried at his greasy, grey beard and slapped his skeletal thighs with delight.

And that had given Stryker an idea. 'Well? What say you?'

Gardner had initially refused Stryker's offer outright, but now, having met these men again, it was clear he had begun to allow the proposal to snag in his mind. He glanced back up at the lonely, wind-bleached crag, then back at Stryker. 'You're certain your colonel would allow it?'

Stryker nodded. 'I'm told our old preacher died of an ague a month ago. Besides, he is aware of my habit of collecting strays.' He turned to look at Skellen, mounted at his left flank. 'Wouldn't you have said, Sergeant?'

Skellen sucked at his rotten teeth. 'Right enough, sir. It's a sickness, the colonel says.' He glanced meaningfully at the diminutive man seated on a piebald gelding nearby. 'He'll have you treated soon as someone finds a cure.'

Simeon Barkworth sneered back, muttered something acerbic in his throttled voice, causing Skellen to grin broadly.

'What say you, Seek Wisdom?' Stryker asked. 'You won't regret it.'

'Aye, boy,' Seek Wisdom and Fear the Lord Gardner replied with a roguish wink, 'but you bloody might.'

LONDON, JUNE 1643

Clouds scudded across the capital's sky, cloaking the stars and dimming the moon. A cold breeze whipped at the waterman as he eased his boat into the freezing river.

'Where to?'

His passenger, faceless beneath a voluminous black cowl, did not speak but simply pointed to the opposite bank.

'Temple Stairs?' the waterman asked, pushing off when the passenger offered a single nod and turned a thin coin between thumb and forefinger.

The small boat rocked, its hull slapped the surface, the splashes of the paddle seemingly cacophonous in the quiet night, but it sliced through the inky water stealthily enough, waterman and fare keeping watch over the north bank in silence.

At the stairs the cowled figure alighted, tossed the coin into its new owner's waiting palm, and slipped into the city.

The figure was swift and alert, scuttling along the filthy streets like a feral cat, footfalls a mere whisper, eyes glinting from the cloak's sepulchral recesses. The human shadow ghosted along Fleet Street, up into Shoe Lane, then right, passed Ely Place and over the stinking Fleet River. It darted into a narrow lane when a racking cough broke the stillness up ahead, and waited, patient and calm, for the noise to abate.

Off it went again, swift and nimble, aware of the danger a city teeming with soldiers posed, but utterly unafraid.

The figure arrived at a small building on Pie Corner, the stink of Smithfield invading the air even at this hour, and knocked three times on the worm-eaten door, then once more to complete the code. A man appeared, lantern in hand, wart-infested face glowing demonically in the illumination.

'In.'

The figure slipped inside. The door clicked firmly shut behind.

They whisked up a slender corridor, never speaking, turning left through another doorway. And then they were in a tiny chamber, unfurnished and stinking of damp.

The figure lifted a hand and tugged back the hood. 'Well? Where is she?'

The warty man gazed in amazement, almost dropping his lamp. 'What is the meaning—?'

The figure was a woman. A woman with long, blonde

537

hair, eyes like a pair of sapphires, and a temper akin to a powder keg. She stepped close, arm snapping out like a snake, fine dagger in her delicate hand, and she let the tip just nick one of the warts at the man's stubbly chin. It began to bleed profusely, but he knew better than to move.

'No more chatter,' she hissed, her accent rich with a Gallic tone. 'I am come from the Queen herself. Where is she? Cecily Cade.'

The man swallowed as though a boiled egg had been stuffed down his throat. 'We—we received word only yesterday, madam. She is kept in a house up on Corn Hill.'

The woman frowned. 'A house?'

The man nodded swiftly, eyes still firmly fixed on the knife. 'The home of a grand man. One of the rebel generals, named Erasmus Collings. God place a pox on him.'

She lowered the blade at the last remark, smiled at his sigh of relief. 'It is guarded well?'

'Very well, madam.'

She thought for a moment, sheathed the blade, made to turn. 'You will show me this house, sir.'

'You'll never get her out, madam,' the man warned. 'You'd need an army at your back, an' that's no word of a lie.'

Lisette Gaillard, Queen Henrietta Maria's most trusted agent, looked at him then, flashing a broad, gleaming grin. 'I have one, monsieur. And he is on his way.'

The man looked nonplussed. 'He?'

'*Oui*. A man named Stryker.'

ACKNOWLEDGEMENTS

First and foremost, thanks to my editor Kate Parkin, whose expertise has, as ever, been crucial. Much appreciation must also go to the whole team at John Murray and Hodder, including Caro Westmore, Lyndsey Ng, James Spackman, Ben Gutcher, and Hilary Hammond, to name but a few.

Huge thanks to my agent, Rupert Heath, who has, once again, been a priceless source of advice and guidance.

Many thanks to Richard Foreman and everyone at Chalke, and to Martin Abbott of the Sealed Knot, whose knowledge of the Battle of Stratton was absolutely invaluable. And thanks, yet again, to Malcolm Watkins of Heritage Matters, for casting an expert and insightful eye over the manuscript. Ultimately, though, all mistakes remain my own.

Thanks to my son, Joshua, for doing his bit for sales (shouting excitedly whenever he spots one of my books in a shop window). And last but not least, love and thanks to my parents, John and Gerry, and to my wife Rebecca, for their constant support and encouragement. The novels really wouldn't happen without you.

HISTORICAL NOTE

When the truce in the south-west (in place since 28 February 1643) expired on 22 April, war was resumed in earnest. After victories for both sides (at Launceston for the Royalists and Sourton Down for the Parliamentarians) the factions gathered at Stratton for the decisive encounter of this phase of the war.

As I have noted in the book, the rout at Sourton Down cost Sir Ralph Hopton more than weapons, stores, and gunpowder. In the confusion the rebels also captured the Royalist general's portmanteau, containing letters from King Charles ordering the Cornish army to join forces with the Marquis of Hertford and Prince Maurice in Somerset. This crucial piece of intelligence compelled the Parliamentarian commander, the Earl of Stamford, to take the initiative.

Acutely aware of the need to prevent the two enemy armies combining, Stamford mustered all available forces at Torrington, Devon, with the view to destroying Hopton while he was still weak. With a force of 1,400 horse and 5,400 foot, he crossed the Cornish border.

The Battle of Stratton unfolded much as I have described. On 15 May, Stamford sent the bulk of his cavalry under Sir George Chudleigh (father of Major-General James Chudleigh) on a raid on Bodmin in order to prevent Sherriff Grylls raising the posse comitatus in support of the king's men. The rest of his force advanced to Stratton and took up a strong defensive position on a hill to the north of the town.

Stamford's opponent, Sir Ralph Hopton, marched immediately to meet the threat, but could muster only 2,400 foot and 500 horse. But despite the disparity in numbers, the Royalist general was determined to attack Stamford's encampment while most of the Parliamentarian cavalry was absent.

When Hopton approached early on the morning of 16 May, he divided his infantry into four columns of about 600 men each to attack the hill from different directions in a great arc. Hopton and Lord Mohun led one column from the south, Major-General Basset attacked from the north, while Sir Bevil Grenville and Sir Nicholas Slanning led the two remaining columns from the west.

Beginning the assault at dawn, the Cornish infantry fought their way doggedly up the steep slopes under determined enemy fire from the surrounding hedges. The skirmishing was bitter and drawn out, with neither side gaining any real advantage, and by mid afternoon the Royalists were down to their last four barrels of powder. After an impromptu council of war, Hopton ordered that (keeping the dire situation from the men) the Royalists would make a last, synchronized assault, with orders not to fire until they reached the summit.

That remarkable 'silent march' has become part of Cornish folklore, but it might still be argued that, had the Parliamentarians simply held their position, the victory would surely have been theirs. The day's pivotal moment was, in fact, the counterattack led by Major-General James Chudleigh. Whether he was disconcerted by the Royalists' refusal to fire, or simply sought personal glory, it is difficult to say, but his headlong charge against Sir Bevil Grenville's column committed a large portion of the rebel army's best troops. As described in *Hunter's Rage*, Grenville himself was hurt, but Sir John Berkeley rallied the Royalists and made a desperate counter-charge that turned the tide of the battle. Witnessing the disintegration of Chudleigh's force – not to mention the capture of the major-general – must have been a truly inspirational sight for the three remaining Royalist columns, and they surged onwards with one last push.

Such a sight, of course, would have had the opposite effect on the hearts and minds of the Parliamentarian reserve as they peered down from the hill's summit. And when, towards the end of the afternoon, all four Royalist columns converged on the crest, the Roundhead ranks finally capitulated.

Despite traditional accounts of the battle, I have taken the view that the Earl of Stamford arrived late on to the field that day. It is said he kept his cavalry – those not engaged at Bodmin – in reserve at the top of the hill, but my contention is that it was not possible for more than a hundred horsemen to gather on the summit alongside five thousand pikemen and musketeers and not become embroiled in the fighting. The area is simply too small. Moreover, it was the cavalry – seemingly intact after the fight – that escorted Stamford to the safety of Bideford. My contention is that Stamford was not there until the latter stages of the battle – certainly too late to affect its outcome – and effectively turned his cavalrymen around when he saw the day was lost.

But present or not, one thing is certain; the Earl of Stamford's grand army was destroyed. Three hundred Parliamentarians lay dead on the slopes of what is now known as Stamford Hill, while 1,700 prisoners were taken. The Royalists captured all thirteen Parliamentarian cannon and a large quantity of powder and ammunition. Most crucially, Hopton's victory secured Cornwall for the king.

The Cornish army was famous for its reckless bravery, its savagery in battle, and its sheer bloody-mindedness. But above all else, it was – and is – best known for the charismatic men who marched at its head. Chief of these was the Somerset MP, Sir Ralph Hopton, later Lord Stratton, but the Cornish, perhaps more than any other regional army, were fiercely loyal to their own 'home-grown' commanders. It is fair to say that Hopton's achievements might never have come to pass were it not for the support of local leaders such as Godolphin, Slanning, and Trevanion. But of those well-known Cornishmen, perhaps the most famous remains Sir Bevil Grenville.

Grandson of the Elizabethan hero Sir Richard Grenville, captain of the *Revenge*, Bevil Grenville inherited large estates in Cornwall and became an ardent Royalist, serving in the king's bodyguard during the Bishop's Wars of the late 1630s. At the outbreak of civil war he raised an army of infantrymen, which, under his leadership, became one of the most effective fighting units in the early campaigns of the English Civil War. Grenville, in turn, achieved something of a talismanic status amongst his men. Indeed, without Grenville's personal endorsement of Sir Ralph Hopton, the general might never have enjoyed the loyalty of his Cornish troops.

At the Battle of Stratton, Grenville's brigade, as I describe in the book, probably made the most rapid advance. To a modern reader it may seem as though my depiction of Grenville fighting on foot, becoming entangled in a press of pike, and then marching on despite his injuries, might be a little far-fetched. But Grenville had 'previous'. At the Battle of Braddock Down in January 1643 he had been at the head of his men in an uphill charge that won the day for the Royalists. Moreover, at the rout at Sourton Down it was Grenville's last stand that saved Hopton's army from complete annihilation.

But all would not go well for the dashing Cavalier. In the summer of 1643 the Cornish army joined forces with a detachment from Oxford and marched eastwards against Sir William Waller. At the Battle of Lansdown, near Bath, the Royalist cavalry was routed, but, true to form, Grenville led a counterattack against the Parliamentarian position at the top of the hill. The manoeuvre was again successful, forcing Waller to withdraw, but Grenville was wounded by a halberd blow to the skull. He died the following day.

At his side to the end was another man whose life – and physique – seem stranger than fiction. Anthony Payne, the Cornish Giant, was a real figure. Born in the manor house on the Grenville estate, now known as the Tree Inn, he was taken into the Grenville household and excelled in both academic subjects and at sports. By the time he was twenty-one it is said that he was 7 feet, 2 inches tall, and later grew a further two inches. But games and academia were to fall by the wayside for Payne, who, by the time war was declared, had become Sir Bevil's bodyguard. He was a key figure in recruiting, organizing, and leading Grenville's force, and must have been a truly formidable sight on the field of battle.

He was, as described in *Hunter's Rage*, in the thick of the fight at Stratton, and it does not take a great deal of imagination to picture his imposing figure cutting a swathe through the enemy ranks. But it seems proper to note that he stayed behind long after the battle to help bury the dead. Moreover, the fearsome warrior even showed great compassion for one badly wounded Parliamentarian, taking him home to be nursed back to health.

I am reluctant to say more of Payne's contribution to the war, for Stryker may meet him again in due course, but his story is certainly a remarkable one, and I am pleased to say that he survived to see the Restoration of the Monarchy. Upon Charles II's return from exile, John Grenville, Sir Bevil's son, received great reward for his steadfast support, including money, the Earldom of Bath, and several other lofty positions. He duly appointed Anthony Payne as Halberdier of the Guns at Plymouth.

Upon retirement, Payne returned to his old home at Stratton, affording himself time to rest and to enjoy his 'daily allowance' of a gallon of wine! When he died in 1681, his coffin was so large that it had to be taken out of a hole cut into the ceiling and lowered to the ground!

Though the Cornish Giant most certainly existed, the same cannot be said of some of the book's other figures. Colonel Wild is pure invention. So too are Cecily Cade, Erasmus Collings and, I'm sad to say, Seek Wisdom and Fear the Lord Gardner.

Osmyn Hogg and José Ventura are also figments of my imagination, but witch-hunters most certainly existed